DJINNS

DJINNS

FATMA AYDEMIR

Translated by Jon Cho-Polizzi

THE UNIVERSITY OF WISCONSIN PRESS

Publication of this book has been made possible, in part,
through support from the Brittingham Trust.

The translation of this book was supported by a grant from
the Goethe-Institut.
The translation was also made possible by the support of the
TOLEDO-Mobilitätsfonds, which facilitated the translator's spring 2023 residency
at the Literary Colloquium Berlin and participation in the Internationales
Treffen der Übersetzer·innen deutschsprachiger Literatur (International
Meeting of Translators of German Literature).

The University of Wisconsin Press
728 State Street, Suite 443
Madison, Wisconsin 53706
uwpress.wisc.edu

Printed in the United States of America
This book may be available in a digital edition.

Library of Congress Cataloging-in-Publication Data

Names: Aydemir, Fatma, 1986– author. | Cho-Polizzi, Jon, translator.
Title: Djinns / Fatma Aydemir ; translated by Jon Cho-Polizzi.
Other titles: Dschinns. English
Description: Madison, Wisconsin : The University of Wisconsin Press, 2024.
Identifiers: LCCN 2024002387 | ISBN 9780299349240 (paperback)
Subjects: LCGFT: Domestic fiction. | Novels.
Classification: LCC PT2701.Y43 D7313 2024 | DDC 833/.92—dc23/eng/20240412
LC record available at https://lccn.loc.gov/2024002387

A previous version of the opening chapter, "Hüseyin,"
was published online in *Columbia Journal*.

Contents

Translator's Introduction

Jon Cho-Polizzi

How does one properly introduce a translation of a novel that requires
no introduction in the cultural context of its source language? Perhaps
through a brief overview of the work's translatability: Since its 2022
German-language publication, Fatma Aydemir's *Dschinns* has already
been adapted for three separate stage productions: at the National-
theater in Mannheim, the Maxim Gorki Theater in Berlin, and the
Schauspielhaus in Düsseldorf.[1] Plans are also underway for a forth-
coming cinematic adaptation of the book as well. In addition to these
German-language medial "translations," the novel has begun to circu-
late beyond the German-speaking world too. From Finnish to Bosnian,
Polish to French, Danish to Dutch to Turkish, it has been or is currently
being translated into more than a dozen languages. *Dschinns* was selected
this year by the Kunststiftung NRW to be workshopped for the twenty-
fifth Straelener Atriumsgespräch, a multiday conversation and reading
series held between an author and their respective translators to facili-
tate the best possible translation of a contemporary German-language
novel. Having had the honor of participating in this conversation as
the novel's English-language translator, I was struck by the multiplicity
of ways this novel spoke to its respective readers across languages and
communities.

A journalist, publicist, writer, and public intellectual, Fatma Aydemir
is also something of a household name herself. The granddaughter of
Turkish-Kurdish immigrants, Aydemir was an editor for the Berlin-based

periodical *Die Tageszeitung* (*taz*) and writes for the feminist culture magazine *Missy Magazine*. She was also an initiator of the bilingual news portal taz.gazete, combating state media repression in Turkey. Her breakthrough 2017 novel *Ellbogen* (Elbow) was the recipient of both the Franz Hessel and Klaus Michael Kühne Prizes for best authorial debut. The 2019 essay collection *Eure Heimat ist unser Albtraum* (*Your Homeland Is Our Nightmare*), which Aydemir coedited with Hengameh Yaghoobifarah—with its scathing social critiques and poignant personal confessions—became an overnight sensation in German-speaking Europe, encapsulating the discontents of a new generation no longer willing to conform to the social norms of a patriarchal, heteronormative, white Christian identity. Bringing together fourteen contemporary authors whose styles, interests, and life experiences span the polyphony of the German-speaking world, the volume has already become standard curriculum for contemporary German studies in university classrooms across much of the anglophone world and has been reprinted well over a dozen times in the few short years since its publication.[2]

Dschinns, Aydemir's second novel, was shortlisted for the German Book Prize. It has been described as *the* book cultural critics will reach for in a hundred years in their attempt to make sense of the zeitgeist of Germany today, while another critic described it as a novel "as moving as it is disturbing."[3] And indeed, the critical reception of this work has reignited debates on the very function of literature in the German-speaking world: At once lauded for its precision, its scope, its intimacy, and its daring, *Dschinns* has simultaneously been lambasted for its bold, no-holds-barred critique of German society and its open rebuttal of modern Germany's well-guarded public image as the refined, redeemed, and reconciled successor of its violent mid-twentieth-century self. *Dschinns* joins the ranks of an increasing body of recent German-language literature grappling with the traumatic aftermath of German Unification. It documents the xenophobic violence and pogroms that characterized the migrant experience of 1990s Germany—a history that has long been eclipsed by the national narrative of unity, the end of the Cold War, and the triumph of West German capitalism and democracy. Literature, so goes the age-old German adage, dare not be too openly or immediately political—it must maintain critical (and chronological) distance. Literature should operate in the abstract realm of aesthetics, not the concrete realm of an often deplorable reality. Proper German literature "sounds different," one establishment critic wrote of this novel.[4] But the contemporary cultural-creative scene seems, overwhelmingly, to disagree.

How, then, does one approach a novel that in many ways successfully defies the expectations of its reading public? In recent years, the attribute *postmigrantisch* (postmigrant) has increasingly become a catch-all for the reception and evaluation of an ever-expanding body of cultural productions by racialized creatives in the German-speaking world. Used in academic discourse since at least the late 1990s for scholarly classification and interpretation, "postmigrant" also became a self-designation from the early 2000s onward, initially employed to describe the culturally and linguistically diverse actors and writers associated with Şermin Langhoff and Berlin's Ballhaus Naunynstraße Theater. But this self-designation has fallen out of favor with both critics and creatives alike in recent years. In a 2023 publication of the literary journal *Politisches Schreiben*, cultural critics Jeannette Oholi, Maryam Aras, Kyung-Ho Cha, and Maha El Hissy describe the devaluation of the term as an instrument of self-designation. In their conversation, Oholi observes: "Today the term *postmigrant* has lost something of its edge. I no longer have a sense of its radical, empowering potential for resistance. This has to do with the fact that the use of the term 'postmigrant' as a self-designation for resistance among marginalized people—and in reference to their artistic works—has been appropriated by a white, hegemonic culture."[5] Together, the critics argue instead for the necessity of reframing postmigrant discourse through the framework of wider, postcolonial analysis, rather than simply applying it as a convenient adjective for categorizing the diverse and often socially critical works of racialized artists and writers.

Nevertheless, this trend has come to dominate recent approaches to German culture. In their 2023 monograph, *Postmigrant Turn*, Rahel Cramer, Jara Schmidt, and Jule Thiemann define *postmigrantisch* explicitly as "the considerations and incorporation of migrant biographies and migration as a shared social experience. A postmigrant society is shaped by globalization, technologization, and digitalization, presenting complex intercultural structures."[6] But this definition can be misleading. In its broadest and most all-encompassing application, *postmigrant* would then refer to any and all German-language cultural productions after the mid-twentieth century, a period marked by numerous international trade and worker agreements, migration, and rapid demographic shifts. But if German society collectively can be conceptualized as a postmigrant society, that is, one influenced by the ongoing effects of migration, the term *postmigrant* seems to lose something of its utility. And in practice, the term is rarely if ever applied to the works of white German creatives, even if their works engage explicitly with these subjects. It is, instead, applied all but exclusively to the works of German-language creatives whose biographies are somehow perceived as differing from a white German norm—even if their works do *not* explicitly take up the themes associated with a history of familial migration. In its uneven application, the concept of "postmigrant" seems in danger of becoming little more than a marketing label or cubbyhole through which the works of certain creatives become abstracted from the larger German-language creative scene—or at worst, a way of labeling and coaching the expectations around what the works of minoritized creatives "should" look like. Aydemir herself would seem to agree with this analysis. Responding to a follower's question in a 2023 story on her Instagram account, Aydemir observes that the term *postmigrant* "is a tool. . . . I don't use it myself because it throws too many things into one pot and sounds a little bit like saying 'I don't see color.'"[7]

Can *Dschinns* then be classified as a work of postmigrant literature? Yes and no. *Dschinns* is certainly a novel influenced by the confluence of Kurdish and Turkish migration histories. It is a multigenerational story of movement, immigration, and varied attempts at integration and assimilation—and in that sense, the expression of an experience that transcends national borders and narratives. Its prose is translingual and its plotline transnational. *Dschinns* is a work of fiction profoundly situated in the circumstances of life in contemporary Germany, and it is precisely this grounding that may help us rethink established notions of national literature. The postmigrant nature of the Federal Republic of Germany, of course, plays no small role in this. But to limit one's reading of the work to the author's or characters' biographies would also be to limit one's understanding of the centrality of migration in the globalized world we all inhabit today.

I could wax poetic about the merits, achievements, and tremendous impacts of this novel. As a translator, however, it occurs to me that it need not be my task to muddy the waters overmuch with details on the contents or reception of this book. That is simply not the hat I've chosen to wear today. And as an avid reader, I am also acutely aware of the fine line between framing an imported work of literature and descending into unwarranted plot spoilers—cognizant of the risk of unduly influencing the experience of the would-be reader. And so, it strikes me that it should be my task, instead, to discuss some of the specific linguistic facets of this novel and to shine light for the English-language reader where the opacity of translation might overshadow some of the work's special qualities.

Even the most casual of German-language readers would be struck by the high number of Turkish-language words in the source text. These words appear in the German narrative without gloss or italicization—as if to imply that they need no further explanation—as if to highlight their de facto presence in German society. After all, according to German state authorities, by the end of 2022, there were nearly 1.5 million Turkish nationals living in Germany, a country of just over 84 million residents (by far and away Germany's largest immigrant population[8])—and this number does *not* include the even larger number of German citizens of Turkish heritage (many estimates place this number closer to 3 million). And yet the novel's intervention is of tremendous significance precisely because nearly all these words do, in fact, require additional explanation for the "average" German reader. Despite the omnipresence of Turkish culture in Germany these days, the Turkish language is rarely taught in German schools. It's no secret that the bilingualism of Turkish-heritage speakers is actively discouraged in most social and professional contexts. Many German speakers cannot recognize more than a mere smattering of highly Germanized Turkish words for food, such as the inevitable *döner* or perhaps a *çay*. It has been more than sixty years since Germany's first 1961 Recruitment Agreement with Turkey, facilitating state-regulated labor migration for the Turkish diaspora. And so, Aydemir's insistence on writing the Turkish presence into the linguistic fabric of her novel demands a certain reckoning from her reader with what has, by now, long since become a lived social reality.

In keeping with the author's choices, but in recognition of the diverse experiences and socialization of an English-language readership, I, too, have both retained a large number of these untranslated Turkish words in my English-language translation and eschewed their italicization in my formatting. But I have opted to include a short glossary of English translations and explanations—not only for the untranslated Turkish words but also for the untranslated vestiges of German, Kurdish, and Serbo-Croatian in the novel. Unlike in the author's original German, I have also chosen to use English orthography for a number of words where the English equivalent bears a recognizable similarity to the original Turkish or Arabic (words like azan [Turkish: *ezan*], arabesque [*arabesk*], or hodja [*hoca*], for which the author chose to privilege Turkish words over their German-language counterparts). I believe, in many cases, this was a deliberate choice on the part of the author to highlight the different associations with specific Turkish vis-à-vis German vocabulary. But because English is often much quicker to accept loanwords from non-Indo-European languages than German is, I found it simpler to work with the English-language equivalents rather than to present the Turkish orthography for what are already established English-language words.

While it is certainly not my intention to provide anything resembling an introduction to the Turkish language here (I would be utterly unqualified to do so), I would also like to include a small guide for the English-language reader when it comes to Turkish letters whose pronunciation differs markedly from the English:

C/c—[dʒ]—similar to the English *j* in jar
Ç/ç—[tʃ]—similar to the English *ch* in chop

Ğ / ğ—[ɰ]—pronunciation differs by association, but often similar to an
unstressed English *w*, or something like a placeholder indicating a brief
pause between letters

İ / i—[i]—similar to the English "long e" in speed

I / ı—[ɯ]—similar to the English "short u" or the *e* in roses

Ş / ş—[ʃ]—similar to the English *sh* in shop

In addition, the German consonant *ß*, the "Sharp S" or "Eszett," is
pronounced:

ß—[s]—equivalent to the English *s* in street

while the German *s* (before most consonants) is pronounced similarly
to the English *sh*:

s [before most consonants]—[ʃ]—similar to the English *sh* in shop

Thus, for example, the name *Cem* would be pronounced more like the
English noun *gem*; *çay* is pronounced more like the English transliteration of the Hindi *chai*; the first *s* in the German word *Straße* (street) is
pronounced more like the English *sh*, while the *eszett* is pronounced
more like the standard English *s* (ˈʃtʁäːsə). I am aware that this is, at best,
a cursory overview and that some linguistically minded readers might
prefer a longer, more thorough, or more scholarly introduction to the
languages. The brief phonetic table provided here is intended as a reader's aid and not as a substitute for in-depth engagement with the Turkish
(or German) language.

Likewise, the glossary included at the back of this book is short. It is
intended to be used solely as a reader's reference for untranslated vocabulary. Although I began my work by compiling a comprehensive list that
included the vast number of references to cities, films, people, songs,
TV shows, and so on that appear in this novel, I eventually opted to
restrict the glossary to specific non-English vocabulary, as deciding which
cultural references to explain to a global readership became frustratingly
arbitrary in the context of such a transnational work. The elucidation

of every Turkish, German, or US cultural reference would have been untenable. I also chose to eschew explanation of most specific Islamic vocabulary (including the names of figures or places as well as the titles of passages from the Quran), though I did, at times, provide more common English-language equivalents. I have endeavored to ensure that further explanations for most unglossed references or terms are readily available online for the interested reader. Except in specific cases, I also did not provide glossary entries for the names of businesses, companies, or commercial items, though the incident with the Kinder Surprise Egg (Turkish: *Kinder Sürpriz* / German: *Kinder Überraschungsei* or *Kinder Ü-Ei*)—a beloved toy-filled chocolate candy that was famously banned from import to the United States due to its choking hazard—might require some explanation, if for no other reason than because it is simultaneously referred to with different names by the various characters in the novel and because it is rarely available to US consumers in its original form. Suffice it to say that the interested reader would also benefit from reviewing the biographies of the various Turkish celebrities and political agents referenced throughout the novel, particularly to the extent that they often provide important cultural cues and subtle foreshadowing.

The word *kanak* (variously *kanake, kanakin* [feminine], *kanaken* [plural]) plays a central role in the German-language novel. A word of Malay and Polynesian origin meaning "child," "human," or "brother," the term has come to be used disparagingly in modern German (presumably by way of Dutch or Low German colonial derivation) to denote those of perceived Mediterranean, Middle Eastern, Muslim, or North African heritage. During the 1990s, with the influence of imported US hip-hop culture and a discourse and affect inspired by Black activism in the United States, the word was increasingly reappropriated as a term of self-empowerment within these minoritized German communities. This application was popularized in mainstream German culture through the use of *Kiezdeutsch* (literally: neighborhood German)—the youth jargon spoken in predominantly racialized inner-city communities, German hip-hop culture, and the work of anti-racist activist collectives such as Kanak Attak. The word appears throughout the novel with varying nuances according to the positionalities of the individual characters. The reader should be aware that this word carries significant derogatory connotations in standard German and that its casual use is never appropriate outside the communities who have endeavored to repurpose it as an emancipatory tool.

References in the novel to Mölln and Solingen (potential spoiler) refer to two of the most infamous cases of right-wing terrorism in the immediate post-Unification period. Both were the sites of fatal arson attacks by German neo-Nazis who set fire to the homes of Turkish immigrant families. Although many such xenophobic attacks occurred during this period (and indeed, continue to occur in Germany today), these particular attacks received widespread media attention due to the deaths of several victims in each case (two children and one elderly woman died in Mölln, while nine others were seriously injured; five family members died in Solingen, while fourteen others were injured). Particularly in Sevda's chapter, the word *Solingen* acquires a complex relation to the character's own socioeconomic ascent, as the city is also associated with the production of high-quality cutlery and knives that have become something of a hallmark for an affluent German household. As aforementioned, *Dschinns* is one of many recent literary publications in Germany to rework the trauma of right-wing violence in the post-Unification years, following a relative hiatus in the treatment of the subject by German-language authors after the initial works of contemporaneous poets in the early 1990s such as May Ayim and José F. A. Oliver.

It is also necessary to acknowledge the author's use in the novel of the Turkish pronoun *o*—a word that snowballs in importance over the narrative arc of the story. Turkish, unlike English and German, is a highly inflected language, meaning that the endings of its words change to denote a word's grammatical function in a given sentence: for instance, whether a substantive is functioning as the sentence's subject, direct object, indirect object, and so forth. Inflection can also be determined by specific vocabulary. Certain verbs might demand the use of one declension (word ending) or another. While German retains some elements of inflection in its articles and adjective endings as well, modern English has largely moved away from this grammatical feature. One exception is retained in English pronouns; for example, the English-socialized speaker recognizes that the words *I, me, my,* and *mine* may all refer to the same person, although their specific use depends on the function of the word in a given sentence. *O* (the gender-neutral Turkish pronoun equivalent to the English *he/she/it* or the singular *they*) appears extensively throughout the novel, and is declined as *onu/ona/onun* in accordance with its use in the original German text (*onu/ona* are equivalent to the singular *them; onun* is equivalent to the singular *their*). Although perhaps inconspicuous to the casual reader, the declination of this Turkish pronoun in *Dschinns* is highly idiosyncratic. It follows the grammatical rules of the German language rather than the Turkish—creating a distinct linguistic hybridity at the very heart of the novel and explicitly highlighting the translingual and transnational framing of the narrative.

Finally, lest the minutia of my introduction convince you otherwise—I would like to end by stressing the incredible readability of this book. Preparations for the translation took me on physical journeys from Eastern Anatolia to Istanbul, Oakland to Detroit, and the Black Forest to Berlin. The pages of the novel alone, however, should suffice to carry the engaged reader on a similarly harrowing journey: back into the volatile decade following Germany's Unification, from the mountains of Kurdistan to the factories and labor domiciles of West Germany, and onward through a new nation's reluctant transformation into one of the most culturally diverse and dynamic countries in Western Europe today. *Dschinns* is at once a touching family narrative, a sweeping modern-day epic, and a timeless examination of the lies, loves, and losses of a life lived navigating between worlds. It is, truly, one of the definitive novels of our generation.

NOTES

1. Adapted for stage by Selen Kara, Nurkan Erpulat and Johannes Kirsten, and Birgit Lengers, respectively.

2. Originally published by Ullstein Verlag; English-language translations of the collection are available online through UC Berkeley's *TRANSIT Journal* (2021) and in print from Literarische Diverse Verlag (2022).

3. "Auf Platz 3 der 10 Bücher des Jahres 2022," *Die Zeit* (Hamburg), December 29, 2022; Olaf Przybilla, "Das Erlanger Poetenfest wird immer weiblicher," *Süddeutsche Zeitung* (Munich), August 23, 2022.

4. Iris Radisch, "Verficktes Land," *Die Zeit—Feuilleton*, no. 9 (Hamburg), February 24, 2022.

5. Jeannette Oholi et al., "Postmigration Reloaded: Ein Schreibgespräch," *Politisches Schreiben* 7 (October 2022): 63.

6. Rahel Cramer, Jara Schmidt, and Jule Thiemann, *Postmigrant Turn: Postmigration als kulturwissenschaftliche Analysekategorie* (Berlin: Neofelis Verlag GmbH, 2023), 11–12.

7. Fatma Aydemir (@fatmaaydemir), "Postmigrant is a tool," Instagram (story), April 16, 2023.

8. "Foreign Population by Place of Birth and Selected Citizenships," Federal Statistical Office of Germany, accessed June 1, 2023, https://www.destatis.de/EN/Themes/Society-Environment/Population/Migration-Integration/Tables/for eigner-place-of-birth.html.

DJINNS

Hüseyin

Hüseyin . . . do you know who you are, Hüseyin, when you see the shining contours of your face in the reflection on the balcony door? When you open the door, stride across the balcony, and a warm breeze caresses your face while the setting sun glimmers between the rooftops of the apartments in Zeytinburnu like a giant tangerine? You rub your eyes. Maybe, you think, maybe every obstacle and every conflict in this life was only there so that, one day, you could stand up here and know: *I've earned this for myself. With the sweat of my brow.*

You hear the first evening call to prayer from the balcony of the apartment—this spacious, three-bedroom apartment on the fourth floor. The apartment you worked and saved for—for almost thirty years—while raising your four children and providing your wife with an admittedly humble but never meager life. You lived your days to the rhythm of three shifts, Hüseyin. You took on every Sunday, every holiday, overtime. Took advantage of every available bonus in the metalworks to make sure your family could get by. To buy new football cleats for the little one, pay off the older one's debts, and still set a little something aside. And now you've finally done it. You're fifty-nine and a homeowner. In a few years, when Ümit finishes school and you can finally leave Germany— that cold, cold-hearted country—there'll be an apartment waiting for you in Istanbul with your name at the door: Hüseyin! You've finally found a place you can call home.

Enjoy it, Hüseyin. Listen as the blaring music from the shops in the streets below grows quiet. Now there is only the azan. The azan and the honking and the cries of the millions who must still navigate the streets and go about the business of their days. Hear the call of the gulls. Inhale the humid air tinged with exhaust and the smell of burning rubbish. Let your gaze fall for a few moments on the bustle between the houses below before you go to pray.

Look, across the way, a new location of İbrahim Tatlıses's lahmacun restaurant has opened. You used to love his music so, Hüseyin. You bought one of his albums. Every evening, at the boarding house, you'd pop open a bottle of Kristallweizen; the hum of the record player followed the hiss of the bottle cap. The bağlama in the opening notes of "Tükendi Nakdi Ömrüm." Do you remember, Hüseyin, the countless cigarettes you smoked to this song? How your body dissolved into one single white puff of smoke inside the narrow kitchen of the home? The kitchen at the end of that long, dark hallway. You could feel İbo because he sang of the people in his songs—of those to whom no one else lent an ear. The poor, the darkling, those hardworking people from the countryside. Those people like you, Hüseyin. And you felt İbo because, like you, he, too, had discarded the language of his parents. Discarded it like an unused sack of stones.

But now you can no longer stand him. You despise İbo, Hüseyin. How he hops around on his show on Friday evenings. Speaking nonsense. And gaping at his belly dancers. This honorless man who had a simple merchant shot at the Urfa bazaar because the merchant did not want to serve him. Or at least, so the papers had said.

No, Hüseyin, this is by no means the kind of man whose cassette tapes you'd want to buy or listen to. And besides, İbo has long since transitioned from folk music to arabesque. And you've long since given up both alcohol and tobacco. And without alcohol, it's almost impossible to tolerate arabesque. And even if you could, what could the songs of such a man provide? A man who beats his women and wears this crime in public like a badge of pride? Nothing. But still, Perihan and Hakan and Ümit will no doubt be impressed by this restaurant. It belongs to the most famous person in the country, after all. You won't be able to say a thing, Hüseyin, when your children rush over there each day to stuff themselves.

And you will pay for their food. You'll watch them peacefully. And silently, you'll be glad that you can finally provide them with the opportunity to spend each summer here in Istanbul from now on. Istanbul, this splendid city, over which so many centuries of wars were waged and so much blood was shed. And all for naught. For no one has ever understood that this city will never permit itself to be conquered. In the end, the city always conquers you. In the end, you will be nothing more than another layer of dust on the earth beneath the feet of new conquerors, always with the same desires. And Istanbul will absorb and devour all of them, reducing all to dust. Nourishing itself on them, forever growing in its incandescent splendor.

And you, Hüseyin, you already knew that someday you would return to Istanbul. Already, the first time you arrived in this city. Back then you'd come by train from your village. You disembarked here for a week, you stayed with relatives before you boarded the bus and then the train to Southern Germany where you were assigned a job. They put you in a line with other workers there, they inspected your naked bodies, and they examined the contents of your underpants. That was in the spring of 1971.

Germany was not what you had hoped it would be, Hüseyin. You'd hoped for a new life. But what you received, instead, was loneliness. And loneliness can never be a new life. For loneliness is a cycle, the constant repetition of the same memories inside your head. The perpetual search for new wounds within your long-departed ego. The longing for those people you left behind. But what could you do, Hüseyin? You couldn't just return to your village. And so, you stayed. And you did the things you had to do so that your coming here would at least make sense.

How time flies, Hüseyin. In the last twenty-eight years of your life, you've earned more money than you would ever have dreamed of in Turkey. You earned it because you were never too good for any work. The kind of work no German would do. You could not have known, Hüseyin, that your body would soon—far before retirement age—grow

as weary as the German economy after Unification. Like your many
colleagues, in that moment when the two exhaustions came together
and the doors of the metalworks closed, you, too, had wanted to go
into early retirement. But you received no certification. Although after
all those long years bent before the furnace, your back had twisted
inside like a C. And your knee had begun to ache dreadfully, after even
the shortest walks.

But even this had some validity, Hüseyin. For how else would you all
have gotten by back then? With three children at home, on a pension of
only 900 marks? From your savings? Would you have wanted to give up
this apartment, Hüseyin, just so that you could have started to relax
a few years earlier? A few years earlier, but in Germany forever more?
Of course not, Hüseyin. And so, you went on to a different factory for
less pay and even lesser benefits. But it was still enough to amass the
necessary savings. To put away a bit more toward your pension. And
besides, it was hard to call folding cardboard work—especially after all
those years melting scraps of metal at 1500°C. And so you drudged
through five more years, Hüseyin, until last year, you personally asked
your cardboard boss—as politely as you could—to be discharged. And he
acquiesced. And you finally found time to look at apartments in Istanbul. Time to rededicate yourself to your faith that had, for long years,
wilted like an unwatered flower. Time to listen to yourself and time to
make peace with your demons. And next week when you turn sixty,
your pension will finally kick in, Hüseyin. They call it early retirement,
but nothing about this feels early.

How the time flies. Who knows, maybe you'll never go back to Germany again. Maybe you'll just stay here. Maybe Emine and the children
will stay, too, after they arrive and see how perfectly you've arranged
the apartment for them. Maybe Ümit will just finish his schooling here.
Maybe Perihan and Hakan will both fall in love here and finally want
to get married. You tremble at the thought, Hüseyin. But why? Was it
not you, back then, who wrung your hands and wanted to deliver your
eldest daughter, Sevda, to a man? Who gave her an ultimatum when

she was seventeen-and-a-half years old? You'll marry this one or that one, you can decide, but you will take one of them and start a family. And then, at least, we won't have to worry what Germany will do to our Sevda. Our Sevda, who always wants too much from life, who's never satisfied with what she has, with what she can achieve. Was it not your idea, Hüseyin, to deliver Sevda into safety in this fashion? Was it not your idea to kill her dreams?

But poor Hüseyin, Sevda did as she pleased. And even with two children on her lap, she kept doing it, all the same. Can you not see? So now, instead, you worry about Perihan and Hakan. But you should have realized long ago, Hüseyin, that your fears for your children seldom guide you to the right decisions. Yes, you smile, Hüseyin. And well you should. For today is a good day: perhaps the best day of your life.

All the furniture has arrived. The men arranged the furnishings according to your plan: the mirror and the heavy double bed for Emine and you in the back bedroom, the patterned futons for the children in the two smaller rooms. In the living room stands an ornate dresser of dark, polished hardwood, just how Emine would want it. She will like the dresser, of this you are sure.

Emine, whom you have loved since you first saw her in the neighboring village. You had just come back from your military service then, a little crazed from the experience, a little broken. And this young woman passed you in the alleyway with her head lowered, white as a cotton blossom. The very next day, you'd called to ask for her hand. Called at her aunt's, for by then, Emine's parents were long dead. Her aunt had tried to suppress her joy, for she had not wished to reveal her toothless smile, and yet she had seemed gladdened by the notion of one less mouth to feed. That was thirty-three years ago. And you have always loved Emine—more than you love yourself. Even during those eight long years when you were so far away from her in Germany. You always thought of her, you fell asleep each night on dreams that carried you to Emine. To the smell of the rosewater she rubbed each morning behind her ears. To the coolness of her skin—cool, even beneath two thick layers of blankets. None of the German women you met in the

bars along the river during those lonely years could still the yearning
you felt for Emine. Quite the contrary, Hüseyin: the closer you drew to
these women, the greater your longing grew.

And then it became possible to bring her and the children after
you. The long wait came to an end. You moved together into the dim
ground-level apartment of a yellow high-rise building across from the
factory. A building where only Turkish and Italian workers and one
ancient German widow lived. And you made the best of everything; you
sent your children to better schools than you ever could have dreamed
of in Turkey. You did everything. You gave your all—except, perhaps,
with Sevda. But the firstborn child is always an experiment. What could
you do? People make mistakes. And you could do better with those
who followed after, isn't that right, Hüseyin? All but the firstborn. Only
your firstborn child.

And now, Hüseyin, you're waiting for Emine, again. For this time,
it is she who is in Germany, and you: here in Turkey. Next week she
will follow, with Hakan, Perihan, and little Ümit, who finally has summer break. You flew earlier to prepare the apartment. Halime Bacı,
your friendly neighbor from the apartment below, already arranged a
cleaning woman for Sunday to look after the details. Your glance falls
on the kitchen, Hüseyin, through the balcony's French doors. The pile
of apricots—still wrapped in newspaper—that Halime Bacı brought
this afternoon. You were lucky, Hüseyin, to find such a helpful and
respectable neighbor. Such things are no longer the rule these days, not
even here.

The call to prayer has already ended. But it doesn't matter if you
pray five minutes late, today, Hüseyin. And so, you push open the doors
to the kitchen, unwrap the newspapers, and let warm water run over
the fruit. You leave the balcony doors open so the synthetic smell of the
new furniture can waft away. The apricots are already slightly fermented,
just the way you like them. Sugary sweet and almost mush.

You eat one, and then another. And you're just about to walk to the
bathroom, Hüseyin, to prepare yourself for prayer. You've just decided
not to wash your sticky fingers in the kitchen but to head straight to
the bathroom, where you will wash your hands and your face and your

arms and your head and your ears and your neck and your feet anyway. You've just taken one step from the kitchen toward the hallway when you feel a sharp twinge of pain in your left arm.

You wonder whether you overstrained yourself earlier helping the men carry those two sofas and three futons down the hall, even though they had said graciously that they'd be fine. The furniture wasn't that heavy anyway. But the pain does not subside. A stabbing pain. Again and again. Like an ax, cleaving your flesh apart.

Hüseyin, cold sweat beads on your neck. Your body does not know this kind of pain. And suddenly, a tightness spreads across your chest as if your whole torso were contracting to no larger than a button. You remain on your feet, Hüseyin. You stand, crossing your arms over your chest as if hugging yourself. And then you have to sit down anyway. You take two steps toward the living room where the brand-new dining table and the matching upholstered chairs are waiting, but after these two steps you're overcome by such a wave of nausea that you turn toward the bathroom instead. But it's too late for that, Hüseyin. Your body bends in half, and you vomit then and there, before the entryway, in the middle of the hall.

You cough, falling to your knees and crying as loudly as you still can for your neighbor, Halime Bacı. You hammer with both hands on the floor, but you don't know whether she will hear you knocking. The world is spinning. You see bits of apricot on the oak-finish laminate of the floor. Your body struggles to right itself from this crouch, but you just can't manage it, Hüseyin. Everything is too heavy. Too much. Too tight. Your chest is rocked by sudden cramps, and while you're screaming for Halime, you jerk upward, lose your balance, and your body tumbles to the floor amid your vomit.

You keep your head high, with all your strength. You scream, struggling for air. You scream again. And suddenly, you hear Halime Bacı's voice outside in the main hallway. The slip-slap of her rubber slippers ascending the stone stairs. The cramp in your upper body releases for two seconds. Somehow you manage to heave your arm against the doorknob, to open the front door. And then another cramp, more forceful still. A pain so deep, so bitter, the likes of which you've never known

before. Cries flood from your body. They sound so odd; you can't be
sure whether they're yours at all. They must come from somewhere
else, outside. It's not possible for you to make such a noise.

You see the long frame of Halime Bacı's frightened face above you.
You can't understand what she's saying, but she quivers. She looks terrified. Pale. Her face is a mirror in which you see the reflection of your
own fate, Hüseyin.

The fuzzy thoughts inside your head grow suddenly clearer: This is
the end. Finished. Over. This is how you'll die. Covered in your own
vomit. A sticky mess of fruit in the apartment you dreamed of all your
life. You'll die like this, without a glimpse of the sparkle in Emine's eyes
when she first sees the place, without feeling the youthful excitement
of your youngest daughter and two sons. You'll never know what they
think of the furniture you chose, of the bustle of the neighborhood. Of
Istanbul: a city they know only from postcards and a few short stop-
overs during their youth—and of course, from TV.

Just like you, Hüseyin. Why did you want to move to Istanbul, anyway? What do you truly know about this place? Was it really the place
you dreamed of, or merely a memory? A memory of leaving home, a
layover on your way to the factory—a place between forgetting and the
toil that followed. The first place where you could breathe.

You want to breathe, Hüseyin. You don't want to die. Not now, even
though you are devout. Even though you've always said that you'll be
ready when Azrael comes for you. Maybe, you think now, maybe you've
secretly hoped your faith would grant you a long and healthy life. How
naive you've been, Hüseyin. You are not ready. It just can't end this way.
Not like this. You would pray to Allah if your tongue were not as heavy
as lead, your mouth so cleft with the pain roiling inside you like an
uncontainable wildfire: set to scorch the earth and burn away all hostile
life. You would beseech Azrael that he—or she, or it—grant you just
one week more. Please, just one week more. Just this short period of
grace. To open the apartment doors to your dear family, the doorway
here before you, and lead them into the bright rooms. This is Hakan
and Ümit's bedroom; this room is for Perihan. This is the living room,
and here, our balcony. Over there is another balcony attached to our

bedroom, Emine. Just one week more to walk along the water with them. To pour your children a çay, to hold your daughter's hand and tell her how very much you love her. To tell your sons you're proud of them. To call Sevda and beg her to forgive you. To hear the voices of the grandchildren you've missed for all these years. Maybe a bit more than a week. You stopped smoking long ago, Hüseyin. That was meant to prolong your life. How can you die of a heart attack now, of all times, and miss everything that was meant to happen in this apartment? Your apartment, Hüseyin.

Hüseyin, you strain your eyes. You keep them open. You look around. Halime Bacı was gone, but now she's back again. You understand that Halime has called an ambulance, is begging you to hold on. She wipes your brow with a damp towel. Ice cold, it runs across your forehead and nose—over the twitching corners of your mouth. For a moment, it feels as though a hole has opened in your heart. A hole through which all the pain is vanishing, is sinking. Disappears.

Hüseyin, you know that this will only last a moment—this respite from the pain. You know it will return, come soon. The pain will return. You can't say how you have this knowledge, how you know with such certainty, but the next cramp will surely come. And it will be monstrous. It will carry you far from here. You know this. And so, you use this yawning emptiness in your chest, use the final strength you find within you, to move your lips. Panic-stricken and pale, Halime stares questioningly. She lowers her ear to your mouth to better understand what you have to say, Hüseyin. You whisper it. One word. And Halime asks, "What was that? Come again?" But you cannot. You see a shadow fall across the wall. You feel those cold beads of sweat gathering at your neck. But you need not be afraid, Hüseyin. That shadow is only me. I promise you, I will tarry here. In this house. In this apartment. I will watch over your family when they arrive. I give you my word, Hüseyin. I promise. But it is time for you to go now, Hüseyin. Even I can do nothing to change this.

Don't be afraid, Hüseyin. Come. Just take one breath. Just take one little breath. Only as much air as you need to compose yourself. To murmur your words. You've held onto them for a lifetime. For this moment, Hüseyin. But now you don't want to say them. Because you don't want to give up yet. But that is no longer in your hands, Hüseyin. There's nothing in your hands, Hüseyin. And you want to do it, before it is too late. You take a breath. One breath to let go. To decide for yourself this is the moment to let go. And so, you take a breath, and you whisper: "Eşhedü en la ilahe illallah . . ."

Ümit

The call came in the night. A scream.

Ümit wasn't sure whether the scream was just another remnant of those recent dreams that had been leaving him tied up in knots. He lay in bed until he heard the apartment door open and Hakan's voice inside. Barefoot, Ümit tiptoed from his bedroom only to find everyone—Peri, Hakan, his mother—huddling together in the night. Stony-faced, no one so much as noticed Ümit's presence in the room. *How could it have happened? Just like that? Why hadn't they sent him to Germany immediately? How exactly? With a helicopter! What would that have changed? They don't have decent doctors there! That can't be. It can't be . . .* Their murmurs filled the darkness of the apartment until the sun rose, ushering reality in with it.

Baba was dead. And they needed to go. Immediately. Find a flight to Istanbul with four seats free in the middle of the summer holidays. Forget it. Peri sobbed over the telephone with every travel agency, her glittery face crumpled as though she'd just returned from a long night out partying. Hakan scowled, chain-smoking cigarettes on their balcony. And Ümit's mother. Ümit's mother had become a collapsed heap of limbs strewn across their sofa, as impossible to reconstitute as the stew meat in a pot of goulash.

Peri found a flight from Frankfurt rather than Stuttgart. Three seats instead of four. Hakan popped open a can of Red Bull and began calling around to find a separate flight. Secretly, Ümit was glad to be missing his appointment with Dr. Schumann, but he was also ashamed of these thoughts. Feraye Teyze's son from next door shuttled them through traffic in his BMW 3 Series. They flew on an airline none of them had ever heard of, leaving their in-flight meal—sausages in some kind of gruel—untouched until the flight attendants collected their trays. Peri and Ümit's mother cried incessantly while Ümit stared out the oval window at the cotton-candy clouds. He was thinking of the tectonic plates he'd learned about in geography. Floating above this continent toward a rough landing at its outermost limits. The people around him clapped their hands. The sun was setting twenty kilometers from Asia.

And now it's shining again, completely indifferent to the fact that a life had ended and a family had been broken. The sun drips from the windowpane to claw at Ümit's eyelids. The rush of a thousand motors bores its way in from the outside world while Ümit lies here in the same unfamiliar apartment that had taken his father from him. Lies here wishing that the world would grant him one small reprieve, if only for a moment. That the world would stand still so he can find time to pre-pare himself for everything to come. To come up with a plan to sneak away, or simply remain lying in this room—still reeking of fresh paint—to lie here and let the day pass by without anyone coming to bother him.

Ümit shuts his eyes, squeezes them tight, trying to return to that un-encumbered place he sometimes reaches just before sleep. Just before he finally nods off, clocks out. Drifting. Lost. Wandering in the dark, endless shadows of a tangled German forest. Just before he sinks there is that span of time between sleep and unsleep that envelops him in velvet, lifts him from the floor, and carries him away. That moment his mother calls şekerleme. Sugar sleep.

But it's useless. The heat is grilling him alive in bed. A metallic taste he can't identify coats his tongue. For some strange reason, it reminds Ümit of childhood. Something clatters in the kitchen, someone's talk-ing in the room next door. Cars are honking on the street below, music drifts up from the storefronts. Anything is better than those unearthly wails the night before. Guardedly, he opens his eyes. The ceiling has the color of vanilla ice cream. Ümit could puke. The way everything in this apartment smells so new. Like it's still waiting to be brought to life. But it will never be brought to life. Death lives in this place.

Ümit peers over at the empty bed beside him, the green sheets folded neatly on the extended pullout sofa. Hakan still hasn't been here. Hadn't he planned on taking the redeye from Strasbourg? Hopefully he'll make it on time for the funeral, Ümit thinks. There's no way Ümit wants to be there by himself with his sobbing mother and sobbing sister, whom—truth be told—he'd gladly do anything to help if only he knew how. Hakan knows his way around these things. No doubt he'll be here any minute, breezing in freshly shaven with his hair trimmed down smartly at three millimeters, his steel jaw chewing away every uncertainty like bubble gum. Hakan can bolster everyone, at least a little bit. Hug his mother, pat Peri on the shoulder. And Ümit will stand beside him, like he always does, watching—trying his best to do everything the same way.

The room is stuffy; Ümit can barely breathe. But he wants just a little more time to himself here on the pullout sofa before he has to go face Peri and his mother. When they'd arrived last night by taxi from the airport, there was already a line of men waiting there, chain-smoking apathetically, ready to gather up their luggage from the driver as they tried to make themselves useful. In front of the apartment door upstairs, there'd already been a mountain of dusty grandma shoes: semi-open, black, brown, dark blue. Leather or plastic that looked like leather. Inside, at least fifty women pressed together, praying, crying, praying again, as if they'd studied the art of mourning for years with the self-same piety with which they'd learned their prayers. The men withdrew to wait downstairs at the street below. But who the hell were all these people? How had they all learned the news about Ümit's father so quickly? Who invited them anyway?

Ümit had sped as quickly as he could from his room to the bathroom and he'd locked the door behind him. He listened to the muffled lamentations from the room next door while seated trembling on the edge of the bathtub. The one crying the loudest was not his mother. He couldn't place her voice at all; she sounded like a crazed monkey. When Ümit finally turned the key and opened the door cautiously—crossing the darkened hallway to creep into the crowded space his father had once decorated to be their living room and that now stank unbearably of old women's sweat—he saw that the crazy ape was, in fact, his Auntie Ayşe.

He could identify her by her left eye with its white lashes and the missing eyebrow. It seemed oddly naked. Ümit noticed that this eye was also a different color than the right one. It was strange how Ayşe Yenge cried so much: She couldn't have been that close to her brother-in-law. Ümit's father had rarely spoken of his brother Ahmet or his wife, Ayşe. They had never come to visit. They had never called. Not even on Bayram. Ümit only recognized her from a black-and-white photograph in which she and Ahmet Amca had posed arm-in-arm in front of a rosebush. It must have been taken after they'd moved to Vienna. Ümit's parents had similar pictures from their early days in Rheinstadt, standing before floral arrangements or next to the fountain on Poststraße. Ümit liked these kinds of pictures, and he'd spent a lot of time studying them. Maybe because they told a story of searching: about the search for beauty in a new life.

Ayşe Yenge had been seated cross-legged, thick and imposing, in the middle of their living room. Seated between two women dutifully counting their prayer beads who looked like bodyguards. These two were the only ones who weren't crying. Their bodies were draped in long black garments resembling bedsheets, revealing only the round globes of their faces. Ayşe's headscarf, on the other hand, had long since slipped down around her shoulders. She slapped her hands again and again against her knees, emitting rhythmic cries. Maybe she's afraid she'll be the next to go, Ümit had thought. Maybe that's why she's crying so much. Or maybe she was still mourning her own husband, who had passed the year before.

Ümit looked around for his mother and Peri, noticing at the same time that he himself was slowly becoming the center of attention in the room. There'd been nothing he could do about it. The many women seated around him on folding chairs or on the floor rattled themselves to their feet, one after the other, in slow motion. They reminded him of zombies in the horror movies Hakan sometimes watched late at night.

They formed a zombie waiting line to express their condolences to him one by one with wet kisses and hugs. Some spoke to him in a language Ümit didn't understand. They all smelled the same: like bad breath and Kolonya perfume. Each time they came in, Ümit did his best to leave a bit of room between his scrawny chest and the women's soft warm breasts, but it was hopeless.

He hunted around the room for Peri out of the corner of his eye. When he finally found her, he tried to signal to her to come to his rescue. But Peri remained standing in a corner, staring at her feet. The way she was rubbing her cheeks in disgust with the backs of her hands told him that she, too, had fallen victim to this eddy of commiseration. And yet Ümit couldn't help but feel terribly alone surrounded by all these unknown women's kisses. He felt like a little orphan boy, wept over and pitied by a world that knew he'd never amount to anything now without his father's shielding hands over his head. A loser.

Ümit hasn't left the bed. But he can hear scraps of conversation and footsteps in the hallway where his father died. The air hangs smoldering in the bedroom. Unbearable. Ümit wants to move, but he can't. He's lying in his own sticky juices. He has to think about the strange language of those zombie women, and the way his mother spoke to them yesterday in the same tongue. Why hadn't he known his mother could speak a foreign language? And why hadn't he ever heard this language before himself? He always thought his mother could only speak Turkish and about three words of German. And suddenly there she was, responding to these women and Ümit didn't know what she was saying. Where had she learned it?

Ümit guesses it must have been Kurdish because the Kurds are always in the news these days. Ever since they captured that Öcalan guy. But how can it be that Ümit never knew his own mother was Kurdish? Had his father been Kurdish too? What would that make his siblings? What did that make Ümit himself? Had he just not been listening properly when they'd talked about these kinds of things? Had he been too busy daydreaming? You're supposed to know what you are by the time that you're fifteen. Ümit can't just walk up now and say: *Anne, are we*

Kurdish? That would be ridiculous. Embarrassing. You're supposed to
know these things.

Ümit finally manages to get up. He does it quickly, cracks a window,
reaches for his Walkman, then slips back onto the sheets. He's gotten
up too quickly, and the room is spinning. Ümit's head feels heavy. That
metallic taste isn't just on his tongue anymore, it's spreading into his
brain. Each new breath into his body feels mechanical, and his ears
squeak like his thoughts were creaky hinges. Ümit sighs and switches
on his Walkman to tune out the squealing in his ears. Biggie raps: *And
if you don't know, now you know.* The sound rattles straight through Ümit's
tinny brain. Hakan had given him this cassette tape recently, just before
he moved out. At first, Ümit had been happy to finally not have to share
a room with his big brother anymore. But as soon as Hakan was gone,
Ümit was overcome by a strange fear: what if he suffocated in his sleep
and no one was there to notice?

   At least he gets to share a room with Hakan here again. That is,
whenever Hakan finally makes an appearance. Ümit fast-forwards to
Mariah Carey. She wasn't on Hakan's original tape, of course. Mariah
was not his jam. But Ümit had recorded over one of Hakan's more boring tracks with "The Beautiful Ones" when it played on the radio. Unfortunately, the DJ had started talking over them right at the climax of
the song, just when Mariah and Dru Hill were really getting into it.
Which is why Ümit has decided to get himself a copy of the *Butterfly*
album here. Peri told him there were shops in Turkey where you could
put together your own mixed tapes with any song you can think of, or
else buy bootleg albums for just a mark or two. Ümit wouldn't know
these kinds of things on his own; he was only nine the last time he was in
Turkey. All he can really remember are the sugar crystals on the Haylayf
cookies and the little girl who got run over by a semitruck on the street
in front of the cookie shop. They'd scraped her body up before his eyes:
tiny and delicate as a lifeless bird on the roadside.

   Normally, Ümit has to cry whenever he thinks about the cookie
girl. And usually whenever he listens to this Mariah Carey song too.
But ever since the news about his father, everything's been different.

Since that phone call yesterday, since that scream in the night. Or no. Really, more precisely, ever since the moment Ümit padded half-asleep into the living room and found his family—or what was left of it— seated before him, tear-streaked and in shock. Now Ümit can't cry anymore. He tells himself from now on he's going to be somebody else. The damage has been done, but he can't feel it yet. Its presence hasn't registered in Ümit's body. Nothing hurts. There's only this one feeling: regret.

Ümit always has to think about that day at one of his home games when his father came and stood at the edge of the soccer field. He'd stood there all by himself on the sideline, and all of a sudden he had shouted: *Saldır! Koş oğlum!* Ümit had kept running. He hadn't even looked at his father, his head throbbing instead with swirling thoughts and shame. Shame that his father had yelled commands at him in Turkish across the entire soccer field instead of standing around with the other fathers drinking a light beer and making the odd commentary in German. He'd been ashamed of his father for stopping by just like that on his way home, a full bag of groceries in one hand—a bag from the discount supermarket. All Ümit had wanted was not to be associated by his teammates with those discount groceries. And that same night, he'd begged his father not to come to his games anymore. He'd stood meekly in their kitchen, hands in his pockets, and said only: *Baba, you distract me from the game.* But his father had known precisely what this was really all about. His father had responded with a single look. A look Ümit now wished had never been.

There is an emptiness. It's been there for a while. It was already there when his father was still alive. And, of course, at some point Ümit will get used to his father's absence. One gets used to anything. But how long do these things take? And more importantly: When will the others get used to it? When will he be able to speak to his mother again without being afraid of seeing that fear in her eyes?

Ever since yesterday, she's looked like she's in a constant state of panic. Panic, perhaps, because she doesn't know if she can survive this pain? Will Ümit only be able to share in missing his father, too, after he no longer has to worry about his mother and sister? They seem like they've completely lost it ever since that phone call in the night. They'd broken down at the airport. They broke down on the plane. They broke down going through customs. And they broke down at the taxi stand. They were both so haggard by the end that they had had to hold on to each other, crouching, trying not to get lost while they dragged themselves through the garbage-littered street. But Ümit could only stiffen, lower his gaze, try to be as unobtrusive as possible: like a stranger lost in thought who only happened by chance to be standing next to these two broken women. Willing himself away to another world entirely, or maybe just ten paces further because this world seems to expect something of him that he cannot provide.

Dead. He is dead. But what exactly is death anyway? Is death a state like sleeping, only longer? Never-ending. Like a dream, but without those flights of stairs one sometimes stumbles down into waking? A kind of sugar sleep? And aren't we all just dying constantly over the course of our lifetimes? Because we wake each morning as a different person? Every day a bit sadder, a bit more afraid? Awaken each day as someone with just a little bit less faith. Hadn't the person Ümit was only yesterday also died during the night? Can we ever find our way back to the lightness we felt in ourselves at, say, the tender age of ten? No? Then where was that boy now? Where?

Ümit pulls the sheets up over his head, thinking of Jonas. Of course, Ümit had promised Dr. Schumann he would block out every thought of Jonas like an unwelcome storm cloud. And that when he had difficulty doing so, he would tug at the rubber band he was supposed to wear around his wrist. That thin rubber band, like the kind they put around bunches of green onions at the supermarket. Dr. Schumann had presented it to him like some priceless treasure: an essential instrument for bringing the thought carousel in his mind to a screeching halt. But Dr. Schumann is far away now, and his rubber band is lying in a dumpster at the Frankfurt airport. Ümit is trapped in this apartment of mourning today, and the only thing that can help him escape the moment is this carousel. The laughter in Jonas's eyes when he made a goal. After games, Ümit always congratulated Jonas with a fleeting hug, a hug that would then repeat itself a thousand times over in Ümit's head during the night. Evolving with each repetition, growing longer and more intimate, until finally, Ümit and Jonas lay together in the middle of the soccer field, their bodies rubbing together with enough force to start a fire.

Ümit is trying to remember the smell of Jonas's jersey he had sometimes sniffed in the locker room when everyone else was in the shower. Jonas's sweat smelled like Juicy Fruit gum. Ümit's hand slips beneath his underwear. But nothing happens there. The cassette tape is back on one of Hakan's songs: "Ruff Ryder's Anthem." Ümit's right hand makes a couple more passes before giving up. Weird. This never happens. But maybe it's part of his mourning—the sadness he could not feel yesterday, at least not like the others. He couldn't cry; he did not collapse. Ümit could only stand there feeling the presence of the monster inside him. A monster growing ever greater, all-consuming: his thoughts, his feelings, his hunger.

Now, in the sticky half-light under the sheets, he's thinking about how sadness and mourning might be different for everyone. For his mother and sister, it's these constant breakdowns, but for Ümit, it's his dick: lifeless and limp. And then, suddenly the bedsheets are torn back, and Peri is standing over him blank-faced with a towel around her head. She says something, but Ümit can only hear DMX bellowing his refrain. He jerks his hand from his underpants, instinctively. Peri remains expressionless, turns around, exits the room. Maybe she hadn't noticed. Ümit tears off his headphones, throws on a pair of shorts, and heads for the bathroom.

He splashes cold water on his face until the lump in his throat loosens. Ümit hasn't eaten for a day and a half. In the living room, his mother and sister are already seated at the breakfast table. The table is large. Round. It tells of plans for family meals and game nights with Turkish rummy tiles. Things his family doesn't do. Ümit hates this table immediately. But he sits down anyway because he doesn't know what else to do. The neighbor woman with the thick glasses from the apartment below is back again. She's filling their tea glasses. The murmur of the hot water in the kettle hurts his head.

"Where's Hakan?"

His question hangs in the air.

Everyone keeps chewing on their rubbery bread, drinking tea the color of rabbit blood. Pretending like they're having breakfast. But no one tries the apricot marmalade or the watermelon or any of the other things on the table that might actually taste like something. Emine only stares with her puffy eyes into the glowing russet of her tea glass, sitting there like an empty husk. Peri, on the contrary, looks wide awake. More awake than yesterday, anyway. Her freshly washed hair lies in wet braids. She's almost back to the Peri Ümit usually knows: seated cross-legged in her chair, slurping earnestly at her tea, a hundred thoughts competing in her head.

"Peri. Where is Hakan?"

"Missed his flight. Arriving this evening." Peri casts a fleeting glance to her right, trying discreetly to gauge their mother's reaction. Ümit's mother sets her tea glass down with a heavy sigh. Peri's dark eyes meet Ümit's in warning.

"This evening?" he asks anyway. "So, he's not going to make it to the . . . ?"

A spasm convulses through the room.

As though Peri and the neighbor woman were trying to flinch the word *funeral* away with their shoulders.

This neighbor takes a seat next to Ümit, laying her clammy hand on his. Her face is long and narrow like the mask from *Scream*.

"Your father has been waiting for more than a day. We cannot leave him any longer. We must return him to the earth."

Return him to the earth? What's the rush, Ümit thinks. But this time he doesn't say anything out loud. His mother removes her silken head-scarf and fans herself with her hands. Her pale face begins to flush. Grows angry. The neighbor woman rises from the table and brings her a glass of water from the kitchen.

"Here, Emine."

"Thank you, Bacım," Ümit's mother says with a strained voice. She takes only a tiny sip.

"And where is Sevda Abla?"

Peri clenches one eye shut and casts Ümit a withering glare with the other: *Just shut your mouth*, the look says. *Keep it shut.*

His mother braces her elbows against the table and raises her open hands as though she wants to offer up a prayer.

"Rabbim! Grant me patience!"

Peri shakes her head, still glaring at Ümit, already anticipating what's to come. *Now see what you've done.*

"These children," his mother snarls, her torso swaying like a heavy ship at sea. Ümit knows what's coming too. Everything with his mother has always been dramatic. Each new emotion is always heralded by gesticulations and sighs. The crescendo always arrives with a frenzied spike in blood pressure. It's easy to upset her, it's always been this way. But even Ümit startles when she slams her fist down on the table.

"These children! They have only one duty," Emine cries, shaking her index finger at the heavens. "Only one! That they should bury their parents with dignity. But this is too much for them! Even this is too much!"

Peri scoots her chair closer to their mother.

"Anne! Ümit and I are here. Don't get so excited, remember your blood pressure," she says, rubbing Emine's back softly with one hand, as though this could stave off the coming avalanche.

"But what's up with Sevda Abla? Where is she?" Ümit repeats quietly to the neighbor woman. She merely serves a bit of sheep's cheese onto his empty plate in answer, shaking her head obliviously.

In the meantime, his mother has progressed into a full rage. She slams her fist against the table a second time. This time, they all startle at once.

"Your sister missed her flight too! Can it be? Can it? Sevda, who thinks she is the cleverest one of all, thinks she is better than us because she made a little money. But see: she cannot even make it to the airport on time. She is completely useless!"

Her head falls on the palms of her outstretched hands, her body trembling as she begins to sob.

"How did he deserve it? Your father did not deserve this . . ."

Peri rolls her eyes and rises silently to her feet. She shakes her head helplessly. The neighbor woman nods to her, taking over. She moves to settle into Peri's empty seat and comforts their mother as though they hadn't just met only yesterday for the first time. Why is this neighbor woman so involved? Doesn't she have anything better to do? Probably not. But how can she act with such compassion, as though it were her own family, her own loss? Ümit knows he should be grateful to her for this actually, but the performance seems so artificial. And her mask of a face still creeps him out.

His mother wails louder than Ümit has ever heard her wail before. His chest tightens. With half-sunk head, he looks from side to side. Can he manage to cry along this time and take his mother in his arms? Or can he do what he really wants to do and follow Peri out into the other room, the one with the second balcony? Can he just go and share a cigarette with Peri on the balcony? But Ümit's not sure what the right decision would be, and so, he stays put where he is.

He has to think about Sevda now. He's never understood what the problem is between his mother and his eldest sister. He was just a baby when Sevda got married and moved away. It's an old story. As far back as he can remember, there has always been a coldness between them. Ümit stares at the ornate cupboard in the corner, at the square mirror hanging over it. Everything smells new. Like paint. Like wood. Like the plastic tarps Ümit imagines being spread over the furniture for transportation. He can't help but hate this apartment because it was his father's dream. And because it now belongs just as much to the past as his father does. The whole apartment is nothing more than a museum, the museum of Hüseyin Yılmaz's dreams. And who needs museums anyway?

His mother's crying has grown softer. The neighbor woman is stroking her back, extending a tissue to Ümit with her other hand. He grasps for it, trying his best to jerk a couple tears. Something is building in his eye, something is there. But it's not honest enough to spill out over his cheek. Ümit rubs the tissue over his dry face anyway.

Hakan hadn't cried yesterday either. But maybe he had done so after the others left. There are only two times in a man's life when he's allowed to cry: at the death of his mother and at the death of his father. Of course, there are also the deaths of your wife and your own children, but these things have little relevance in Ümit's life. And not because he's never interested in women per se: it just doesn't happen often. But still, you can't rule out the possibility entirely.

After all, the very first time he had touched himself had been during one of those movies with Banu Alkan in her skimpy bathing suits. A daytime movie showing on some Turkish TV channel. It happened during that summer when Ümit had to stay in after school and hadn't been allowed to play outside because his mother thought the old metalworks was poisoning the neighborhood.

But the idea of living together with someone and having his own family seems absurd to Ümit, who is far more concerned with impatiently counting down the days until he can finally leave the family he already has behind. Not because he doesn't love them. They mean everything to him. But this *everything* also includes the very air he breathes, along with the noose around his neck.

Ümit had cried a lot over these past months. During those meetings with Dr. Schumann. Because of Jonas. Because of the incident with the letter. But now? Now that something far worse had actually happened, crying no longer works. His tear ducts are all used up and empty. Despite the heat, they, too, have been cast over with the same coating of cold metal that had already hardened over his head. It lies heavy on his bones, permitting him no softness. Not on the skin around his hips, not on the surface of his eyelids. Nothing feels the same as it did before that phone call last night. No part of his body and no part of his family—a family that will never be whole again. And yet, all the same, Ümit still feels terribly indifferent.

Breakfast ends abruptly. The plates all seem to have wandered into the kitchen on their own. Ümit sees only one half-empty tea glass on the table in front of him. He's growing impatient. Peri and his mother rush around the room, looking for a long skirt, the headscarf without the flowers, a purse. Everything they need today: the day of the funeral. Ümit has never been to a funeral before. His head is flooded with images he knows from American movies: everyone in black. He looks at his mother; she's not wearing black. He looks at the neighbor woman, who is certainly coming with them too. She isn't wearing black either. Only Peri's wearing black. But Peri's goth. She always wears black. Ever since Kurt Cobain blew himself away.

The neighbor woman is drawing wet circles on the table with a kitchen rag. She whispers to Ümit: "Drink your tea and then go get ready, my son. We must go to the hospital and collect your father."

Collect his father? Ümit jumps to his feet and carries his glass of tea with him to the bedroom. His heart is racing. The packet of pills is waiting for him in a sock inside his backpack. Dr. Schumann had given him these pills a week ago when Ümit told him that the trick with the rubber band wasn't working. *Only take these when you feel like you can't take it anymore,* Dr. Schumann had said. But Ümit didn't trust him. He'd sworn to himself he'd never touch those pills. And then, yesterday, on the airplane, for the first time he really had felt like he couldn't take it anymore. He'd swallowed his first pill right after landing, and it helped. Helped him not take everything happening around him so hard; helped him be there without really being there at all. Now he swallows a second, chasing it down with the rest of his tea because he's supposed to go collect his father now from some hospital, and there's nothing he wouldn't rather be doing. How was he supposed to *collect* him anyway? In a box, like those Americans in the movies? Or would he have to stare his dead father in the face: the thickness of his grown-together eyebrows, the mole on his cheek, his eyes now closed for eternity. Ümit hoped they would be closed. Some people die with their eyes open; he's seen it on TV. Ümit takes another pill and stashes it in his pocket. Just in case.

"What are you doing?"

Peri is standing in the doorway, her right eyebrow elevated like it always is whenever she's annoyed.

"Nothing."

"Come on. Let's go outside for a minute while they get ready. Hurry up."

Peri throws a blue headscarf around her neck like a shawl at the door. Later, she'll probably wear it around her head like at the mosque. Maybe you're supposed to do that at a funeral? She's wearing skinny jeans and looks even more angular than usual. When she lights a cigarette, Ümit asks if he can have one too.

"You shouldn't even get started," Peri says, but she lets Ümit take a couple drags off hers while they pad down the street.

The high-rise apartment buildings are all painted different colors, and all seem to be leaning in different directions. Green and yellow balloons are billowing in front of a shop window. A lahmacun shop, named after İbrahim Tatlıses. Lahmacun: Ümit's favorite food. Under normal circumstances, he'd be begging Peri to buy him one, but the metal in his stomach leaves no room for appetite. Ümit feels nothing. Even when the smell of freshly baking dough and spicy ground meat waft into his nose.

A group of small children, maybe six years old, runs past them in excitement. A little boy with only one shoe on stops and screams after them: "I'll fuck your mothers, you sons of whores!"

"Interesting neighborhood Baba chose," Ümit whispers to Peri, not wishing for anyone to hear him speaking German here.

"What do you mean? I like it!" Peri replies, staring bemusedly after the children. Of course. Peri likes everything somehow distant and grungy. Otherwise, she wouldn't have moved away to study in Frankfurt a few years back. Ümit could never do that. He doesn't like being places he does not already know. He likes knowing in which houses the biggest assholes live, likes knowing the best places to hide when someone wants to beat him up.

"You have to be more careful with her, you know?" Peri says suddenly, and Ümit knows immediately whom Peri means.

"She was never exactly the most stable person, and she's got a tendency to overdo it. We know that. But I'm really worried she won't be able to handle this thing with Baba now."

Ümit nods. He looks down at the ground. The sidewalk is littered with candy wrappers, crumpled plastic bottles. He feels relieved not to be the only one who's worried about his mother. At least Peri's got things back under control today. She was barely approachable yesterday. That worried Ümit almost more than his mother's condition. He doesn't know Peri that way.

Someone is blocking the path in front of them. An old woman with extremely massive breasts. She smiles at Ümit and Peri, balling her hands against her hips. Her clothes look like she's wearing Emine's pajamas.

"Well, my pretties. Shall I look into the future for you? You two must be wondering what fortunes await you in this life. What loves? What perils?"

Remnants of blue eyeliner are gathered in the bags beneath her eyes. Her canine tooth glistens; it's made of gold.

"Why not," Peri says, shrugging her shoulders.

"We don't have time for this," Ümit hisses, but Peri is already seated on one of the tiny plastic stools the fortune teller has set out on the sidewalk like an impromptu office.

"I've got three minutes and five million lira, so let's do this," Peri says, spreading the bills out on the table. Impatiently, she lights another cigarette, extending her left hand.

Ümit is surprised that Peri's interested in this kind of thing. Cautiously, he takes a seat on the third plastic stool.

"Hmm," the gold woman murmurs, running her fingertips across the palm of Peri's hand. "Hmm."

Ümit leans forward to peer at Peri's hand as well, but he sees only a network of fine lines like the brightly colored Metro map Peri always has at her disposal.

"I see grief, my love."

Ümit and Peri exchange exhausted glances. It isn't hard to read in their faces that something isn't right.

"How many siblings do you have, my love?"

"Yeah. You tell me," Peri counters.

"Hmm." The gold woman closes her eyes. "I see four. With you that would make five."

"Wrong. There's four of us."

"Strange," the gold woman says, counting something on the map of Peri's palm. "Very strange, indeed . . . In any case: you've traveled a long way to be here."

Peri rolls her eyes; she's starting to get bored. And Ümit too. It's not hard to recognize their Almancı accents either.

"Hmmm," the gold woman says again, studying Peri's hand further, pulling it in closer. Silver bracelets with sparkling stones and tiny round mirrors jingle on her arms. Peri's wrist has only one black hair tie. When she was younger, Peri wore lots of jewelry too: lots of rings and necklaces, that kind of thing. Only a single, round nose ring has remained with her from those days. Nothing more. Ümit remembers how she used to wear makeup back then too. They used to fight about it sometimes because he used to like opening her makeup bag and sniffing curiously at the tiny bottles of nail polish. Peri had still been in school. But since moving away, she doesn't wear any of that anymore. No nail polish. No lipstick. Not even a bit of mascara. And she's still beautiful with her big dark eyes and long, glossy hair. But she could do with a bit of color too.

The gold woman looks up at her, staring earnestly.

"This isn't the first time that you've lost someone close to you."

Ümit doesn't understand at first. He shakes his head, then looks questioningly at his sister. Peri looks shocked.

"Is it so?" the gold woman asks her.

Peri shrugs her shoulders, wordlessly.

Ümit wonders whom the fortune teller means. Who else did Peri lose? And why doesn't he know anything about it? Okay, he knows next to nothing about Peri's life in Frankfurt. Only those things she tells him and the others on her weekends home. And that's not exactly a lot.

The fortune teller takes a deep breath, as though preparing herself for a difficult duty. Her breasts rise and fall. It looks like she's searching for the proper words, so as not to overwhelm Peri.

"I want to tell you nice things, my love. But you've trusted me with your hand, and so I must speak the truth."

Ümit stares back at her; his eyes hang on her lips. Now what? Somehow, he'd imagined this whole thing would be more entertaining.

"It is what it is, and so I tell you: I see a coming funeral."

Ümit's heart begins to pound.

Peri smiles bitterly. "It's all good. You're not telling us anything new, Abla."

"I understand, my child. But brace yourself for what I have to say: In truth I see two funerals. One will follow quickly on the other."

"Wait, what?" Ümit exclaims. "What is she saying?"

He hears his voice mutedly, as if he has water in his ears. He presses his fingers nervously against them, while Peri and the fortune teller continue their conversation. Suddenly, Peri stands up, glaring down at the plastic stool as though she'd like to kick it.

"Come on, we've gotta go!" She grabs Ümit under the arm, hurrying away with him in the direction of the apartment.

"I speak only the truth! I never lie!" Ümit hears the gold-toothed woman cry out behind them. But Peri only shakes her head in anger.

"That old bag's out of her mind. I paid her to cheer me up, not tell me more psychotic bullshit."

Ümit's mother and the neighbor woman are already standing in front of the door, waiting for them arm in arm like twins in their broad summer coats. They're wearing the same coat, the one made from that material that gives you a light shock of static electricity every time you brush against it. Ümit's mother's coat is grayish, and the neighbor's is beige. Ümit wonders why this neighbor woman is coming with them to the hospital, but then he notices a white cat and bends down to pet it, completely forgetting what he was just thinking about. The cat's fur is unbelievably soft, softer than anything Ümit has ever touched before. He can't stop petting it. Peri squeals, *oooh*, and bends, too, to scratch the cat behind its ears.

"Tell me, have you both gone completely mad?" their mother cries. "Why are you touching that filthy animal?"

The neighbor woman soothes her, says it's not that bad, reminds her that they will have to perform abdest in the hospital anyway.

"Abdest? Shit, Peri, I don't remember how that works!" Ümit whispers nervously in his sister's ear. His heart begins to race again.

Peri rolls her eyes. "It doesn't even matter."

"Yes, it does! We're going straight to the funeral from there!"

"Just wash yourself all over till you're clean. It's not that hard."

A man with a thick moustache and sad eyes arrives to pick them up. He flicks away his cigarette and opens the doors of his white jalopy. This man had been there last night standing in front of the apartment too. He'd introduced himself as Ümit's father's nephew. The son of so-and-so. He's about as old as Hakan, but he already dresses like an old man. There's a tiny cushion embroidered with some words of Arabic hanging from his rearview mirror.

Ümit sinks into the passenger seat. He rolls down the window, allowing the warm outside air to swirl through his hair, while Peri squeezes into the back seat between his mother and the neighbor woman. Ümit can hear them sobbing. But he'd rather not turn around. The combination of the noisy chaos of the city and the pill in his bloodstream makes it easier for him to tune out the three behind him. He fixates instead on the faces of the people rushing by outside, one, then another, then another. They look familiar, like distant acquaintances with whom he could enter into an easy conversation beginning with the question: *Borussia Dortmund or Bayern München?* And followed by: Did his father drive a Mercedes or a BMW? People had always asked him that on previous family holidays in Turkey.

The streets are distended, full of potholes, as if they were driving on the moon. The car's engine howls; it's moving in such a way that Ümit imagines it could defy gravity at any minute and blast off over the rooftops of Zeytinburnu. He's reminded of plate tectonics again—the Eurasian and Anatolian plates—how they collide here, directly beneath them, grinding against one another, building up a tension that could release at any moment in a colossal earthquake. Or not for thirty or even a hundred years.

For the first time, Ümit thinks he can understand just what it was his father saw in this city. Yesterday, Istanbul had seemed to him like nothing more than a giant trash heap filled with far too many tragic children pawing at the car windows with their dirty fingers, begging for a couple spare lira. But today, Ümit sees the mystery and the familiarity too.

Sees the crumbling facades of houses and the brightly colored carpets fluttering from windows, the faces of the men wreathed in smoke, the old women huddled together in the shadows as they rush past him. They all seem so familiar. As if Ümit had already been here innumerable times before. He can feel the joy welling inside him. The joy of being among so many people and yet remaining anonymous to all. Perhaps Ümit has nothing to be afraid of here, perhaps the entire city is one giant hiding place because you don't stand out among so many strangers, because you can simply be normal here because everyone else is busy with themselves. Is that why Peri moved to Frankfurt? Maybe Ümit should escape and study something too.

When they arrive at the hospital parking lot, Ümit's legs are as limp as yeasted bread dough waiting to rise, waiting to be kneaded. While everyone else hurries from the car, Ümit only slowly manages to extend his feet from the door and place them on the asphalt. He braces himself against the hood of the car while Peri, his mother, and the neighbor woman rush toward the rear entry of the hospital as if time were still of some significance to the dead.

Suddenly, Ümit sees a black, veiled figure flit across the parking lot behind his family, as though it were stalking them like prey. There are two figures. On second glance, he recognizes them: it's Ayşe Yenge with one of her two bodyguards. What are they doing here? Ayşe Yenge is saying something to Ümit's mother. They exchange only a few words before Emine sends them packing with an angry hand gesture. Peri and the neighbor woman drag Ümit's mother into the hospital while Ayşe Yenge and the ghost beside her scuttle back across the parking lot with bowed heads. Ümit takes a deep breath, uncertain now whether he really saw these two women at all. He decides to take the second pill in his pocket. Ümit doesn't have any water to wash it down with, and the pill sticks somewhere halfway down his throat.

"Is everything okay?"

With a start, Ümit realizes his cousin is still standing next to him. He nods, slapping himself on the chest. The pill slides down a bit further. Cautiously, he places one foot in front of the other. And they work:

dependably and purposefully, as though operating of their own free will. Ümit's cousin follows after him. The metal coating inside Ümit begins flaking away, and suddenly the parking lot feels as soft as a freshly laundered bathmat.

The sounds at the entry to the hospital invade his ears like insects. A shrill peep, a creaking wheeze, a constant rush like a radio with bad reception. Bodies are being transferred back and forth in the sharp light of the neon tubes above them: sleeping bodies, bandaged bodies, hysterical bodies. A white filter of smoke hangs over everyone. Is there a fog machine running somewhere in this hospital? Ümit's mother droops beside the neighbor woman on a row of green plastic chairs. Ümit decides to head for Peri at the reception counter instead. Peri looks sidelong at him, a single eyebrow cocked. She lays two fingers on his damp forehead, wiping them across his face like a fogged-up mirror.

"Why are you so sweaty?"

"Who, me?"

Idiot. What kind of question was that: *Me?* Of course, she means you; who else would she mean besides the person she's looking at, the person whose face she's touching. She means precisely the person she believes you to be. But who does Peri see when she looks at you? Who are you to her, who is this Ümit person? A small, helpless pubescent brother with a perspiration problem? Or an insufferable boy, a sicko, who can't cry for his own dead father and whose apathy seeps from his pores like poison, infecting everything around him? Is that white smoke actually coming from him? Is that Ümit's poison floating in the air?

Ümit's sister knows him better than do any of their other siblings, even though Hakan slept in the same bedroom with Ümit all his life and Sevda fed and diapered him as a baby. It's still Peri who really sees him. Peri knows what's happening to him; Peri's been through stuff herself. And Peri can keep a secret without Ümit even revealing it to her.

Peri takes Ümit's hand. Who did she lose? What had the gold woman meant? Had Peri loved someone and lost them? This unknown cousin and another man in white scrubs come down the corridor toward the waiting room. The man is dressed like a doctor, but he doesn't seem to be one. Their cousin calls him "Hodja." The hodja says something to

Ümit, but the words don't register. There are still insects buzzing in his ears. He watches his unknown cousin nodding at the hodja's words and simply imitates his nodding. Ümit tries his best to do it at the same tempo as his cousin, who has also begun to fiddle with his pack of cigarettes and stare nervously toward the exit. Why doesn't he just leave? Why does he think he needs to be here anyway? His job is done; he drove them here. Is he waiting for a "Thank you and goodbye"?

The hodja gestures at something behind him with a nod of his head. The neighbor woman pats Ümit's mother on the shoulder and remains seated in the waiting room. Ümit's mother, the unknown cousin, and Peri all follow the hodja. Peri takes Ümit by the hand, and his feet pad along automatically behind her. Together they hurry down the hectic length of the hallway where exhausted strangers huddle waiting on the floor. Some are crying; some simply stare blindly into space. Still others call out after the hodja, babbling excitedly until they realize he's not a doctor.

The four of them pile into an elevator. It's filled with a soft mist too. The elevator descends to a stop two floors underground. His mother is breathing heavily, close to Ümit's ear like a whisper. Like a storm. A threat to Ümit's sanity. Ümit has felt this breathing in his ear since childhood. Whenever he feels it, it means his mother has ventured far too close. That there's no space left between them. That she can do with him as she pleases because she is his mother and mothers can do these things. Not that Emine would ever do anything specifically to harm him. At least not on purpose. And yet this kind of proximity still feels wrong. Feels threatening. Because it isn't consensual. Because Ümit cannot escape. Because he can't do a thing about it without behaving like a disrespectful bastard.

Ümit gasps. The others are panting too. Only the hodja maintains his composure at the elevator door. They exit, continue down to the end of another corridor, but this time there's no one else waiting in the hall. It's cooler down here too, and it smells more severely of medicine. Like iodine on bloodied knees. Their shoes click-clack over the stone floor until they arrive at a large, white-tiled room with nothing but a wardrobe in one corner, a large metal table in the center, and two hoses next to an enormous soap dispenser.

"You can deposit your things here until we collect him," the hodja says in his white scrubs.

Ümit looks around himself uncertainly.

Deposit? Deposit what? Were they supposed to undress now? And then what? Open the spigots? Should they throw a foam party with the soap dispenser like they do in those nightclubs in Bodrum he's seen on TV? Ümit giggles to himself at the thought. Or had he just giggled out loud in the tiled room? He looks around himself again, fearfully, locks eyes with his unknown cousin. This cousin still has an air of sadness about him, but then, all of a sudden, he winks at Ümit with one eye and then the other, like he's trying to encourage him somehow. Ümit is beginning to understand what this cousin is doing here. He's a Hakan substitute. The man of the house. He's there to accompany Ümit because Ümit's not man enough to survive the challenge on his own. That's probably what they were thinking. And whoever *they* are, they were right. Ümit doesn't know how he's supposed to behave at this sort of thing. He only knows that he's got to keep himself under control, that he shouldn't laugh out loud at any cost.

But of course, just when Ümit's thinking this, a wave suddenly rolls across his stomach, a ripple of laughter scheming deviously to escape. Ümit tries to contain the wave by crossing his arms tightly. This laughter must not make it to his throat! Ümit needs to smother it; he needs to think of something else. Death. He peers around him. His mother seems to be having difficulties taking off her coat; Peri gives her a hand, then hangs Emine's coat in the wardrobe. Sleeves are being rolled up. Hands washed. Prayers whispered. Ümit swallows, trying not to listen. Whenever people pray, Ümit immediately feels guilty. As long as he's in the room, it seems to Ümit that their prayers are all in vain. His very presence will prevent these prayers from being answered. He decides to simply imitate the others' movements—particularly the washing—like following warmups at soccer practice. He'd learned to perform abdest as a kid, but really only to show his father that he could. And now, Ümit's having difficulty remembering the order, just like all the other things he's had to memorize. Ümit's done a lot of things for no other reason than to impress his father. Little things. But also, big ones. This he's discovered during his sessions with Dr. Schumann.

Ümit had gotten good grades, said his prayers, broken a tenth grader's nose, and gone to soccer practice twice a week despite the fact that he had not enjoyed it. Ümit hadn't known all these things had to do with his father. But Dr. Schumann had known it instantly. The week after his hypnosis, Dr. Schumann explained to Ümit that he had been suffering since childhood from the repercussions of a cold relationship with his father. Ümit understood the things his father valued and tried to make a good impression through effort and acquiring knowledge: prayer, sports, school. Yeah, could be, Ümit had thought while Dr. Schumann explained all this to him. But what did that have to do with breaking the tenth grader's nose?

"Go clean yourself off. You stink, you filthy wetback kanake!" the boy had said. Out of the clear blue. For no other reason than because he'd happened to pass Ümit on the schoolyard. Because he could. And without giving it a second thought, Ümit had wound back and hammered his fist into the boy's freckly face. Now, had he given it even a moment's consideration, things would have transpired differently: Ümit would have lacked both the courage and the strength to defend himself against a tenth grader. But Ümit hadn't thought at all. His fist had acted of its own accord, from a place over which Ümit had no control.

"This type of masculinity," Dr. Schumann had later said, "is precisely that which your father taught you by example. The young man's insult was directed at your father. Against his temperament and disposition. And you tried to react in the same manner your father would."

Ümit had simply nodded along. Back then, he'd thought he could rid himself of the whole situation quicker by just nodding. What good would it have done to tell Dr. Schumann that he didn't understand a word he was saying and that his father was definitely not the kind of man to break somebody's nose. It would have been pointless, and so, Ümit held his tongue. He'd kept silent, too, about the fact that it was this broken nose that had inspired Jonas to talk to him in the first place. That they had only started hanging out after this incident.

The door opens and two men in blue uniforms roll a cart into the tiled basement room. Verbally, they express their condolences, but their eyes are as distant and empty as those of people who find their own work boring. A long gray bag is lying on their cart. A bag the length of Baba. The two men roll the cart up to the metal table, bend forward to unzip the gray bag. They pull the zipper down the entire length of the Baba-bag.

Neither of the men so much as look at Ümit or his family. The bag lies open there, and Ümit hears a tiny cry. A moment's jolt. An *ah*. He doesn't know who it came from, but he closes his eyes, willing himself to be somewhere, anywhere else with all his might, imagining his bedroom, then the changing room of his soccer club, the warm stone ping-pong table in the park he sometimes sits on with Jonas. But nothing works. Something new has mingled with the medical smell in the room. Something pungent. It forces Ümit back, preventing his escape. It smells old and sweet like dried lavender. Ümit can hear the two men rustling around with the bag. He hears a strained exhalation, then listens as they roll the cart away. Hears the hodja's voice as he begins reciting a prayer. Someone touches Ümit's arm, pulls at him, draws him a few steps forward, taking his hand as if inviting him to dance. They open his hand palm upward while Ümit squeezes his eyes tightly shut, allowing himself to be guided along.

～

The splash of water. His team was at a training camp somewhere in the country and pollen was drifting over Jonas's head like snow where he stood on the field. It was the final evening and the rest of the team had taken three cases of beer down to the lake. Only Jonas and Ümit had stayed behind at the hostel, telling the others they'd come along later. They were seated together in an empty stairwell, beer bottles in hand, when Jonas first told Ümit about his father. Jonas couldn't really remember him because he'd gone back to America after his service time in Germany had ended. Jonas and his mother never heard from him again.

Ümit said: *But you can look for him. Fly to America someday and find him.* Jonas just shook his head, smiling softly. There was something in his eyes that Ümit had already seen before, though he could only read it now. Shards telling him that something inside Jonas was broken. Ümit could understand this; he had always believed something was broken inside him too. *Yeah. Maybe I'll go to America someday,* Jonas said. *To feel less alone. Because there's other people there like me. Not like here, where everyone looks at me like some kind of intruder, like someone who can't belong. I'm always the only Black person in the room. When I go home, I'm still the only Black person, even with my mom. And sometimes I feel like she thinks I'm an intruder in her life too. I don't know, maybe I'm just imagining it. But I hate feeling this way. And I can tell you one thing: I'd never go to America to look for my fucking father. Fuck him. If he doesn't want me, I sure as hell don't want him.*

Silence fell over the stairwell. The air smelled like greasy meat and stale fruit tea. Jonas said: *I heard there was a pool down in the basement.* They drained their beers and commenced searching the darkened building for an entrance to the basement room. They found an unlocked door. *Why would we go down to that dirty lake when we have our own private pool?*

Jonas took off his shirt and pants and jumped into the water. Ümit followed his example and was surprised by the coldness of the water. They swam toward each other, then after one another, racing back and forth, diving to the bottom, dunking each other's faces underwater. Their laughter echoed from the grouted tile of the pool, reflecting back from every corner to their ears.

The water prickled Ümit's skin like tiny needles; he needed to keep moving to stay warm, and Jonas too. They made a game of it, danced in the water rapping the intro to *The Fresh Prince of Bel-Air*. They knew every line, every single word. Their movements grew sillier, maybe because they were drunk or maybe just because the others weren't there. Jonas's arm brushed Ümit's shoulder; Jonas's belly, Ümit's back. Knees against his hips. Skin to skin. Ümit's body yielded, sinking backward. Jonas's chin on his head, his fingers laced across Ümit's face. For one

moment. Then another. They sank into the water as if melting together;
they stopped moving completely. Until finally, Jonas let go, pushed off,
and swam a couple strokes away. Ümit stayed under, holding his breath,
just a few seconds, a few seconds more, and then a few more seconds
still. Until his lungs began to burn and tiny bubbles gathered around
his nose and started rising. A ticklish happiness, a sultry lightness of
being. As if he could soon burst into a thousand tiny feathers. Suddenly,
Jonas grabbed him under the arms, pulling him close before kicking
to the surface. It felt like an embrace. Oxygen shocked Ümit back into
the moment. Jonas was screaming at him: *Hey man, did you forget how
to swim or what?* He inhaled the smell of chlorine, struggled for breath,
and laughed.

That night, after the other boys had returned and long since fallen
asleep, Ümit sat awake on his mattress, the lower berth of a squeaky
metal bunkbed, watching Jonas sleeping in the bed across from him.
Not that there was much to see, but a beam of light from the streetlamp
fell across the floor between their beds. Ümit could only just make out
the contours of Jonas's slender torso, a thin and bony violet, a lovingly
drawn line. Uneven. Somewhat clumsy. As if drawn without a ruler.
And for that reason alone, unique. Jonas's chest rose and fell peacefully.
Ümit thought back to the swimming pool, to their underwater embrace.
Repeated the scene over and over in his head until Jonas was no longer
in the pool but standing in the showers they'd passed by. He imagined
them washing each other, lathering until every inch of their bodies was
slippery, slick as glass. He slipped below the blankets with his notebook
and a flashlight, drawing Jonas, the softness of his close-shorn curls. The
long curve of his eyelashes. The M of his lips. Ümit wrote Jonas a letter,
describing the line he made in his sleep. Describing how he'd sunk into
the depths of the pool with the weight of Jonas's body and felt the wish
never to emerge again.

Ümit folded the letter, crept two paces through the room of sleeping boys, and tucked it into Jonas's backpack. Later, Ümit would ask
himself again and again why he had done this. And he would always
tell himself that he simply could not have done otherwise. That he'd
yearned for nothing more badly than to show Jonas who he really was.

Completely. Just as he was. That he had not wanted to hide anymore, even if only for a moment. That he'd wanted to feel stronger than he ever felt before, wanted to reveal the things inside him that weren't right, the things that made no sense. Everything he'd always hidden from the world to avoid catastrophe.

And then he'd awoken the next morning to precisely this catastrophe. Lying in a puddle of sweat, fear pulsing in his throat like a second heartbeat. He'd spent the entire bus ride home in terror that Jonas might open his Eastpak, wondering if he would discover the letter right away. Or would he first find it at home? Or the next morning when he packed his bag for school?

That night, Ümit dreamed of Jonas, and he went to practice the next afternoon with a smile on his lips. It was not a happy smile but one of panic that had frozen on his face because now everything, everything in his life revolved around the single question of whether Jonas had read his letter or not. When Jonas finally arrived in the locker room, he threw his Eastpak on the bench at the opposite end of the room. He was already changed; he only needed to switch shoes. And he did so with violence, concentrating on not looking in Ümit's direction. Ümit sat among his clothes and stared into the emptiness around him. He finally knew at last: the letter had been a bad idea.

At their next practice three days later, Jonas only looked at him once. A look that told Ümit nothing. Not even anger. The thought that just the week before Jonas had laughed with him, touched him, shown him his broken pieces, and that it would never be this way again now was enough to suffocate Ümit. Jonas seemed disappointed. As if Ümit had somehow betrayed his confidence. And then, the first signs began to show with his teammates on the field. An elbow in the side here, a foot to trip him there. "Watch out, faggot!" someone called out once across the field. Did they mean him? And did they mean faggot like gay? Or did they mean it like idiot, dumbass, douchebag, fool?

Ümit only knotted his brow, willing his body to run on as though nothing had happened. He saw himself from the outside as they mocked him with little gestures, pushed him a bit too roughly to the ground. Watched and shook his head, as if it wasn't happening to him at all but to some other boy Ümit could only recognize from a distance and think to himself: *What a loser.* Soon the entire team had turned against Ümit, to the extent that even their coach noticed it at their next practice. By the fourth week, Ümit did not show up to practice anymore. He stayed home, lying in his bed, listening to one of Hakan's Biggie tapes. That evening, his coach, Walter, called. Ümit's mother brought him the phone. The coach suggested a meeting at the clubhouse. Just Ümit and him.

"You've got a real problem, kid."

Walter was seated before him, hands folded one on top of the other, doing his best to appear understanding. There were two bottles of carbonated apple juice in front of him. Ümit had always hated this drink: it reminded him of piss. Especially when it wasn't cold. But he took a sip anyway to combat the dryness in his mouth. Walter's fleshy fingers reminded Ümit of the canned sausages in the jars the other children used to eat at birthday parties while Ümit had to eat a cheerless slice of toast with cheese. A too-small golden ring bit into a sausage on one of Walter's hands. Ümit imagined Walter's pink face on his wedding day at some creepy altar in a cold, dimly lit church.

Once, years back, Walter had given Ümit a red book after practice. It was in Turkish and had the word *İncil* on the cover. He liked to read so much, Walter observed. Said he'd always noticed Ümit with some book or other when they went to away games. Maybe he'd like to read this book too. Ümit had shoved it into his duffel bag and simply thanked his coach rather than telling Walter that his Turkish was lousy and barely sufficed for the kitchen table. On his way back home along the riverbank, he'd also noticed that the book was written in some strange, archaic Turkish Ümit couldn't understand at all. When he got home, he'd simply slipped it into the display case on the bookshelf in the front room. The only other books there were a twenty-volume encyclopedia set bound in brown leather and purchased at a discount with coupons from *Hürriyet*, a thick volume on dream interpretation, and a thin green book with Surah Ya-Sin from the Quran. Their actual Quran was wrapped in a headscarf, locked in a special drawer, and tucked away horizontally like a sleeping baby.

Ümit's father had noticed the new book right away and raised the subject with everyone in the apartment. He waved the tome about the room and had worked himself into quite a frenzy by the time Ümit explained the book was from Walter.

"Who does that dog think he is?"

He'd run straight to the clubhouse with the book and thrust it back into Walter's sausage fingers. Peri explained to Ümit later that *İncil* meant Bible in Turkish. *Yeah, and?* Ümit had thought.

"Baba thinks he's trying to convert you," Peri had said with a look of exhaustion on her face, switching on the tiny television in Hakan and Ümit's room and surfing through the channels to Viva. "I don't know."

"You've got a real problem, kid."

Walter's lips were cracked and gray.

"But you know what the good thing about this problem is? There is a cure."

Ümit had gasped for air. He'd tried explaining to Walter that the letter was just a joke, that Jonas had misunderstood. But Walter would have none of it. His chapped lips opened into a Grand Canyon. *No, no, it was all a misunderstanding*, Ümit said once more, rising to turn and run from the clubhouse. But Walter rose too, and grabbed Ümit by the shirtsleeve, dragging him back down to his seat. He tore Ümit's T-shirt. It was important that Ümit listened to him now, Walter said in a pointedly calm voice. He was only trying to help. Ümit looked from his ripped shirt to Walter's face and the depths of the Grand Canyon and then back at his sausage fingers, wondering how many other T-shirts they'd destroyed. In a panic, he thought that he might be unable to refuse Walter's so-called help no matter what it looked like, and he grew even more convinced of this when Walter threatened that it was his responsibility to inform Ümit's father about the letter.

Ümit inhaled and exhaled. Every bit of energy had left his limbs, and he clung with his right hand to the tear in his T-shirt like a bleeding wound. He gaped at Walter. That was definitely not going to happen. Walter would not speak with Ümit's father if there was anything Ümit could do about it. He'd cave to Walter's demands, of course. Ümit said only yes and yes and yes, again. He allowed Walter to arrange him an appointment with some doctor, and from then on, he no longer went to soccer practice Mondays and Thursdays at five. On Mondays he took a comic book and a bag of Haribo Color-Rado to the riverbank, and on Thursdays he went to Dr. Schumann's office, where they tried to cure him of being in love.

Dr. Schumann's practice was next to a plant nursery behind the train station. It stood at the edge of an industrial area that seemed a strange location for a doctor's office. Every other doctor Ümit had ever been to had their office in the city center or next to the unemployment office. The sign at the door said: *Dr. Richard Schumann, Psychological Advisor.*

Dr. Schumann opened the door himself. There wasn't a waiting room or a receptionist or anything. There was only Dr. Schumann, who led Ümit down a small, dark corridor to an airy room with a writing desk in one corner and two large, black leather chairs in the other. It was only here that Dr. Schumann finally gave him his hand. Ümit first dried his own sweaty palms against his jeans before extending his right hand to Dr. Schumann. Dr. Schumann's grip was not merely firm; it was like a meatgrinder pounding Ümit's hand into mincemeat. They took seats on the cold leather chairs while Ümit tried to calm his breathing. Dr. Schumann's manner of speaking was unlike that of any other doctor. He also bore no stethoscope around his neck, nor did he wear a white coat. The plaid collar rising from under his green knitted waistcoat made him look more like a math teacher than a doctor. Dr. Schumann crossed his legs and folded his hands, exactly like Walter had done at the clubhouse.

"Would you like to tell me why you're here?"

"Walter Hartmann sent me."

Dr. Schumann raised his eyebrows.

"Did Herr Hartmann *send* you here? Or did he simply arrange the appointment for you because you asked for his help?"

Ümit stared back in bewilderment. He could tell Dr. Schumann was expecting a particular answer from him. And that he would survive whatever it was that happened here best if he gave Dr. Schumann exactly what Dr. Schumann wanted.

"Yes," Ümit said haltingly. "Yes, it was just like that."

Dr. Schumann's eyebrows remained floating in the air. They demanded that Ümit continue. But Ümit's lips could not form any further words. He didn't know how he was meant to continue and felt as unprepared as if he'd just landed in the middle of a history test without so much as opening a book. Ümit had always been a diligent student.

"Very well." Dr. Schumann slapped his armrest. "I understand that it is difficult for you to speak of yourself and of your problem. And so, I will assist you, if I may? I'll formulate a few assumptions, and you will tell me whether I'm correct. Would that be suitable?"

Ümit nodded.

"Let us begin."

Dr. Schumann drew a notebook from his desk and thumbed through it until he arrived at the page he was looking for.

"Ümit, I've heard from your coach, Herr Hartmann, that you are in need of help. And this, due to the fact that you have developed a certain inclination that is bothering you. Is this correct?"

Ümit was wondering how Walter and Dr. Schumann knew each other. He was looking for some similarity between them, but there didn't seem to be one. Dr. Schumann had a silky way of talking, obviously soft by design, that gave off a distinct air of confidence. Which was very different from Walter, who always tried to exude a certain strength but who nevertheless always came off instead as if he had something to hide or push away. As though he were somehow ashamed. Dr. Schumann, on the other hand, had everything under control: his feelings, his voice, other people.

"Ümit, is that correct?"

"Um, what? I'm not sure . . . I don't know. What does inclination mean?"

"Ümit. There is a certain young man, and you purport to love him. Is this correct?"

A fist was pounding inside Ümit's ribcage. He squirmed to and fro in his seat, seeking some position that might protect him from falling off the chair completely. He stared at the pale watercolor of half-timbered houses hanging on the wall behind Dr. Schumann. Dr. Schumann's words reverberated in his brain.

"So, you're saying, I'm pretending to be in love?" Ümit asked cautiously.

"Yes, precisely. One could say: you've convinced yourself of this?" Was that a question from Dr. Schumann? Or had Ümit misinterpreted his intonation at the end of the sentence? Ümit stared at his hands. His fingernails were a fraction too long. His mother hated it when you could see the white of his fingernails. He concentrated as hard as he could. He wanted to tell the doctor he was right, but Ümit wasn't sure he'd understood the question.

"What's the difference?" Ümit asked. "I mean: between being in love and thinking you're in love?"

"An excellent question," Dr. Schumann replied. He nodded approvingly at Ümit and clicked his silver ballpoint pen. Dr. Schumann wore a wedding band, as well, but his ring seemed to fit his finger perfectly. Unlike Walter's ring that was so tight Ümit had to wonder how any blood got to his fingertip at all. Dr. Schumann's hands were slender and well manicured. Did Walter and Dr. Schumann perhaps know each other from church?

"The difference," Dr. Schumann explained, "is as follows: Sometimes we admire people of the same sex for their particular qualities. We would like to be like them, and we identify quite strongly with them. But, of course, this has nothing to do with being in love."

Ümit could feel the tip of his nose tingling. His eyes burned. He held his breath.

"In most cases, there is already some sort of identity disorder, such that one does not perceive oneself as masculine enough. Such a disorder can begin in the parental home . . ."

And so, it began. Those endless conversations. *Das Elternhaus. The parental home.* Each time Dr. Schumann said *Elternhaus*—which was incessantly—Ümit asked himself whether it had ever so much as occurred to Dr. Schumann that his family didn't own a house at all but rented an

apartment. But of course, Ümit imagined that Dr. Schumann would
have told him it had nothing to do with the concrete building itself—
das Haus—with its walls and roof, and rather with the things transpir-
ing under this roof. All the same, Ümit felt like there was some distinct
connection between the idea that everyone lived in their own house,
and Dr. Schumann's particular choice of vocabulary: *Elternhaus*. Because
of course, if you said someone *came from a good house*, didn't you also
mean the wealth that came with it: the wealth required to own a house
in the first place? Didn't it signify precisely those neat little half-timbered
houses in the watercolor on Dr. Schumann's wall?

But Dr. Schumann's questions were never about money. They were
always about his childhood, his religion, his culture—all things Ümit
told himself had nothing to do with money. Or did they? Those hours
transformed into an unending search for flaws in Ümit's life. And the
thing about it was: seek long enough and you shall find. After a few
such Thursdays, Ümit could no longer imagine how anyone could walk
around without suffering the weight of their own childhood, their culture, this world.

At first, Ümit made an effort not to tell Dr. Schumann too much. He
didn't want to embarrass his parents, did not wish to betray them by
confirming the many assumptions Dr. Schumann made about them.
But it was no use. Dr. Schumann cracked him like a cheap bike lock.

At some point, all his poor acting and beating around the bush
became meaningless. At some point, this educated doctor with his lus-
trous silver hair, his rimless glasses, and his silky superiority bored his
way into your head, convinced you there was something wrong with
you. And then, all of a sudden, you started talking despite yourself.
Telling him about those nights you'd wet the bed and your mother had
made you feel ashamed. Telling him how she had forbidden you from
drinking water in the evening, how you lay awake for hours trying to
fall asleep with a parched mouth. How you still wet the bed anyway.
And then there were those awful quiet fights between your parents.
Early in the morning. Late at night. The oppressive silence between
them. Those nights when the light from the living room fell through

the crack in your and Hakan's bedroom door. Your mother's endless whispering, her attempts to sooth herself with surahs from the Quran. The fear it made you feel. Those days when you wondered whether your father loved you at all. Those days when Peri took you in her arms and cried, and you had not known why, but you'd cried along with her. Those days when Hakan sat there bleary-eyed and told you not to call the cops no matter what happened. Those days when your mother forbade you to leave the house because she thought the air was poisoned.

Dr. Schumann wrote diligently in his yellow notebook, only glancing up from time to time with a slight tilt of the chin to signal that Ümit should keep talking. Ümit left each one of these appointments with a terrible noise inside his head. The noise of church bells clanging over what seemed like every three minutes of his childhood, overwhelming every conversation, suffocating any thought.

At home, he made his mother chamomile tea as though to compensate for his betrayal, and she kissed him unwittingly on the forehead.

According to Dr. Schumann, Ümit was gay because his father hadn't shown him affection. Because they'd lacked physical closeness. He was gay because his mother made all his decisions for him. He was gay because he'd spent too much time during his childhood with his sister instead of with boys his own age. He was gay because all the women in his *cultural milieu*—Dr. Schumann loved this term too—were so submissive that he couldn't find them attractive.

"But I thought you said my mother made all the decisions?"

"Ümit," Dr. Schumann answered with measured patience, "you must learn to endure life's many inconsistencies." As if it was merely life that was inconsistent, and not the many things Dr. Schumann said about Ümit's family every Thursday.

"Did you not say that in your parental home it is exclusively your mother and sister who see to the household?"

Ümit wanted to know what the hell this had to do with anything. Instead, he asked: "Who cleans up at your place?"

"In our house, each person is responsible for his or her own things."

"No, that's putting things away. That's not what I mean. I meant *cleaning*. Who scrubs your toilet?"

Dr. Schumann shook his head fiercely.

"That is the responsibility of the housekeeper. But this is neither here nor there."

Of course, Dr. Schumann never said the word *gay*. That word likely did not exist for him at all because the concept did not exist for him: men did not love other men. That was an invention of the liberal media. A very dangerous one, particularly for young people who were inclined to copy everything and believed what they saw on TV was normal. There was no such thing as gay love. There were only people with very serious disorders, people in desperate need of professional help. Ümit was such a case.

Only once did Ümit try to contradict Dr. Schumann. Ümit, who rarely contradicted anyone, and who—when he did—had to clear his throat so many times that he could barely make himself understood. But this time, he gathered his courage and simply spat it out: said there were different opinions on every subject and there were certainly far worse ailments that could have befallen him than simply being in love. He surprised even himself with how clearly and intelligibly the words flowed from his mouth. But Dr. Schumann only stared at him indifferently and asked: "Have you learned about AIDS at your school yet?" And Ümit nodded, deciding never to attempt an intervention like that again.

∾

The splash of water. Ümit opens his eyes and stares at the white tile wall, at the grayness of the grout between the tiles. He looks around himself and notices his mother and Peri are no longer in the basement with him. He's alone with only the hodja in his white scrubs and this unknown cousin standing beside him at the metal table. The two of them are washing the naked, bloated body on the table in front of them, softly repeating their prayers. They're both wearing surgical masks. Ümit touches his own face and determines he's not wearing one himself even though he finds it hard to breathe. He takes one step closer to the table.

The skin on the body is mottled; only the groin is covered with a small white cloth. The spots are blue and purple; they look like the bruises Ümit sometimes had after soccer practice. Only these are bigger, much bigger, covering entire regions of the body. Ümit looks at Baba's hand, lying swollen and colorless like the little inflatable floaties kids wear in the swimming pool. He can still smell sweet lavender in the room, but also something else entirely. With an effort, he tries breathing only through his mouth because he can barely stomach it. Ümit tries to remove the surgical mask he isn't wearing, takes another deep breath, but it still isn't enough. He can feel his legs reverting into bread dough, his knees giving way. He watches the white tile room dissolve into those glowing points of light. Ümit feels his body crumbling into a thousand tiny feathers. Only this time, Jonas isn't here to pull him back up to the surface.

Sevda

Sevda is saying a prayer. She's wearing her big black sunglasses and sitting in the back seat of the taxi with her children while she prays. Surah Al-Fatiha and Surah Al-Ikhlas: the first two prayers she ever learned. Sevda still has no idea what they're about, no idea what the words she had to memorize as a child mean. She doesn't speak Arabic, so how is she supposed to understand? She merely learned to repeat the sounds and rhythm. The tone. And yet, whenever she feels like she's losing herself to panic, it's these two surahs that come to mind. These and nothing else. They're like her handrail on the staircase through a darkened house. Stability. A crutch.

The news of her father's death had barreled through Sevda's life like a steamroller, like an indisputable sign from above. As though Allah were punishing her for what she had been doing now for months without feeling so much as a hint of shame. So, there is justice in this world after all, she thought. Justice waiting to crash down around Sevda's head like the wreckage of a burning house. Sevda hurried down the stairs that morning to her restaurant before stopping by to ask Frau Meyer from the third floor to hang a handwritten note on the door next to her opening hours with the words: *Closed due to family tragedy.* Sevda hadn't closed her restaurant outside normal hours for more than two years; usually it was open six days a week. Actually, it had been Frau Meyer who suggested the wording for her note. A German would say it this way, she had said, rather than hanging a sign on their windowpane that said: *My baba is dead.* This had been Sevda's suggestion. Sevda then called her two employees and told them to just stay home. She didn't want them destroying her business while she was away. Davide and Moni were useless without someone there looking over their shoulders every minute and telling them what to do. They'd probably spend their entire shifts meandering around the kitchen flirting, completely oblivious even if customers came in and seated themselves. The only person you can depend on in this world is yourself. And who knew this better than a woman who'd been betrayed by those closest to her?

The taxi rushes through the empty, treeless landscape. A landscape that seemed strangely unfamiliar to Sevda. But of course, she knows this thoroughfare. It leads not only to the airport but also to a wholesaler where she sometimes makes purchases for her restaurant. She's never noticed how bleak it is before. Alternating green and yellow fields, flowing so seamlessly into one another that Sevda starts to feel queasy trying to keep track. She continues her prayers, observing from a distance how the tears are streaming from her cheeks down to her chin. Sevda removes her sunglasses, wipes one hand over her face, and notices her black, mascara-stained fingertips. She glances down at herself and sees a bright, watery stain on the jacket of her rose-colored twinset. Just what she needed.

Who puts on makeup on the way to their father's funeral anyway? For whom? Why bother? Or is this simply her way of trying to cling to life, of warding away death? I'm a woman. I'm alive. So, I wear makeup? How pathetic.

But then again, maybe makeup has a way of stealing into Sevda's life, maybe it just happens automatically whenever she doesn't have to open the restaurant. Mondays, her day off, she spends a few precious minutes of her time putting on a bit of makeup before she starts with the billing and her trips to the shops. Sevda fills every other day of the week with running back and forth between her restaurant on the ground floor and her apartment on the floor above: serving her children and her restaurant guests alike, cooking, keeping the business afloat and

her two employees under control, who recently—foolishly—decided
to shack up and now only have eyes for one another. These days, Sevda
only has time to brush her hair and put on a little moisturizer before
she has to appear in front of her customers. That's it. But at least one
time per week, Sevda wants to feel pretty. Just once a week, she wants
to take a bath. Put on a facemask. Massage a bit of that special condi-
tioner into the tips of her curls. Finish with a thick streak of black eyeliner on her top lids. Just once a week, Sevda likes to spend an hour on
herself alone.

Bahar leans her head against her mother's shoulder. Sevda is still snif-
fling like one of Bahar's little school friends crying in embarrassment
after falling down.

"Please, Mommy, not sad!" Bahar says.

Cem only stares at her sidelong in fear. Sevda's children have never
seen their mother cry before. She's always managed to hide from them
whenever she breaks down in tears. But this time is different.

"*Don't be* sad," she corrects Bahar, wiping the mascara from her face
with a tissue. "It's: Please, *don't be* sad. You have to use all your words,
Bahar. Don't talk German like a foreigner."

The little girl turns away and stares out the window. Sevda readjusts
her sunglasses.

～

Sevda had learned Al-Fatiha, the first surah of the Quran, from her
grandmother when she was as old as her daughter is now: seven. Never
complain. Always be grateful for what you have. Her babaanne had
taught her this, too, while providing the exact opposite example through
her actions. Babaanne did not let anyone tell her anything. Especially
her husband. She always thought that she was right, and usually, it
seemed like she was. And yet, she still demanded meekness from everyone around her, preached humility as though it were the greatest vir-
tue and could guarantee a well-shaded spot in Paradise.

When, at the age of only twelve, Sevda was left behind with her
grandparents in Karlıdağ while the rest of her family followed Hüseyin

to Germany, she was particularly confused by the things people expected of her. They didn't seem to apply to anyone else. But it wasn't until her thirteenth birthday that she finally built up the confidence to say *No!* To say it loudly and clearly. It became a matter of life and death then.

"NO! I. DON'T. WANT. TO. GET. MARRIED." Sevda hissed with so much emphasis her whisper reverberated like a scream. Babaanne looked up at her from the gas stove in surprise. And then she caressed Sevda's cheek with her gnarled, henna-red fingers, as if rewarding the girl for finally standing up for herself.

"Child, no one will force this upon you. But one day you must marry, and I tell you this: This man is a teacher. You will not find better than him here in this place."

She removed her icy fingers from Sevda's face and squeezed her hand. Tears were already gathering in the corners of her eyes. Sevda turned away from her babaanne, panting for air to keep the tears at bay. Her eyes drifted to the great enamel tablet leaned against the wall on which Babaanne would most certainly serve freshly cut hingel for this teacher, the same way she did whenever particularly exalted guests came to dine.

"I don't care if he's a teacher, Babaanne. He's too old. I don't want him!"

Only two days earlier, when Babaanne had informed Sevda that the elementary school teacher had declared his intentions to Sevda's dede to ask for her hand, Sevda's ears had glowed with excitement. Sevda liked the idea that someone was in love with her, and that she might soon have her own home with this person, with her own oven and her own TV. That they would lie arm in arm on Sunday evenings and watch *Dallas* together. That they would maybe even kiss on the mouth afterward like Pamela and Bobby. Sevda downright caught her breath at the idea. She threw herself down on the divan, closed her eyes, and imagined how things might transpire after this kiss.

But now, with every passing hour, it was becoming clearer to Sevda how little the world around her had in common with the world in which Pamela lay by the pool in her bathing suit slurping brightly colored cocktails before sitting to dine at her long table. There wasn't any pool in Karlıdağ. Nor were there any women who so much as owned a bathing suit, much less sat at fancy banquet tables to eat. And so, Sevda's *Dallas* fantasies eventually reverted back into the life led by every woman Sevda actually knew. A life that always stank of stewing onions. A life of children tumbling from your lap. A life where people ate on the floor. A life where you sweated through the winter from the incessant heat of the oven and froze during the summer.

"I'm going to move to Germany, Babaanne."

Babaanne sat on a kilim on the kitchen floor, peeling an apple. Her gleaming, green velvet dress with the floral print reminded Sevda of those meadows in the village that would miraculously burst into bloom in just a few days after lying dormant under six months of winter snow. Maybe Babaanne wore this flowered dress to remind herself of the mountain village she'd never wanted to leave and never would have left if her son Hüseyin had not compelled them to. Sevda was only eight years old when she, along with her mother, siblings, and grandparents, had moved to the city. Ever since that time, Babaanne traveled each summer for a few days to visit relatives in her village. Relatives who grew ever scarcer in number as they themselves moved one after another to Karlıdağ or to some other city.

Babaanne dragged slow circles around the apple with the knife Sevda's baba had brought back with him from Germany. Until the entire peel fell in one spiral onto the flowering meadow of her lap. "I'm going to go to school in Germany," Sevda continued, without being prompted to do so. "I'm going to become a businesswoman, Babaanne."

Babaanne shook her head and smiled, as though she'd heard a joke. Wrinkles spread across the dry leather of her face like a thousand tiny rivers, merging together in the yawning darkness of the gap beside her canine tooth.

"Why are you laughing, Babaanne? Baba said I can come too, soon. Do you know when he's coming back?"

Babaanne extended a slice of apple to Sevda.

"He'll come get you when Dede and I are dead. Who will take care of us otherwise?"

"Well, who will take care of you if you marry me off to this teacher?"

"You'll still be close, my child. He wants to move into a house in this same neighborhood."

Sevda swallowed hard. So, it had all been planned. Everything except for Sevda's own desires. The slice of apple hung in the air. As if these two ancients would ever die with all the vitamins they swallowed. Sevda snatched the slice of apple before her babaanne changed her mind and decided to eat it herself.

"What is this anyway: a businesswoman?" Babaanne asked, wiping her hands on one of the crocheted washrags that hung above her sink like a garland of flags on a national holiday. And then she left the kitchen without listening to Sevda's answer.

A businesswoman was a woman with style and perfect clothes. A woman who held her chin a whole floor higher than all the normal women and who made her own decisions without asking her husband or her parents for permission. Sevda had only seen such a woman one time in real life. She'd still been very small, maybe only four or five years old. In any case, they had still lived in the village where the snow lay piled much higher than it did in Karlıdağ below. The village where no one ever came whom she did not at least already recognize by sight. Packed tightly like a watermelon with two tiny toothpick legs, Sevda had stood in front of the green door of her house staring out into the endless white that stretched on in front of her day after day, when suddenly a woman appeared in the midst of all that white. A woman with a bob cut and enormous black sunglasses. The woman was staring hard at a piece of paper like she was searching for a particular person or house. She was the strangest being Sevda had ever seen. She wore a coat of light-brown fur that ended just above her ankles and high-heel boots beneath that did not seem well suited for the muddy pathways of the village. But the woman hadn't looked like she needed to walk much, Sevda thought later, any time their chance meeting occurred to her again. She'd looked like someone with a chauffeur and a Mercedes or something. She'd carried a small boxy blue handbag around her wrist, and when she'd removed her sunglasses for a moment, Sevda had seen cat-eye eyeliner like the women in the movies.

Even today, Sevda still doesn't know who that beautiful woman in her village was, who she was looking for, or whether she had found what she'd been seeking. Years later, when she had told her dede about their meeting, Dede had called her memory nonsense. Sevda had only imagined it. What would such a woman be doing in their village? Nothing. And it was true that Sevda had always been a dreamer. She'd always imagined things for herself, but that was also why she knew exactly where to draw the line between reality and dream. Much clearer than someone who'd long since ceased to dream at all, someone who believed in nothing more than what was preached at them in the mosque. The woman with the bob cut and the sunglasses was real. Sevda was sure of it. It was just that no one but Sevda had had the good fortune to meet her.

Sevda managed to deter this teacher who came to ask for her hand. But she could not manage to dissuade Ihsan. Several years transpired before he came into her life, several precious years in which she managed, bit by bit, to come closer to the person she'd always wanted to be. The first step had been escaping the dismal house of her grandparents. This opportunity finally came shortly before her fifteenth birthday: Her father arrived to collect her and bring her back with him to Germany. By that time, Hüseyin had been living there for nearly ten years. Two years before, he'd returned to Karlıdağ and taken Sevda's mother and her two younger siblings, Hakan and Peri, back with him. This was Sevda's last chance to follow them, for only guest workers' children under the age of sixteen were permitted entry to Germany, and Sevda's yellow identity card said that she would soon be turning sixteen.

In truth, this card had been issued for another child who'd been born the year before Sevda and died after only a few weeks. It, too, had been called Sevda. And because the road from the village to the city was treacherous even during summer and nigh impassible in winter, no one had ever made the effort to register one child's death and another child's birth. What did it matter; they had both been girls.

Sometimes Sevda imagined she was the reincarnation of this first baby Sevda: since she had already lived once before, she had to use, to relish this second chance by living the best possible life she could. Other times, however, Sevda was also overcome with sadness at the thought that she did not even have her own name, and in that sense, that her entire existence was merely something borrowed. Something that could be taken back away from her at any moment, without so much as the right to shed a tear.

It was one thing to have the life of a dead baby imposed upon your own. It was another to be left behind with your grandparents like a broken piece of luggage. The reality of having been left all alone at the tender age of twelve while the rest of her family started a new life in an exciting country on the other side of the world came to define Sevda's entire destiny. She would never recover from this loneliness; the feeling of isolation would remain a part of her forever. She carried it with her wherever she went, even to the small town in Southern Germany where her younger siblings had already long since learned to speak a new language she couldn't understand. She carried it onward with her to Lower Saxony, where only a few years later, she would sit, heavy with child, another baby in her arms, crying alone to the songs of Tracy Chapman.

But loneliness is also a kind of freedom. Sevda's loneliness taught her to form her own thoughts and listen to herself. Because the things that happened in her head belonged to her alone and nobody could ever take them from her. Which was why, during those two years alone with her grandparents in Karlıdağ, Sevda had determined to teach herself to read and write. Each day, as soon as she finished her chores, she paid a visit to the tiny neighbor children while they sat doing their schoolwork. Sevda brought them gifts of dried fruit and nuts in exchange for the right to peer over their shoulders.

When Sevda had been their age, she'd still lived with her family in their mountain village. There had not been any school. And when they'd

moved down to the city—if you could call a town where more chickens
and sheep occupied the broken asphalt of the streets than cars a city at
all—Sevda had already been eight years old. No longer a small child.
And school was only something for small children. At least that's what
her mother had said. And Emine would have known. For unlike her
daughter, *she* had attended elementary school in *her* village and could
proudly read aloud the quote on the calendar sheet each evening to her
assembled family.

Before her family had departed for Germany and left Sevda behind,
Sevda's mother had called her over and pointed to the two small bulges
budding on her chest. Sevda was a big girl now, she'd said, and Sevda
would have to take care of herself now. She must take particular care
if she ever left the house alone. Especially if there were men around. It
didn't matter if they were strangers or acquaintances, friendly, young,
or old. This did not matter. All men only wanted one thing, and Sevda
must fight with all her power to deny them this. If she did not, they
would kill her, cut her up in little pieces, and hide her dismembered
body away so no one would ever know about it. Sevda had nodded
dutifully, promised her mother from now on that she would always
take care. And then, only a few months later, she'd awoken one night in
shock to find that she had failed anyway: there was blood between her
legs! How could it have happened? Her uncle from the village had spent
the night with them. And so, that morning, Sevda's gaze had darted
back and forth between her uncle and her dede until she couldn't take
it anymore and crawled away to the kitchen to cry over her wasted life.
Her uncle's wife found Sevda in the kitchen and took her in her arms.
   "But Sevdacım, what is it? What is wrong?"
   When she learned about the blood, she'd only laughed and told Sevda
that this was normal. That it would happen again each month from
now on. On the first day, she should wear a long dress and squat over
a pit. For the remaining days, her aunt cut an old undershirt into little
strips that Sevda should always boil afterward.
   Another thing Sevda learned in her first years of loneliness was how
to wash her grandparents' laundry, so they had nothing to complain of.

Already in the years before, she'd had to wash Hakan's and Peri's soiled diapers. But Babaanne's dresses were another thing entirely and required greater effort and skill, for they were made of thick velvet that, when wet, was as heavy as a thigh-high sack of potatoes. Sevda developed a technique for wringing them out by herself, wrapping the sleeves around a small tree trunk, and pulling the other end of the dress tight before twisting it until the excess water began to drip out. She twisted them again and again until her chubby arms could do no more. Babaanne wore her velvet dresses over a thin cotton dress, and beneath that, another even thinner cotton dress, and beneath that an undershirt and a thick pair of long underwear, and beneath them, yet another thinner pair. And so, Babaanne's clothing comprised more dirty laundry than a lifetime of Sevda's and her dede's clothes combined. When Babaanne undressed in the evening, removing one layer after another, she grew smaller and smaller until, in the end, there remained only a tiny, frail figure in the room, like the innermost matryoshka doll. A tiny doll who had nothing in common with the powerful Kurdish woman who set the tone for her husband and spent her days rushing to the aid of every neighbor and fellow villager. At least until that fateful morning in September 1980 when the Turkish Armed Forces seized control of the country. After this, Babaanne rarely left her home. Half a year later, Hüseyin finally came and took Sevda away.

In no time, Hüseyin found a family to check in on his parents each day now that Sevda would no longer be around. For 100 marks and a used Telefunken TV, they also agreed to take over Sevda's laundry duties for her grandparents. On the night before Sevda's and Hüseyin's departure, Sevda promised her distraught babaanne that she would come back to visit soon. But secretly, she hoped she would never have to come back. Not back to this ugly city, not to this neighborhood, and certainly not to this awful, desolate house she'd been confined to ever since the coup.

She and Hüseyin took the train to Istanbul. For two days and two nights they traveled together across soft green and barren stony land-scapes. They clambered over sleeping passengers in the aisle on their way to the toilet, and played a guessing game where Sevda tried to say

how long they had been waiting each time their train made an unexpected stop in the middle of nowhere without looking at her father's
watch. For Sevda, this train ride was the beginning of a new life filled
with unfamiliar faces and dialects. For Hüseyin, the ride seemed to offer
a respite from his work shifts in the factory. Sevda watched her father,
examining the brilliant white of his collared shirt beneath the earthtones
of his jacket as he sat across from her and leafed through his newspaper. The way he pressed his thick black eyebrows together sternly as he
read, and how his expression softened into a smile whenever he noticed
his daughter's gaze and returned it. Then Sevda would smile back shyly
in return before staring out the window and wondering whether she,
too, would someday find a husband anywhere near as handsome as her
father.

After their arrival at the Haydarpaşa Train Station, Sevda's baba
bought her lunch served with paper napkins and water in a tiny glass
bottle with colorful impressions on it. Then they took the ferry over
the Bosporus to the other half of the city. Sevda ate her first ice cream
that day, a cold little ball in a waffle cone that tasted like sweetened milk.
She ate it as slowly as she could to savor the taste on her tongue. But it
began to melt, dripping over her hand and down onto her dress until
Sevda wanted to cry. Nothing could ever just be beautiful. Instead, something seemed beautiful and then it ruined your only good dress.

Luckily, you couldn't see the stain in the passport picture they took
at the photographer's while Hüseyin got Sevda's travel documents in
order. Sevda held the picture in her hand, staring back at the little girl
with her braids and bashful expression. She was so pretty, Sevda had
to blush. When Hüseyin finished her paperwork more quickly than expected, they still had an entire day before their flight to Germany. The
relatives they were staying with explained the way to the Kapalı Çarşı
to Hüseyin. Its market hall was hidden like a diminutive, secret city of
its own, right there in the center of Istanbul, its unobtrusive entryway
leading under the great vaulted ceiling where brightly colored birds sang
from their cages and golden chains shimmered in illuminated cabinet
displays. Suddenly, Hüseyin squeezed Sevda's hand tightly in his. He
was giddy, enjoying the hubbub, but worried at the same time about

losing his daughter in the crowd. Sevda could see this in his wide, shining eyes and in the happy arch of his eyebrows. In the way he greeted complete strangers with a little nod of his head, as though they were all his brothers.

A young man stopped them in the crowd to show them a white leather handbag. It was not as big as the purse from the woman in the snow, but it was every bit as stylish. Hüseyin bought it for Sevda, along with an embroidered handkerchief so she'd have something to put inside it. She didn't have anything else besides her passport and her German papers, but Hüseyin preferred to look after these himself.

The next morning, they took a taxi to the airport in Yeşilköy. Sevda looked out from the windows of the car at the glimmering blue of the sea, as if in farewell. It was not until they were seated in the airplane and the turbines had already started that Sevda realized she'd left her handbag in the taxicab. She began to cry. Hüseyin's lips formed only a sad smile. "Don't worry, Sevdam. In Germany, there are even more beautiful purses. We'll just buy you a new one."

∼

"Where is my purse?" Sevda hears herself asking her children when they arrive at the airport in Hanover, and she needs to show their passports. "Bahar, have you seen it?"

The little girl points to the leather satchel dangling from her mother's shoulder.

"No, the other bag. The big black one with the passports and your change of clothes," Sevda says.

Bahar shrugs her shoulders. Where is her big brother?

"Where's Cem?"

Bahar points with one finger to where Cem is standing under a distant display screen of flights. He's staring up at the metal panels in the ceiling of the terminal that look like the scaly skin of some giant fish.

"CEM!"

Sevda's voice echoes through the building and other travelers turn to gawk at her. Cem gawks, too, both recognizing and fearing the sound of his mother's voice. He hurries over.

"Cem, stay with your sister, and don't move. I need to check if I left my black travel bag outside at the taxi stand."

"But you left it at home," Cem says.

"What?"

"On the chair in the kitchen. I saw it lying there before we left."

"Then why didn't you say so? Our passports are in there! How are we supposed to fly without our passports?"

He stares at his mother in terror. Cem is only ten, but he knows exactly what will come next. He can hear it in his mother's tone of voice. No matter what he says now, it will be the wrong answer.

"Tell me, Cem. How are we supposed to board the plane without our passports?"

He looks down at his tennis shoes and shrugs. "Can't we just say we forgot them at home? Tell them that we're sorry?"

Sevda can feel her veins throbbing.

"Oh, is that right? You think we can just say sorry and then everything will be fine? You're a very stupid boy if you think that, Cem. Very, very stupid! And your stupidity is going to make us miss your grandpa's funeral. Do you know what that means? Do you?"

Sevda digs her fingernails into her son's shoulder. She can hear her own voice breaking.

Cem looks up at her with watery eyes and says haltingly: "I'm sorry, Mommy . . ." Fuck, did he really just say he was sorry again? Sevda wants to hit him. As hard as she can. Right in his stupid little face. So he will understand. So he will realize saying this word over and over again does nothing. So he will know that this word changes nothing about the mistake he made. That he deserves a slap in the face anyway. But there are too many people watching. And she knows some German will probably start preaching at her about how they do things differently in this country. Right. They don't hit children here. They burn them alive.

Sevda drags her suitcase behind her with one hand, her son with the other. Luckily for her, Bahar is not as capricious as Cem. She can take Bahar everywhere with her; her daughter follows Sevda around like a miniature shadow. At seven, she's already such a clever and well-behaved little girl. Sevda has big plans for Bahar.

Ever since her separation from Ihsan, she's felt the constant, merciless stares directed at her and her children. As though there were no way this could not go wrong: a foreigner with her own restaurant trying to raise two children on her own. And, as if in answer, Bahar and Cem have transformed into Sevda's walking, talking business cards. The more flawless their appearance, the more successful Sevda feels. If she discovers so much as a tiny speck of food on either of their outfits, they have to change immediately from head to toe. Sometimes as many as four times a day. If Cem slumps at the table, he'll be punished with no TV for the rest of the day. There's nothing wrong with Bahar's posture; the ballet course Sevda sends her to is far too expensive for that. But the little one garbles her words: she says things like *sunshrine* and *shreet*. Sevda has already made an appointment for her with a speech therapist and hopes Bahar will get her situation under control before the other children start mocking her at school.

They hurry back to the taxi stand and ask a driver whether he can make it to Salzhagen and back to the airport in an hour. He laughs as he steps on the accelerator. But he has to slam his foot down on the brake as soon as they reach the highway. A blinking wall of motionless vehicles. On the radio, reports of a multicar pileup. Fuck, Sevda thinks. Her only consolation is the thought that—at the very least—this will mean a few extra hours before she has to face her mother.

The truth is that this is not the first time Sevda lost her father. It already happened in the summer of 1981, the summer he brought her back with him to Germany. Then, too, Hüseyin suddenly vanished from her life without a trace: This loving father whom she had only known for the last ten years of her life from fleeting four-week holidays in which he'd brought her gifts from Germany. Dresses with silk ribbons and dolls with red braids. He'd nestled Sevda in his arms, kissing her and smelling her hair. And then he vanished completely after his journey with Sevda, just after they arrived in Germany.

In his place, another man appeared. A man who greeted her, at most, with a nod of his head when he returned in the mornings from his night shift. A man who looked exactly like her father except that the warmness of his eyes had been replaced by a cold obstinacy. Sevda could never say for certain when or why it happened. Suddenly, he looked infinitely tired and old. Far older than he had been on the train ride across Turkey or in the bazaar in Istanbul. The radiance of his face during his visits home—it simply did not exist anymore. And after their arrival in Rheinstadt, he no longer hugged her, no longer gave her presents. Of course, there was never a new purse. Hüseyin didn't even speak to Sevda anymore. He just stood there silently whenever Emine spat her poison out of nowhere at their daughter: *Do not wear this, do not wear that, do not go out, do not talk to him, do not talk to her, you look hideous.* Hüseyin just stood there listening, and sometimes muttering: *Do what your mother says.*

But Germany had changed Emine, too. She had always been severe, but now she also looked exhausted and old, although hardly two years had transpired since moving to Rheinstadt. Some days, Emine spent the entire afternoon on the sofa in tears. She complained of pains in her entire body, though the German doctors could find no cause for her ailments. At night, Sevda heard her wandering listlessly through the apartment, softly reading whispered lines from the Quran. Sevda would have liked to get up as well, sit down beside her mother, and hug her tightly. But she knew Emine would have pushed her arms away.

Because from the first moment Sevda had set foot in their apartment in Rheinstadt, Emine had eyed her like an unwelcome stranger passing through. A fundamentally untrusted guest one could not be rid of because, as a pious woman, one could not do such things.

Sevda had thought she and her mother might need to get used to one another again. Maybe it was normal to grow apart after two years. She did her best to help her with the housework, hoping that in return Emine would show her their new neighborhood and tell her all about this strange new country. Everything she'd learned over the past two years. But Sevda soon realized that Emine knew nothing. The only places Emine knew were Hakan's school, Peri's preschool, and the discount supermarket by the bridge. Emine didn't seem to have any interest in exploring anything new. For her, all these things were only temporary.

"Let's go for a walk!" Sevda had suggested to her mother one afternoon soon after her arrival. Emine only stared bewildered at the wool cardigan in her daughter's hand.

"We already went to the store yesterday," Emine responded without meeting her daughter's eyes.

"No, I didn't mean the supermarket, Anne. I meant let's go for a walk!"

"What? Just like this? When you know that my back hurts me!"

"Oh, okay. I'll go by myself," Sevda said, wriggling nervously into her cardigan, conscious of her mother's stare. She had wanted to ignore it and just slip out of the apartment as quickly as possible, but then she'd glanced at her mother and seen the way Emine had ogled her clothing as though it were not simply a light jacket knit from butter-colored wool but some kind of dangerous, loaded weapon.

"Yes, of course, you will go by yourself, Sevda. You know your way around. Just like you know the language here. Some Hans will kidnap you immediately and rape you and hack you into little pieces. Haydi, put that jacket away right now before you give me a nervous breakdown!"

Germany was not like Sevda had imagined. If she were to believe her mother, it was little different from Karlıdağ: she lived under the constant threat of being kidnapped, raped, and hacked to pieces, and so she was not to trust anyone or leave the house at all. Sevda thought her mother acted here in Rheinstadt exactly like Babaanne had in Karlıdağ during the months after the military coup: She did not want to be seen. It would be best if no one even realized that she existed. In public, Emine only whispered. There were unseen dangers lurking around every corner; she and her family were only safe inside their home. Sevda couldn't explain any of it. Neither her babaanne's fears nor those of her anne. She only knew that she never wanted to become like they were, for other people's fears had become Sevda's prison.

But there were some things about Germany that did remind Sevda of Karlıdağ too. It was always cold, dead silent at night, and when Sevda and her mother encountered other people on their walk to the supermarket, they were stared at like a curious riddle that needed to be solved. Except that no one here so much as greeted one another on the street.

Nor did they plant anything in their gardens. There was only grass, trimmed regularly to a uniform height and framed by a tiny fence composed of many little Xs. The purpose of these fences, never more than waist high, eluded Sevda. They neither protected their inhabitants from burglars, nor were they high enough to keep out wolves or bears. Their only purpose seemed to be to delineate the beginning and the end of each property. And to prevent Hakan and his little friends from so much as thinking of playing on any grass their parents hadn't paid for.

Those were the only things Sevda could observe from the kitchen window of their street-level apartment. For she spent the majority of her first year in Germany there, in the kitchen. Only twice a week was she permitted to leave their home with her mother. These trips to the supermarket were the highlights of her week. Both of them hung their enormous, checkered plastic shopping bags over their shoulders and walked along the river that separated the area around the metalworks from the rest of the city. When they reached the supermarket at the bridge, they walked up and down each aisle with their shopping cart, always in the same order, in search of ingredients with which they could still never truly re-create the dishes from their homeland but at least could achieve some kind of semblance of approximation. When they reached the checkout, Emine always stared anxiously at the dizzying movements of the cashier's brightly colored fingernails as they typed madly at the register. She could only ever relax when the sum of her purchases had been totaled up and she knew that she'd brought enough money with her to pay for their groceries.

"37.92 marks," Sevda once said.

Emine had only just begun to unload her items at the checkout, and she stared at her daughter in confusion.

"That's how much it's going to cost, Anne. We have that much, right?"

"Yes, yes," Emine had snapped, piling the remaining contents of her cart onto the conveyor belt. Emine's mouth remained silent, but she cast an incredulous look over her daughter out of the corner of one eye: Where had Sevda learned mental math?

Around ten o'clock each day, while Hakan was at school and Peri at preschool, Emine often collapsed back into bed, exhausted, trying to reclaim some of the sleep she'd missed out on the night before. During these times, Sevda usually sat by herself in front of the TV, trying to memorize a few lines of German. Kids' shows were the easiest: *Löwenzahn, Sesame Street, Sendung mit der Maus*. They all spoke slowly and clearly, and Sevda bent over a piece of paper, trying to write down some of the words, so she could ask her little brother and sister later what they meant. *Dallas* was on here too, but Pamela and Bobby and all the others spoke German now. When they showed reruns Sevda already knew, it was easier for her to translate some of the snippets of conversation in her head. Soon, she could hardly wait to try out her new vocabulary. When she met their neighbor from the second floor in the stairwell—an elderly woman who wore bright red lipstick every day although one could hardly identify the lips on her face anymore—Sevda wanted to give her a compliment. It was her very first sentence in German. Slowly and carefully, Sevda pronounced: "You stink very good!" The old woman had laughed and tried to explain something to Sevda, who only smiled politely before slinking cautiously back into the darkness of their ground-floor apartment that always stank like the bleach Emine used.

At some point, the neighbors from the house at the other end of the street came to visit. A family from Hatay. Latife Teyze and her daughter Havva brought them a box of pralines and embraced Sevda and Emine as warmly and as tightly as if they were long-lost relatives. Both of them spoke with an accent Sevda had never heard before. It sounded dark and raw, as if it were being formed somewhere deep in the back of their throats. Later that night, Sevda would quietly practice imitating them because their voices sounded so pleasant to her ears.

While both mothers sat in the front room gossiping about half the neighborhood, Sevda and Havva went to the kitchen to make them coffee. Havva opened a window and lit up a cigarette with a composure that shocked Sevda to her core. She then undid the top two buttons of her shimmery blouse, revealing the Y of her cleavage along with a tiny silver chain that hung between her breasts. There was a round pendant on her necklace with an engraving of a woman in a headscarf. Later, Sevda saw this woman on TV: it was Meryem Ana, whom Christians called the Mother of God.

"So, what do you do here all day?" Havva asked, languidly blowing her smoke out the kitchen window. Sevda shrugged her shoulders. "Nothing. What about you?"

"I go to school, girl. What else am I supposed to do? I'm trying to get my diploma, so I can start working right away. I need the money," Havva explained.

"What for?"

"Makeup. Cigarettes. I don't know. Everyone needs money. What's wrong with you?"

"My parents don't send me to school," Sevda said apathetically, stirring to dissolve the Nescafé in their hot water.

"What do you mean they don't send you to school? School's mandatory here until you turn fifteen. Didn't you just say you're only fourteen?" Havva asked, blinking in disbelief.

"But my passport says I'm fifteen."

Havva took a long drag from her cigarette, musing over this information.

"Okay, just wait. We'll find a solution. Otherwise, you're gonna die on us cooped up here all day in this dump."

Sevda wasn't sure what she should make of Havva's desire to help her. Of course, Sevda had always dreamed of going to school. She'd dreamed about this all her life. Even if school was supposed to be the most miserable place in the world—something she personally could not believe—Sevda would have been willing to go there if for no other reason than to finally be able to leave the apartment. But could she trust this girl? Sevda wasn't even sure whether she liked Havva. Or whether Havva liked her. It seemed to Sevda that Havva was constantly making fun of her. There was something distinctly mocking about the way Havva spoke to her.

"Yeah, whatever," Sevda finally muttered, trying to keep her voice as free of emotion as possible, as if she really didn't care whether she had to spend the rest of her life in this kitchen.

Havva was unlike any girl Sevda had ever met before. There was something so mature about the way she guided her cigarette between her splayed fingers and pressed it between her full, pink lips. With her eyebrows plucked gossamer thin and her curly hair bobbed short, she even reminded Sevda a bit of the businesswoman in the snow. There was always a half smile on Havva's lips, as though she were constantly amused by everything happening around her. But the way Havva spoke like a woman who had already seen and experienced everything, although she was barely a year older than Sevda, also bothered her. Still, it was better to have Havva to talk to than have no one at all. And so, Sevda was happy when Havva soon began to stop by every few days to smoke out her kitchen window and complain about the other students in the class she took for foreigners.

"There's this one guy, Mahmut. My goodness, Sevdacım. I tell you, he's a real kıro. He's only got one pair of 501 jeans, and he wears them to school every single goddamn day. And I mean, good, that's his decision. But do you know what he wears with them? Black leather shoes! The kind with pointy toes. With light blue jeans? Ewww!"

"Ewww," Sevda repeated.

"But seriously, when I look at the guys at school, the Turks are honestly the worst. You know, at least the Italian boys have style. They don't need a lot of money to look good."

Sevda nodded, looking down at her own clothes and thinking that she wore this same blue blouse every day. She decided to pay more

attention to the clothes people wore on TV. Maybe she could convince
Emine to buy her something new. Right. Not even in Sevda's dreams
would her mother ever concede to buying her something.

"I'm serious. You've got to be ashamed to call yourself a Turk
here," Havva continued on about the leather shoes, rolling her eyes
emphatically.

"But you're not Turkish, are you?" Sevda asked.

Havva stared at her wordlessly with the half smile frozen on her lips
before removing another cigarette from her purse. "What are you trying to say, darling?"

"Nothing. I'm sorry. I didn't mean anything by that," Sevda replied
uncertainly.

"Yes, you did. You mean because we aren't Muslims?"

"No, no," Sevda assured her.

"Yes, you meant exactly that."

"You misunderstand me, Havva. I meant because you speak Arabic
at home. You and your mother. That's all."

"Okay, listen up, girl." Havva shook her head. "Maybe you're right.
And maybe you're not. Honestly, I don't even care. But don't you ever
tell me what I am and what I'm not, okay? Isn't it enough that they tell
us on the street: *Go home, you fucking Turks!*"

"Who says that?" Sevda asked in surprise.

"Oh, Sevdacım. You really don't know anything, do you? You sit here
in your little hole all day with no clue about what happens in the outside world. And besides, don't you even know what people say about
your people? They call you 'mountain Turks'! And that sounds like a
mix between a mountain goat and a human, doesn't it? So, just because
you've unlearned that mountain goat language you used to speak, it
doesn't make you any less of a farm animal, Sevda. Don't you ever forget it."

Sevda didn't understand what hornet's nest she'd just stepped into.
She only knew that she would never tell another soul where her family
came from. She had spoken Kurdish with her grandparents as a child.
Only she couldn't remember when she'd stopped doing that. Probably
after they'd moved to the city? Yes! She could remember a box on the

ear. Emine had slapped her across the face and said: *If you answer me in Kurdish one more time, I'll kill you.*

Havva continued talking to distract Sevda, changing her tone now, as though it were all just fun and games and nothing was serious. But Sevda could still see the anger glimmering in Havva's eyes.

"Seriously, Sevda. We're in Germany now. And the Germans don't give a fuck how many languages we speak or who we pray to. They see us all as fucking Turks, and so that's what we are. End of story."

Of course, Sevda wasn't allowed to buy new clothes. "We do not have money for that kind of thing," her mother said, with a look that asked how stupid she must be to ask this kind of question at all. And so, Sevda rummaged around in her parents' closet until she found a dress she was certain her mother would never wear again. It was a full-length dress of brown polyester that shimmered like silk. She had Havva call and convince her mother that Sevda should visit her the following afternoon. Together, they attempted to use Latife Teyze's sewing machine to make the dress a bit tighter and a bit shorter. But because neither of them knew how to sew, in the end, it came out looking like a kind of oversized pillowcase.

Sevda looked longingly at the ruined length of fabric. Havva tugged it away from her indifferently.

"Oh, whatever. Forget it. I have a better idea."

She opened a brown cabinet and removed a bottle with a clear liquid inside that looked like water.

"K-or-n." Sevda read aloud from the gold-colored label. "What is that?"

"We'll see, darling, we'll see. My father seems to like it anyway."

They locked themselves in the room Havva shared with her sister, who was still at school. Sevda had always wanted to know what it felt like to be drunk. When they were small children, they used to sniff at poppy flowers because they'd heard poppies could make people go crazy. Then they had spun around in a circle, as quickly as they could, until they fell to the ground in the meadow giggling: *We're sooooooo druuuuuunk.*

Sevda twisted the cap and took a mighty swig out of the bottle before spewing half of it back out onto the carpet.

"Shit, what are you doing?" Havva laughed.

"I'm sorry . . . but this stuff tastes like gasoline. Who drinks this willingly?"

"Just hand it over."

Havva pinched her nose, bringing the bottle to her mouth with her other hand. She took an experimental sip.

"Shit, girl. That really burns the throat."

She switched on the tape player and began to hop around the room with the bottle.

Sevda rose and began to dance as well, shyly at first, and then with increasing gusto. Her hips became infatuated with the music, the song was so giddy, so awake, you couldn't possibly sit still. You had to wiggle your shoulders, your butt, your head. She took another swig of the disgusting liquid and threw her hands into the air. Later she would learn that this was a song by Prince—a staggeringly beautiful man who wore ruffled shirts and smeared kajal around his almond eyes. Sevda felt a growing flame well up inside her with each subsequent mouthful of the vomit-juice. Her face was glowing with it. She couldn't stop laughing at Havva, who alternated between wild grimaces and solemn, seductive stares before shaking her bosom like the belly dancer on the poster above her bed.

Sevda knew this dancer. Her name was Nesrin Topkapı, and she was the first woman ever to be permitted to belly dance on Turkish television. Wide-eyed, Sevda had sat in front of their TV in Karlıdağ, five minutes after midnight on New Years 1981, only a few months after the Turkish Armed Forces had marched through the muddy streets of their city as the occupation spread across the country, and only a few months after her babaanne and dede had begun to only whisper when they spoke among themselves. There must certainly have been other films with scenes of belly dancers in them that had played in the nightclubs, but for a dancer to be invited to dance for the entire country on national television—especially in such a skimpy little outfit—this was something unexpected and scandalous indeed! It was particularly absurd at that time when they could think of nothing else but those armed soldiers patrolling their neighborhoods each day. Half of the neighborhood had been gathered there in the living room because hardly anyone else other than Sevda's grandparents had owned a television. Their breath caught collectively in their throats. No one made a sound, and even the wheezing respiration of the old people grew quiet in veneration of the movement of Nesrin Topkapı's hips.

Next to this poster in Havva's bedroom hung a second image: an older movie poster with Bülent Ersoy, whose performances, Havva reported, had been banned ever since the military coup. She, too, like them, had also moved to Germany. It was Havva's dream to one day visit Bülent Ersoy. Havva had put makeup over Bülent's face in the photo on the poster—bright pink lipstick, thick dark eyeshadow, and a bit of rouge— for in this film, she had still starred as a man. Havva had also crafted her a scarlet dress of paper, high-heeled shoes, and a handbag of silver aluminum foil that she'd glued onto the poster as well. Apparently, Havva had always been a fan of Bülent Ersoy, she was perhaps even a bit infatuated, and she knew her older films inside and out: those films in which Bülent had performed heartbreakingly tragic songs and all the women had fallen instantly in love. But ever since Bülent Ersoy had announced she was a woman and appeared in the tabloids in photos from London where she'd undergone multiple surgeries, Havva had venerated her like a goddess. She saved clippings of articles in a drawer that showed a jubilant Bülent posing in a hospital bed, a blue nightgown flattering her new body, a sea of flower bouquets around her. Once, when Havva was rearranging these clippings in a notebook to stow back inside the drawer alongside other books where she'd pressed dried roses and daisies, she said: "My father says the coup happened so they could break up the trade unions. But I'll tell you what I think: The real reason for the military coup was Bülent Ersoy's tits. She whipped them out on stage one month before the coup d'état!"

As Sevda drew her finger over the poster, she felt herself growing hotter. She pulled at the collar of her sweater, fanning herself for air with

her free hand until eventually she had to stand and open Havva's bedroom window. Havva followed her to smoke a cigarette.

"Here, Sevdacım, take a drag!" she said, pressing the cigarette between
Sevda's lips.

Sevda inhaled and had the feeling she was licking one of her father's
ashtrays. She had to cough. Havva laughed until she, too, broke down
in a rasping cough.

"No, no. You've gotta learn to inhale gently. You're pulling too hard.
Come on, let me show you something."

Sevda never wanted to smoke again. Her body shook in disgust, but
she still watched Havva with fascination as she took another long drag
from her cigarette, its filter already stained lipstick pink with the impression of her mouth. Sevda watched as she held the smoke inside her. As
her pink mouth drew closer to Sevda's own. Havva's lips pressed softly
and gently against Sevda's until, with one single movement, she pushed
them open and slowly exhaled the warm smoke into Sevda's lungs as
though Sevda were inhaling a ghost. Sevda's body accepted it without
objection. She wanted to keep it inside her forever, like a guardian angel
to protect her from ever growing as bitter and lonely as her mother.

Not only did Havva know what she wanted from life, she also knew
what everyone else wanted too. And so, one afternoon, while the four
of them sat together over Nescafé, she very casually mentioned to Sevda's mother that there was a new program from the federal government that would pay money to foreign families each month if they sent
their children to German classes. Particularly those children who were
too old for mandatory schooling but did not yet have a job.

"That could even be something for Sevda," Havva suggested, completely deadpan, as she stirred white powdered milk into her mug by
the spoonful.

"I do not know what Hüseyin would say," Emine replied, revealing
nothing of her usual austerity in the presence of guests. Quite the opposite, in fact: She seemed like a sweet, if somewhat naive woman. She
assumed the role of a wife who couldn't make her own decisions, who
needed to ask her husband at every turn because she was so painfully
helpless on her own. In truth, she was merely killing time so that she

could blame every disappointment and refusal on Hüseyin. *Such a pity: I wanted to, but he wouldn't let us.*

"Oh, but Emine Teyze, if you think it's important, surely you can convince your husband of this! What would it hurt to earn a few extra marks, a bit more money for the family budget?" Havva suggested, turning sidelong to Sevda and rubbing her thumb and index finger together discreetly, as though she already held the three hundred marks with which she was enticing Emine in her hand.

Havva's mother nodded, agreeing that it sounded like a good and simple source of extra income. And that very evening, Emine spoke with Hüseyin, in hopes of acquiring a new set of porcelain or a Rowenta steam iron or even a Singer sewing machine. And Hüseyin said, on his way to the shower into which he sprang each day as soon as he'd come home from his shift, that he would have to think about it. But of course, he did exactly what his wife said, for this was always their way. And so, the very next week, at fifteen years of age, Sevda stood in front of the mirror tying her hair into two braids for her first day of school.

~

By the time Sevda unlocks their apartment, they've already long since missed their plane. Exhausted, she boils pasta for her children and collapses beside them at the table, observing as they make a mess of themselves with tomato sauce. Cem watches his mother timidly. He's waiting for Sevda to scream at him and frantically tug his soiled T-shirt over his head. But Sevda lacks the strength for this right now. She's not even thinking about her dead father and the others in Istanbul. She can only think of her own failure. She stares down at the table, regarding the tiny, untouched portion of penne on the plate in front of her and the silverware beside it engraved with the letters *Solingen*. She can smell something, and only for a moment, she imagines it's the smell of smoke. She rubs the back of one hand over her forehead. *Stop it. Don't go crazy now,* she tells herself, taking a deep breath. *Please, please, don't go crazy now.* And then Bahar cries, "Mama!" and points to the stove. Sevda turns around and sees the empty pot smoking on the burner. She rises slowly, switches off the stove, and opens the window. She sends her children to their room.

"Take your food and go play Gameboy."

The two can hardly believe their luck. They run quickly before their mother has time to reconsider. Meanwhile, Sevda drags herself to the living room. She throws herself onto the sofa with her phone and a bar of chocolate with hazelnuts and prepares herself to book them a new flight. The sugar helps wake her up. She pulls herself together just long enough to receive a new booking confirmation. At least it's for tomorrow, even though it won't be until afternoon. Sevda hangs up the phone. The children's bedroom door is closed. She takes one of the embroidered cushions from the couch and hugs it to her chest. She's going to miss the funeral. She won't even be able to say goodbye to her father—to whisper to him that she'd already forgiven him long ago. It's too late now. Her mother will have hours to get worked up about her absence with the others. Emine will wave her arms in the air and cry and curse and wail. But secretly, she'll be happy, too, because Sevda has failed again. Sevda raises the flowered cushion and presses it to her face. She screams. She sobs into the cushion until her lungs feel like a giant burn hole in her chest.

~

Sevda's head had felt like it was on fire. She walked downriver to her German class Monday through Friday for an entire year, trying to learn all the rules of German grammar, the exceptions, the exceptions to the exceptions, and the exceptions to the exceptions to the exceptions—cramming all of it into her brain. When school got out at noon, she sometimes went to the library she'd received a card to as part of her studies. She borrowed issues of *Burda Moden* and a copy of *Little Women* by Louisa May Alcott because she'd heard about it on the radio when she was still living in Karlıdağ. But she hardly made it past the third page.

Part of her class also required participating in two internships. Sevda did her first internship at the hospital in Rheinstadt, where she distributed meals to patients there. She did her second at the department store Hertie, downstairs in the wool and textile department. After two Turkish customers spotted Sevda working there, Turkish women began arriving each day to consult with her, and later just to chat. In the end, they always left without making a purchase, but Sevda thought that she was useful anyway. At the very least, there was something Sevda could offer that the other saleswomen couldn't.

Her internship was unpaid, but every minute away from her mother, her father, and her other spoiled siblings was worth its weight in gold to Sevda. She saw Havva less often now as well. One day, Sevda went to visit her and found Havva lying on her bed under the patched-up wall where the posters of the belly dancer and Bülent Ersoy had hung, her eyes red from crying. Havva's parents had, like many others, decided to move back to Turkey. It was 1984, and the German government was paying money to guest workers who volunteered to leave—enough money to buy themselves a house in their home country. Havva had lived in Germany since she was ten years old. She was acting like she could stay in Germany if she wanted to, as if it were her decision to leave.

"They don't want us in this country. It's better to leave now before they chase us out," she said. She no longer even made the effort of going to her window when she smoked. Instead, she ashed her cigarette on the dresser by her bed.

Back then, Sevda didn't understand what Havva meant. She'd never had the feeling people didn't want her here. No one had ever called her a *fucking Turk*. No one had ever treated her poorly at all. Okay, the Germans at her work were not the friendliest of people, but they weren't exactly friendly to each other either. Germans were like that. Sevda's real problem was the look on her mother's face—a look that hadn't changed over the three years since her arrival. It was a look of mistrust, a look constantly seeking for her flaws, her mistakes. A tear-stained expression impossible to rectify. And then there was the constant uproar from Peri and Hakan, who argued incessantly. Sevda had nowhere to hide in the room she shared with her sister, a room constantly invaded by Hakan's angry presence. And now there was a fourth child on the way. And this new pregnancy was certainly not transforming Emine into a more tolerable person. Meanwhile Hüseyin slunk around as always, a wordless ghost in their apartment whenever he was home from work. From time to time, he ordered Sevda to help her pregnant mother more. But Sevda already did everything, and if he meant

something other than the housework, well, no one could help Emine
with that.

Sevda was organizing the bolts of reduced-price fabric in the stuffy
basement of the department store to pass the final minutes of her shift
more quickly when suddenly Emine appeared before her, round as a
bowling ball and beaming. Sevda started at the sight of her, less surprised by her mother's unexpected presence than she was by her friendly
demeanor. Emine said she wanted to buy Sevda a dress, and that she
should pick one out upstairs. Sevda was not entirely convinced. She could
sense that there would be some catch involved, but she also wanted to
take advantage of the situation anyway. After all, it was the first time in
her life that Sevda would be allowed to choose an article of clothing for
herself. She chose a sky-blue dress with padded shoulders and a wide,
white belt of artificial leather, and Emine nodded along. They had the
dress wrapped in tissue paper at the register.

There were to be visitors on Saturday, and Sevda didn't recognize the
names of her parents' guests. But the moment Emine told her to put
on her new dress, it all suddenly made sense. A couple arrived whom
she had never seen before and behind them, a son approximately Sevda's age. He had a perm and giant square-frame glasses; Sevda couldn't
see much more of him from her vantage point in the kitchen. She sent
Peri and Hakan out to the adults as her mini spies, both of them also
clad in their finest. "Find out what they're talking about!" The little ones
enjoyed their new mission. They ran giggling into the living room and
returned moments later somber-faced, reporting back: "They're only
saying blablabla."

Shortly thereafter, when Sevda brought tea into the living room,
she could feel their eyes sizing her up and down as though she were a
juicy cut of lamb at the butcher's. She distributed their tea glasses and
retreated into the kitchen in shame, without so much as giving the young
man a single glance. She'd only managed to catch sight of a bit of one
light-blue pant leg. Bored out of their wits, Hakan and Peri began to
punch and yell at each other in the hallway in front of the apartment
door until Emine emerged to pinch Hakan's upper arm. Under the cover

of this commotion, Sevda crept to the front door to examine the guests' shoes. The brown ones with the worn-out heels belonged without a doubt to the father. The low tops with heels belonged to the mother. That left only one other pair: pointed toes and shiny black leather. With blue jeans!

"I don't want him. There's no way," Sevda told her mother later that evening.

"Why not? He is a good-looking young man. He has a job. Do you think you can do better?"

Sevda had no answer for this, but she remained obstinate, storming out of the kitchen without saying another word. Hüseyin sat in his chair by the television. Sevda wanted to march right up to him and tell him that she didn't want to get married at all. But what would the alternative be? To waste away forever in this apartment and listen to Emine's bitching? She wanted to escape as soon as possible. And marriage was the only road leading away from this place. That much was clear. And how could you know, anyway, whether you could love someone or not? Certainly not from their shoes. Nevertheless, Sevda only had these pointed shoes, the blue jeans, and the curly perm to hold on to. And they sufficed to tell her that he was not the one. Not him.

And so, two Saturdays later, she put her sky-blue dress back on and another couple came to visit. This time, Sevda recognized them: Orhan and Güldane were good friends of her parents already. Their children and grandchildren lived in Holland, so each time they visited, they brought wet kisses and presents for Hakan and Peri. Sevda thought they were obnoxious because they gossiped too much and always stayed late into the night to tell just one more and then just another story while Sevda had to boil pot after pot of tea. This time they brought a nephew of Orhan's with them who lived alone somewhere in northern Germany. He wore a modest black T-shirt under a mint-green suit with trainers. He didn't open his mouth much, but he spoke with his eyes. Sevda looked shyly away when he made eye contact at their meeting. He looked her directly in the eye rather than staring at her dress or at her hips. The second time, when he was leaving, she returned his gaze. She knew she wanted to see him again.

And so, Ihsan returned the very next weekend in his black Opel Manta, driving five hours down from someplace called Salzhagen, just to see Sevda. The two chatterboxes did not accompany him this time. He and Sevda sat on the balcony, a half story above the ground, and talked, staring out from time to time toward the metalworks, looming over the parking lot like a giant smoking monster. The balcony door stood open with little Peri on a chair beside it, keeping watch.

"How was the drive? Are you tired?"

"No."

"I see. So do you like driving?"

"Yeah."

Sevda reentered the apartment, passing Peri on her way in to make them two cups of Nescafé. And to think of more questions she could ask that might require more than a one-word answer.

"Did your parents move back to Turkey without you?"

"Yes."

"You didn't want to go with them?"

"No."

Sevda stirred her coffee around and around, although the sugar had long since dissolved.

"There's nothing in Turkey," Ihsan said at some point, out of the blue, craning his neck to stare down over the balcony railing. Sevda followed his gaze and could see Hakan and his friends admiring Ihsan's Manta in the parking lot in front of the factory. "I have a car here. And a job," Ihsan continued.

"I understand," Sevda said quietly.

She could hear Peri's bored sighs coming from inside.

"Don't you sometimes feel lonely in Salzhagen?"

"Sometimes," he said. "I go out with friends. But it's pretty lonely at my place."

Sevda liked the idea that Ihsan had his own apartment. Where he could do whatever he pleased. She wondered what he saw when he looked out his window.

"My uncle says that's why I should get married. But to be honest, I don't necessarily want to." His eyebrows drew together, as if he were thinking. Sevda could feel a lump in her throat. What was this then? Was he leading her on? But before she could say anything, he added: "I mean, I do want to get married. But not to just anyone."

"Of course. I don't want to marry just anybody either."

They sat quietly on the balcony for a while, sipping their coffees and looking down at Hakan and the boys, who had now moved on to playing soccer. They did not look at each other again until it was time for him to go. A simple handshake, during which Ihsan's thumb moved ever so slightly to caress the back of Sevda's hand.

One week later, they talked again on the phone. And two weeks later, Ihsan returned with the two gossips and two engagement rings.

"If the wedding is in June, I'll miss my exam," Sevda said during her next balcony conversation with Ihsan. Peri was keeping watch again from her chair behind the door and humming loudly. "I still want to try to get my diploma. Do you think I can retake the exam in Salzhagen?"

"Of course," Ihsan promised with a shrug. "There're schools everywhere."

~

Sevda is still lying on the sofa, staring at the ceiling. It's gotten late. She tore the telephone cable from the wall, only to plug it back in ten minutes later. And she's waiting. Waiting for some kind of a sign. She's already put the kids to bed and changed her clothes. The TV is still on, but only so it doesn't get too quiet in her apartment.

On nights like these, her life seems like one long series of bad decisions. She hadn't spoken a single word to her father in years. She only ever asked Peri or Hakan at most how he and Emine were doing. She hasn't visited Rheinstadt, hasn't sought out her parents' company, she doesn't even know what her father looked like recently—what the past five years had done to him. Five years. She hadn't even realized their radio silence had lasted that long. Those five years had flown by while Sevda ran after her children, took over the restaurant, wanted to separate from her husband, forgave him, and then eventually left him anyway. But simply changing the locks is not enough to shut a person out. Tearing the phone from the phone jack doesn't suffice either. Because Ihsan isn't just some nobody. He's the father of her children. The man with whom Sevda had learned what it meant to love someone completely, along with all his flaws.

Yes, Sevda had loved him. She knows this now: now that the love is gone. The words never passed her lips. They were never part of her language. Nor were they part of Ihsan's language. Or the language of her parents. *I love you* was something the people in *Dallas* told each other, not real people in real life. *I love you*, that sounded like Pamela and Bobby. Like a scarlet-red bathing suit and brightly colored cocktails at the pool. Here in real life, Sevda first had to lie bludgeoned by her sadness, staring at the ceiling, afraid of the doorbell and the phone, before she could acknowledge that she had loved her husband. That she had loved her father. And that she hadn't even known it then, back when it had been so. Because Sevda thought that love was when you have nothing but beautiful thoughts and feelings for somebody, from morning until night. But that's not what love is. How bitter for this to first dawn on her now. Sevda, whose very name means *love*, despite the fact that she herself never had so much as the faintest glimmer of what love truly means. That love always also means discord and strife. Always also a yearning for more, a dissatisfaction. That nothing can be perfect. That you can never be enough. That you can never just be satisfied with the way things are. No, Sevda and Ihsan weren't Pamela and Bobby. No, not even close. Their love was not a *Dallas* love. Not a love at first sight. Not love head-over-heels. No kara sevda.

And yet it was love nonetheless. In the way that, at some point, it always becomes love when two people spend enough time together. When they show each other their best sides and their worst. Argue and reconcile. Injure and forgive. Until one of them is no longer willing to do so. Sevda rises from the sofa and tears the phone cord from the wall again.

~

It was just after Sevda's eighteenth birthday. Her actual eighteenth birthday. Emine held ten-month-old baby Ümit in one arm. In her other hand, she held a tiny bottle of water, the contents of which she emptied onto the street behind the Manta as it sped away, assuring that Sevda and Ihsan would finish their journey in happiness and good health. Peri and Hakan were waving. Hüseyin stood a bit removed from the rest of their family. From the window of the car, Sevda saw him light a cigarette.

They arrived in Salzhagen late at night. Sevda was still wearing her oversized wedding dress, at least three sizes too big. She could hardly wait to change out of the thing. But upstairs in the apartment Ihsan had rented for them, it was all she could do to keep herself from bawling.

The attic apartment was freezing cold. Filthy. And it stank worse than the rest stop toilet earlier that day on the road to Salzhagen, where Sevda had been afraid she might catch some disease. Sevda swallowed her initial disgust and wandered about her new home. A German couple had grown old together here. In any case, the wallpaper was straight out of the 1950s, along with the furniture Ihsan had simply acquired with the apartment. Including their bed. The mattress not only sagged; it had two brown stains in the shape of the two bodies that had lain upon it every night, falling asleep in the same position and at the same distance from one another for decades.

Sevda spent her first days combating the stench of what was likely the long-dead couple with chlorine-based cleaners. Their stink haunted each and every crevice of the rooms like two persistent ghosts. When she was finally finished, she asked Ihsan, who was lying on the sofa with a newspaper: "So when can we register me for school?"

"What school?"

"Well, the school where I can finish my diploma?"

"Why did you get married if you wanted to go to school?"

Sevda had no answer for this. Ihsan put down his paper and sat for another half hour in front of the ghost couple's TV before departing for the bar. And Sevda went back to her cleaning until she had infiltrated every joint and seam of the apartment and her body was so weary there was nothing left but to collapse onto their rancid bed.

Weeks and months passed by, and Sevda felt increasingly isolated in Salzhagen. She befriended two women from Afyon who lived on the two floors beneath her and were both cousins and sisters-in-law. Both

styled their hair in the same perm. But Neslihan and Neriman could
only still Sevda's loneliness for a half hour per day. Their mother-in-
law or mother who lived on the ground floor did not permit them any
more time than this away from their apartments. She ordered them
around day in and day out. Apparently, she could not abide their having suddenly taken to stealing away to the courtyard to smoke and gos-
sip with this stranger. For the rest of the day, Sevda sat in the ghost
couple's apartment, trying to find distractions from her boredom. She
scrubbed the rusty bathtub, watched *Lindenstraße*, and thumbed through
sticky dime novels Ihsan brought her from the flea market. Ihsan himself spent less and less time at home. His path from work to the bar
led only briefly past Sevda for food. It now seemed he simply planned
to continue living as he had before, with the only difference that he
could now fetch himself a warm meal at home. In the beginning, Sevda
endeavored to prepare a fresh soup and salad with the same effort she
devoted to the main course every day, hoping to convince her husband
to stay home just a bit longer. So she could talk to him and get to know
him better. But it didn't work. His friends were waiting. It was his right
to have free time. He needed to recover at the bar after his hard work in
the factory. He told her these things with such irritation in his voice. It
was as if she were not his lover at all but some obnoxious and infantiliz-
ing mother, and he, her sulky child. He devoured his food as quickly as
possible, thanking Sevda as if it were an obligation, before disappearing
quickly out the door.

On one such evening, their furnace stopped working. Sevda sat on the
sofa under the pitched roof wrapped up in blankets, staring out the
window. Not a soul could be seen on the street below. Not even a car.
But lights were on in all the windows of the house across the way.
Sevda had escaped her parents' desolate apartment only to be trapped
in another that was every bit as desolate. But also cold. And uncannily
quiet. She imagined her neighbors drinking herbal tea and chatting
with one another. Tucking their children into bed and reading them
bedtime stories. That night, Sevda decided to do something about these
lonely evenings. She would stop taking the pill and make herself a best

girlfriend of her own. That was the plan at least. But her new friend turned out to be a boy.

She named him Cem, like *gathering*, like *crowd*. Because together they would build a new clique of their own, the smallest clique in the world. Cem kept her busy twenty-four hours a day; Sevda lacked the time for boredom now. She nursed him, bathed him, and massaged his chubby legs with oil. She made him laugh, rocked him to sleep. She watched him while he was sleeping. The silence of the apartment was no longer intimidating. It was comfortable and pleasant. Ihsan came home, ate something, held the little one in his arms for a moment, and then left again. Sevda no longer cared that he sometimes spent whole nights away from home now and came back with bruises and scuffs from the fights he got into with Germans at the night clubs he went to. All the love and affection she could muster were reserved solely for Cem.

Cem had barely begun to speak his first sentences, and already a new child was growing in her womb. The same joy Sevda had felt for her first child transformed into a fear now that she would not have the available attention for two. What if she cared more for this new baby than for Cem? What if Cem realized he'd been relegated to a second-tier position for the rest of his life, the way Sevda—as her family's firstborn—had always been forced into last place? Ever since his birth, Sevda had had to think back constantly on her own childhood. She incessantly compared the things she did with the things she could remember Emine doing. Sevda made an effort to do the exact opposite. And yet, despite herself, she often found herself slipping into the same patterns of behavior she knew from her mother. She'd became short-tempered, loud. She caught herself striking Cem on the fingers when he did something he wasn't supposed to, even before he was old enough to understand. Sevda was about to fall victim to the same battles Emine fought: the constant struggle not to overindulge her children. As if the worst thing that could possibly happen to a child was for it to be given too much freedom and shown too much love. As if such excesses were even possible.

On the TV, they were showing footage of neo-Nazis attacking a refugee shelter and setting it on fire. It was too late now for Sevda to think about how she was supposed to raise two children in a country whose citizens set people on fire while others stood by and filmed rather than trying to intervene. So Sevda turned the TV off instead. She asked Ihsan to buy her a CD by Tracy Chapman because she'd heard the song "Fast Car" on the radio. At night, she rocked Cem to sleep on her lap, while Tracy's soulful voice sang of a yearning Sevda could comprehend without even understanding the words. Tears rained thick and heavy down over her swollen belly.

How had she wound up here, twenty-three years old and saddled with two lifelong obligations when all she'd ever dreamed of was a career, a handbag, a life of her own? With two children and no diploma or qualifications, living in a city where every day the words *Ausländer raus!* were graffitied on a new and different wall. Sevda could forget about her prospects of ever finding a real job. Her grandmother had been right when she'd told her back in Karlıdağ: "Sevdam, you dream and dream, and one morning you will wake up and curse your life because it will have nothing to do with the life that you have dreamed. Be a clever girl and appreciate the things you have: two arms, two legs, your beauty. Is this not enough? We cannot have everything."

When her second child was born, Emine, Peri, and little Ümit came to help Sevda out. By that time, Peri was in the midst of the throes of puberty. She was constantly running to the phonebooth in the city center, supposedly to call her girlfriends. Ümit played with Cem, and Emine found surprisingly little to criticize. She cooked their meals and left Sevda in peace, lying in her bedroom with the baby. She even knocked on Sevda's door before bringing in her tea; she took the baby in her arms whenever Sevda asked her to. Sevda had never experienced the kind of respect and empathy from her mother she felt now in the presence of her newborn child. And she would never experience Emine this way again. The baby seemed to have flipped some kind of switch inside Emine.

Sevda enjoyed her peace, concentrating on her daughter's breathing and the movements of her tiny hands. She named her Bahar, like *springtime*, hoping her arrival would herald the end of the dark season of Sevda's life. Her love for Bahar wasn't any greater than her love for Cem, but it was different because Bahar was a girl. And girls needed encouragement. Girls needed to be taught how to say no, so they could live life on their own terms rather than only endeavoring to fulfill other people's desires. Sevda told herself that Cem, on the other hand, would already know how to get his way. She stared down at the coffee table where Ihsan had left a pile of sunflower seed shells and an empty can of beer. A puddle of amber liquid was pooling underneath the empty can.

Back then, Sevda was still convinced she needed to accept Ihsan's selfish behavior. This was what a loving wife must do. The truth that this concept of love was a fatal lie leading only to a life in which Sevda swaddled their children, tucked them in bed, cooked, and cleaned without so much as ever uttering a peep: this was something she still had to learn for herself.

Money was always tight. Ihsan constantly worked overtime at the assembly line, but by the end of each month, there was still only enough to buy potatoes and rice. And after Ihsan broke a flowerpot against the wall because she asked him what he did with all the rest of his paycheck, Sevda didn't ask again. But she could hardly wait for the time to come when both Cem and Bahar could go to preschool, and she could look for a job of her own. In the summer of 1994, when Bahar was finally three, Sevda went downstairs to Neriman and Neslihan and asked them to recommend her for a position at the laundry service where they worked. The two of them worked night shifts while their children slept and slept during the day while their children were at preschool.

"I don't know if they're looking for anyone right now," Neriman hemmed and hawed.

"I don't think any positions will free up," Neslihan said, in a distinctly colder tone.

"Well, maybe I can go and ask myself?" Sevda tried not to sound too much like she was pleading.

"No, no, that won't do any good," Neslihan said, frantically clearing away Sevda's glass of tèa. "You don't want to go all that way for nothing!"

Sevda didn't understand why the two of them were being so evasive. But she did know that without a high school diploma, she had very few options. And if the laundry service had even hired Neriman and Neslihan, her own chances couldn't be so bad. And so, on Bahar's very first day of preschool, Sevda walked all the way across Salzhagen to the laundry facilities out in the industrial zone. She got the address from the phone book because Neriman had forgotten to write it down and put it in her mailbox as promised.

"Boss not here!" the blonde secretary screamed. Her makeup was two shades too dark, and the color of her face reminded Sevda of a peach. Her name was supposedly Frau Schmidt.

"When is he coming in then?" Sevda asked uneasily.

"Boss not here! No understand or what?"

"Yes, I understand you, ma'am. But when is he coming back?"

"Tomorrow. Come. Early here!"

And so, Sevda made her way back down the turnpike to the preschool, picked up her sobbing daughter—who, unlike Cem, had difficulties adjusting to this new environment. She returned the next morning along the same route as soon as she had dropped the little one off despite her protests.

"Hallo, Frau Schmidt. I was here yesterday. Is Herr . . ."

"Yes, un momento. I getting boss. You waiting here!"

Sevda got the job. That evening, she made Ihsan's favorite meal: mantı with garlic yogurt sauce. While they were eating, she held a monologue—how things could not go on this way any longer, how they were always broke. How he always had to say no to any purchases besides their normal groceries. And so, from now on, Sevda would work too. Ihsan would need to stay home three nights a week and watch over their children. He wouldn't need to do anything; the children would be sleeping anyway. Ihsan did not like this idea at all. Sevda could see it in his eyes. But he resigned himself to his fate. He didn't have much choice. After all, in the end, it was he who spent his entire monthly earnings at the bar.

Monday, Wednesday, and Thursday nights, Sevda and her neighbors drove to the laundry service in Neslihan's father's rickety Mercedes-Benz.

Sevda could tell from her two companions' faces that they did not think her inhaling the same hot, humid detergent-laden air they did was a good idea. But it was only after some time that Sevda realized what the problem really was: Neriman and Neslihan were afraid Sevda would take their jobs. Of course, this was ridiculous: the two of them were full-time employees, and Sevda only had a temporary, part-time job. But all the same, a feeling of distrust had grown between them. They glared at Sevda with the same expression the Germans did if you came too close to their property or car.

And so, in addition to her own tasks, Sevda rolled up her sleeves and did her best to help Neriman and Neslihan with their work as well.

"Neriman, you can take a cigarette break if you want to. If Frau Schmidt says anything, I'll tell her you're in the bathroom."

"Neslihan, I'm finished with this load. Should I help you with the rest of yours?"

At least they still took Sevda to work with them in their car. It didn't bother her that they began to give her more and more of their own tasks at work. The job wasn't easy, but she liked it. Her arms ached the next morning from carrying and hanging and ironing the bedding and the heavy curtains; everything was infused with the awful smell of fabric softener. But Sevda felt useful at last. When she finally received her first paycheck, she stood with her children by the fountain in front of the bank, crying quiet tears of joy. Then she took them to the toy store and watched proudly as they skipped excitedly through the aisles looking for playthings.

When Sevda received her second paycheck, Ihsan asked her over dinner to pay for the month's rent. This way, he could pay off the debts he allegedly had. The next afternoon, without going into too much detail, Sevda marched to the bank and transferred the money, humming happily to herself on the way home. Finally, she and Ihsan were on equal footing.

But then came that December morning. It was just after five. Neriman and Neslihan were smoking an after-work cigarette in the parking lot in front of the facilities. Sevda sat wearily in their Mercedes, watching her cold breath turn into fog. She was trying to calculate in her head how much money she could save that month and how long it would take before she reached the next thousand-mark milestone. Neriman and Neslihan got in and sat silently for the length of their drive. They were exhausted, but they also enjoyed these final moments of peace before returning to the chaos of their apartments.

They drove along the empty streets. The houses where lights were already burning in the windows must belong to other workers preparing for their early morning shifts. The sky was black as coal. But it wasn't merely the sky. Smoke was rising over the rooftops of the low, postwar housing complexes. Lots of smoke, Sevda suddenly realized. When they turned into their street, they were greeted by flashing emergency lights. The fire department. An ambulance. A crowd of people standing around wrapped in thick blankets stood in front of the roofless, burned-out apartment building that just that evening had still been their home.

"What the hell?"

Sevda leapt from their vehicle before Neslihan could even park the car.

"Cem! Bahar!" She ran through the crowd in her work uniform, frantically searching for her children. The smoke tickled her throat and she thought she could taste ashes on her tongue. Neslihan's mother-in-law stood swaying in her nightgown, holding a blanket over her head with both hands because she didn't have her headscarf. Neslihan's husband stood beside her in his slippers. He took a few steps toward Sevda, pointing with one finger in the direction of the fire truck. As if in some kind of nightmare, Sevda pushed her way through the crowd to the hulking red vehicle that looked like an oversized version of one of Cem's toy cars. Its back doors were open. The little ones were sitting on a stretcher, Bahar in her pajamas with the little horses on them, Cem in his pajamas with the lions. They were drinking something warm out of two mugs. Ihsan sat beside them in his winter jacket, absentmindedly stroking Bahar's head.

Sevda climbed up into the fire truck, emitted one single stifled sob, and hugged her children tightly.

"Oh, thank God. What happened?"

"There was a fire. But luckily no one in the building was hurt," Ihsan said. He stood clumsily, bending down to kiss her on the cheek. He had never kissed her in public before. Not even in front of their children. Sevda looked him up and down.

"Why are you fully dressed?"

He returned her gaze in silence. He even smiled. He didn't appear uneasy in the slightest. He maybe even looked a bit relieved.

"The amca from downstairs carried us out," Cem blurted in excitement.

"What?"

"He broke down the door like Rambo and carried us through the fire!"

Cem wiggled his arms around enthusiastically, imitating the roaring flames. Exhausted, Bahar could no longer keep her eyes open.

Sevda grew silent. She couldn't find the words. Her mouth became a hole, deep and dark, empty of all contents. She clambered down from the fire truck, staggered a few paces away from the others, and took in the house—the house in which she'd gone to bed night after night without so much as a single doubt that she was safe. That this was her home. Part of the facade was charred away, particularly the bits over the windows, as if the flames had sought to free themselves from the house there. Only the roof had completely burned away. The roof under which their own apartment had lain. The roof under which her children had slept while their own father was out God knows where.

Sevda did not say anything. She did not say anything while they spent the first three nights in a motel. And she did not say anything when the police questioned them. The authorities already knew from others that their children had been home alone. She did not say anything when Ihsan sent them off by train to Rheinstadt, where they were to stay with Hüseyin and Emine while he looked for a new place. And she did not say anything while Ihsan stared mournfully at her from the platform as their train pulled away.

In her parents' apartment, Sevda watched Peri and Ümit happily playing with the little ones on the carpet. Saw Hüseyin positively blossom with his grandchildren on his lap. Even Hakan came home early every

day to take Cem and Bahar to the playground. After a time, Sevda came
to realize that maybe she was not nearly as isolated and alone as she
had felt. And so, after a few days, she called Ihsan's favorite bar and
asked for them to fetch her husband. She could hear her own breathing over the heavy tones of arabesque music and the echoes of men's
voices in the bar she'd never seen from the inside. When Ihsan finally
made his presence known on the other end of the line, she cleared her
throat and said: "Don't bother coming here for me. It's over."

He probably didn't take her seriously. But in any case, Ihsan didn't contact Sevda for an entire week. And then he started calling multiple times
a day. Each time, Emine called for Sevda, and Sevda sent Cem to the
phone to tell his father that Mama was busy right now. Whenever the
phone rang, Sevda went to the basement to wash or hang the laundry or
simply just to breathe in the smell of the cellar. Until one day, she finally
answered the phone herself to tell Ihsan over the leaden receiver that
she was serious about what she'd said. And that she would look for her
own apartment here in Rheinstadt. He needn't bother calling her again.

"And how do you plan to pay for this?" asked Emine, who had of
course been listening from the kitchen. It was New Year's Day. The little ones were on a walk with their dede. Peri had been lying around
since morning in Hakan and Ümit's room with a book and a long face.
Hakan and Ümit were in the living room marveling at the video camera
Hakan had somehow acquired. The entire apartment smelled like the
goose roasting in the oven because Emine had overheard at the mosque
that it was a sin to make a turkey for New Year's.

"I'll find myself a job," Sevda told her mother. "Don't worry, we
won't be sleeping on your sofa forever."

Emine clicked her tongue. "Your father does not approve of you being
away from your husband."

"Ihsan won't be my husband for much longer. Does that solve the
problem?" Sevda replied.

"What do you want from him? What did he ever do to you? Does
he not feed your children? Does he mistreat you? Does he hit you?"

"Anne!" Sevda cried out in irritation.

"Tell me, Sevda. Does he hit you?" Emine persisted.

"No, Anne. He doesn't hit me." Sevda rolled her eyes.

"You see? It is as I thought. There is no reason for divorce besides your own whimsies."

"He's never home. We don't talk. He left our children alone. The children almost . . . What don't you understand about that, Anne?"

"No, Sevda. This is not the truth. *You* left your children alone. *You* were away night after night. Are you not their mother? Is it not your responsibility to watch over them while they sleep?"

"I'm sorry, Anne, but you don't know what you're talking about. You never had to work. Baba's salary was always enough. But you can't throw us out as long as Baba says we can stay."

"Your father feels the same way I do!"

"You know what? I don't believe you. You always say that. Supposedly Baba always feels the exact same way as you. But I only ever hear it from you! I won't fall for that again. Baba needs to tell me this himself!" Sevda retorted.

There were voices in the stairwell. The children were back.

"Oh, yes? Go right ahead. There he is. Go and ask your father what he thinks of your behavior with your husband!"

A short while later, standing before Hüseyin in the kitchen, Sevda sought in vain to find the baba she had once known in this man. She remembered how he'd sat across from her in the train to Istanbul, how they had laughed together. But now, he only looked away; it was so difficult for him to talk about anything of substance that he couldn't even meet her eye. He took one sharp breath and finally responded: "It would be best if you went back to Ihsan, Sevda."

"But I want . . ."

"I already spoke to Ihsan yesterday on the phone while you were shopping. He has found a new apartment. He is coming here to get you tomorrow."

That was the last time Sevda ever spoke to her father.

The new apartment in Salzhagen was only a few hundred meters from their old building, but it was on a busier street. The first time Sevda

stood before the building, her eyes swept over the last names on the
buzzer by the door. She breathed a sigh of relief. There were only German names. There was also an Italian restaurant on the ground floor,
but it seemed to be popular with people who could afford to have someone else cook for them and whose own names sounded like the last
names at the door.

This apartment was well lit and better than their last one. The bathroom had been freshly renovated, and Ihsan had even installed new
appliances and cabinets in the kitchen. Sevda didn't ask with whose
money he'd paid for it. In fact, she did her best to avoid speaking to
him at all, which didn't pose much of a problem. Ihsan had never been
one for conversation, and he'd never been interested in what was going
on at home. He'd only ever stopped in briefly with itchy feet; he was
always there with one foot out the door. But now, he spent every single
evening at home, even if he did secretly wish he could be somewhere
else. His foot tapped and fidgeted, and Sevda did her best to ignore him
while she made herself a tea without preparing a glass for Ihsan. She
settled down on the sofa to listen to the muffled noises from the restaurant below.

One question was still burning on Sevda's tongue while the smell
of warm pizza dough seeped in under their door to tickle her nostrils.
Finally, she had to ask.

"What did the police find out about the fire? How did it start?"

"They don't know."

"What do you mean they don't know?"

"It was probably something technical. A cable or something. But it
could even have been a cigarette."

"A cable or a cigarette? Tell me, do the police not even watch the
news?"

Ihsan nodded wisely. He certainly watched the news. And Sevda
watched it too. She'd known what was happening the moment she
saw the smoke and fire against the sky over her building. She'd simply known. She could still smell the smoke and ashes. And so, it wasn't
merely disappointment at her incessantly absent shell of a husband
that made her never want to return to Salzhagen. It was also the knowledge that somewhere in this dismal little city with its twenty thousand

inhabitants, there were people who wanted to see her dead. People who wanted to see her and her two children and her husband and her neighbors dead. Incinerated. Burned to dust. Exterminated. Unlike in Solingen and Mölln, there had not been any casualties in their fire. All of them were okay, thank God. Sevda had begun to repeat her grandmother's prayers again silently every time she watched her children playing. But the fact that there had not been any deaths also meant that the cause of the fire would never be properly investigated. That no one would ever leave flowers in front of the scorched ruins of their home. That the city would never apologize to them. What for? No one would ever even hear about this fire; no one would ever care. And even if there were thousands of other fires just like this one, no one would ever hear about them either. It was like none of this had happened to Sevda, her family, and her neighbors. It was as if Sevda's fear of Nazis who wanted to burn her children to death in their sleep was nothing more than a figment of her own imagination. As if the nightmare in which Frau Schmidt from the laundry service flicked her burning cigarette into Bahar's little bed was nothing more than an irrational fantasy. And that was all it was. Of course, that was all it was. But wasn't there some shred of truth there all the same? Sevda would walk through the neatly trimmed streets, shop, pick up her children from preschool, and she would never know whether she was passing by the perpetrators on her way. She would spend the rest of her life walking through the world with the smell of ashes in her nostrils. And no one would ever know. Not the cashier at the supermarket. Not the friendly preschool teacher. And even if they did know, how could they understand?

During those first weeks in her new apartment in Salzhagen, Sevda often had to think of Havva's warning: *They don't want us in this country. It's better to leave now before they chase us out.* Slowly, hour by hour, as Sevda washed the parsley, tidied up her children's room, and cleaned the foggy mirror in the bathroom, the meaning of her friend's parting words grew clear. It had been eleven years now since Havva moved back to Turkey. Eleven years until Sevda could understand. The roof had literally had to burn up over her very head before she finally understood Havva was right. They didn't want her here.

But Sevda made a different choice than Havva and her family had made. Sevda wasn't going anywhere. She would not do them the favor. Never. If they didn't want Sevda here, they would damn well have to chase her out. She would stay and live here and do her utmost to be happy. Here, in this shit town. Come what may. She didn't have any other choice anyway. Where else could she go? Not even her parents would take her in. They'd sent her back to Salzhagen like an ill-fitting suit from a mail order catalog. But maybe Hüseyin and Emine had done their daughter a favor. Maybe it was finally time for Sevda to cut ties with everyone. Even those who were supposed to be closest to her. Yes, Sevda found herself in an impossible situation, but she would turn the situation around and make a conscious choice of it. She would awaken from her powerlessness and take matters into her own hands. She'd set goals for herself and create room for hope. And even if her hopes were only tiny, she would take them seriously from now on and keep them ever present in her mind. She would no longer hide. She would make herself useful and make her children into useful people too. Raise indispensable members of this society, so there would always be others around who needed them and would stand up for them if someone did them wrong. Sevda would take the suspicion that had burned behind her eyes ever since the fire and lock it away. She could not extinguish it, no, she would never be able to extinguish these flames, but she would keep the fire small. She'd do her best to look back on her life up to this moment as the beginning: the beginning of something new. She wouldn't sugarcoat things, no, and she would never forget what happened on that December night. But she would also not surrender to her fear. Because this was what they wanted. No, Sevda would never be afraid. She would work her way out of her invisibility and make sure that people knew her name. That they were interested in her, so at the very least someone would notice if she or her children suddenly disappeared. Because wasn't that the absolute worst thing that could happen to a person: to be erased without anyone so much as noticing?

Sevda peered out her open bedroom window, daydreaming until she noticed a woman below her in the courtyard. She was wearing a red apron and leaning against the wall of the building drinking coffee from a tiny cup. She probably worked at the pizzeria. It was late afternoon, and the restaurant was still closed. The woman's curly black hair reminded Sevda of Havva. After a moment's hesitation, she plucked up her courage.

"Hallo!"

Her voice echoed through the courtyard and the woman started. She glared up at Sevda angrily.

"Are you trying to give me a heart attack?"

Sevda could only look back at her aghast, shaking her head.

"What then?" the woman asked. "And now you can't talk at all? What do you want?"

"Nothing," Sevda replied, raising one hand in apology and quickly closing the window.

Only a short while later, someone knocked at the front door. Sevda crept on tiptoe to peer through the peephole. It was the woman from the courtyard. She had her hands behind her back and was staring up at the ceiling in exasperation.

What did she want now? Was she crazy? Why, oh why, had Sevda drawn the attention of the crazy person in the house?

"Mama, who's there?" Bahar cried, bounding from her room.

"Shhhh!" Sevda hissed, but it was too late. The woman had certainly heard Bahar. And now, Sevda had to open up. Anything else would be embarrassing.

"Oh, hello," Sevda said, trying to act surprised as she opened the door and stood before the little woman with the wrathful gaze. Up close, she no longer looked so young. She might even be older than Emine. Her mouth was lined with innumerable wrinkles that reminded Sevda of her babaanne. But her body was so slim and fit, her curly hair so thick and black, that from a distance Sevda had thought they might be the same age.

"Earlier, I didn't mean to . . . ," Sevda began, but the woman reached out and gripped her under her arm, shaking her head.

"No, no, it was nothing. I was only startled, that is all. You are new here, yes?"

Sevda nodded. Her eyes wandered to the woman's other hand, in which she held a paper plate with pastries on it.

"These are cannoli. For you. And for the children, of course. It's something sweet. From Sicily. What a cute little girl you are! What is your name?" the woman said, bending down to Bahar.

Bahar looked away shyly, hiding behind her mother's legs.

"This is Bahar. And my name is Sevda. That's very kind of you," Sevda replied, accepting the woman's plate. "Please come in. I'll make us tea."

"I have to go back down and open the restaurant. But stop in for a coffee. I usually have time to chat between five and six o'clock, before we open."

"I'd love to. But only if it doesn't bother your boss to have me sitting there."

The woman smiled mischievously. "No, it will not bother my boss at all."

Sevda nodded, watching the woman as she descended the stairs. Halfway down, she turned again and pointed to herself. She called out: "Mariella!"

"It's nice to meet you, Mariella," Sevda said with a smile.

It was only a few days later, when Sevda took Mariella up on her offer and drank one of those bitter little coffees in the restaurant below, that she found out Mariella herself was the owner of the pizzeria. The realization that she'd simply assumed Mariella was just a waitress made Sevda feel uncomfortable. Mariella ran the business entirely on her own, without a man at her side, and it seemed to be doing great. From her apartment every evening, Sevda could hear the customers' bursts of laughter and the sound of clinking glasses. Mariella had only hired a single cook, and she ran from table to table herself. Her son helped out on the weekends.

"But he is a lazy slacker," she said with a wave of her hand. "I have to tell him everything three times before he does it. And I could never leave him alone with the restaurant. Otherwise, I would have retired long ago. I'm only fifty-five, Sevda, but my back cannot keep up with me anymore, you know? At some point you wake up and you just feel old. There is nothing you can do for it. Enjoy your youth as long as you can!"

Sevda took to visiting Mariella more and more. She liked to watch how devotedly Mariella prepared her restaurant before the first customers arrived. Mariella polished the silverware, arranged fresh candles on the tables, and wrote the daily menu on a large board with chalk. From time to time, she went into the kitchen to admonish her cook, Davide. She always returned with a smile on her face, as though it had been nothing. She would put on a melancholy Italian tune and hum along to the melody, while deftly preparing an espresso for Sevda.

Sometimes, she gave Sevda a large, family-sized pizza to take upstairs with her, so Sevda wouldn't have to cook herself. The children loved it—they'd never eaten takeout anything before. Ihsan seemed to like it too. "That lady knows what she's doing there!" he'd rave while cramming the last slice into his mouth.

"I'm glad you think so too," Sevda said one evening, removing the empty pizza box and sweeping the crumbs into the trash. "I'm going to start working for Mariella. She'll pay me a good hourly wage and the guests leave decent tips."

Ihsan stared at Sevda in surprise.

"What is it, Ihsan?"

"Working as what?" he asked her.

"Well, as a waitress."

"You want to *wait tables* down there?" Ihsan said it like it was some kind of obscenity. Sevda did her best to ignore this.

"You know as well as I do that they fired me from the laundry service when I didn't show up to work after the fire. I need to find a job, Ihsan. You know this," Sevda explained as calmly as she could, folding the pizza box into the trash.

"Then you find yourself a different job! My wife will not be down there serving other men while they drink red wine thinking God knows what!"

Sevda wiped the table clean and shook the rag out over the sink. Then she turned slowly to Ihsan and said calmly: "Well, that's a shame

then, Ihsan. Because I'm going to work there. My first shift starts tomorrow at five. So, I guess that means you'll have to find another wife."

Ihsan stared at her for a moment in silence. Then he leapt up in a rage.
He threw everything on their table within reach against the wall—the
saltshaker, the sugar bowl, Cem's pencil box. Sevda ducked out of the
way. He screamed at her. Called her a whore. Said she had lost her
mind. Threatened to throw her out of the house if she ever spoke this
way to him again. Sevda said nothing. She walked slowly to the children's room, where Bahar and Cem were cowering on the rug, staring
up at her in fear. She closed their bedroom door behind her and sat
down on the carpet with her children, smiling softly at them while the
sound of her husband's screaming continued from the kitchen. Sevda
said nothing. But her heart beat wildly. Not from fear but from excitement. It felt good to contradict Ihsan. It felt better than anything in the
world. And this was only the beginning.

As the first rays of sunlight start creeping across the living room, Sevda
can't say whether she's slept a wink. For a moment, she hopes it was
all just a bad dream. But then her eyes fall on the enormous suitcase in
the corner of the room, and she emits a deep sigh. Tears well up in her
eyes. It was not a dream. Her father is dead, and she won't even make
it to his funeral. She'll never forgive herself for missing the opportunity
to say goodbye, the last opportunity for contact.

Sevda rises from the sofa and pulls the curtains shut to block out the
sunlight. Then she pads to the kitchen to make herself a tea. The water
has hardly begun to boil before both Cem and Bahar are awake.

"Mama, can we watch TV?" Bahar asks, while Cem pours himself a
bowl of cornflakes.

"Yes, you may."

"Can we eat breakfast in front of the TV too?" Cem asks in excitement.

When Sevda reaches out to pat his head, he flinches. Sevda stares at
him aghast. Did he really think that she would hit him? Is it really that
bad?

"Yes, this morning you may eat breakfast in front of the TV," she
says, kissing her son on the forehead.

Sevda knows she's a strict mother. And it might be that she some-times pinches her children on the arm or raps them on the hand. But she would never hit them. The thought comes to her head often enough. She certainly has felt the urge to put them in their place with physical pain. But she would never do it in reality. Never. She doesn't want her children to be afraid of her. She only wants them to obey. To pay atten-tion. Because if they didn't listen to her, none of these things with the restaurant would be possible. And now that they live alone with her, it's even more important for them to follow her rules and keep the pace. For them to take care of each other. Sevda can't watch them twenty-four seven. She works way too much for that.

In the beginning, when she'd first taken over the pizzeria from Mari-ella, Sevda had worked even more. Sometimes sixteen-hour days. She'd done everything herself in order to pay off her debts to Mariella for the inventory as quickly as possible. She'd only retained the cook, Davide. Everything else had been up to Sevda: purchasing, cleaning, bookkeep-ing, serving. Ihsan had still been around back then. But they'd already slept separately: he, in the bedroom; she, on the sofa. It had never occurred to him to help her out in any way. He'd been frozen with rage from the moment Mariella had offered to let Sevda take over the busi-ness. Mariella wanted to finally retire and move back to Sicily, where she still owned a tiny house in her village.

"Mariella, I'm flattered that you trust me so much. But I don't know anything about running a business," Sevda had responded, sadly polish-ing the wine glasses.

"Oh, yes you do, Sevda. You understand it all. I've seen it over the past two years. You can do the calculations, you're organized. You're not afraid of responsibility. And you have a friendly face the customers appreciate. You're the only person I would trust to take over my restau-rant with dignity."

Of course, Sevda had always dreamed of having her own business. Especially a restaurant as nice as this one: built up block by block with love over many years, a family business cherished by its customers. But she could never see herself the way that Mariella saw her. And even if she didn't ever want to hear Ihsan's opinion, in secret, she still thought that he was right when he heard about Mariella's offer and snorted:

"Sevda, what do you know about Italian food? You're a Turk, and you want to sell pizza? Who would eat pizza from a Turk, Sevda? Don't bullshit me."

Mariella, on the other hand, thought Germans wouldn't even know the difference as long as Sevda always repeated the three magic words: *prego, ciao,* and *grazie.* Sevda still had her doubts.

But when Ihsan lost his job at the factory only two weeks later, was fired with such short notice that he wasn't even eligible for unemployment benefits, things suddenly looked very different to Sevda. Mariella's offer now appeared like a promise of salvation from her misery.

"What do you mean, you beat him up?" Sevda asked her husband the day he was fired.

"He had it coming. He should be happy he's still alive."

"What are you talking about?" Sevda was so angry she would have liked to throw Ihsan out that very moment.

"I've been working at that factory for ten years. He's only been there for three months. What makes him think he can treat me like that?"

"Like what?"

"Like a slave! Like his own personal fucking kanake. Do you know what he calls me? Ali! I've told him a thousand times my name isn't Ali. And he told me he doesn't give a fuck what my name is."

"And that's why you put him in the hospital?" A smile of satisfaction flitted over Ihsan's face at the mention of the hospital. Sevda wanted to slap him.

"Ihsan, you know perfectly well what the Germans are like! Why did you let him provoke you? Do you think anyone is going to hire you now once word of this gets out? Do you think no one will find out?"

"Bullshit. It won't take me a day to find another job, Sevda. You'll see. I just need to ask around at the bar."

Ihsan did not come home that night. Nor the next morning. When he stumbled past Sevda on her way to work, he still hadn't found a job. He did not find one in the week that followed. A month later, he was still unemployed.

And so, Sevda went to the bank, and then to another. She sat for hours with Mariella while they worked out their business agreement because she couldn't read it on her own. Then, with a simple signature, she assumed ownership of the pizzeria. She stared incredulously at her signature for a long time in the stairwell. Then she headed upstairs to ask Ihsan to at least look after the apartment and the children while she got the restaurant ready, even though she hadn't wanted to ever leave them alone with him again after the fire. But Ihsan refused. He continued sleeping till noon, ate the rest of whatever leftovers Sevda had brought with her from the restaurant the night before, and then made a beeline to the bar. He did manage to stop by briefly in the evenings to tuck the children in bed before he disappeared again. Sevda didn't mind. After all, the children were only a floor away from her now, and she could be back with them in less than a minute if she needed to.

"And what are we supposed to eat now?" Sevda demanded of Ihsan one morning, after waking up after just four hours of sleep to find their refrigerator empty. "If you can't cook anything yourself, the very least you could do is buy some groceries," she continued in a tone intended to provoke him.

"Why don't you eat the profits you're always hiding from me?" Ihsan shot back at her. "Why should I do your work if you don't even pay me?"

Before Sevda could answer him, Ihsan began running through their apartment, frenzied, dumping out the contents of the shelves in search of hidden money. Clothing, toys, and pantry goods flew through the air, landing in untidy heaps. But Ihsan didn't find her hiding place. He would never find it. In desperation, he began smashing the potted plants against the floor. He shattered the mirror on the wall for his crescendo. Sevda stared from the shards of broken glass and back to her husband. He gazed helplessly at her before storming away from the chaos he had made and slamming the door behind him. By the time he returned later that night, Sevda had already changed the locks and disconnected the doorbell.

~

Cem and Bahar are singing along to the theme song of *Pinky and the Brain*. Sevda bends down to plug the phone back in and fishes her address book from the drawer. She dials a number she should know by heart, considering how often she's called it.

The phone rings a few times before someone answers.

"Emergency shelter, City Mission. Hallo?"

"Hallo. This is Frau Demirkan," Sevda says with one hand over her mouth as if trying to keep her last name a secret from her children. She glances over to them. They're only interested in the two cartoon rats on the TV. "I'd like to know if an Ihsan Demirkan spent the night with you last night."

"Who?" the voice demands.

"Ihsan Demirkan."

"What about him?"

"Did he spend the night there?"

"Umm. We can't simply reveal that kind of information. I don't even know who's calling . . ." The voice sounds irritated.

"I call here all the time. Your colleagues tell me whether he's there or not." Sevda does her best to try to sound friendly.

"Then I'll have to have a serious word with my colleagues. This is not some kind of hotel where we have time to run a reception."

Sevda lets out an exhausted sigh. Her breathing turns to static on the line.

"I just want to know if he's okay. Can't you make an exception?" she pleads.

"Who is this anyway? I can't even understand you."

"Sevda Demirkan. My name is Sevda Demirkan. I'm looking for my husband, Ihsan Demirkan." Cem turns away from the TV and stares at his mother. She tries to smile back at him; it feels artificial. But it works. His eyes return to the TV.

"I'm sorry, I don't know that name," says the voice. "And I have too many other things to do for me to worry about your marriage problems. Take care of it yourself, okay? We all have to carry our own . . ."

Sevda hangs up the phone and slinks away to the bathroom to be alone.

～

After Sevda locked Ihsan out, he didn't show himself for two weeks. That was actually all Sevda had wanted: not to have to see him anymore. But they were two awful weeks all the same because Sevda was constantly worried Ihsan would show up unexpectedly. And because she was no longer sure what he was capable of in his newfound rage. And so, she was almost relieved when he finally did appear at the pizzeria, a little out of it, and simply started screaming. Screaming at Sevda in front of her customers like a little child. Sevda tried to calm him down, asked him to leave and call back later if he wanted to see the children. But it didn't help. Ihsan continued screaming at her, insulting her, claiming that she owed him money. The Germans looked up from their tables, glasses of red wine in their hands, as if Sevda and Ihsan were acting out some kind of tragic play in front of them. At some point, Davide came out from the kitchen, grabbed Ihsan, and hauled him away. Somehow, he managed to push Ihsan out the back door with a bottle of grappa before Sevda was forced to call the police. The same police who hadn't given a shit about the arson at their former apartment. These were the last people Sevda wanted to rely on. Instead, she started giving Davide a hundred marks each week to deliver to Ihsan at the bar. And so, she managed to have a few months' peace.

After she had paid off a good amount of her debts to Mariella, Sevda could finally afford to hire an experienced waitress. A half-Italian woman named Moni who could carry five plates at once, who forbade their customers from leaving their umbrellas open in the restaurant because she believed it brought bad luck, and with whose icy blue eyes every man, Davide included, fell instantly in love. Unfortunately, Moni had no head for mathematics. It was a great mystery how she had managed to work so many years in restaurants. Sevda had to stay behind each night in the restaurant and redo the books. But she also had the luxury now of taking a half hour off mid-evening to rush upstairs and give Cem and Bahar a kiss on the forehead while she put them to bed.

"Hey, check it out. He was here yesterday too," Moni said one evening when Sevda returned from her children. She pointed at a young man sitting alone at a table, still wearing his jacket.

"Didn't he order any food?" Sevda asked in confusion.

"No," Moni replied. "He's a weirdo. He only orders beer. He did the same thing yesterday."

"Hmm," Sevda said, measuring this stranger with her eyes. She hadn't noticed him yesterday with all the commotion. He appeared to be well groomed; he did not look like an alcoholic. He also looked to be about her age, and his bushy unibrow betrayed him as one of her fellow countrymen. Which was unusual, since such people never frequented her restaurant.

"He's gotta be here on your account," Sevda said to Moni, but it was more a question than an explanation.

"That's the weird thing about him," Moni said quietly, shaking her head in disbelief. "He's not interested in me at all. He only watches you the whole time."

Sevda and Moni exchanged a worried glance. Evidently, Moni was thinking the same thing as Sevda.

"I'll take care of this," Sevda replied, tugging her blouse straight before marching over to the young man's table.

He sat up stiffly when she drew closer and looked up at her expectantly. Sevda was certain now he was a spy.

"I'm sorry, but I've got to clear your table," she said, removing his glass of beer.

"What do you mean?" he asked in irritation.

"Unfortunately, this table is reserved. All the tables are reserved. My colleague just forgot to mention it to you. But the guests are coming soon. I'm afraid I have to ask you to leave." Sevda spoke politely, but she made no effort to smile. She wanted to make sure he did not come back.

"I understand," he said, to her surprise. He reached into his inner jacket pocket.

"That's okay, this one's on the house," Sevda said, before wondering whether this was really the right technique to chase someone away forever. He looked baffled, then stood, nodding to her in thanks.

"Give Ihsan my regards," Sevda hissed. The question in his eyes remained. "Tell him he should call next time he wants something. Otherwise, it will be me calling the police instead."

His face looked like he had no idea what Sevda was talking about. But at the word *police* he turned quickly and left. The young man did not come back.

The next time Ihsan showed up at the restaurant, the first thing Sevda noticed was his smell. It wasn't merely the reek of alcohol—he'd already had that the last time he stopped by. This time, the stench was different, more penetrating. It was so pungent that Ihsan only needed to take one step through the door before the entire room filled with his odor. The smell of urine. Stale man piss that had been marinating in his unwashed clothing for days.

Luckily, it was still early, and the customers had not yet arrived. Only Moni was already in the restaurant. She held a napkin over her nose and stared at Sevda helplessly. Sevda rushed across the room to Ihsan, casting Moni an apologetic glance as she slid past her. Sevda wasn't sure just what she was sorry for. But she grabbed Ihsan and dragged him through the back door and into the stairwell. It was easy. Surprisingly easy. His body had dwindled into an unhappy mass that reminded Sevda of Bahar's brightly colored playdough: waiting for someone to give it shape. Ihsan's eyelids were only half open. He barely managed to expel his children's names through his lips before he began to cry. Sevda was shocked. She wanted so badly to be angry at him; she wanted to give him hell for showing up at her place of business in this state and risking frightening her customers away. Who of these suburban Germans wanted to sit next to a bum in her restaurant and still pay twenty marks for some red wine? Did he have any idea what he was even doing? How were his children supposed to get by if Sevda did not have any customers left?

But she couldn't do it. She could not be angry with Ihsan. In fact, she had to pull herself together not to break down in tears right along with him and take him in her arms. She could only feel sorry for him. Ihsan had aged significantly. He looked many years older, and he had a gaping wound on his head from God knows where. There was black filth under his fingernails, and his fingers themselves were stained yellow from nicotine. All at once, a realization dawned on Sevda that struck her on the head like a prickly chestnut: Ihsan had no one. No one besides Sevda. And when Ihsan had lost her, he had lost everything.

Sevda brought him up to her apartment, pushed him into the bathroom, and ordered him to wash himself before going directly to the bedroom without showing himself around their children. He slept for two days uninterrupted. And then he left, without saying a word. He took only a few fresh articles of clothing and the money-filled envelope Sevda placed on the nightstand. She hadn't heard from him since.

That night, when Sevda returned home from work with tired legs and her head still reeling, she lay in the warmth of her bed, interrupted only by the occasional poke of a stray pizza crumb against the back of her neck. But she couldn't sleep a wink. She could only lie and wonder what had become of Ihsan. She tried imagining possibilities that weren't cold or wet or out of doors. At a friend's? Maybe he had real friends after all? Real friends, not the kind with whom he played poker at the bar, the ones who fleeced him mercilessly although they knew he was a man with problems, serious problems. A man who needed help. A man who needed the money they stripped from him with cards to buy himself something to eat or find somewhere to sleep. And then Sevda had to ask herself why she believed that any of these bar men she imagined would feel any sense of responsibility for Ihsan. Wasn't that Sevda's job? Was she only trying to escape her own sense of guilt by pinning it on someone else? She brooded over whether she would have to take him back. Could she do it?

The next morning, sunlight tumbled through Sevda's smudgy windowpanes and into her messy apartment. Dust swirled like glitter in the air. And Sevda knew her answer. Before she could so much as think of sweeping the crumbs from her bed, of getting up, her hustle had already begun: racing after the children, racing against the chaos, racing around her restaurant. And she knew. The answer was no. She didn't need to take Ihsan back. He was not her responsibility. He was a grown man and could take care of himself. For he had been capable of doing so before Sevda came into his life. The fact that he had let himself go like this now, that was his decision. His decision alone. The decision to do nothing. To have no work, no home. Those were his problems. Sevda had tried with him. She had tried and tried. But it hadn't worked. At the end of her next workday, Sevda lay again with a heavy head in her crumb-filled sheets, and her cycle of thoughts and worries began anew.

~

Now Sevda is sitting on the closed lid of the toilet in her bathroom shivering. Disjointed question marks swirl inside her head, each one discharging in a new bout of sobs. How could she have been so stubborn? How could five years have gone by without her ever once picking up the phone and calling her baba to tell him she'd forgiven him? How could she be so stupid—missing her flight, and with it, her final chance to say goodbye? What if the same thing happened with Ihsan? How could she explain it to her children? Sevda holds her mouth closed to dam in the desperate scream that has been clawing for a way out of her lungs. She chokes it back and swallows it like a giant, stringy lump. She can't wrap her head around the idea that another human being is living on the streets because of her and that she hasn't done anything for months now, even though she knows about it. What has she done with this disgrace? Nothing. It robbed her of a few hours of sleep. But nothing more. She'd gone on living as if nothing had happened, kept Ihsan at bay with envelopes of cash. Sevda gasps for air. Rising, she looks at herself in the mirror. Stares into the tearstained face of a hypocrite. Someone who gives herself credit for all her successes while remaining trapped in the same impasse from which she will never escape.

The only way would be to take Ihsan back, she thinks. Forgive him. Yes, Sevda should look for her husband and bring him home. Should let him go on doing and not doing what he wants. It doesn't matter. What matters is that he has a roof over his head and food to eat. What matters is that he's alive. Sevda won't be able to take it if another person in her life . . .

The doorbell rings.

Sevda's heart skips a beat. These thoughts freeze in her head. She looks up at the mold spots on her bathroom ceiling. Is this some kind of sign? It was quick. Too quick, even. She could have used a little more time to think. The doorbell rings again, and Sevda's heart starts beating wildly in her chest. She feels trapped. At someone else's mercy.

"Mama, the door!" Bahar calls from the living room.

Haphazardly, Sevda washes her face and throws open the bathroom door. Bahar is already standing in the hall, pressing the buzzer to the main entry of the building.

"Who is it?" Sevda asks nervously.

Bahar shrugs her shoulders.

"Bahar, haven't I told you a thousand times to look out the window first before you buzz open the door? What if it's someone coming to kidnap you? What would you do then?"

The little one knots her hands together, staring up at the doorway in fear.

"Come. Go back to the living room!"

Bahar hops away.

Sevda can feel her cheeks reddening. She peers through the peep hole, waiting a few seconds until someone comes into view. Suddenly, the knot in her chest loosens. A wave of relief washes away the tightness in her neck. She straightens her shoulders, runs one finger through her hair, and opens the door.

"Sevdacım, I couldn't come any earlier, I'm so sorry!"

"Nonsense, you didn't need to come all this way at all!" Sevda replies, shaking her head. And yet Sevda's overcome with joy that she came all the same: the one person in this world from whom she doesn't need to hide her tears. And here they come again, already pearling in the corners of her eyes and running down her cheeks until they're caught up in a tight—almost too tight—embrace. They trickle off into the fabric of their T-shirts, T-shirts emblazoned with English words neither of them understands. Sevda lets herself collapse into those slender arms. Slender but strong enough to raise entire buildings on their own. Instead, those arms have had to accomplish something far more difficult; they've freed themselves from the clutches of a violent and brutal husband. Sevda slowly pulls away from this other woman, wiping her eyes with the back of both hands. Bahar hops her way back down the hallway.

"Havva Teyze!"

"There's my little princess," Havva cries, kneeling down and wrapping Bahar in her arms. "Look what I've brought you: a Kinder Sürpriz!" The little girl giggles. "Sürpriz? It's called a Kinder Ü-Egg, Teyze!" "Üüüü-Egg!" Havva repeats with a frown, handing the little girl her chocolate egg.

Sevda wants to march directly to the kitchen and make tea. But Havva tugs at her T-shirt.

"It's all good, Sevda. I don't need a tea. You need to hit the road soon, anyway."

"We still have five hours till our flight," Sevda says, shaking her head. But Havva already has one arm around her shoulder and guides her into the living room instead. Sevda gives in. She takes a seat on the floor with her back against the sofa and watches Havva and the children assemble the plastic pieces inside their chocolate eggs, transforming them into tiny toys.

Cem and Bahar have been crazy about Havva, ever since she first visited a few months back. They're constantly asking Sevda about her: when she's coming back, why she has to live so far away, and when they might get to visit her at her place. Sevda has tried explaining to them what a woman's shelter is. "Does Baba live there too?" they asked.

The first time Havva called, Sevda had just separated from Ihsan. And Havva, from her own abusive husband. It had been such an odd co-incidence that they'd started to giggle nervously into the phone until they both fell silent. A moment of silence. Because their separations had, for such a very long time, been nothing to laugh about. Sevda had been surprised. It seemed Havva had already been living back in Germany for many years. In the country she had said she never wanted to return to. The country where they didn't want her. But now Havva said the same thing about Turkey too. In Germany she'd been a filthy fucking Turk; in Turkey, she became a filthy Arab infidel. And so, Havva and her husband, the abuser, had come back together. She'd thought he wouldn't hit her anymore in Germany. Because he'd only started doing so in Turkey once he'd realized that despite his college degree, his status as a Christian would forever bar him from becoming a civil servant. He couldn't even work as a security guard in front of a police station. Havva had convinced him to move to Germany with her. They might not be treated any better here, but the one thing they could count on was that there was work in Germany. Shortly after their arrival, they'd learned that their status as asylum seekers officially prevented them from working here as well, for the time being. And many things had changed in the ten years since Havva left Germany. There were far fewer jobs now, and competition with the East Germans who had dispersed across the country was steep. Her abuser hadn't proved to be particularly ambitious. After two days of construction work, he'd thrown in his hat and broken Havva's collarbone.

Sevda examines Havva's delicate shoulder. She still wears the Virgin Mary pendant around her neck she's always worn. Havva smiles at Sevda. "Come on, darling, let's have a smoke," she says.

The children are glued to the TV again.

Havva and Sevda retreat to the kitchen. Sevda opens a window, and Havva takes a seat in the breakfast nook and lights up. Sevda draws a cigarette for herself from Havva's pack. Ever since Havva's been back in her life, she's taken to having an occasional cigarette. She still doesn't like the way they taste, and her throat burns during the night afterward. But whenever she sees Havva smoking, the temptation is too great. Smoking forms a magical bond between them. Sevda feels like an accomplice to a crime: every cigarette, a tiny negation of this life.

"Why did it take you so long to leave him?" Sevda asks, trying to exhale her smoke in little rings. It doesn't work.

"Because I was stupid!" Havva exclaims, but she knows immediately what Sevda means. "I thought I owed him something. Because I dragged him here and he didn't speak a word of German." She shakes her head, rolling her eyes. "I thought: He can't help the way he is."

"And then what changed?" Sevda asks.

Havva only shrugs. "I just came to understand I was the stupid one." She extinguishes her cigarette on the saucer Sevda has set out for them as an ashtray. "But Sevdacım, I didn't come here to burden you with all my worries. You're the one in mourning. Can't I do something for you? Please, just tell me."

Havva tilts her head and stares up at Sevda. Her hand rubs Sevda's back.

Sevda shakes her head, extinguishing her cigarette as well. She's only managed to smoke half. She watches the smoke as it swirls for a while suspended in the air.

Suddenly, Havva's eyes fill with concern. She draws her face in closer. After a moment, she stands up and reaches into one pants pocket. She fishes around with her hand until she finds what she's looking for. Proudly she holds aloft the infamous bit of thread she's taken to carrying with her recently.

"Put your head back, darling," she says, looping the thread into the form of a figure eight between her thumb and index finger. She leans over Sevda's head where it rests against her, and she draws the thread between her brows. Havva taps Sevda on the forehead, demonstrating to her that she should raise her eyebrows and tense up her skin.

"You look like my dead uncle's neglected garden," she says, pressing one end of the thread between her lips. With a deft movement of her thumb and index finger she pulls it back and forth like a zipper, yanking the stubble from the skin on Sevda's tightly drawn face like little weeds.

Sevda enjoys the prick and burn. When the thread draws closer to her eyelids where the skin is particularly sensitive, Sevda's face begins to hurt so badly it provides a momentary respite from her other pain.

"Move in with us," Sevda says, without opening her eyes, while Havva drives this silent lawnmower across her face.

"What?" she hears Havva exclaim through her pursed lips, still pinching tight the end of the thread.

Sevda opens her eyes and tries to smile at Havva without relaxing her face. "Why not? We have room. You wouldn't be alone," she says, and wonders how the words must sound to Havva in combination with the hideous expression she's making and the redness of her irritated skin. Sevda can feel it burning. "You could help me out a little with the kids?" she adds in an attempt to make her offer sound more reasonable.

Havva grins in disbelief while she continues plucking. "I mean, of course I could. But what would happen then? What would the others think?"

"Since when do you care what other people think of you?" Sevda asks, almost a bit offended.

Havva doesn't answer. She's thinking while she operates on one end of Sevda's left eyebrow.

"Don't pluck them too thin," Sevda warns her out of habit.

"Yeah, yeah," Havva says, making her way back to the right eyebrow to make sure they're even. "Just get to your family first. We can talk about this when you're back. Okay?"

Sevda emits a quiet sigh as Havva's fingers leave her forehead.

"The last thing I want to do right now is see my mother," Sevda says.

Havva puts down her thread and begins brushing the loose hairs from Sevda's face with her fingertips. "I know, Sevdacım. I know."

Peri

Peri sits in the darkened living room, cracking çekirdek. Everyone else is sleeping. The salt burns her lips. Her left hand slowly ruffles Ümit's hair while he's dreaming, soft as a kitten, on her lap. Her right hand jitters nervously between her bowl and mouth, while the blue light from the new television flickers over Ümit's pale face. He still hasn't woken up. It's been a very long time since their bodies have been this close. Ever since Ümit grew his first beard hairs and sprouted his first pimples, he's done what everyone else does at his age: he withdrew into himself, shielding his body beneath hunched shoulders and crossed arms. As if to prevent the impending crash landing of his broken heart onto the floor.

Peri is watching one of those disturbing late-night TV shows where people describe their encounters with the supernatural. Semiprofessionals act out the narration in dimly lit sequences while the real-life eyewitnesses sit behind baffle screens, speaking through grotesque distortion effects. Furniture moving of its own accord. Lights that turn themselves on and off. Footsteps in the hallway when no one is home. Usually, it's some deceased family member trying to send a message. The worst kind of entertainment for a day like this. Or maybe the best. The whole ceremony was so toxic that a ghost show might just be the antidote. And watching still comes easier to Peri than closing her eyes. She won't sleep anyway.

For days now, Peri has been hugging people she wants to lend strength to. Her mother. Her brother. All those aunties and cousins she's never

met before. But in reality, she's been propping herself up against their
bodies, struggling to remain standing on her own two feet. Every touch
has been a promise of life. Each proximity, a tiny bit less death. Peri
can already feel them coming: those shadows from her past. Phantoms.
She cannot see them yet or hear them, but she knows that they're not
far away. With seductive whispers and beckoning fingers, they wait at
open windows and busy intersections—in the lonely hours in bed between her dreams—hoping for Peri to meet their eyes. But it's been a
long time since she's taken hard drugs. Maybe a little coke or speed to
dance during those raves she rarely frequents anymore. Maybe a little
weed to calm her nerves in the kitchen of some random party friends
whose company she can hardly stand these days. But nothing more. Even
though Peri knows the shadow figures aren't simply waiting for her
next ecstasy or mushroom trip. Instead, they lurk in hopes that Peri will
give in to her self-doubt. That she will ask herself: What's the point?
Has there ever been any meaning to this life? But she knows she mustn't
think of these things now. No. It can't begin again all over like before.
It's better to dream as seldom as possible. Better to remain clear-headed.
To be there for the others and to focus as little on herself as she can. Peri
reaches for the TV remote control and turns the volume up a bit. On
screen, a woman lies in bed watching a shadowy figure floating toward
her. Boo.

Who would have thought that having already stood at the grave of a
loved one once before and learned that it's still possible to go on just
doesn't help? This knowledge means nothing to Peri now. Fuck it. All
those years it took her to get over Armin's death were buried in a single
moment. Drunkenly stumbling back to her mother's home two nights
ago after her high school reunion at the lake, she was suddenly struck
sober by the sound of her mother's cries. And now she's back there
again, back at the beginning of the same uncanny road with no idea
what to expect at its conclusion. The only difference now is that she
has no coordinates left for orientation, no security, no way of knowing
who she really is. *Baba.* Because what is a father other than a corner
marking, a demarcation for the space in which one grows, and from

which one finally breaks free? A problem to resolve, a mirror in which to constantly see one's life anew and know what it shouldn't be. A kind of anti-ego.

But please. How insincere. Missing someone whom you haven't wasted a single thought on in years? Of course, Peri had still seen her father during those weekends she'd come home. She'd greeted him, eaten beside him, and then taken her leave. But had she ever truly worried about how he was doing? How he *really* was? Had she even once tried to lighten his load? To ease one of his worries or resolve a problem the way she always had for her mother? Peri had never so much as considered that her father, too, might be every bit as broken as her mother was. That he was simply better at hiding his pain than she. At making things invisible. In truth, Peri hadn't given a thought to him in the five years since she'd moved away to Frankfurt, fleeing into that tiny room in the high tower of dormitory cells whose window she could only crack ajar. There was simply no more reason to fear Hüseyin, and so, there had been no more reason to think of him at all.

And now, he was presented to her on a silver platter, his broken body lying there powerless. That body she had avoided all those years. As if to offer some final proof of just how pointless her fear of her father had always been. Peri almost wished now that Hüseyin truly had been the authoritarian father figure she had—at the very latest since joining the women's study group in her department during her first semester of university—imagined him to be. Domineering. Self-centered. Ignorant. But he had never really been that way. Or at least, not only this. He had also been nurturing. And he had been quiet. Most of all, he had been withdrawn. A sealed vault, all feelings locked away. A closed door. The note with the passcode to his personal safe had been thrown out the window of a speeding car. But to truly realize all of this, Peri had first needed to see him lying there, cold and lifeless, tucked away in the underground morgue of a hospital in Istanbul. And now, she has to sit in the dark herself—crouched in the living room of this lovingly renovated, big-city apartment: the grave her father had dug himself for an entire lifetime. A grave in which he lay down and died at the very first opportunity.

"Freedom means not having to work." Peri had picked up this quote during a seminar. It came from a conversation between Horkheimer and Adorno. And for days now, it had been reverberating in her brain. It had had to be this way. Hüseyin had had to die one week before the start of his freedom, one measly week before his official retirement. Die from a depleted heart. And while her classmates would inherit jewelry or fine cutlery or even entire houses to remind them of rainy summer holidays at their grandparents', Peri had always assumed nothing would be left to her and her siblings. They didn't even have a story. But now they did have this one thing: the apartment in Istanbul. The apartment for which her father had sacrificed the best years of his life. Four rooms to remind them of exhaustion and death and nothing else.

No one should have to wash the corpse of their own father. No one should have to stretch his bloated arms and let the stream of water run down into his armpits. This morning, for the first time in her life, when Peri had been made to leave the room before they commenced with the washing, she'd seen the gender segregation of religious rituals as a blessing. Just seeing the dead body of her father had been enough. She would not have been able to touch him. She had tried to push herself, but it just wasn't going to happen. She couldn't do it. There was a barricade inside her she just couldn't overcome. She could only watch as her mother lifted the pale, spotted, swollen arm and caressed it. Held it to her own face lovingly, as she began quietly to moan. Peri's own hand had caressed her mother's back instead. As if her mother's back could convey her own touch onward. And perhaps, indeed, it had. For suddenly, Peri, too, could imagine how it would have felt to touch her father's arm—she imagined his skin would feel like that of an orange overwintering in the cold of their balcony. Not a frozen orange, but rather, a very cold orange that had absorbed the winter night into its flesh, saving its chill away in the tension of an empty, lifeless peel. And then, she and Emine had left the washing room, and poor Ümit had remained behind, alone in the room with their new cousin and some official corpse washer. It hadn't taken five minutes before they'd had to carry Ümit out as well.

"Ümit? Canım, can you hear me?"

He had collapsed. The nurses gave him an infusion while Peri held his clammy hand. Then they drove on to the funeral. Ümit remained lying in the car. The nurses had said there was no reason to worry. He was simply in a very deep sleep. Some kind of state of shock. Peri had envied her little brother's condition. He hadn't had to stand there in the cemetery staring at the same swollen faces that had already assembled the night before in their apartment. Most of them had never even known Hüseyin. They merely came from neighboring villages in the same region, had all moved to Istanbul, and apparently, they met up at every funeral or wedding to mourn or dance together.

Peri had always hated weddings, and she realized now just what it was that always bothered her—in addition to her contempt for the very insti-tution of marriage. There was something more: the inability to express rejection. Honesty isn't desired at a wedding. No one goes to a wedding scowling only to stand and proclaim: I hate this life and the bride here is betraying the feminist struggle! No. Instead, everyone stretches the corners of their mouths together, fakes a smile, and thinks about fifty other things they'd rather be doing at that moment than hunkering down in a sweaty room and listening to the blaring music, eating chicken from paper plates, and becoming just another extra in this cheap stag-ing of memories for a bridal pair who will long for divorce in two years' time anyway.

It's different at funerals. When confronted with death, no one is strong enough to maintain these facades. Cracks form whether one wants them to or not. And in between the cracks, the horror is revealed. This narcissistic fear: the knowledge that we, too, are only transient. That every little stroll might end in a heart attack; each cigarette, in cancer; each pang of heartbreak, in suicide. And so, Peri had to watch all these

complete strangers bawl their eyes out at her father's funeral—not crying for the man who'd died, who really didn't interest them at all, but
crying for themselves. She'd watched these people mourn their own
impending deaths and bury their own desires and their heres and nows.

Peri's gaze sweeps through the darkened room. It's still bizarre for her
to see the extravagance with which Hüseyin had furnished this apartment. The walnut paneling and the carefully plastered walls. The sump-
tuous molding and the baseboards, the giant television—all of it spoke
of a life utterly incomparable to the life Peri had always known. For
while they had changed virtually nothing over the past twenty years in
their cramped, rented apartment in Germany—replacing each broken
thing at the flea market and diligently undertaking every necessary ren-
ovation by hand—Hüseyin had, in one week, reveled in all the luxuries
he had denied himself for a lifetime. Indulged in the finer things. Peri
could imagine how Hüseyin had watched the workers with satisfaction,
his hands clasped behind his back. It would have been the first time in
his life that strangers had worked for Hüseyin and not the other way
around. He must have enjoyed the feeling.

Peri had probably been as old as Ümit when she had first stood in the
imposing entryway of Armin's home. She'd waited for him to come
down because she hadn't found the courage to simply follow his mother
into the house. Even after removing her shoes and edging onto the
cold, terracotta tiles in threadbare stockings to wait for Armin by the
door, Peri had had to ask herself just how her own problems would be
different had she, too, grown up in such a home. Two cars in the driveway: a small one for Armin's mother, a large one for his father, and in
all likelihood, soon a third, sporty car for their son. What would she
have worried about in such a house? Certainly not her desire to one day
just fuck off and leave this place behind as quickly and as permanently
as possible. And then, just as she began to ask herself what it might be
like to actually enjoy being at home, Armin had come down and told
her to put her shoes back on because no one took their shoes off in
his house. He'd led her through the building, its rear wall built entirely

of glass with a view over a pond with fish and frogs. First, they had
gone into his bedroom, where he'd gathered a few cassette tapes, and
then he'd led Peri down into the party room in the basement with its
pool table and dartboard. Led her back into the furthest corner, where
he had arranged himself a second room. It smelled stuffy in there, and
the brightly upholstered couch had always felt a little damp. Only a
few beams of light trickled down through the bars of the small basement window where the cellar wall ran into the ceiling. And then he'd
switched on a string of purple lights, ensuring that they could still make
out the dim contours of each other's bodies.

He first placed a cassette into the stereo, and then he'd shut and
locked the door so that his prying mother could not intrude while
he and Peri sat demurely side-by-side on the clammy sofa, listening to
Nevermind and waiting for someone to make the first move and repeat
the kiss they had exchanged a few days earlier in the gym behind their
school. Repeat this kiss and then extend it, imbibe it like fresh air, like
a new self without the fear of being seen, there in the safety of this
musty cellar room. The purple string of lights. The cassette tape from
Nirvana. An electric heater that mingled the slight stench of burning
with the musk of the basement. A smell that Peri liked. This, and the
way that Armin had already tasted like mint and honey to her back
then. Not the sharp, artificial mint of toothpaste. No, different. Something else. Maybe breath mints, Peri thinks now. But he always tasted
that way, even years later. Late at night and early in the morning. Could
it have been possible that he always carried the same box of mints around
with him? Over all those years, and even when he was naked? Even
when they were far from home? Lying in an empty field or in the back
seat of a car. Behind a bush in the park. In the bed of some friend's
parents at a high school party. Or with their bodies entwined, grinding
together against the wall of some squalid nightclub restroom.

There are thoughts that only come to us in darkness. The glow of
Armin's skin. Like a freshly filled hot water bottle. Peri had never again
felt this warmth in another's embrace. And she'd hugged many people.
Kissed many people. Seen the vulnerability in their eyes. Felt good when

she had thought of them as equals. Felt bad when she'd seen something
in their faces she could not reciprocate. Been honest—perhaps as honest as she should never have allowed herself to be with Armin. But she
had never again felt so warm and so secure: the way she'd felt with her
face pressed against his neck. Never.

There are thoughts that only come to us in darkness. The pounding
in Peri's chest when she ran down the narrow path to Armin's house
on winter afternoons, the gray sky when she had rung at his door, the
darkness when she left his house again just after five. They had only
disappeared into his basement during those afternoons. They'd told
Armin's mother they were studying math down there. Peri had told
her own parents she was studying math with Sarah or Lisa or Caro
or Elena. Hüseyin and Emine had never prevented her from spending
afternoons away when it came to her education. After all, Peri was in
her last years of high school, preparing for university—this strange and
unfamiliar place that filled her parents with pride and reverence. Hüseyin and Emine assumed Peri was always studying with others to catch
up. Just like they also believed that preventing her from leaving their
house after 6 p.m. would keep Peri from doing those things all young
people thought about incessantly. That this would somehow protect
her virginity. As if you couldn't lose your virginity before six pm. As
if you couldn't bathe in the warmth, the kisses, the sweat of another
body before six pm. As if there weren't thousands of other activities
you could engage in to feel pleasure without breaking your so-called
hymen—the very existence of which had long been refuted by science,
as Peri would later learn in her women's study group. As if you couldn't
shower and shave and apply body lotion in the morning before school;
as if you couldn't hide lotion in your school bag and reapply it after
class in the school bathroom so your skin would be soft and smell good
on your date. As if you couldn't finally buy a bra with the few marks
you had earned stocking shelves at the supermarket—finally, a bra that
wasn't already worn out and beige and many sizes too big because it
was a hand-me-down from Mother. A black, see-through bra worn only
for those basement afternoons. As if anyone could have noticed when

she came home at 5:30 that her face wasn't puffy from too much studying math but swollen and flushed from other things.

Maybe it was this obsession with her virginity that half the world seemed
to have that made Peri want to dispense with it as soon as possible. The
half of the world on her one side—her mother and their female neighbors, her kanaken side—which never really offered her any specific
instructions but always simply told her with such certainty and con-
viction that her first sex would transpire on her wedding night. This
message came across plainly without anyone ever needing to have a
real conversation about it. But the other half of her world consisted of
school friends, teen magazines, American films, and TV shows—all of
which seemed to insist that a teenager need only wait for the right person, your first serious boyfriend, stall a little bit, push back just a few
times to test, so that after a year or so you could reveal during a make-
out session that you were "ready." So he could pluck a condom from
his pants pocket, put it on carefully, and, while gazing placidly into your
eyes, penetrate the timid, passive female body—always in the mission-
ary position, of course. Peri was nauseated by both sides.

And then, without so much as asking, Armin tried to sleep with her
one afternoon. Peri had been a bit irritated but was generally okay with
it. Except that her body hadn't played along. It hadn't let Armin inside
her. And after this snafu, they had gone their separate ways. Armin—
who had always written her love letters and recorded mix tapes for
her—suddenly began avoiding her at school. And so Peri, in her pride,
avoided him back, acting like he wasn't even there while still worrying
at the same time about her uncooperative pussy. Because after all, this
had been the cause of her failure. Although maybe it was Armin who
had failed after all. Who could say? In any case, that was the first time
Peri and Armin had broken up. And then Peri had met someone else.
Known him only a few days before she did it with him on a Saturday
morning in the untidy room he still occupied in his parents' apartment.
On the yet-unbroken half of his unmade double bed. Alongside piles of
gray, unopened official letters and bills. His mouth had tasted like he'd
drunk a big glass of orange juice that morning instead of brushing his

teeth. Peri was sixteen, and he was ten years older. He came quickly. Peri never heard from him again.

A few months went by, and with them came Peri's first more or less serious thoughts of suicide—along with the reoccurring fear that the condom might have been compromised. That she had fucked up her life with this trainwreck of a man. But even after her fears had proven themselves to be unfounded, a new fear arose: Perhaps there really was some higher power that might now be judging Peri by the condition of her hymen. A power that would now transform her, after its loss, into some unhappy witch. Eventually, she got herself back under control and did the one thing that could free her from the loneliness that had been the real source of her panic after all: she went back to Armin. And lo and behold, he welcomed her with open arms—and conspicuously smaller eyes from the weed he'd taken to smoking in the meantime. And he simply gaped when Peri proceeded to sleep with him just like that—without any shadow of a doubt, like it was second nature—then took her first rip from his green bong. And they started all over again.

Armin no longer played Nirvana cassettes on the stereo in the basement. These had been replaced by vinyl records like *Step in the Arena* and *Enter the Wu-Tang*. In front of the clammy sofa, there now stood a tiny table Armin had commissioned from a friend who was apprenticing as a woodworker. Its black tabletop was formed like the round *W* logo of the Wu-Tang Clan. Armin wore baggy clothes himself now and had taken to acting like he didn't live in a boring little town on the Rhine River but in the Bronx. Armin's mother pounded furiously on the door whenever the smell of marijuana curled up from the party basement, but Armin only giggled back, calling out that he couldn't open the door because he was naked. This, of course, was more than humiliating for Peri, but she simply smoked herself into a state in which she could no longer even comprehend comparing Armin's relationship to his mother with her own. This basement and her home existed in two parallel universes; their only point of convergence was Peri's ability to exist in both. Nothing more. Emine, in all likelihood, would not have waited to detect the smell of cannabis but would, instead, have already poked out Peri's eyes with a knitting needle the moment she tried to disappear behind a locked door with a boy.

And yet, all the same, the weed and the sex did something to Peri. For a while, she grew strangely reckless: testing the limits of the little box she'd drawn with chalk inside her mind to see just how far she could stretch herself beyond its boundaries. This box had been firmly delineated years before, the borders Peri must mind in order to exist in peace without her parents making her life a living hell. Sharing news of her abortion with the neighbor's daughter lay definitively outside these boundaries. And yet, nevertheless, on her way to the doctor's, it spilled out anyway. Peri had stood waiting at the bus stop when Burcu, the intrusive daughter of the even more intrusive Feraye Teyze, who had just moved in next door, came walking toward her.

"Where are you going?" Burcu asked, glaring disparagingly at Peri's ripped-up jeans.

"To get an abortion." Peri stared back into her eyes, doing her utmost to repress her laughter at the look of shock in Burcu's eyes.

"But Peri, what are you saying? Who did this to you? Don't you know that you will go to hell for this? You will go to hell, and you will see your baby waiting there for you."

"My baby is going to hell too?" Peri feigned her shock.

"It will only be there to torture you. Because you will have murdered it!" Burcu warned, peering around to see whether anyone else was listening, beginning to feel a share of Peri's shame.

"But Burcu, I'm not even going to see the baby. It's not even as big as a pea."

"Oh, yes, you will see it, Peri!" Burcu insisted, pointing with her index finger at Peri's belly. "It will be big and strong. And it will torment you for what you did to it!"

Peri just shrugged her shoulders and got on the bus. She blew a kiss to Burcu out the window as she rode away. Burcu's forehead furrowed with lines of self-righteous concern.

∾

Peri can feel the warmth of her brother's breath against her thigh. She knows. She knows that Ümit is in love with someone. And she knows this someone doesn't love him back. She can read it in his every movement. In the naked pain he wears on his face. Unrequited love is like a sickness. It makes Peri sad to see Ümit this way. She would like to switch places with her little brother, so he wouldn't have to feel this pain. Ümit more than anyone. He's such a softy. And Peri loves softies. But the others are—well, the others are the way the others are. For them, combining manliness and softness is wrong. And so, Ümit has begun to foster a quiet hatred for himself. And why wouldn't he? In this shitty family and in this shitty town, both of which Peri fled as soon as she possibly could—the moment she had her diploma in hand. Even now, she only visits every second week for Ümit's sake. And for her mother.

Ümit had only been eight or nine the first time they tried humiliating him. At least the first time Peri was there to see it.

"Hey, kid, did you paint your nails or what? Why do they look so shiny?" Burcu's mother, the fiery red-haired Feraye Teyze from next door, called him out, gawking in amusement.

Ümit balled his hands into fists and hid them behind his back.

"Let me see!" Emine wrenched on Ümit's tiny arm.

He'd kept his hands balled tightly into fists, fighting to resist her before finally breaking down in silent tears.

"Leave him alone! It was me," Peri had lied. "We were only playing. And it's just clear nail polish. I thought no one could tell the difference."

"Of course you can see it, Peri, just look how it shimmers," Feraye Teyze had exclaimed, stretching her hand expectantly for Ümit to present his fingernails again.

"Yeah, well, I guess your eagle eyes don't miss a thing, Teyze."

"You should not do such things, Peri," Feraye had scolded her. "All these men they show on TV, running around in women's clothes. God forbid the boy grows up and thinks such things are normal!"

And what *is* normal? Peri wanted to ask her, but Emine had already sent her away in exasperation, banishing Peri to the kitchen to make coffee.

Normal. As though any relationship in this family had ever been normal. How normal was it that Emine always started talking like those actresses in old-fashioned Turkish movies—Türkan Şoray or Filiz Akın—whenever Feraye Teyze came to visit? How normal was it that Emine suddenly said *mersi* when Peri brought coffee to her and Feraye Teyze? Peri could hardly keep herself from laughing out loud at the absurdity of hearing such sounds from her mother's lips. How normal was it that whenever Feraye came to visit Emine always began cursing those Kurdish fighters in the mountains out of the blue, as though she needed to prove her loyalty to this woman in whose parlor hung a framed portrait of Atatürk? How normal was it that Hüseyin forbid his mother tongue from being spoken in his own household, while he and his wife spent half their lives living in a country whose language they only fragmentarily understood? How normal was it that Emine didn't sleep at night, that she hardly smiled during the day, and could only ever wallow in self-pity?

That something wasn't right with Emine, that she was obviously suffering from depression, was something Peri only came to understand after she left home. After she herself suffered a loss she couldn't share with anyone. After Armin's death, Peri continued traveling back to Rheinstadt every other weekend, simulating some sense of the normalcy she couldn't re-create inside her tiny dorm room in Frankfurt with the window she could only crack ajar. Peri entered her parents' apartment like a ghost and sat on their couch thinner, paler, and more silent than she had ever been before. She rarely wore color. She was always out of sorts. Perhaps her family—which had never seen the inside of a university—accepted this change as Peri simply being stressed out from studying. Perhaps they also guessed that it was something more and respected Peri's inability to speak of it. Who knows? They must have thought something. But Peri came and came again, and even this semblance of regularity created such a convincing routine that no one ever found it necessary to start a conversation that might have extended beyond their practiced words and familiar conventions. Normal: that simply meant going on, refusing to acknowledge the obvious.

It went on this way for a couple of years, and then, when Peri finally found herself capable of moving past those constant slides back into the mineshaft that had opened in her mind, she came to recognize that her mother, too, was stuck inside a hole. Except Emine never managed to climb back out of hers. Emine would never manage to do so on her own.

At one point, Peri pushed her mother far enough to actually book an appointment with a therapist. That was shortly after the incident with the bleach. Supposedly, Emine was convinced Hüseyin was cheating on her. She didn't know when or with whom; she only said she could tell by the way he was acting that he loved somebody else. And one afternoon—Peri had just arrived home from Frankfurt and was taking a shower—Emine rushed into the bathroom, opened a cabinet, and reached for the bottle of bleach she used for cleaning the toilet. Peri stared at her mother in wonder from the shower, watching as Emine unscrewed the cap and brought the mouth of the bottle to her own. Peri leapt from the shower like a frog, but Emine had still managed to take a swig before Peri could tear the plastic bottle from her hands and knock it to the floor. The smell of chlorine burned in Peri's nose like crazy, and over the days that followed, she began to look for a psychologist. It was important that she be a woman. It would, of course, have been even better if she had spoken Turkish, but where could you find such a therapist in Germany besides maybe Cologne or Berlin? Peri made a special trip from Frankfurt to Rheinstadt to bring her mother to the consultation and translate for her. Emine sat in her chair in the brightly lit office, staring severely, pulling the knot of her headscarf ever tighter. The therapist found it odd to communicate with her patient through an interpreter, and she found it even odder that this interpreter was her patient's daughter. But she tried her best to keep an open mind.

"And, what brings you here to me, Frau Yılmaz?"

Peri translated: "The doctor is asking why you came here, Anne."

"Well, because you forced me to. That is why I came."

"Anne, I didn't force you!"

"Can you please just translate what she's saying. If possible, one sentence at a time, yes?" the psychologist suggested.

"She claims I forced her to come. But I'm only trying to help . . . ," Peri began.

"That's quite all right. Please translate without any further commentary. Tell me only what *she* says. Now, Frau Yılmaz." She glanced soberly at Emine. "Can you please tell me how you've felt recently?"

Peri translated: "She wants to know how you feel. Recently."

"How I feel?" Emine asked, as if the question were offensive.

Peri nodded patiently.

"How should I know how I feel?"

Peri shook her head.

"Yes, please?" the psychologist murmured.

"She says she doesn't know how she feels."

"Have you had the feeling that you are often sad? Or angry?"

"Anne, are you often sad? Or angry?"

Her mother looked down at her knees.

"Say something, Anne."

Emine turned her head to Peri; her eyes were glassy.

"Let us go home, please," she pled quietly. "Please, take me away from here, Kızım."

And that was that. Five minutes later, they were back outside again, and Peri really couldn't even accuse her mother of anything. How was Emine supposed to talk about her feelings after spending a lifetime swallowing every single thing that might make her vulnerable? All these things had melded together inside Emine into one single, solitary conclusion: no one will ever understand my pain.

And Peri knows this feeling too. She carried it around inside her as well, after what happened with Armin. That was her second semester at university. She'd dragged herself around campus with bloodshot eyes and begun clinging to every depressing book her study of German could offer. Nietzsche, Schopenhauer. In fact, she'd wound herself up so tightly in this German pessimism that she now found herself chipping away at a useless master's thesis on Nietzsche's aphorisms. A thesis she might now be able to postpone due to her father's sudden death.

Fuck it, Armin would have said. *Fuck that piece of paper, that's only for squares who think they need things like a degree, a car, a house. Just fuck it all.* And he would have taken another hit from his bong inside Mommy and Daddy's massive, two-story, single-family home. Just like he'd done with his own high school diploma. In the middle of his final math exam, he'd just decided to throw it all away. Turned in an empty sheet of paper and marched coolly from the room straight out to the parking lot and his VW Golf—his parents hadn't sprung for a sports car after all—and rolled himself a blunt, cranking up *The Low End Theory* on his car stereo. Wow. What a bad boy. Peri had been beside herself with rage. How could he have been so flippant with his life? After all those hours she'd actually tried to study math with him—at some point during their last year of school they'd taken to fucking less often. Peri had to at least pass her math exam. Because this diploma *was* important to her. Because her freedom depended on it. Because she could only ever move out with her parents' approval if she enrolled at a university. And because maybe, someday, she might actually want to be one of those squares. Probably not. Whatever. But to at least maintain the possibility of one day owning a house, a car . . . That *would* mean something to her.

Peri shakes her head at herself. As if a German degree would ever make her rich. Who the hell was still waiting to read another master's thesis on Nietzsche in 1999? No-damn-body. And yet Peri would still write it anyway. She'd write it and turn it in alongside her proof of a real, bona fide family emergency. Extenuating circumstances. Even if she wasn't the slightest bit interested in her thesis anymore, even if the guy was a complete, misogynistic sack of shit. Even if her only reason for choosing the fucking topic in the first place was to prove to all those shit-eating professors and those shit-eating classmates of hers with their shit-eating grins that she, too, was capable of reading Nietzsche and getting something out of it. And it was true. Peri had found what she was looking for in Nietzsche. Even if just for a little while.

Of course, Peri's classmates' interest in Nietzsche was completely different from her own. And while Peri searched in *Human, All Too Human* for answers to the questions that haunted her, those questions that tortured her day and night like an endless migraine, throbbing in her eyes like the display of some ticking timebomb named survival, the others looked at Nietzsche like some old demented uncle. Someone they had to be acquainted with but someone who meant nothing to them personally except as an extra bit of cultural capital. They did not do battle with him. They did not need to vanquish him. They saw themselves as his worthy equals, as parts of a greater whole: a cultural history stretching back for centuries to a time to which they all secretly wanted to return. A desire they could maintain because for them it was self-evident that they would always have existed on the same side of the power dynamic. They could be certain they would never have been servants or serfs, but always the savants—the wealthy—those from the finest houses who passed their time drinking wine, reading for leisure, and fucking their concubines.

Peri, on the other hand, had never seen herself as part of anything. She didn't even know where she came from. Karlıdağ was simply the name of some distant place that remained every bit as enigmatic as Hüseyin's imprecise tapping on the upper-righthand corner of the map of Turkey. Somewhere just before the border of Armenia. Her own search for her heritage ended in the silence beneath her father's mustache and those unpredictable phases between her mother's blank stares and tears. Assimilation, Peri thought, had no history. Assimilation was the opposite of history. It was history's end; history's extermination. It was that empty feeling in her heart whenever someone spoke of homesickness. It was the absent impulse to correct people who mispronounced her name. Because what if it wasn't their pronunciation that was wrong but Peri's name itself?

At the end of the day, like so many other things in Peri's life, her master's thesis had grown out of the impulse not to simply conform to the image others had of her. And while people like Armin or Peri's classmates at university enjoyed the freedom of deciding for themselves what they liked and didn't like, Peri was constantly being told from the outside what her interests should be. And she seemed and still seems to be condemned to always do precisely the opposite. And so, yes, she really was interested in Nietzsche. And no, she didn't believe in monogamy. And yes, she read feminist theory, but she also went to raves and listened to hip-hop even if the other ladies in her women's study group did not approve. And no, she didn't have to turn her back on her family to emancipate herself. She could do it all and still wear the same hat. Albeit, always with a tightness in her chest. But at least she could.

There are thoughts that only come to us in darkness. After her high school graduation, Peri had walked to Armin's house, dragging her long evening dress behind her. Armin sat in his bedroom playing Nintendo. Peri acted like the celebration had meant nothing to her either.

There are thoughts that only come to us in darkness. *Maybe I'll move to Frankfurt with you and look for a job. You can go to uni, and afterward we'll go to the video parlor at night and rent movies. How does that sound, babe?*

There are thoughts that only come to us in darkness. Armin, in Frankfurt, in Peri's dorm room, rolling one joint after the other while Peri tried not to sound completely incompetent during orientation events. While she worked nights at the cider bar.

There are thoughts that only come to us in darkness. Armin at the intersection when Peri's shift ended and she locked up the bar. Armin saying he'd just come to pick her up, and Peri wondering how long he'd really been standing there.

There are thoughts that only come to us in darkness. That handsome guy with the five-o'clock shadow who always smiled at her on campus sitting at the bar one night in front of her. Peri pouring him a shot and writing her number on the coaster.

There are thoughts that only come to us in darkness. *Armin, maybe it would be better if you just went home and we saw each other on the weekends. I really need to study.*

There are thoughts that only come to us in darkness. The little one with the pierced tongue and bob cut who came to the women's study group for a while to stir things up. She'd tasted like green salted plums. *Armin, maybe it would be better if we took a break. No, I'm not breaking up with you, I just need some space. It's all just too much right now.*

∿

"Peri," she hears Ümit murmur.

She strokes his cheek, sensing him trying to free himself from her. But he doesn't have the strength. His upper body relaxes again, and he remains lying on her lap.

"Peri, what is a djinn?" Ümit asks.

Peri feels the cold creep through her skin. Like anyone who's grown up in a Muslim home hearing this word. In this house of death. At night.

She looks up, notices that the same creepy show is still running on the TV.

"Is it something like a ghost?" Ümit asks. His eyes are glued to the ceiling.

"Yes," Peri says. She thinks for a moment. "Or maybe no. Not entirely."

Did Ümit just pick up the word *djinn* from the TV? Or had he simply built up the courage for the first time to finally ask her what a djinn was? Hadn't all her siblings, cousins, and neighbors grown up with the same constant fear of these invisible beings—despite the fact that they were seldom spoken of. People wouldn't even speak their name aloud. In Turkish, djinns were often called *those with the three letters* rather than *cin*, for fear one might accidentally summon them with the word and then be unable to rid oneself of them again. And what was the plural form of djinn? Djinns? Maybe the fear of djinns was really more about not understanding what a djinn really is. And was this any different with death? Wasn't it the vagueness, the uncertainty, the darkness that people feared because these things remain intangible? Because we have to fill them with our fantasies and nothing is truly more wretched than our own fantasy? Does Lauryn Hill really rap in her new song about *a muslim sleeping with a djinn*?

"The Quran says djinns inhabit the earth like we do. Actually, the entire holy scripture is addressed to both humans and djinns. It's just that we can't see them."

"Hmm," Ümit murmurs. "Then they *are* something like ghosts."

"Yeah, something like that. But when people talk about djinns, they usually mean something different."

"Like what?"

"They mean the things they can't explain. Just check out this TV show, for instance. These people are having hallucinations. A lot of them probably have some kind of psychosis or something."

"So, djinns are like a sickness?"

"Well, it's not just that. Djinns are everything we think is strange, different, unnatural. When we don't live up to the expectations most people consider normal, they're often quick to say: *So-and-so has been possessed by a djinn.*"

"Because djinns are evil?" Ümit asks.

"Some people think so, but I don't think that's true. Djinns are neither good nor evil . . . at least not according to the Quran. They can be both. Or neither. Just like people."

Ümit remains silent. The quiet hangs heavily, and Peri almost feels like she can hear the gears turning in his head.

She is surprised at herself. Surprised at how much knowledge has stuck with her from those Quran study groups her mother made her attend for a year until Peri was old enough and clever enough to claim she couldn't concentrate properly on both school and all the *elif be te* on the weekends in the mosque.

But then again, Peri might actually have acquired her knowledge of djinns during one of those childhood trips to Turkey when some distant relative warned her not to whistle at night, not to sing on the toilet, not to stand under doorways, laugh too loudly, or even utter the word *djinn* for fear of being possessed by one.

But what did this constant fear of djinns *really* mean? Why did people still warn their children about mythological beings instead of teaching them about the real dangers? Things like fascists, for example, or capitalism? Could it be the same with stories of life after death? Subordinate yourselves, suffer, never rebel, don't have too much fun, because your time on Earth is fleeting anyway compared with the eternity that awaits you on the other side. Compared with the fire, the Azaab.

Was it just easier to worry about djinns rather than worrying about Nazis? After all, both live among us. Both are capable of remaining unnoticed until the moment of catastrophe when the reality of their existence finally becomes undeniable. Like when Sevda's house was set on fire.

Peri is happy to have put her *God-is-dead* phase behind her. Not that she's exactly found Him in the meantime, this God in whom you should place all your faith. But the self-righteousness of nihilists can be every bit as obnoxious as the proselytizing of the faithful—their constant blather about djinns and Jahannam. And after having spent a while running around as a godless nihilist and rubbing the meaninglessness and emptiness of life in everyone's faces, Peri had finally pulled herself back together. Because despite the lofty pretense with which she'd turned up her nose at her parents' way of life, after some time, she'd come to realize that an attempt to fill one's emptiness with rituals, stories, and beliefs did not automatically equate to grounds for pity or scorn. And those who staged and worshipped their emptiness on a pedestal instead more often than not also wound up losing their connection to those around them: those human needs and human desires. Because how can you really feel empathy for others while being occupied exclusively with the tragedy of your own existence? How can you truly oppose injustice if all things are equally meaningless? And how can you make life worth living if you deny its every significance?

Perhaps it was for this reason that Peri eventually found it necessary to distance herself from Nietzsche: because he, too, had made her numb. Because he—along with all those diluted drugs, those monotonous parties, and those uninspired acquaintances—had spiraled into a deadly undertow threatening to drag Peri down forever into its oblivion. Into insanity. And isn't the break with sanity, the break from your own sense of reality, the worst torment we can endure? The greatest fear? Greater even than the fear of death. Because at least in death there is also finality: nothing more to fear. But to become insane, to truly lose faith in your own sense of comprehension, in your perception—to find no escape from the spiral in which you find yourself—that's actually

the real terror. Living on without participating in your own life. Anyone who's ever accidentally taken too much LSD certainly knows this
feeling—panic stricken, laid out prone across the vinyl floor of your own
apartment. Staring at the ceiling, watching windows open one after
another, new windows out of the old, and then newer windows still.
Until all the open window frames compress into one single mineshaft:
a pit into which you see your own self falling. Because it is no longer
clear which way is up and which way down. Because none of this is
relevant, the physically possible and the improbable. And then that passage from Nietzsche's *Joyous Science* comes to mind, that passage where:
some day or night a demon steals into your loneliest loneliness and says to you:
"This life, as you now live it and have lived it, you will have to repeat innumer-
able times more; and there will be nothing new in it—every pain and every
pleasure, every thought and every sigh, and each thing ineffably great or finite
in your life will have to return to you, all things in the same succession and
sequence. Even this spider and this moonlight between the trees, and even this
moment and I, myself."

One always speaks of "mental derangement" in the literature on
the last ten years of Nietzsche's life. That decade in which he no longer
spoke or wrote. Some researchers claim he suffered for decades from an
untreated case of syphilis that ultimately led to the uncoupling of the
neural networks in his brain. Derangement. In German: *Umnachtung*—
from *Nacht*, the German word for night. Peri likes this word, enjoys
the connection between nighttime and insanity, relishes the idea that
unprotected sex with a whore might have brought about the end of
this oh-so-meaningful German philosopher's sanity. She likes imagining the tenacity with which Nietzsche surely must have watched his
own last reserves of reason—his thoughts, his head, his brain—slowly
decay. Nietzsche had also had a djinn of his own. A djinn who ultimately
wrested away control. Nietzsche was consumed by his own ideas, sitting for the last ten years in his room like a vegetable while his Nazi
sister zealously falsified his legacy from the room next door.

Everyone probably has their own djinns. Hüseyin had a djinn he'd
tried to hold at bay with his incessant labor. Hüseyin kept himself so

overworked that he never had time to stop and ask why he no longer spoke Kurdish. Why he'd forbidden Emine from speaking Kurdish. Forbidden them both from teaching Kurdish to their children. Why had he wanted things this way? Peri had never asked. She had never asked him what had happened during his two years of compulsory military service in Turkey—after which, as far as Peri could tell, he had first come to this decision. Peri had also never asked him how it had been later on to move alone to a new country whose own history he didn't know. She hadn't asked because she'd known that he would have no answers for her. There were rarely answers in this family. They all simply repeated the same stories—stories that wouldn't cause them any pain. And yet, each time, the stories sounded a little different; sometimes new details emerged—harmless trifles that always hid more than they revealed. But perhaps a family is nothing more than that: a construct strung together out of stories and stories and stories. And what then could those holes within them, those silences, mean? Are they the gaps that will eventually bring about the collapse of the whole? Or do they instead provide the air we need to breathe? Because to reveal the truth, the whole truth, would be more than we could bear?

Sevda had never spoken about the night of the fire. Never spoken about how it had been to then return to Salzhagen. She never spoke about why she had divorced Ihsan. She only spoke about her restaurant and her stress. And yet everything seemed to be going well for her. She'd bought herself a Mercedes and sent Bahar to ballet. And yet Sevda, too, was haunted by her djinn. She simply sought to evade it with the same ambition with which she'd brought about her own success. From illiterate to entrepreneur. But of course, her djinn remains to show her her limitations. Because ambition alone can't save you from those who would murder your family in their sleep. Peri hardly sees her older sister anymore. Last winter, she and Ümit and Hakan drove to Lower Saxony together to visit Sevda and her children because Sevda never came to Rheinstadt anymore. She always said she was too busy with work, but everyone knew Sevda didn't visit because of her fight with Emine. But no one knew the reason for this fight. The last time Sevda and her children had visited was the New Year's when the goose dinner had burned.

That had also been the New Year's after Peri had lost Armin. The entire apartment filled with smoke. Peri lay the whole day in Hakan and Ümit's bedroom thinking about death, only showing herself briefly to pretend to eat like a normal person. And there in the smoke-filled living room, her gaze had fallen on Sevda's embittered stare—Sevda, who had only just survived an arson attack on her home but left early the next morning with her children without saying goodbye.

Yes, Sevda did work a lot. Peri had seen this with her own eyes when she visited in January. She'd seen the axis around which Sevda's world revolved: seen how important for her was the approval and acknowledgment her work could provide—the approval of others, and most of all the approval of the Germans. The importance of her reputation. Her sense of belonging. Her ability to pass. Mediocrity in mediocre, small-town Germany. Because Sevda believed this mediocrity could save her. And who knows? Maybe she was right. But Peri still had her doubts.

And Hakan. Hakan and his obsession with the never-ending, one-man show of his life. His permanent act. No one knows who Hakan really is because he presents a different version of himself to everyone. Peri isn't sure whether Hakan really knows who he is himself. Or whether he has long since come to believe his own stories—the stories he tells, depending on his current company—so that the people around him either love or hate Hakan immediately. So that they can't help but give him their full attention. Hakan can never enter a room without standing at its center.

And Emine . . . with Emine, Peri isn't sure where to begin. Peri always has to think of a hopelessly tangled ball of yarn when she looks at her mother.

"Peri."

Ümit has freed himself from Peri's lap and is now sitting beside her on the couch. He used to always call her Abla until Peri had told him to stop one day because she thought there was something authoritarian about allowing yourself to be called something like that. Now she sees things differently. Now, she can also recognize the tenderness, the connection, in the word. Abla. Yes, also the intimacy. Because no one else in this world but Ümit ever called her that. Because only he could ever call her his big sister. And yet to change course now and ask him to call her that again would also be silly.

"Peri?" He looks at her questioningly.

"Yes, canım?"

"Who else did you lose?"

Peri is reminded again of the passcode thrown from the window of a speeding car. The code for the safe in which her baba locked away his feelings over a lifetime.

"That woman today. The fortune teller. She said you'd lost somebody else. And you didn't say that she was wrong. Who did you lose?"

Peri can hear the strain in Ümit's voice. It was a breakthrough for him to even ask the question. And why not? After all, he and Peri are both part of this same family. A family that speaks incessantly without ever revealing anything. It's more than unusual for someone here to ask these kinds of questions. Uncomfortable questions. Intimate questions. Important questions you should avoid at all costs. Intuitively. Like a deer on the highway. Even when you know the greater danger lies in injuring yourself.

"It wasn't Kurt Cobain, was it?"

"What?" Peri stares at him, confused.

"The suicide."

Peri has to think for a moment until she can connect the dots. And then she starts to laugh. "Cobain? Seriously? Ümit, how did you come up with that? Oh my God!"

"I dunno. I mean. You always used to listen to Nirvana. And ever since he died, you've been different. You're always sad."

Peri's laughter becomes louder and shriller. She tries to suppress it. After all, Emine is sleeping just across the hall in the master bedroom. She shouldn't be awakened, much less by this kind of inappropriate laughter. But Peri can't help it. She can't stop. Kurt Cobain. Wow. Kurt Cobain. Tears of laughter cascade from Peri's eyes. When was it again that Kurt Cobain had blown his head off? Had it been the same year? She holds her stomach, the laughter vibrating through every muscle. Yes. It had been the same year! Peri graduated in 1994, started at university, and then everything with Armin happened. Kurt Cobain. Was this for real? Kurt. Fucking. Cobain.

"Well then, who was it?" Ümit insists.

Peri struggles to compose herself.

"That was all just bullshit," she says, still wiping tears of laughter from the corners of her eyes. "You don't really believe anything that old lady said from her plastic stool, do you? I'm sure she always prophesizes the impending death of somebody at some time. How can you believe something like that?"

Ümit falls silent. She can feel his disappointment. His shame. Ümit had just tried to do something and Peri left him cold. This was actually the last thing she wanted to do. The last thing in this family. In this dark fucking apartment, which had already changed so much for all of them. Why can't Peri simply do differently herself? Finally break this cycle of silence with honesty. Ümit deserves this honesty from her; she wants to gain his trust. She wants him to feel strong with her. Feel safe. Feel understood. And yet she still does what generations of ablas have done before her. She acts like there's nothing. And maybe these are djinns too. Truths that are always there. Always in the room. Whether one wants them or not. Truths that no one speaks aloud in hopes that they will keep their peace. That they will remain forever hidden away.

The key. It had been stuck in the lock from the inside. They had to break the door completely. Break into the corner room in the cellar. Into Armin's second room. Into their one-time love nest. That's what they told Peri later on. But they hadn't broken up in there. They'd broken up in the driveway, in front of the house. They'd smoked in Armin's Golf, ashing the butts out the open windows against the car doors. Armin wasn't angry anymore. He had stopped screaming at her. He simply sat there like a sick, exhausted child. His look still pleaded, but no further words came from his mouth. One could say it hadn't been Peri's idea to break up. One could say Armin simply didn't agree with her conditions. One could say Armin had simply wanted the relationship to keep going the way he'd envisioned it. The way everyone else's relationships seemed to work. He'd wanted to hold on to Peri the way she had been without recognizing that she had already moved on. Maybe she had simply tried to take him with her to this new place with her conditions. But none of that would have been the whole truth. Because in the end, it was Peri who had hugged him, pressing her face one final time against his neck to feel his warmth, before exiting the car and leaving him behind.

"My boyfriend."

Ümit says nothing, but he slowly turns his upper body to face her.

"I lost my boyfriend. Or my ex-boyfriend. He's dead. He hanged himself."

The chain of purple lights.

Peri presses both hands to her face. Not because she needs to cry but because she's growing angry. And she shouldn't do this, she's already told herself a thousand times. It can't begin all over again like before. The tip of her index finger traces over her nose ring, pushing it back and forth. Peri had been so angry at Armin, angry at what he'd done to her. Although that wasn't really it, and she had known it even then: he hadn't done anything *to* her. It hadn't all been about her. It was his thing. Armin had made the decision for himself, and Peri had to accept this. She needed to show him the same respect she had so stubbornly demanded from him back when she'd first realized how her studies, her living alone, her reading, the women's study group, her own ability to determine the course of her days and nights, were changing her.

She could still remember the flippant manner with which she'd made the suggestion to Armin:

No, I don't want to break up, Armin. I just want an open relationship. Do you know what that means? It means we can stay together.

Remember the desperation flooding out of his tear ducts. His mouth forming words that did not belong to him.

Who is it? You have someone else, don't you? Or do you just want to whore around? What would your father say? Your mother? Your brother?

Remember the serenity Peri had fought to maintain. The patience with which she'd tried to convince him of something he would never be ready to understand. Something she had hardly understood herself.

That's just the patriarchy talking through you, babe. And that's precisely the problem: I don't believe in it. We don't have to be like everybody else. We can still love each other without needing to possess each other. Babe, don't you understand? Don't you want us to be honest with each other? Wouldn't that be the most perfect love of all?

Remember the fear swelling in Armin's veins. The red blotches spreading across his throat when he had nothing more to say.

That's just those fucking bra burners from the uni talking. That isn't you, Peri. That's not who you are. They've brainwashed you. You don't mean what you say.

The rage turned Armin into a different person. Led him to Hakan in his favorite café, where Armin told him with crazed eyes that his sister had become a whore. And Hakan slammed his fist into Armin's face. That evening, Hakan had called his little sister and told her with unsettling composure that she'd better take care who she spent her time with. This Armin guy was nuts.

Peri feels Ümit's hand against her arm. He's too unsure of himself to give her a proper hug, but he's still showing her he's there. Peri takes a deep breath, strokes the back of his hand. Then she reaches for the remote control and turns off the TV. She crosses her legs, turns sideways on the couch, watching her little brother. He looks back at her expectantly. Peri searches his face trying to determine whether he's ready too. Whether he's going to tell her now. She searches his eyes—sometimes you can tell if someone has something to say, sometimes it's already burning on their lips. She searches guardedly, fearful she, too, might destroy something at any moment.

"And what about now?" Ümit asks.

Okay. He isn't ready yet. If he's only asking questions, he's not ready to speak himself. He still wants to divert the attention away. Play for time. Peri wants to be patient with her little brother. He can tell her everything or nothing. They have all the time in the world. At least tonight. As long as Emine is sleeping.

"What do you mean, now, canım?" she asks.

"Do you think you're ready to love someone again?"

Peri smiles back at him sadly.

"I don't know."

"But it's been such a long time. Didn't you meet anyone in Frankfurt?"

"I've met lots of people, Ümit. But meeting and loving are two different things."

Ümit nods like he understands. But what does he know at fifteen? And then Peri has to smile herself because it's foolish to think this way. How could she possibly know what Ümit is capable of? What difference should it make whether he's fifteen or thirty-five? Maybe he already knows more about love than Peri because his feelings haven't been buried under a hundred thousand other problems.

"You look like Baba when you nod like that," she says.

"Really?" Ümit looks genuinely surprised. "I always thought I was the complete opposite of Baba."

"No. You're not. You two have the same eyes, Ümit. The exact same eyes."

Ümit looks down, plays with his hands.

"Okay, actually, I did meet someone," Peri says.

Ümit looks back up at her, his eyes flashing.

"But it's not like that. It's not what you think. It's different."

"How is it different?"

"It's completely different."

"Is it . . . Is she . . . ?"

"No, it's not a woman!" Peri says this a bit too forcefully.

Ümit freezes for a moment. He looks shocked. He begins to blush.

"But . . ." Peri lays her hand on his, tilting her head to one side. "That's not really important."

"What?" he asks hesitantly.

"Whether it's a woman or a man. That doesn't matter to me."

Ümit shrugs his shoulders and pulls his hand away from hers, intimidated.

Peri shakes her head reflexively. What kind of answer was that? Was that supposed to comfort her brother? *Whether it's a woman or a man, that doesn't matter to me.* It sounds so hopelessly naive. Why can she never find the right words to encourage the people around her, to free them

from the prisons in their minds? Why is there always such a divide
between the things she's feeling and the things she's able to say? Peri
can remember lecturing her mother about Simone de Beauvoir. She
was still in her first semester and had just started attending the reading
circle of the women's study group. She had felt like she knew everything.
She had thought she only needed to explain things to her mother about
what she'd read and heard in order to wipe away generations of oppression, poverty, and lack of education in one ten-minute conversation.

"You know, Anne, you're not really born a woman. This world makes
you into one."

"Tövbe estafurullah, Allah created us as women."

"No, Anne, if Allah . . . if Allah created us at all . . . Allah created
people. And people created all the rest. This world. Our upbringing.
All of it!"

"What are you trying to say to me, Perihan?"

"I'm trying to say that you're just trapped . . . stuck in this passive
role, stuck in this place in your mind that tells you you can't take charge
of your own life. But that isn't true, Anne. Or at least, it's not completely true."

"Tamam. Are you telling me to be like a man?"

"No, Anne . . . Or maybe, yes. Yes, yes! Maybe just a little bit. I'm
trying to tell you you don't have to spend your whole life living and acting the way they taught you to be. You don't just have to act the way
women are *supposed* to be. You're free."

"Oh, no, I am not free, Perihan. You have no idea what you're talking
about."

Only two years later, Peri was already over Simone de Beauvoir: her
reading circle had introduced her to Judith Butler. And she tried again
to explain things to Emine.

"Anne, listen up. In German, when you talk about me, you'd say
something like: *She* goes to university."

Emine was peeling onions.

"But how would you say that in Turkish?"

Silence.

"You would say: *O* goes to university. Right?"

Emine glanced up from her onions, staring blankly in Peri's direction. It was a look that said: *What do you want now?*

"And what would you say, if you wanted to say the same thing about Hakan?"

"I do not say the same thing about Hakan, Perihan. Hakan doesn't go to university. Hakan is a lazy good-for-nothing."

"Yes, but let's just pretend he did. Or, no: Hakan goes to kahve. How would you say that? *O* goes to kahve. Or let's say: *He* gets in *his* car. *O* gets in *onun* car. You see? There's no such thing as *he* or *she* in Turkish! Because it doesn't matter whether it's a man or a woman. Or whether it's *his* or *her* car. It doesn't matter at all.

"But Perihan, women do not go to kahve."

"Okay, right. I mean, it's not that it doesn't matter. But it's not more important whether it's a man or a woman that's going somewhere than, say, a poor person or a rich person. A foreigner or a German . . . It doesn't make sense that the defining aspect of my being should be my womanhood when you say: *She* goes to university."

Emine poured a generous amount of sunflower oil into the frying pan and waited for it to heat.

"Do you understand what I'm trying to say, Anne?"

Emine pushed the diced onions off the cutting board and into the pan with her knife, stirring them together with a wooden spoon as if Peri weren't there.

"The German language is always, always, *always* re-creating, staging these differences between women and men. With every sentence. Every *she* and every *he*. I know you're probably thinking: Yes, well, we're just describing a person. But there are hundreds of thousands of different ways to describe a human being. Why does it always have to be about whether they're a woman or a man? Why can't it be something else? Have you ever asked yourself that? Because every language is also a tool, a tool to build and uphold the structures of its society. Holding the system together . . ."

"Yani," Emine interrupted, to Peri's surprise. Peri nodded, but Emine continued stirring her onions for a while, adding cubes of meat, then stirring again vigorously.

"Yani, I understood you, Perihan. But this is nonsense."

"What do you mean? What's nonsense, Anne?"

"All of it," Emine said, shrugging her shoulders. "Just because we say *o* in Turkish and there is no *he* or *she* does not mean things are better for us women there."

"Well, no," Peri began. "Of course, it's not that easy to dismantle power structures with a single word."

"Excuse me, Perihan, but why do you make my head hurt with all this chatter when you already know it does not change a thing? Go. I have things to do. Go, haydi!"

And then came Ciwan.

Hindsight often gives new meaning to each little thing that led to an encounter, as if everything were all part of a greater puzzle. Every speck of dust suddenly has weight, every casual decision that brought you to a certain place at a certain time. But this was not the way it happened with Ciwan. It was neither fate nor coincidence that brought Peri and Ciwan together. One day, Ciwan was simply standing there in front of Peri. Ciwan had found her.

Peri sat in that dingy campus bar with the Adorno quote on its facade. She'd been staring at an open book without reading it, scooting around on the uncomfortable wooden chair. And then, when she looked up from her daydreams, someone had been standing awkwardly at the bar across from her with empty hands and hunched shoulders. His hair shone black like his leather jacket; his round face was shaven clean. He stared directly at her, and Peri had to smile. He seemed somehow lost or abandoned, as if he did not really belong. There was something surprised, something incredulous, in his look. Peri felt flattered that a stranger would stare at her this way. She nodded to him. A nod that meant he could approach her. He stuck both hands in his jacket pocket and shuffled toward her with downcast eyes. Then he looked up and said: *Hello.* That was it. Nothing more. He didn't ask her for her name. He didn't offer to buy her a drink. He only stood there without any expectations. Full of possibilities. *Let's do what you want to do*, Peri read in Ciwan's eyes. And his eyes immediately looked so familiar to Peri. She'd felt like she knew everything about him instantly. But maybe that was only because he was also a foreigner like her. Every now and then, Peri had caught sight of other lonely foreigners in the library, hunched over heavy law books, scribbling their notes. But she'd never seen one hanging out in a dingy student bar like this before.

Peri pointed to the chair across from her. He took a seat.

"Another loner, huh?" she asked.

He nodded.

"Don't you want a drink?"

He shrugged his shoulders inside his huge, oversized black leather jacket.

Peri slid her beer bottle over to him. He took only a tiny sip, out of politeness. And then he thanked her.

"This place is such a dump. I don't know what brings me here. Boredom, I guess," Peri said to break his silence.

He looked around them, assessing the bar.

"Is this your first time here?"

He nodded.

"Weird. I always ask myself: What *do* students do at night, if they're not hanging out in places like this?" Peri laughed.

"I'm not a student."

His eyebrows were dark; they drew together in the middle in a fine spiral just like Peri's had, too, before she'd started plucking them meticulously each morning with tweezers.

"I see. Yeah, well, I am, but I'm not really sure why, to be honest. My mother's always asking me what I'm going to be when I finish. And I don't know what to say. I study German. But I'm not going to be a teacher. And if you're not going to be a teacher, my mother asks, what are you going to be? I've started telling her I'm going to be a librarian, just so she'll leave me alone. Of course, she doesn't know you have to study library science for that!"

Peri noticed how attentively he listened to her. As though she were telling him her darkest secrets. She was no longer sure whether she found it creepy or flattering.

"What's your name, anyway?"

"Ciwan."

"Ciwan. What a pretty name. Where does it come from?"

"From Kurdistan." The words shot from his mouth like they'd been fired from a pistol.

Peri caught her breath. She hadn't expected this answer. Not because it came with any particular association. But simply because she'd never heard someone say that before: *Kurdistan*. It sounded so beautiful. And yet, at the same time, like something one could only whisper carefully and quietly. But Ciwan had not been quiet. He'd said it like it was the most natural thing ever. Just like if he'd asked her where she came from and Peri had said: *Turkey*. Completely natural. Even though she didn't really know herself if this was true. Whether the place from which she'd acquired her name was really Turkey at all, or whether it was really someplace else.

"My name is Perihan."

"Perihan," Ciwan repeated.

"But everyone calls me Peri. Like faerie."

Ciwan stared at her wide-eyed.

They left the bar and went out walking. Meandering through the narrow, empty streets of Bockenheim, Peri felt like she told Ciwan half of her life story that first night. He did not speak much himself. Peri learned only that he'd just been in Frankfurt for a few days. That he wasn't sure yet how long he would stay. And that he'd lived in Berlin before that. He didn't say what kind of job he had, or whether he worked at all, and Peri didn't ask him. She let the conversation take its own course and spoke of anything that came to her mind while he listened, rapt. Sometimes he asked careful little questions. They talked and walked for hours. For a small eternity. And when morning came and the sun was just peeking over the horizon, they stood in front of Peri's apartment building.

"I had a really good time with you," she said, rubbing her tired eyes.

"Yes," Ciwan replied, not looking the least bit tired himself. "It *was* really good."

"Will I see you again?"

He nodded.

"Do you have a number?"

He shook his head.

"Do you want to meet me here again tomorrow? Right here, at 8 p.m.?"

He left without so much as a hug or a handshake.

And that was how it began. Peri and Ciwan met every evening Peri didn't work at the cider bar. At 8 p.m. In front of her apartment. For a walk. It didn't matter if it was raining, storming, or the mildest of spring evenings. Ciwan always came empty-handed, in the same over-sized leather jacket. He never had an umbrella or a bag. He always wore the same clothes, though they never looked dirty. He smelled nice; the scent reminded Peri of Hakan's aftershave. And his hair was always gelled back like the delikanlıs who stood at the doors during weddings and smoked. But Peri was sure Ciwan had never been to such a wedding. His appearance and demeanor were oddly matched. In fact, Peri had a hard time sorting him into any of the categories of men she'd known before. She couldn't even say how old Ciwan might be. His face looked smooth and young, and his hands were remarkably delicate. So much so that Peri sometimes suspected he might even be younger than she. But Ciwan's manner of speaking, the depth of his aura, also made him seem at least ten years her senior.

And still, in other situations, Ciwan seemed strangely reckless. Particularly when it came to negotiating traffic. He never paid attention to the street signs on their walks. A few times, Peri even shrieked in panic when he stepped out directly onto a busy street. A car honked, swerving wildly to avoid him.

"What the hell are you doing, Ciwan? He could have run you over, man!" Peri had screamed.

Ciwan simply shrugged his shoulders. "But he didn't."

Whenever Peri asked Ciwan where he was staying, he always said: *with a friend.* But he never told her anything about this friend or about where their apartment might be. After a while, Peri began to realize Ciwan had little contact with anyone but her. It was just something she could tell: lonely people recognize their own kind.

One day, Ciwan told her that he'd been to a demonstration. They were walking, like always. They never stopped at cafés or bars. Peri had very little money anyway, and she guessed Ciwan had even less than she. But on that evening, he'd appeared with a bottle of wine and two plastic cups. They sat together on a bench in Grüneburg Park.

"Okay. Now are you finally gonna tell me where you're really from?" Peri asked after a half cup of wine, a warm feeling filling her belly.

"I grew up in a village."

"Wow. So much information," Peri exclaimed, laughing at him. "I better stop, I need to process all of this."

He looked at her questioningly. "What do you mean?"

"Well, does this village have a name or something? Or is that top secret?"

"You wouldn't know it anyway." He took a slow sip of his wine.

"Let me guess. It's in Bavaria, isn't it? And you speak a funny dialect there. You're always trying to hide it, but I hear it anyway: There's some sort of lilt!"

"A lilt?" He smiled.

"*A lilt?*" Peri repeated. "And when did you move to Berlin?"

"When I was twenty."

"And your family. Are they still living in this village of yours?"

Ciwan cleared his throat. "Um. I don't have family."

"What do you mean you don't have family? No parents? No siblings?"

Ciwan just shook his head.

Peri searched his face for some sign that would tell her more than this single, curt sentence. Sorrow, maybe. Anger. Something. Anything. But Ciwan's face remained expressionless. It was as though he'd pulled down a steel gate hiding everything from his past behind it. Peri could only nod. She decided to accept this, guessing there was something more to it. That perhaps it was better for Ciwan not to speak of these things.

"And what about you?" he asked instead.

"My family? Ah, you know: the usual, normal working-class family."

"What does that mean? *Usual, normal?*" he asked with irritation.

"My dad is either working or sitting in front of the TV. And my mother has depression."

"Why?"

"Yeah, I've been trying to figure that out for years," Peri said, downing the rest of her cup of wine.

Ciwan watched her, as if hoping she might go on. Peri was thinking.

"Maybe the problem isn't just my mother. You know. It feels like there's some kind of fissure running through our family."

"A fissure?"

"Yeah. Like something just broke at some point. Or disappeared. A crack opened and now it's just been covered up with silence. Do you know what I mean?"

Ciwan nodded, but his face looked less than certain.

"I think my parents never truly *arrived* in Germany. Never settled in. And I think that's why they're so unhappy."

"Where did they live before?" he asked.

"In northeastern . . ." Peri paused. "Or, no. In Kurdistan?"

Ciwan smiled softly. "Tu Kurmancî zanî?"

"What's that?"

"You don't speak Kurdish?"

"No. Unfortunately not."

"But you're Kurdish?"

"My parents are, yes."

"And you are not?"

"I don't know what I am."

Ciwan only nodded.

"I think it's weird to say I'm Kurdish," Peri tried to explain.

"Why's that?"

"Well, I don't know what's Kurdish about me. Because no one ever even told me we were Kurdish. I don't have the same problems the Kurds you see on the news do. I can't even speak the language." Peri poured herself another cup of wine.

"But lots of Kurds can't speak Kurdish," Ciwan protested. "Today, at the demonstration, I met many of them. It's not the language that makes you a Kurd."

"What is it then?" Peri asked.

Ciwan set down his plastic cup, rubbing his hands together as though he were growing cold. "Acknowledgment. Commitment. Saying: *I am a Kurd.* That's what makes you one."

"It's that easy?" Peri asked.

"I wouldn't say it's easy. You should have seen how many cops were at the demo today."

"What kind of a demonstration was it anyway?"

"A protest."

"But what for? What were you protesting about?" Peri insisted.

"For the release of Abdullah Öcalan."

"Excuse me?" Peri could feel goosebumps rising on her arms. She measured Ciwan again, hoping he was making some kind of joke. But Ciwan didn't make jokes. Never.

"What do you mean, *excuse me*?" he asked her.

"I mean: Why would you demonstrate for him?" Peri shook her head in disbelief. "He killed so many people. Or had them killed? It doesn't even make a difference. Why wouldn't you want someone like him to be brought to justice? Why wouldn't you protest for the release of someone like, I don't know, Leyla Zana instead? Someone who resists by democratic means?"

Ciwan nodded, gazing at Peri sympathetically.

"Don't worry, we do that too. But tell me this: Who do you think has more dead bodies on their conscience, Apo or the Turkish Army?"

Peri shook her head again, fumbling for a cigarette in her jacket pocket. Her pulse was rising. She suddenly found herself in the middle of a conversation she had never had before.

"I don't think it does any good comparing dead bodies with other dead bodies, Ciwan. Supporting Kurdish rights? Sure, I'm with you there. That's an important fight. But taking up arms? Sorry, I can't support something like that."

"*You* don't have to," Ciwan murmured, shrugging his shoulders. "The question is: Can you accept that I do?"

"But why?" Peri burst out. "Why would you support people with guns? You're so . . . so . . ."

"What am I?" he asked.

"You're so intelligent. And . . . kind. Caring. I don't know. I didn't think you were like that."

"Peri," Ciwan replied, slowly growing impatient himself. "People are being tortured. Burned alive. Exiled. Leyla Zana got seventeen years in prison for saying a single Kurdish sentence at parliament in Ankara. Seventeen years! How else should people defend themselves against that? By throwing daisies at the apparatus of the state? You tell me!"

But Peri had nothing to say. There wasn't a proper answer to this kind of question. She took a long drag on her cigarette. Her head felt so heavy, like she might fall forward at any moment and crash into the footpath. Her gaze swept the gravel trail and the weeds around her feet. Everything Ciwan said made sense. And yet there was a red line that Peri wasn't prepared to cross. She couldn't just say: Yeah, well, when you think about it that way, sure. She couldn't just say: Yeah, I guess I'm just supporting other people with guns when I say: Öcalan should be brought to justice. Because wasn't the state just other people with guns? Why could its use of violence be justified while others' could not?

Peri felt a rage building up inside her, but she wasn't angry at Ciwan. She was angry with herself. She couldn't process what she was hearing, couldn't believe that she had never heard it told this way before. She felt genuinely shocked to be confronted by this question now for the first time: Wasn't armed resistance justified in the face of decades of massacres and brutal oppression? Peri had simply never had contact with people who thought this way before. Because she'd never taken the time to really think about the people and stories behind the headlines in the newspaper her father bought each day. Yes, of course, she knew that it was Turkish propaganda. And she also understood that her father didn't necessarily share the same opinions just because he read this paper. It was simply the only Turkish newspaper he could buy at the kiosk. Wasn't it better to read this paper rather than not read any news at all? But still, Peri had never dared to take that extra little step. The leap that would have meant asking: What does all this have to do with me? What do I think about it? *Weapons are bad.* What kind of opinion was that?

"You think I'm some kind of terrorist now, don't you?" Ciwan asked suddenly.

Peri stared back at him blankly, realizing now her silence had unnerved him.

"Huh? What? Sorry."

"Are you afraid now that I'm some kind of terrorist?" he asked again.

Peri measured Ciwan up and down. "I'm not sure."

Ciwan nodded this answer away. And Peri understood for the first time just what it was that she found so attractive about him. He was not the kind of guy to go on the offensive immediately, nor was he the type to just retreat into himself when he was hurt. Ciwan made no attempt to hide his vulnerability. Peri was suddenly overcome by the urge to kiss him.

But instead, she continued: "Yes, I am scared. But only because you look so good to me."

Ciwan started. A smile fled over his face for an instant, but then it vanished. He cleared his throat and fiddled with his jacket.

"Acknowledging it. Committing," Peri repeated, hoping to relieve Ciwan of his shame. "That would make me a Kurd? Just saying that I am one?"

Ciwan turned to her gratefully. "If we don't say that we are Kurdish, then we Kurds do not exist."

Peri was astonished by the clarity with which Ciwan spoke of these things. When it came to Kurdistan, nothing remained of the shy and timid person Peri believed him to be. In the days that followed, Peri came to realize the only thing that actually seemed to unsettle Ciwan was her. There was something between them. Something she could not explain. Particularly because they always maintained physical distance. At some point, Ciwan had begun to shake Peri's hand in greeting or in farewell. They spent as much time together as lovers or best friends, and yet this handshake remained so formal that the physical contact only made Peri more confused. She did her best to leave it at this. Without titles. Without categories. Was that not precisely what Peri had wanted? Hadn't she wanted to have liberated relationships? Relationships without descriptors? To be together without possessing one another. But still, there was something different with Ciwan. Peri felt like it was growing harder and harder to navigate the undefined boundaries of their relationship each time she met with him. She hadn't spent this much time with another person again since Armin. She'd never felt closer to another person—even if Ciwan continued to maintain an arm's length of distance between them while they wandered the empty, nighttime streets of Frankfurt.

One night, Peri convinced Ciwan to visit her during her shift at the bar. There was never much happening after ten anyway, and Peri was happy to have company until she closed up at midnight. She had invited Ciwan many times before, but he'd always refused. Perhaps out of fear that he might have to order something. This time, he had agreed, and as he took a seat at the bar, Peri immediately told him all his drinks were on the house. He thanked her shyly and ordered a beer.

Peri placed two shots of vodka on the bar between them, before downing one herself. Ciwan nipped at the other, making a face. Peri felt a tinge of excitement; for the first time ever, they were not meeting on neutral territory but in a place that belonged to Peri's life. It was almost like he was at her place, but without the cramped confines of her tiny room. She felt like she could feel Ciwan's eyes on her while she was taking orders and serving drinks. They followed her every step around the room. Peri felt like she was on stage. Each trip across the smoke-filled barroom was no longer just a boring moment at her boring job. It had become a choreography. She liked being watched by him.

Peri gave Ciwan a few more shots during the night, drinking one herself each time, so that by the end of the night she needed to count up the day's earnings twice because she kept losing her train of thought.

When she was finished, she shut and locked the front door, realizing only in the coolness of the night air just how drunk she really was. She'd brought two more bottles of beer with her and handed one to Ciwan. She clinked bottles with him, watching as he took a sip.

"Do you ever think about how good we are together?"

Ciwan choked. "Excuse me. What?"

Peri watched him with amusement.

"No, really. There's something to it, right? My boss asked me earlier if you're my boyfriend. Because we're such a good match. Even the way we look."

Ciwan stared at her coolly, clamping the metal blinds down over his expression.

"Maybe he just wanted to know if you were taken."

Well, am I? Peri wanted to ask, but she didn't. Instead, she linked arms with Ciwan. They were walking in the direction of her dorm. It was the first time she'd felt more of his body than his hand. She could feel the arm beneath the thick leather jacket he hadn't once removed, not even inside the bar. Now, his arm remained tense for the length of the entire walk, preventing their bodies from drawing too close. But, nevertheless, his arm remained interlocked with hers. Ciwan didn't use the excuse of a curve or intersection to loose himself of Peri. They arrived at her building arm-in-arm like an old married German couple.

"Are you coming up?" she asked, doing her best to sound nonchalant.

"I don't think so," Ciwan said with determination, nodding, as if in farewell.

"But I want to show you something."

"What?" Ciwan asked.

"Well, you'll see when you come up!"

He looked down at himself.

"Don't worry," Peri said with a wink. "You don't have to take off your jacket."

The white halogen light of the foyer shone on their drunken faces.

"Come on, let's take the elevator."

Ciwan let Peri lead the way and then asked her which floor.

"The ninth."

He pushed the button, then remained standing by the door with his back to Peri, while she shifted from one foot to the other in excitement.

They walked together down the long hallway that always smelled like frying food, down to the far end, and Peri's room. Skunk Anansie was playing behind another closed doorway, the melancholy guitar riff from the opening of "Hedonism."

"Come in, come in," Peri sang, pushing open the door to her room, and she had to laugh at herself—she sounded like a deranged circus conductor in a cartoon.

Ciwan entered and stood waiting in the tiny entryway that separated the sink from the rest of the room. He watched Peri hesitantly.

"You can leave your shoes on."

Ciwan made the few steps over to the other side of the room. He looked around. Bed. Desk. Refrigerator. Hot plate. You couldn't fit much more into the space.

"That's it," Peri said, stretching her arms wide. "This is how I live. That's what I wanted to show you."

Ciwan nodded at Peri's furniture. "Cozy."

"Nah. You can go ahead and say it: This is a tiny little shithole. But it's my shithole. And I've tried to make the best out of it."

By that, Peri meant the lava lamp on her desk, the bright pattern of the '70s-era curtains she'd had Emine sew for her, and the many photo cuttings from magazines she'd posted to her walls. They were mostly of women smoking, drinking, or protesting.

"It's not a shithole, Peri," Ciwan said with a seriousness that seemed almost offended. Ciwan didn't seem to have a home of his own. He stayed here or there with people he knew. In Peri's head that sounded romantic. But the reality was probably just exhausting.

"I'll make us some tea, okay?" she said, stuffing her backpack onto a shelf. She took off her overshirt, quickly rearranging her cleavage in the lacy, black spaghetti-strap top she wore underneath. Ciwan looked away in shame.

"You can sit in my chair or on my bed. Whatever's more comfortable."

He sat down carefully on the chair, bending over her desk to examine the pictures on the wall. Peri filled the kettle and set it on her hot plate. The music from next door grew louder. It seemed to be playing on repeat. *I hope you're feeling happy now.*

While Peri fished two teabags from a drawer, she noticed the concentration with which Ciwan was examining the pictures on her wall. He drew his fingertips across one of the pictures.

"Is that . . . ?"

Peri drew closer, peering over his shoulder.

"Yep, that's my mother when she was still young. I think she had the picture taken for her passport before we moved to Germany. Doesn't she look beautiful?"

Ciwan grew quiet, staring at the photograph.

Peri lay one hand on the cold leather of the jacket over his shoulder. Ciwan flinched. He stood slowly, sliding out from under Peri's grip.

"I think I should get going," he said, without looking at her.

"But I was just making us tea," Peri protested softly.

"Thanks, but I really need to go. I'm pretty tired."

"But you can sleep here . . ."

Ciwan looked at Peri aghast.

"No. No. I don't want that!"

He took a step toward the door, but Peri blocked his way.

"But then what *do* you want from me?" she asked him in a voice that sounded angrier than she'd intended. She tried to start over.

"I mean . . ." She did her best to sound gentler. More inviting. "We don't have to rush things. We don't even have to do anything. But you know, I do wonder why you would meet up with someone so often, want to see someone so much, but not want to let them come even a fraction of an inch closer?"

Ciwan seemed puzzled. "I . . . I don't know what you mean."

His eyes were shifting nervously. Peri didn't want to believe it at first, but the longer she looked, the less she could deny it. Ciwan was afraid. *Just because you feel good, doesn't make you right.*

Suddenly Peri felt terrible about having lured him here and now not letting him leave. She was drunk and the whole thing had seemed like a game to her. But if Ciwan was afraid, then it was not a game. Peri sat down on her bed, staring up at him. She wanted to say something to take away his fear. She wanted him to know that he was safe here.

"If you think you're going to be some kind of guinea pig for me or something, you don't have to worry," she began.

Ciwan looked at her questioningly.

"It's not my first time," Peri continued.

"Wait, what?"

Peri shrugged. "I've been with a woman before, too."

The fear in Ciwan's eyes was suddenly replaced by something different. A dark cloud settled over his eyelids and an almost inaudible breath escaped his lips.

"I'm not a woman," he said.

The words flashed across the room, colliding with Peri's face like a balled fist.

"I know!" she exclaimed, feeling her face begin to flush. "Of course! That's not what I was trying to say. I just mean . . . I want you to feel good."

Ciwan only shook his head. He didn't leave. He remained standing, looking at her. His eyes glowed with disappointment.

The kettle began to whistle.

Peri didn't know what to do. She smiled helplessly at Ciwan.

"So, you're not in love with me?"

"No," Ciwan said with a forcefulness that Peri found insulting.

"No? Then why are you looking at me that way?"

He drew his hands over his face as if trying to determine what was wrong with his expression.

"Ciwan, are you sure? Because you act like you're in love with me . . ."

"No. I'm not in love. It's more complicated than that."

"What can be more complicated than being in love?"

He shrugged his shoulders. "Not being in love. Not being able to be."

"You can't fall in love?" Peri furrowed her brow. "Or just not with me? Am I too ugly? Is it my nose? Or is it just the way I am?"

Ciwan shook his head again, or simply continued doing so. The kettle was still whistling.

"Just tell me, Ciwan. Am I not political enough? Do you think I'm too stupid? Or just plain ugly?" Peri asked it again, knowing how ridiculous she was making herself. But she was drunk, and she wanted an answer. Needed an answer.

"No, of course you aren't stupid. You're as beautiful as a rose, Peri."

A childish laugh escaped her lips.

"A rose?"

Ciwan raised his hands in desperation, as though he wasn't quite sure how he'd come up with this thing with the rose.

"So, you do like me?" Peri asked him.

"That's not what this is about."

"Then what is it about?"

Ciwan straightened his jacket and looked around himself in Peri's room uneasily. Like a man looking for a taxi on the street.

A carousel of possibilities was spinning in Peri's mind. She wondered what she could do to make Ciwan stay. But Ciwan had already made up his mind.

"Take care, Peri."

He removed the kettle from the hot plate, set it on the counter, and left the room without looking back at her.

Peri had never heard from him again.

"Never?" Ümit asks excitedly, cracking çekirdek.

Peri shakes her head.

"Where do you think he is? Is he back in Berlin?"

"I don't know," Peri says, standing and stretching. Her limbs feel stiff from so much sitting around. They're literally screaming for rest.

"But all this happened just a few months ago? Aren't you going to look for him?" Ümit asks, cracking open a few more seeds, one after the other. Peri has to distract herself, or she'll start again, too. Her tongue and fingertips are already burning like crazy from this salty crack.

"I don't know, Ümit. I think he doesn't want me to . . ."

A shrill sound startles Peri and Ümit both. They cower together in tandem. It takes them both a moment before they realize it's the sound of the doorbell ringing in the middle of the night.

"Who could that be?" Ümit asks, still frightened.

Peri shrugs. "Maybe Hakan?"

She paces down the hallway to the door and presses the button with the tiny key on it. She glances down at the floor and is reminded of her baba. Peri jerks the apartment door open to rid herself of these thoughts. She can hear the patter of quick footsteps in the stairwell. After a short time, Peri sees Cem and then Bahar running up the stairs.

"What is this, the twentieth floor?" Cem pants in excitement, completely out of breath.

"Yakışıklım!" Peri wraps him in her arms, kissing his face. Then she lifts Bahar and carries her through the door. She looks bleary-eyed.

"Where is your mother?"

Sevda comes cursing up the stairs, an enormous suitcase clattering behind her and a designer handbag swinging from her neck. Her blonde-streaked hair is frazzled; her face is tired and swollen with tears.

"Abla, wait, let me help you," Ümit cries, but Sevda is already inside with her heavy suitcase.

She looks around nervously, as if expecting Emine.

"These taxi drivers," Sevda whispers, strained. She probably assumes Emine is already sleeping. "They're always the same. He drove around the same block five times because *supposedly* he didn't know the way. How do you become a taxi driver if you don't know your way around? What kind of country is this? Why can't anyone just do their job without trying to screw somebody else over?"

Peri takes her sister's purse. Sevda removes her shoes, runs her hands through her hair, then paces toward the living room looking for her two kids. She seems startled for a moment. Her eyes catch somewhere in the middle of the room. She takes everything in from the darkness of the hallway where the neighbor woman found their father. She doesn't move. Hüseyin's furniture. His living room. Then finally, her eyes fall on her sister. Tears are streaming down her cheeks. Wordlessly, the two embrace. Peri holds her big sister tightly while Sevda's arms hang limp and powerless around her. Sevda whimpers softly against the warmth of Peri's neck.

The television turns on. "Aya Benzer" by Mustafa Sandal is playing, and the children sing along half-heartedly.

"Hey, aren't you two tired?" Ümit asks, amused.

"They're so tired, they're not tired anymore," Sevda replies. Then, slowly freeing herself from Peri, she caresses her sister's cheek as if thanking her for the embrace. She wipes her tear-stained face before hugging Ümit.

"Now, Bahar, cutie pie, how are you?" Peri says, settling down beside her niece. She pulls Bahar closer.

"Good! Can we play Ludo now?"

Peri laughs. "You don't waste any time, do you? Tomorrow, little one. It's getting late now, and you two need to go to bed!"

"But I already slept. On the plane. We have a travel game with magnets! Do you wanna see it?" Bahar jumps up without waiting for an answer, skipping over to her pink Barbie backpack in the hall.

"Bahar, it's way too late! Stop it!" Sevda calls after her, exhausted.

"But I just want to show her!" Bahar says, tugging the game out of her backpack. And then suddenly, she screams.

Peri starts, too, leaping up. She sees a silhouette, silent and motionless, standing at the end of the darkened hall.

"Oh, that's just Anneanne. Did she startle you?" Peri asks Bahar.

Bahar runs back to the couch and cowers by her mother in fright. Sevda strokes her head, then rises to greet Emine. She takes two steps in her direction, then she, too, remains standing. No one in the room says anything. No one breathes. All eyes are on Sevda and Emine.

"Anne," Sevda says.

Emine simply stands there, a dark shape at the end of the hallway. It's starting to make Peri uncomfortable. She leans forward and switches on the light. Emine blinks at them.

"Oh, Sevda Hanım," she says, nodding in their direction. "What an honor for you to grace us with your presence."

Hakan

Hakan's Panasonic rings. An anonymous caller. He puts down his phone and steps on the gas. The August sun burns hot against the skin of his left forearm. The dashboard vibrates to the Funkmaster Flex cassette in his tape deck. Two hours till rush hour traffic. Fifty more kilometers to Munich. And then:

Salzburg
Villach
Ljubljana
Zagreb
Lipovac
Belgrade
Sofia
Plovdiv
Svilengrad

That's the order in the notebook on the passenger seat in Lena's flowing handwriting. Right next to his five cans of Red Bull. Hakan blows through the traffic until he's deadlocked with the bumper of a navy-blue Mercedes E-Class. He doesn't clip the other car. Not really. But he's close. Dizzyingly close. Close enough that there's less than two centimeters of air between them. It's like they're dancing. And he loves it. Two cars: flung together at 220 kph, in the outermost left lane. If the car in front of him just taps the brakes, it's over. For both of them. Ciao. But if she surrenders and merges to the right, Hakan will fly on past, in search of another partner for his dance. It's as simple as that, really. The autobahn is full of them: adrenaline junkies, would-be Schumachers, high-speed kanaken. But this E-Class in front of him is different. She neither brakes nor changes lanes. She stays in the left lane, increasing speed. Backs off the accelerator again. Lets her velocity sink. Slowly. Without braking. So slowly. It makes Hakan hard. Like a lap dance. Like she's grinding her ass just millimeters from Hakan's crotch so he can imagine how it would feel to fuck her, without ever tasting the real thing. Not the whole *I'm-playing-hard-to-get-me-in-your-bed* game girls sometimes play when it's the only way they know how to flirt. That's such a major turnoff for Hakan. No, that isn't it. Hakan doesn't even really want to sleep with them because he already knows exactly how it will be: the idea of sex is always so much hotter than the sex itself. That's how it goes.

Of course, he'd never say this to Lena. Lena, who could already have thrown his ass out ten times over after only living together for three months. Except that she doesn't. Because she's the good kind. Loyal. Hakan has to get his shit together and not scare her away with all his thousand problems. He'll never find one like her again. Lena is the only ray of hope in the shitshow of Hakan's life. Lena, who didn't bat an eye at paying the last two months' rent by herself because she knows Hakan is short on cash. Lena, who just three hours ago sat at their kitchen table tracing the roads in her ADAC European atlas with her gentle fingers while Hakan frantically threw his things together for the trip.

"After Svilengrad comes the border! Then all you have to do is follow signs for Istanbul," she yelled through their apartment. "But I really don't know how you plan to do it all by tomorrow, Hakan! And isn't there still an active warzone in the countries you're planning on driving through?"

"The war's over, baby! And I'm not going through Kosovo anyway. Trust me, it's easy. Just look. His operation's gonna happen tomorrow after afternoon prayer, huh? Let's say five o'clock. Five there is four o'clock here. What time is it now? 9:51 exactly. Shit! I've gotta go. I've got thirty hours to get to that hospital in Istanbul. But I can make it, no problem. Check it out, baby, the streets are butter through Slovenia. They're a little bumpy until Zagreb, okay, but it's fine. But between Zagreb and Belgrade it's a disaster, like driving over a cheese grater, seriously. The fucking streets have potholes that could swallow entire villages. Colonies. Everything, you know? But the real issue is the cops there. I should say the SO-CALLED COPS. They stop you every couple kilometers and make a big deal out of nothing, oh, once you get to Bulgaria! But baby, I know what's up. I've got it all planned out. I'm gonna stop at the gas station right across the street here and buy ten packs of Marlboros. Yeah, that's it! Ten packs. Those smokes will be my express ticket for Serbia and Bulgaria. Nah, of course I can't just buy cheaper ones in Slovenia. Hallo? The Yugos want German Marlboros. Nice and fresh, without the dried-out tips and the crackly little bits of lead and all that other crap they sell as cigarettes in their own shithole little markets. No, no, baby, they're not gonna wave me through for that shit. Do you think you could lend me 500 marks? Ah, you're the best. Yeah, come on, baby, let's run by the bank real quick!"

The Panasonic rings. Anonymous again. Hakan crushes an empty can of Red Bull and throws it onto the back seat. He's been hooked on the stuff ever since he got a free can in the supermarket parking lot from that little hottie with the ass. She was the polar opposite of Lena. Which is not to say that Lena doesn't have a sweet ass too. She does. But only Hakan knows about it because Lena's always dressed in her hippie clothes. Humanities student. Teacher in training. She's a natural beauty. She hardly even wears makeup, she doesn't style her hair, and she looks beautiful all the same. But that girl from the parking lot, on the other hand, you could see her hotness radiating from a kilometer away. And her smell. The kind of perfume no one can ignore. Heavy and sweet, so overpowering it drives you mad. Hakan would have liked to lick it right off her tanning-bed gold cleavage. He'd walked right up to her where she stood at the promotional stand, wrapped in a skin-tight minidress the color of the can. Blue. Silver. Scarlet. She'd only needed to give Hakan a wink, and now he was addicted. What can you say?

These people know how advertisement works. And it doesn't even taste good. There's something like Gummy Bear juice about it. But it gets you going like a line of speed. And pretty much costs the same because those cans are fucking expensive. And it's probably a bad idea to try to drive halfway across the continent with a bag of speed in your pants pocket.

The navy-blue Benz took an offramp in Munich. Hakan checks his watch. It's just after 1 p.m.; 2,100 kilometers in thirty hours. Cutting it close. Obviously. But doable without a break to sleep. The next flight would have been a night flight out of Strasbourg. Hakan could have caught it for 800 marks. He would have made it to the funeral no problem. He could have spared himself the stress. It might even have been cheaper than all the tanks of gas he's going to need with his Alfa. But just before the woman from the travel agency wanted to finalize his booking over the phone, Hakan thought to himself: What the fuck am I gonna do the rest of the day until my flight? Sit around feeling like shit? No way, lan. So, let's do it. Hit the road. Do something. Anything. Hakan hung up the phone, and now here he is flying instead down the A8, blasting past rest stop churches, grazing fucking cows, and the Chiemsee. He's still on the German autobahn: anything goes. The only freedom this piece of shit country hasn't taken away yet.

It's a good thing Lena isn't with him. She always flips out in the car and forces Hakan to drive slower. She's always so dramatic about everything. Well, no. She's just worried because she loves him, the poor thing. She even offered to come with him. To stand there by his side. Sweet of her. A very sweet idea. But Hakan hasn't even told Lena the full truth about what happened yet. He'd only said: *My father had a heart attack*, and already she'd stared back at him in shock. Lena's big blue eyes, wide as saucers, started filling with fearful tears the moment her perfect world began to so much as totter. Hakan couldn't bring himself to tell her the rest. *He's having an operation*, he had said, and: *I've gotta be there for it tomorrow by five*. He'd just continued talking: *I have to be there for him.* Somehow the relief he'd seen in Lena's eyes had given him hope too. Hope that it was all just a misunderstanding, hope that maybe his father really wasn't dead and everything would make sense as soon as Hakan arrived in Istanbul to be with him. Hope that maybe, in the meantime, people would have noticed Hüseyin was still breathing. Maybe they'd hooked him back up to all the machines and by the time Hakan would arrive, he'd be in a more stable condition. Then, in the very moment Hakan reached his room in the hospital, Hüseyin would miraculously regain consciousness, awaken, stare up at Hakan with his sad eyes, and say: *Oğlum benim. There you are, finally.*

If Hakan had told Lena what was really happening, she would never have let him go alone. She might even be sitting beside him in the car right now. Which would have been impractical for so many reasons. First, because he couldn't drive the way that he was driving now. They would never have been able to stick to the schedule he'd laid out. Second, because it wasn't exactly the ideal situation for introducing Lena to his family—who still thought Hakan lived alone. He'd get to that first thing after he got back. After this whole thing with his father was over and the horror of it had had time to process. Hakan would propose. Pull a classic, with a ring and everything. Maybe he'd do it at an Italian restaurant. Order tiramisu and get down on one knee like in that movie with Cher and Nicolas Cage that Lena loved so much. Hakan would pull it all together; he just first needed to clear this thing up with the Albanians. And talk to his mother. Lena was waiting for him to propose. And she deserved it. Not having to see the look of disappointment in Hüseyin's face would even make things a little easier.

Fuck, brother, your baba isn't even six feet under yet and you're already thinking like this? How you might benefit from his death? Hakan stares abjectly toward the heavens, drives with his right hand over his face. He pops another can of Red Bull. A new millennium was breaking and kanaken were still living like it was the Middle Ages. Of course, he didn't want to think too hard about what Lena's parents would say about the whole affair. The little darling always acts like everything was perfect: *They just don't know how to show you how much they like you; that's just their way.* Yeah, yeah. Right. Every time Lena brings him over to visit, her mother suddenly develops a migraine and hot-foots it right after dinner to her bedroom with a cap pulled down over her head. Then

Lena's father plops down with them in front of the idiot tube and throws back enough beers until he gets up the liquid courage or just drowns enough of his shame to ask Hakan for the hundred-and-twenty-ninth time how it can be that Hakan's *people* can all afford to drive such expensive cars, even the ones who are unemployed. Sometimes Lena manages to turn the conversation around before Hakan can get a chance to answer. And sometimes Hakan just shrugs his shoulders and tells Lena's father word for word exactly what he wants to hear: *Yeah, Günther, they're all ripping off the German state. They're lazy, they don't pay their taxes, they all open some bullshit business in their grandma's name and syphon off all the welfare money so they can buy themselves an S-Class Mercedes or a 3-Series BMW. Then they all trick out their cars and drive back with them to Turkey on a six-week holiday. Do you hear me, Günther, six weeks! What German can afford to take a six-week holiday, Günther, huh? Can you tell me that?*

And then Günther shouts, *Bah!* and wags his head up and down like the bobblehead on the dashboard of his VW Passat. *Bah!* before he probably jacks off later that night to Hakan's words again because he always knew he was right all along.

But all fun and games aside. Günther is okay. Yeah, of course he's still a leisure-time Nazi, but at least he lets Lena do what she wants. Lets her Turkish boyfriend sit at his dinner table. Which is different from all the kanaken fathers Hakan knows who only want to raise mini carbon copies of themselves and think there's nothing worse in the whole world than for their sons to bring home a German girl. Not cancer. Not a car crash. Not even junkie shit. There's nothing worse. At least Hüseyin will be spared this disappointment.

Hakan's eye twitches. He rolls down his window, lets the air rush in around his ears. The passenger window has been open a crack ever since he started driving. The rush of the incoming air whirls Hakan's thoughts around like a stack of crisp, fresh hundos. Only twenty-five more hours before Hakan sees what he heard this morning with his own eyes. Until he really knows it's true. But until then, it's all only hearsay. Nothing more than rumor. Why should he bust his head now over some empty rumors? Some relative had called from Istanbul claiming Baba was dead. Okay. Who the hell was that supposed relative anyway? Why should Hakan even trust her? Why did his mother trust her? Hüseyin was still pretty young. He'd seemed so full of life, especially in the last few weeks when his face had finally gotten back a bit of color. When he'd finally been able to look at Hakan again without frowning and making some kind of disparaging remarks about his business. As if he doubted whether Hakan had a business at all. The last time Hakan had seen him, just one week ago, Hüseyin had seemed so relaxed. Grateful, even. Filled with happy anticipation for his retirement and Istanbul. Hakan had never seen him like that before. Hakan can't even remember the last time he'd seen his father smile. It must have been a small eternity. He rolls his window down a little further. The wind strikes him like a slap across the face.

Things had never been easy between Hakan and his father. And yeah, of course Hakan had stirred up a lot of shit, but you had to admit that it is hard. Fuck. It *was* hard to be Hüseyin's son. Or maybe better: to be Hüseyin's eldest son. Because Hakan suspects that Ümit, as the youngest son, might have been spared from all the bullshit: *When will you finally be a man?* and *You're a grown man . . .* and *Man this, man that.* It was a good thing for Ümit because Ümit could not have handled it. Hakan couldn't handle it himself, but he feels like he at least understands now where it came from: Hüseyin's ideas about what it meant to be a man. It was all part of this whole working-class thing.

Had Hüseyin ever done anything but work? Ever been anything but a worker? Hakan can't really say. Hüseyin had always kept busy; Hüseyin had always toiled. For other people. For his family. He had always hustled. Always action. Never talk. No extra risks. Everything on the safe side. Always occupied. No unnecessary chatter. No frivolous things. Not a penny wasted. Hüseyin wasn't just any old worker. Hüseyin had been born to work. He had it in his blood. Some people have that. Hakan doesn't. Because Hakan knows there are thousands of ways to make money faster than standing around at a conveyor belt and subjugating yourself to some piece of shit foreman. No chance. He'd rather bury himself in debt and have his own business. Fuck it.

At least he had something of his own. No boss. No master. No fucking overseer. He could always make his own decisions. And yeah, okay, maybe the occasional decision from a business partner here and there. Maybe even a difficult partner. Maybe a partner who mostly exploited your business to wash his own dirty income clean. But not a boss. Nowhere. No bosses. Never. And always, the whole time, the hope that his used car business would, at some point, pay off. Despite the stiff competition. Hope that he'd somehow make a name for himself. And people would flock to his store. Well . . . to his parking lot. There wasn't really a store in that sense of the word. Hakan had only rented out a tiny bit of asphalt in the industrial part of town. There was just a metal shipping container where he could make himself and his buddies a çay. If you could call that a store. But it was a start. The main thing was setting your goals high. Not letting yourself be satisfied with little things and the dismal grind that every bum out there was content to call a life.

The mood alone on the assembly line before Hakan had dropped out of his training program at Weißburg had been enough. The way his colleagues talked to one another: *Hey, what's up?—Working, working. Gotta do what you gotta do.* Hakan could only laugh at this *gotta do what you gotta do.* But not because he thought it was funny. He found it unbelievably depressing. Gotta do. Gotta do. Okay, but gotta do what? Everyone's always gotta work somehow, fine. But who said you gotta work yourself to death here at this fucking cosmetics factory? No one. Hakan could give two shits about all of it. Diligence. Decorum. Et cetera, et cetera. Yeah, of course he could respect these things his father placed so much value in. Yeah, of course Hakan could understand where his father got these ideas. Baba didn't know anything different. But Hakan does. Hakan knows there's another way. It might not be as comfortable as a factory job: go to work, put on your uniform, stamp in, hustle, grind, stamp out, collapse at home in front of your TV, wake up, do it again. But Hakan would rather lie awake at night beside Lena, his veins pumped full of adrenaline because he thinks they're coming for him. They'll knock at his door any minute now. The Italians. Or the Albanians. Or whatever sons of bitches Hakan's just unintentionally made an underhand deal with on what's turned out to be a stolen car. There's always some headache involved. Some headache and some sleepless nights, yeah, that's his business. But it's still better than plodding along like a donkey between the TV and couch and the conveyor belt. This circular pilgrimage. Day in, day out, for your entire fucking life until one day, like Hüseyin you just . . . no.

The Panasonic rings.

Of course, it wasn't exactly Hakan's life dream to sling used cars. Of course, Hakan believes his real calling will be something better than haggling with some kanaken mechanics to give him a good deal on dialing back a few tachometers so he can start with a better asking price before he unloads the cars. Hakan's always been convinced he has an artistic soul. Yeah. He still believes it: he could have been destined for greatness if he had only ever had the chance to concentrate on such things. Whatever they would have been. Breakdancing or rapping. Who knows. Maybe it might even have been that casting call the mentor at the Youth Center wanted to send him to back when he was fifteen. Some movie where they needed a few extra b-boys. Maybe Hakan could have been discovered then. Maybe he'd be a movie star living in LA now or some other place. Okay, I mean, maybe not Brad Pitt or Wesley Snipes. But Hakan would have been content with a few supporting roles in the big films. Some jailbird in Se7en or a vampire in Blade, that kind of thing. Maybe Hakan could have gone all the way and even made his own movies at some point. Boyz n the Hood, German style. It would have been fresh: Jungs und die Straße. It could have been the real deal. If only Hüseyin hadn't forbidden him from going to that casting back in the day. Yeah, who knows? That's how it goes. Hakan never got a chance, and now he has to make the best of it.

They're talking about traffic jams on the radio. Hakan rolls up the window and adjusts the radio. There's something on the A8 between Stuttgart and Munich, but he's already past that. With any luck, he's just a half hour from the Austrian border. He cracks the window again and lights up a cigarette with satisfaction.

Immer wenn es regnet, muss ich an dich denken. Whenever it rains, I have to think of you. Max Herre croons from the speakers and Hakan almost drops his cigarette. He switches the radio off. Hakan HATES this song. And this band. And this guy. And every other professor's son. These rich kids piggybacking on the scene and making it big. How can they still be playing this old shit? Don't Freundeskreis have another new album out already? Guess it's not going so well, huh? You fucking hobby high school stoners. Ah, right. Hakan remembers watching their new video with Lena recently: "Mit Dir." *With you.* He was pretty taken by the voice of the female lead. It sounded just a little bit raspy, like if Hakan were to run one of Lena's hairbrushes gently up and down his neck. And at the same time, thick and heavy like a drop of honey on the back of his hand. Wow. Hakan hadn't heard something like that for a long time. The song was so well written, maybe the first German R&B song you could listen to without a guilty conscience. And then Hakan's jaw dropped down to the carpet when suddenly Max Herre came dancing toward this other singer in the video and Hakan realized it was another fucking Freundeskreis song. Hakan couldn't believe it. It didn't matter how well their music was produced. What badass artists they found to collaborate with. For Hakan they would still always be three spoiled Swabian brats who could just as easily have gone to law school and built their fancy little houses. But instead, they were making hip-hop now with that same overachiever drive they would have brought to their law careers. They would have wound up just as rich either way. Even though they didn't need the money to begin with because their families were already loaded. Even though they didn't have a goddamn thing to say because they'd never had to fight for anything. *Leg dein Ohr auf die Schiene der Geschichte.* Put your own ear on the tracks of history, you fucking meathead. Daddy probably paid for your demo tapes and your equipment and the goddamn history books too. Probably said: *Yes, sonny boy, you should become a rapper, that's a marvelous idea.* What an unjust fucking world.

The only time Hüseyin ever thought something Hakan had done was good was right after he started his training at the factory. Hüseyin had beamed. And why? Because he'd liked the idea of Hakan standing around in another stuffy factory building filling cosmetics into tiny

little bottles for a miserable salary. Hour after hour. Shift after shift. All
while his big-headed boss with the nose hair had one meltdown after
another and let out his filthy humor on the little kanake in Building 3.
He should see what Hakan thought of him and his big head. Hakan
stood in the courtyard during his breaks, headphones on his ears and
hate in his belly, staring at the strictly adhered to no-smoking sign.
Escaping into his own world. Into *Strictly for my N . . .* or *Doggystyle. The
Chronic.* Lit up his cigarettes anyway and toyed each time with the idea
of flicking his butt into the big dumpster with all the leftover chemicals.
Just because.

Hakan grabs another Red Bull from the passenger seat. The sticky
syrup tickles its way down his esophagus. He's starting to get hungry.
But there's no time for that. He hasn't even made it over the first border yet. He fumbles around with his stereo and switches to disc 5 on the
multidisc changer in the trunk. Hakan skips to song 3.

Don't push me
Cause I'm close to the edge
I'm trying not to lose my head
It's like a jungle sometimes
It makes me wonder how I keep from going under

Back in the day, Hakan and Musti listened to this track nonstop. They
shared the headphones of the Walkman they'd pilfered from the Octo-
media shop, sat at the playground in the park, and rapped along to Melle
Mel. After five, they'd gone to the Youth Center to breakdance with the
other kids. Snuck out of the house at night and headed back to the park
to smoke away the pain from their torn muscles and sprained wrists.
Stuck to each other like Siamese twins. Like two brains grown together
into one. Because the same shit was running through both of their heads;
because they were both hooked on the same songs; because they both
burned with the same fire.

Hakan could feel a lump of sadness in his throat. This down trip. It
happened every time. Every time he thought back on those times: back
when his entire world revolved around only this one thing. It burned

inside him until it almost felt like lovesickness, like the pain of a part-ing Hakan could never overcome. Despite the fact Hakan can't even say how the end came about. Maybe that's just how it is. Maybe he'd grown up, given in. That's how people describe it anyway. No one holds on to this kind of puppy love forever. And the ones who do, well, they're stuck in some way too. But secretly, Hakan admires these kinds of people too. The kind who never let themselves get distracted, led astray. The ones who persist, who stick with things even after they're no longer cool. The ones who keep on it, even when life gets shitty, even after the hard realities kick in. The ones who still get after it, even when there's no one left to go along with them.

It all started when Hakan was thirteen. That must have been 1987, when he and his best friend Musti first landed by chance on an unfamiliar planet. This new world lay hidden in an inconspicuous beer tent on the Rheinstadt fairgrounds. Every year the American military hosted a huge festival there for the entire community, and all the soldiers sta-tioned on nearby bases got to choose a band to be flown out to perform there for one single night.

Hakan's parents had allowed him to attend the Americans' party for the first time in his life. And Musti had told his parents he was at Hakan's. They tried that delicious American-style ice cream and the best hamburgers Hakan would ever eat. Of course, Hakan and Musti overdid it. They ate and ate until they could only lean with heavy bel-lies against the shooting gallery and watch the Americans have at it. At some point, just before sunset, they both had long since frittered away their last marks and Musti wanted to go because he was always afraid of coming home too late and taking a beating. But they could hear euphoric cries rising from the beer tent too: one vast cheering crowd. The soldiers beside them broke off all at once and ran for the pavilion.

"Come on, man. Don't piss your pants," Hakan said, staring after the departing soldiers. "We still have half an hour, Musti. It's gonna be fine. Let's check it out."

Musti stared down at the worn-out purple trainers he had just in-herited from his older sister and nodded despondently. He didn't have much of a choice if he wanted to avoid being laughed at and called a pussy by his best friend.

And so, they made their way to the beer tent, pushing themselves through the crowd up to the very front. The air was sticky and warm, and it stank of beer and bratwurst and kettle corn.

At some point, they reached the center of the pavilion, where a vinyl mat had been spread out across the asphalt between the rows of beer benches. A group of Black American soldiers formed a circle on the mat. Hakan and Musti stared in curiosity, watching as they took turns leaping into the center of the circle to dance. Hakan had seen break-dancing before on television, but what he saw here had very little in common with the kind of aerobic drills he'd seen before on the Eisi Gulp show ZDF played Saturday afternoons. This wasn't some choreographed series of fitness exercises; it was its own language. The soldiers' bodies called out and responded to one another, understanding and challenging each other without the need for words. They seemed to be in competition, while still celebrating each individual's achievements at the same time: nodding their heads, smiling, rapping along to the music. Hakan was electrified by what he saw. It was like every fiber of these dancers' bodies, every muscle, every nerve, imbibed the beat thumping through their speakers. Each movement spoke with feeling— a feeling of unity with the music, the circle of the other dancers, the crowd. It was a cypher, Hakan later learned. Spontaneous and raw, yet always hurtling toward the end goal of a finishing pose in the middle of the circle—freezing like an exclamation point at the end of a mighty sentence. Hakan felt his own heart racing as he followed with his eyes. It was almost like he was already dancing with them himself.

And then, when Hakan turned to the stage where the rest of the beer tent attendees' eyes were fixated, he saw three men in Adidas tracksuits with heavy gold chains around their necks. Two of them were rapping while the third spun records on a turntable. They were the three coolest people Hakan had ever seen, and suddenly he knew he had arrived on a different planet. Hakan wanted to live here. A single glance in Musti's direction confirmed that his friend felt exactly the same way. All the tension and fear had vanished from Musti's pimply face. It had been

replaced by fire. A fire Hakan could feel burning too. Hakan and Musti
would do anything to be a part of this scene. To experience this evening
again and again. And not just from outside the cypher. But from inside
it too.

~

Hakan flicks his cigarette out the window, still in disbelief that he had
stood just a few meters from Run DMC back then, before he had so
much as even heard of them. He can still remember how Musti had
said afterward: *Hakan, man, I'm so glad you made me stay. That black eye
the next morning was worth it, I'd take another any day to relive that night
again.*

Hakan can see the black *A* in the white oval on the highway signs
marking the border in front of him. He's debating whether he should
already stop at the next gas station to buy a pass for the Austrian toll
roads. He also needs to take a piss. His bladder's starting to feel like
one of the water balloons he and Musti used to throw in front of girls'
feet from the sixth floor of their building. That was still back before
they'd learned to dance, back when Hakan and Musti had spent their
summers bored to death because they hadn't known what to do yet
with all their time and energy. Their yaramaz times. Hakan wonders
now what they got out of throwing those water balloons. Sure, it had
been funny to hear the girls squeal and watch them run away. But it
wasn't like he and Musti could even see a nipple through their wet shirts
from so far away.

And then he has to think about the girl from the Red Bull stand
again. One of those Germans with long, dyed-black hair: a wannabe
kanakin. She'd worn a pushup bra that made her salon-golden tits look
like two coconuts. Hakan wants to keep her in his mind's eye and take
her with him to the gas station bathroom. He can see the sign already:
Just five more kilometers. Come on, you can make it, he thinks. She
smelled like vanilla. Like small-town carnival nights. Like that American
festival. He tries to imagine how she'd taste. Like cotton candy. Sweet
and scorched. Like caramelized almonds. Candied apples. Gingerbread
hearts . . .

Hakan's heart skips a beat.

Police lights are flashing. They hit him like a punch in the face.

His memories vanish into thin air.

A cop car overtakes Hakan on the right.

The FOLLOW ME sign flashes.

Hakan swallows.

Slowly, he begins to brake. He merges to the right. Follows the cops. As inconspicuously as possible, he reaches for his seat belt and buckles in. Of course. He'd literally thought of every eventuality on his trip. Everything but this. They exit at the next highway rest stop. The one before the gas station. The white stripes of the parking bays, a rancid-looking toilet, and swarms of wasps circling the garbage cans. Hakan can feel his palms sweating on the leather of his steering wheel. He hates rest stops without gas stations. And there's only one thing worse than a rest stop without a gas station: A rest stop without a gas station in Bavaria. With the Bavarian police.

Two cars are already parked at the rest stop. Lucky for me, I'm not alone here, Hakan thinks. He rolls past the concrete picnic tables: a large family is eating there. Jackpot: kanaken! The cops pull in next to the toilets. Hakan parks behind them. He dries his hands on his shorts. In the rearview mirror, he watches the kanaken family, sees the father craning his balding head in the direction of the police. At least there will be witnesses. Whatever happens, there will be witnesses. That comforts Hakan at least a little bit. The two cops exit their vehicle and approach Hakan's Alfa. He rolls down his window.

The smaller of the two cops takes the lead. His cheeks are round but sag downward indolently. He looks like a beaver.

"Grüß Gott. License and registration."

"Excuse me?"

"License and registration."

"You forgot to say *please*, officer."

The beaver gapes at Hakan in amazement. He glances back at his colleague before shaking his head.

Hakan bites his tongue. But he can't leave it alone. Back home he knows how to play the exemplary kanaken son, and he can put on a

show and be the ideal son-in-law for Lena's parents. Even when Günther
starts unpacking his locker room drivel, Hakan can put on an Oscar-
worthy performance. He's got himself under control; he doesn't let himself slip. He never reveals what's really on his mind. Hakan can dispel
or advance entire aspects of his personality to fit the situation. He can
even play the devout Muslim for Turkish customers, the well-integrated
half-Alman for Germans, and the naive salesman for Yugos—appearing
easy to exploit, although he's already padded the price from the get-go
because he knows they'll only bite if they think they've wheedled him
down shamelessly. It's only when he's confronted with the police that his
talent for roleplay suddenly evaporates. He can only be one thing vis-à-
vis the cops. And that's brash and impertinent. Hakan doesn't know why.
It just happens. Well, no. He knows exactly why it happens. He does it
to keep from panicking. Panic means game over. You can never show
your panic to the police. And that's why Hakan has to put on a show.
Cocky is the opposite of panicked. Nothing more. But if you start to
panic, and it shows, then you've already lost. Then they think: *Oh, we've
got a panicking kanake on our hands; he's got something to hide. Let's fuck
him.* But no. Hakan's not about to get fucked. Not today. No chance.

"Young man, listen up. Since when are federal police expected to say
please when they extract an inebriated driver from the motorway?"

"Inebriated? Excuse me? I'm Muslim. I don't drink alcohol," Hakan
lies. He watches the kanaken family hurriedly packing up their things.
They leap into the two cars and speed away. Leaving Hakan here alone.
Bastards. But he can't even blame them.

"You've neither maintained the minimum distance between yourself and other vehicles, nor have you used your signal before changing
lanes. Where are you off to in such a hurry, anyway?"

"To Turkey. To my father's funeral."

The words left Hakan's mouth before he could think properly. Escaped
him. Hakan clamps his jaw shut now, but he can't retract them. They're
out there now. They've become reality.

The cold eyes of the beaver measure Hakan.

"Then you'll agree to performing a Breathalyzer test?"

"Agree to it?" Hakan snorts in irritation. "What if I don't agree?"

"Then you'll be coming with us to the station to perform a blood test," the beaver's partner says.

"Ey, Herr Officer, I don't have time for this. Like I said: I'm on my way to my father's funeral."

"Then you should have left on time, young man. There's no excuse for reckless driving."

Hakan doesn't want to even try to explain that you can't leave early enough for a kanake's funeral because kanaken are supposed to be buried on the same day. Or under special circumstances, on the next day, if their relatives have to come from far away. But that's it. After that, the body's going under the ground and if you don't make it in time, then you're shit out of luck.

"I thought there was no speed limit here?" Hakan asks instead.

"But you're still required to drive sober regardless. And this does not appear to be the case."

"Okay, fine. Gimme the thing."

The beaver motions with his head toward his colleague before heading back to their police car. The colleague remains standing, staring Hakan down with his steel-blue eyes. He's angular and slick, the kind of German man women probably find sexy. A pasty David Hasselhoff.

"Is this a 164?"

Hakan stares back at Hasselhoff blankly.

"You're driving an Alfa Romeo. That's unusual, isn't it. Only Italians drive Alfas."

"I'm half-half," Hakan replies.

"Half-half?" Hasselhoff asks.

"Half-Italian," Hakan lies, drawing an invisible line across his chest. "The better half."

The cop nods, as if he'd already suspected as much.

Of course, this pig doesn't know the Scorsese movie where Ray Liotta does the exact same thing, claiming to be half-Jewish in order to make it with a Jewish girl. And of course, he doesn't know Hakan's sister either, who's become so obsessed with the topic of their heritage lately that Hakan can already hear her voice ringing in his head, whispering: *The other half is a lie too, Hakan. You're not Turkish either.*

Until very recently, a little red cube had hung from his rearview mirror with a white crescent moon and star on it. Hakan's sure the cop would have liked to point and gawk at that as well. But ever since Hakan lent Peri his car to drive Emine to the doctor, the cube has disappeared. Hakan called Peri to ask about it, but she only said: *I've got no idea what you're talking about, Hakan. What would I want with your nasty little fascist knickknack?*

The beaver's back with his breathing apparatus. He orders Hakan to exit the vehicle. Hakan pulls up his pants and steps out of his car. He rolls back his shoulders and cracks his neck. The beaver cop puts one hand on his hip holster in warning. He stretches out his left with the device.

"Take a deep breath and exhale forcefully."

It's just like Hakan was expecting. Hasselhoff is a few centimeters taller than him, and the beaver is half a head shorter. He probably barely made the minimum height for his profession. 165 cm. Just under five foot five. Hakan knows because he'd thought about becoming a cop too. That was in a former life back when he'd still thought it might be possible to switch sides. Before the incident with the graffiti.

Hakan stares the beaver down, then reaches for the device.

"No, no. You're only going to blow while I hold onto it," the beaver says.

"Yeah, whatever," Hakan says, swallowing an *if that's the way you like it* . . .

Hakan takes a deep breath and blows into the plastic tube until he can't blow any more. It takes a long time, and he's sure the cops must be impressed with his lung capacity. He smokes, after all, and he's got a little gut on him, but they don't know about all the years he used to box. They don't realize that he could wipe the floor with both of them if he wanted to with only his bare hands. If only they didn't have their guns.

The device beeps. The beaver stares at it in disbelief.

"Zero point zero."

Hasselhoff nods as if it's all over now.

"Good, so can I get going now or what?"

"Not so fast. We only know you haven't been drinking. But that doesn't automatically mean you're in the proper state of mind to be operating this vehicle."

"What's that supposed to mean?" Hakan's getting annoyed.

Hasselhoff and the beaver exchange a blank expression.

"Do you consume drugs?"

Hakan's heart begins to race. He looks up and struggles to maintain his composure. He can't lose it now.

"You look nervous."

Hakan notices his right foot has been tapping the hot asphalt this whole time. Like some kind of coke junkie. It's gotta be the Red Bull.

"How would you know?" he asks. "You don't know me. I'm always like this," he says, trying to justify.

"And your eyes? Why are they so red?"

"Hey, guy, my father is dead!" Hakan explodes. "He just collapsed last night out of nowhere. What do you want from me?"

"Hey, hey, you just relax, okay?" Hasselhoff exclaims, extending his hand through the air like a stop sign. His other hand reaches for his hip holster.

Hakan raises both hands in the air, as if in surrender. He takes a deep breath. The Red Bull ticks like a timebomb in his throat. He's feeling sick.

"If you're not on drugs, let's take another little test just to make sure. You don't have anything to worry about, do you?" the beaver says, grinning tactlessly.

Hakan is happy now that he decided at the last minute against calling his buddy Reza and throwing together a couple grams of speed for the drive.

"Yeah, whatever. What're you gonna do? You gonna shine a light in my eyes or what?"

"That doesn't work so well in the daylight," the beaver replies. "And your eyes are too dark anyway. We can hardly even see your pupils. And besides, we've had our share of bad experiences with your people before."

Hakan can only stare at a streetlight in the distance behind the beaver, try to distract himself from the twitch in his right arm. He's thinking

about Lena. Then about the smell of the Red Bull girl. But it isn't working. All his thoughts are spiraling together, flowing into a puddle, reflecting the swollen, red beaver face of the pig standing in front of him.
Hakan wipes the sweat from his forehead. Why are they just standing
around in the direct sunlight anyway instead of trying to humiliate him
just a couple meters away in the shade? It's got to be even hotter in their
uniforms than it is for Hakan in his Jordan jersey. But maybe it's never
too hot for them. Maybe they've got blocks of fucking ice installed inside
their rib cages.

"We're going to look at our clocks. And you're going to tell us when
thirty seconds have gone by and tell us: *Stop.*"

"What now?"

"You're going to approximate the length of thirty seconds!"

"Thirty seconds are thirty seconds. What kind of test is that?"

"We're trying to establish your sense of time," Hasselhoff explains.

"My sense of time?" Hakan shakes his head. Tries to choke back his
laughter.

"What's so funny?"

"Yeah, nothing, Herr Officer. Nothing at all. Except there's an invention called a clock that tells people when thirty seconds are up, and . . ."

"Young man, we can take you straight to the station with us instead!"

"Nah, it's all good, Herr Officer. I'm counting."

The beaver nods again to Hasselhoff. He fixes his eyes on his digital
watch and says: "All right. Ready. Set. Go!"

One. Pause.

Two. Pause.

Three.

Am I counting too slow?

Four, five, six.

Am I counting too fast?

The time fuse burning in Hakan's throat. The sticky film of sweat
between his skin and his Jordan jersey. His father's gaze, down from
above, watching as the scene unfolds. The two cops, their legs spread
wide, torturing Hakan with their little game. Purely out of boredom.
Like federal police stationed on the border have nothing better to do.
His father's disappointment that his son has gotten himself caught up

in this thing like a fool. Always the same mantra: *Bu oğlan hiç adam olmayacak.* This boy will never be a man. Hakan is and will always be a loser for his father. Because Hakan got himself into this situation. Because Hakan wasn't more careful. Because Hakan caught these two pigs' eyes. For Hüseyin, it was always your own fault if you got into trouble. For Hüseyin the cops were always right because they had more power. What good did it do to say they'd been unjust? Their violence, brutal. Their scrutiny, racist. What good was it if these realizations didn't take you anywhere. If they, in the worst-case scenario, only made matters worse? The cops had the authority, and you had to obey at any cost. And if you didn't. Well. Then it was on you to deal with the consequences.

∿

The first time the cops brought Hakan home, Hüseyin's face had flushed with shame. He stood with a pinched face at the door in his pajamas, looking a few inches smaller than usual.

"I'm so sorry, I will punish him. Sorry." He said it again and again, as though it could change something. As though a 6,000-mark penalty was not going to follow. As if Hakan had not already been punished in a different way for his bad day in the ticket hall of the train station. They'd tagged *Fuck tha Police* on the wall there. *Fuck the Police* like the song by N.W.A:

Fuck tha Police comin straight from the underground
A young n**** got it bad 'cause I'm brown

Ice Cube was rapping the lyrics, but Hakan and Musti could feel them. Even though they'd never once in their lives had anything to do with the police. Even though they weren't Black and lived in Rheinstadt and not Compton. The message was still obvious. *Fuck tha Police* meant fuck this school that only existed to squander away their time until they obtained some useless diploma and wound up working in the same factories as their dads. Fuck those teachers who let their students know every day they'd rather that their fathers had never come here in the first place, or at the very least, had left their sons behind in those underdeveloped shitholes they called home. Fuck these neighborhoods, separated off from the rest of the city so they had to wander at night through some asshole of a forest on their way home, only to inevitably arrive back too late and muddy up the hallways of the matchbox-sized apartments they lived in with their filthy shoes. The floors their mothers vacuumed and scrubbed day in and day out so they didn't go crazy with boredom themselves in the seven-hundred-square-foot world they shared with their family of five. Fuck these parents, too, who only ever told them to be grateful because they didn't understand what their children went through every day at school and on the street. Who didn't know anything about life in this shit town where every shopkeeper suspected them of stealing, every teacher thought they were stupid, and every skinhead in the city center wanted to see them in the hospital or dead.

Fuck tha Police! Ey, Dejan, check it out! Hakan and Musti called out proudly. But Dejan was busy with his own piece on the wall around the corner. Dejan was a real tagger and could do real work, not just scribble words like Hakan and Musti, who'd only come along with him for a lark anyway. For a lark, and because somehow they still felt like it wasn't enough to dance and write their own rap lyrics. No, they needed to learn how to tag too, because they felt this was also a part of hip-hop culture, and they could only really be hip-hop if they could do it all. Sure, their tag was ugly, but Hakan was still proud of it. Or high on the fumes from the automotive paint they'd stolen from the hardware store earlier that day. Or both.

Ey, Dejan!

And then Dejan glanced in their direction, only one quick look, before yelling *Shit!* and taking off running. Before Hakan could even turn around someone had grabbed him, wrapped up his arms, and slammed him to the ground. Musti lay there beside him looking scared.

Shit!

∼

"Thirty. The thirty seconds are up, yeah?" Hakan asks the cops.

Hasselhoff and the beaver exchange glances. Hasselhoff checks his watch.

"That was . . . one minute and three seconds," says Hasselhoff.

The beaver clears his throat, makes a pinched expression. "We could accommodate a five-second discrepancy. But you've obviously exceeded that. I'd say there's reasonable grounds for suspicion that you've been driving under the influence of narcotics."

"Are you serious? Don't you have anything better to do right now than try to fuck me?"

Hasselhoff puts both hands on his hips.

"So, young man. Now we'll be taking you in for insulting an officer. That's already a punishable offense."

"A punishable offense? *Fuck* isn't even an insult!" Hakan screams, but the cops are already reaching for their guns, and Hakan knows it's better to keep his mouth shut now, if he wants to make it out of here. They already pulled him over for no reason. They can keep him in a jail cell overnight for no reason too. Or worse. They put Hakan into the back seat of their squad car. Hakan stares out the window at his Alfa, where it remains behind in the empty parking lot.

At the station, they make Hakan piss into a cup. And then they make him wait. He sits alone among a row of metal chairs, breathing through his mouth. Staring at the beige wall in front of him.

He doesn't look at the uniformed legs marching up and down the hallway. He doesn't look at the rubber floor. Not through the crack of the half-open door to the office, where the fax machine is chirping and beeping away. He doesn't look at the clock. Anything but the clock.

Hakan's getting dizzy breathing through his mouth, but he's still trying to float away from this place in his thoughts. A young blonde and her boyfriend are seated next to him now, arguing about some other guy. Supposedly this guy had groped her. Her boyfriend is saying she shouldn't wear that dress anymore in the future. It's a red dress.

An older man takes a seat. He's wearing a full suit in the middle of summer. Tiny hairs are growing out of his gigantic ears. There's a stack of papers rattling in the old man's hands. Each time a cop hustles past them, he nods, smiling, and says: "Grüß Gott," as if he were their fucking cousin.

Two women in headscarves and a child sit down as well. The women look worried, whisper together in a language Hakan can't place. The kid makes a gun with his hand and aims it at Hakan. Hakan stares back at the child. The kid has long, thick eyelashes, framing his eyes like barbed wire around precious, imperiled jewels. Hakan smiles softly and shakes his head. The kid only shrugs and maintains this imagined pistol trained on Hakan. Hakan points with his head toward the half-opened office door, behind which a cop is sitting in front of his PC typing absentmindedly. The kid's eyes scan the office door before returning to Hakan. There's a conspiratorial nod. The pistol zeros in on the cop in the other room.

Everybody comes, waits, is called in, leaves again. Minutes pass. Or hours. Or days. Hakan has lost all concept of time. He just sits there, never looking at the clock. His gaze is trapped by the beige wall in front of him, his hands knotted over one another to keep them from acting up on their own. So they don't find their way around the beaver's neck as he walks back and forth in the hallway, purposely ignoring Hakan.

Hakan forgets for a moment that he shouldn't use his nose, only a moment, and then there it is. The penetrating reek of the old dusty rubber flooring. The sweat of an untold number of uniformed bodies. The stuffy air of overheated copy and fax machines. The stench of a building whose only purpose is to make people like Hakan feel unsafe.

Hakan closes his eyes. He sees Musti again, lying beside him. The fear in his eyes. *Shit!* He sees Dejan sprinting like mad around the corner. Hakan lies on the ground. There in the empty Rheinstadt train station, in the middle of the night, in the middle of summer vacation. Everything smells like their spray paint. They're putting him in cuffs and Musti too. They drag them upright, shove them against the wall. The pigs read their tag out loud. *Fuck tha Police. Fuck tha Police. You think we don't know what that means, you little cumin sacks? Fuck tha Police?* The wooden table at the police station slams into Hakan's face next. Or was it the other way around? *Fuck tha Police.* The fax machine beeping in the background, spewing out an endless stream of paper, information about people accused of doing something, people who probably did do something more dangerous than spraying automotive paint on the train station. *Fuck tha Police.* The lighter and the ten-mark bill they find in Hakan's pocket. *Fuck tha Police.* The ten-mark bill tastes like dust and lead. *Fuck tha Police*, the green lighter's pointy corners all but sticking in his throat. Hakan gagging. *Fuck tha Police.* They tell him: *Strip.* Hakan doesn't want to. Hakan wants to know what they've done with Musti. *Fuck tha Police.* They tell him: *Now.* Hakan doesn't want to. They say: *We're going to search you.* Hakan doesn't want to. *Fuck tha Police.* They do it anyway. Search him. Probe him. Reach into his innermost sanctums. They say they're looking for evidence. Evidence of what? Do they think he's got a fucking can of spray paint shoved in there? What kind of evidence? Evidence of his guilt? Evidence of his offense. His failures. His sins. His mistakes. His disobedience. His fear? *Fuck tha Police.* They search inside him, probing for his fragility, for what he holds most dear, most holy. To crush it with their rending fingers. Searching for his pride. *Fuck tha Police.* They search and search but they'll never find it. Hakan's hidden away inside himself, inside his innermost core. Hidden away in the darkest corner of the labyrinth gaping inside him. *Fuck tha Police.* He slinks into every corner, turns out every light. He's never coming back; a part of him will always be here now in this darkness. *Fuck tha Police.* No matter what, they won't win. They won't get to him. How long will they keep searching? Hakan doesn't want to know what they're saying. He doesn't listen. He tunes it out. He only wants it to be over. Only wants it to be over forever. For no one to ever know. Not Musti. Not his father. No one. *Fuck tha Police.* Not a soul knows. No one will ever hear of it. Because what good would that do? It would do nothing. But he did tell his father. Only a tenth of it, max. He told him, and it had done nothing. Because the cops were always right. The pigs always have more power. They are the power. And you had to obey.

Fuck.

"Ah, there you are, young man."

Hakan opens his eyes. The beaver's standing there in front of him, his backpack already slung over his shoulder, ready to clock out.

"I thought you'd already left. I've been looking for you for hours now." He tries to make his lies seem plausible. Hands Hakan back his driver's license. "This is for you. Your tests have come back clean."

Hakan has to swallow. He rubs his hands against his shorts.

"And how do I get back to my car now?" He regrets the question immediately. Because he already knows the answer. The pig couldn't give a shit.

Back outside the station, Hakan hails a cab and pays him 50 marks to take him back out to the rest stop. An entire tank of gas. Shredded. Out the window. Just like that. Hakan gets back into his Alfa. It's almost six o'clock. He should be just before Ljubljana by now. They've robbed him of four hours. Four. Hakan can feel a tingle in his shoulder. The disappointment in his father's eyes. He keeps the radio off and remains obediently in the right lane.

But his body's getting away from him. Becoming one with the Alfa. The Austrian guards check his toll pass and wave him through. A white Porsche Carrera whizzes past him. Hakan feels nothing. He just wants to get away from here. He doesn't want any more trouble.

The case of Marlboro on the back seat of the car. Thirty ten-mark bills in his fanny pack. Hakan unzips the bag to check they're still all there. Runs his finger over the wad of cash. He just wants to cross the next border and be back in a place where he knows how to solve his problems. Hakan knows Yugos. He knows Ivi. Goran. Dragan. He doesn't know any Austrians. Not a single one. Or wait. He does know one: Adolf Hitler.

Hakan stares out the side window, then back at the street. Mountains. Churches. Mountains. Churches. Mountains. He has to think about his mother. How years ago she'd said she finally wanted to leave Hüseyin and move away. Hakan and Peri had tried to reason with her: *Anne, what are you even talking about? Where do you want to go?* Emine only glared at them, stone cold, and said: *To Austria.* Hakan had no idea what his mother saw in Austria. A useless appendix of Germany, just slightly more depressing.

Hakan once had a girlfriend, Hülya. She lives in Graz with her husband now. Her eyes were the color of kiwi skin, and she was the only kanakin

Hakan had ever been with. Hakan was sixteen at the time and used to meet her every morning before school in a park at the other end of town so they could make out without any interruptions. When he'd slowly put one hand up her shirt, he'd paused halfway to make sure Hülya liked it. She'd told him: *Stop.* And he had stopped. Hülya dumped him later with the explanation: She did not like timid boys.

It's grown dark now. The Slovenian border guards don't even look at Hakan's face. But Hakan does: he sees his own face in the rearview mirror, the sadness hanging under his eyes like two sodden teabags. The officer stamps his passport and shoves it back through the narrow opening in the glass window. The Alfa pushes onward and Hakan's body dissolves into a limp mass. Exhaustion is kicking in. His gas tank is already in the red. Hakan exits the highway, fills up, runs a lap around the rest stop to at least wake up his legs. It's only after he's back in the Alfa, making his way back onto the highway, that he notices the giant illuminated letters on the neon gas station sign: HIP-HOP.

~

That night, when the cops took Hakan home, it was obvious he wouldn't be allowed to go to the casting call the next day. Obvious that he would be spending the remaining two weeks of his summer vacation at home. That he wouldn't get to see Musti, talk to him on the phone, or so much as ask whether they'd done the same things to him. And it was also clear to Hakan now that the wind had changed directions in his home. Hüseyin was beside himself. After the police dumped Hakan off at home like a pile of trash, he'd been afraid that he might see his father cry. Hüseyin looked so terrified at the sight of policemen at his door. Submissively, he had apologized again, stammered, begged over and over for forgiveness for his son's behavior.

Hakan couldn't bear to see his father act that way. He didn't want Hüseyin to be weak. He wanted Hüseyin to be like he always was: proud and unflinching. You know, like fathers were. Fortunately, the fear vanished from Hüseyin's eyes the moment the apartment door swung closed, and they could hear the heavy boots of the policemen

departing. Hüseyin grabbed Hakan roughly by his collar. That was easier to bear. Hüseyin dragged him into the living room.

There, he closed the door carefully behind him, because no matter
how angry he was, he was always mindful of his sleeping wife and children. For a shift worker like Hüseyin, sleep was the holiest of holies.
He stretched himself up to his full height over Hakan. What was Hakan
thinking? Did he have no respect for everything his father had done for
him? How Hüseyin had come here without a penny or a single word
of German to his name only so his son could make something more
of himself. How he had worked himself to death over the years for his
children. How Hakan was spitting on all of this now. How Hakan was
spitting on Hüseyin. How he was ruining all of this, everything, sham-
ing his father in front of the entire world.

"But all we did was draw something," Hakan said.

Hüseyin opened his bloodshot eyes wide and clenched his fist. He
raised his balled fist in the air, but only high enough to rest his chin.
Hüseyin closed his eyes and clicked his tongue. It was obvious that
he was struggling with himself to keep from striking his son. Hakan
almost wanted Hüseyin to do it.

"Do you know what they do in Turkey to people who paint words
on the walls?" Hüseyin bellowed instead, momentarily forgetting the
others' sleep.

"Yes, I know," Hakan replied.

"Oh, do you?"

Hakan hung his head. He ran his fingers over the throbbing lump on
his forehead. He showed it to Hüseyin.

Hüseyin clicked his tongue again. "What is this, Hakan?" he asked.

"They beat me, Baba."

Hüseyin's face went blank. He stared away. Anywhere. He didn't
want to look at his son's injury. Didn't want to know what they had
done. He only stared out into emptiness. "Why do you tell me these
things?"

Hakan thought: *Yeah, why am I telling my father this?* He didn't have an
answer himself. Hakan merely stared back at Hüseyin, who continued
avoiding his eyes.

Hüseyin took a few tired steps toward his armchair, faced in the direction of the television and the display cabinet with their crystal glasses and the encyclopedias. The chair in which only Hüseyin ever sat, set apart from the remaining furniture set and the rest of his family. Hüseyin hadn't even been fifty yet, back then, but at that hour long past midnight, he suddenly looked like an old man. White stubble sprouted from his defeated face. Silver gleamed in the thickness of his eyebrows. His loose pajamas made his body—the body of a great man—appear much smaller than it was. The metalworks burdened his shoulders like an invisible weight, bending, contorting his figure toward the ground.

"Why do you tell me this, Hakan?" Hüseyin repeated. "To humiliate me even more?" He settled into his chair beside the little table with the bowl of walnut shells from the evening before. He stared blindly at the blank screen of the television. He was impossibly distant, only his voice still sounded chafed and hurt. Hakan looked away, staring down at the flowers in the rug.

"No, Baba," he said. "I didn't want to humiliate you. I only told you so you would know."

"And now?" Hüseyin demanded. Hakan's eyes followed the pattern of the carpet, observing how it formed one giant flower out of the many tiny blooms.

"What does it change for me to know?" Hüseyin's metallic voice droned on. "What should I do now with this knowledge? Tell me, Hakan."

Hakan shrugged. He tried repeating his father's words in his head, hoping to better understand them himself. But he understood nothing.

"Why do you put me in such a situation?" Hüseyin demanded. "Where I can do nothing. Do you not understand? Why must you show me that I can do nothing? Where should I go? Where should I complain? Should I go back to the police? To report the police? What do you want from me?"

Hüseyin's questions spiraled around Hakan's head. Every question ended in a crater into which the beginnings of all possible answers disappeared. Like pennies in a chewing gum machine. Like water balloons from the rooftop of their apartment house in those summers before

Hakan and Musti had started dancing in those cramped rooms at the
Youth Center. Hakan's eyes were lost in the fabric of the rug.

He only looked up briefly to avoid growing dizzy under his throbbing forehead. Saw Hüseyin sitting there in his striped pajamas at three
in the morning, trying to tell his son in ever more broken sentences that
he could not protect him. Saw Hüseyin's own shame. Watched Hüseyin losing these priceless hours of sleep before he'd have to go back to
the assembly line at six. Hakan stared back at the floor, ashamed himself of everything he'd seen when he'd looked at his father.

"I thought we would come here and everything would be different,"
he heard Hüseyin continue. "I thought such things don't happen here.
But of course, they happen here. They happen everywhere. Why did
you give them this opportunity, Hakan? Why did you give them a reason to treat you this way? If you weren't out hanging around all night
doing God knows what, they could not have done this to you! I can
do nothing, oğlum. Even if I could speak their language, no one would
hear me. It would only make more problems for us. You will just have
to forget it. Do you hear me, Hakan? You will forget it! And I will forget
it. And you will finally learn to be a man."

By the end of the night, it seemed to Hakan that he himself had
shrunk, curled up in a ball on his bed, listening to Ümit's breathing—
Ümit, who in reality was wide awake, lying just across from Hakan on
the other bed in their tiny bedroom. It was like everything had clenched
together. Compressed. Like he had grown microscopically small over
the past few hours. Meaningless. Hakan felt like a bacterium. Like a speck
of dust lying among the shag of the rug, his entire existence spent waiting until someone vacuumed him up and disappeared him with one
single final movement. Shame does this to a person. Makes you feel this
tiny, this small. When your only consolation is the thought that you're
invisible to everyone else around you anyway. That it doesn't matter
what you do. That no one cares. As long as you stay quiet. On the bottom. You piece of shit.

Hakan stayed grounded in the room he shared with Ümit for the rest
of the summer. He wasn't allowed to see anyone. Wasn't allowed to

call anyone. He started writing his thoughts down in rhymes to keep from going crazy with the loneliness that was devouring him. Little Ümit only stared at him with sympathetic eyes. He offered Hakan his favorite toy car. Hakan put on his headphones and hissed: *Piss off.*

He didn't hear about Musti until the first day of school. After cramming his things together and starting off early to meet Musti like he always did, Emine made the announcement as Hakan was heading out the door.

That Musti wasn't here anymore. *Wait, what do you mean, he isn't here?* Musti's father, Cemil Amca, sent him back to Turkey. To his uncle in Sinop. He was living there now. Hakan's mother's words hit him like an electric shock. The top of his skull was buzzing. He thought he'd gotten the worst of it after his conversation with his father, after not being allowed to take part in the casting. But when he heard about Cemil Amca's punishment for Musti, Hakan's own seemed like a joke. Cemil Amca had topped everything. He'd actually followed through on the threats he was always making. And yeah, Cemil Amca was abusive. He had an anger problem. He beat his wife and children sometimes without any provocation. But Hakan hadn't thought he would take things this far. He only knew that Cemil Amca often threatened Musti with this punishment, that he would send him back to Turkey if he didn't stop his foolish breakdancing. That was günah—a sin—one of the devil's many tricks. Musti hadn't taken him seriously either. He and Hakan had laughed about it. They'd even decided to name their crew the *Dirty Devils*: Breakdancers in Satan's Service. But when the cops took Musti home, Cemil Amca had been forced to take action. At the very latest, after he heard about the impending fines. According to Hüseyin: a year's savings.

Hakan fell into a kind of trance. It consumed the first day of school. The second. The first week. The month. The year. He knew his father was not like Musti's father. He knew he should be grateful that Hüseyin was not this way. And yet it also broke Hakan's heart to know now and forever just how helpless his own father was. He never wanted to see Hüseyin that way again. He never wanted to remind him again that he could neither truly protect nor really punish his own son. Hakan needed to forget.

And so, henceforth he made an effort to avoid any conflict with his father. To cause as little offense as possible at home. He tried to hide anything about himself Hüseyin might not approve of. Until ultimately, Hakan had no more personality of his own. Until he wandered around the house like a transparent being. Like Casper the Ghost.

~

The streetlights end after Zagreb. The undulating waves of sky and earth have the same color here, melting into a single dark-gray sea. There's nothing outside the circle of the Alfa's headlights on the pavement. The white stripes separating lanes fly by to the left of the vehicle, one after another. Providing the illusion of safety in the night. Security from death. As if one single, tiny motion wouldn't suffice to ram your life against the guardrails. Or against another life. If it weren't for the fact that Hakan's Alfa is the only car for far and wide in this nonplace on the road to Slavonski Brod. Hakan has to think about the country roads back home around Rheinstadt. Roads he often drives at night on his way home. It's just as dark there. To the left and right, only the black shadows of tall, slender trees. And then that awful road sign on the edge of the street, illuminated only for an instant by the Alfa's headlights before it disappears again. Hakan could easily look away. But he'd still know about it anyway. He knows the sign is there and he knows what it says. Its mere existence suffices every time to remind Hakan how close his own demise is lurking. Four vultures, sitting on a branch, and over them, the words: *Hello Speeder, We're Waiting*.

Those feathers are already circling in Hakan's mind. The rushing sound of water. Waves. Ocean. A faint whistling pierces through the noise. A familiar beeping. More like a ringtone. A tinny melody. His Panasonic! Hakan doesn't see it. It's not there. He tries to orient himself. Why is the sound so far away? Where is his Panasonic? Where is Hakan? Everything is dark. Gray. Like the screen of an unplugged television. He tries to emerge from the dark water. Tries to free himself from the grip of the waves that keep pushing him down. It rings again. The ringing is getting closer, then further away from his ears. It's thunderous now. He's almost there. Hakan remains floating only for a moment longer, allows the heaviness above to hold him down. It would feel so good to just remain under this weight. If only he didn't know he had to hurry.

Hakan's forehead slams against his steering wheel. His skull rattles like someone shaking a piggybank. He looks around, gasping for air. The sunlight is blinding. Cars are flying past him with strange, unfamiliar license plates. His Alfa is pulled over on the side of the motorway. There's no sign of an accident. But he must have been asleep. He had been asleep. He's parked beside a roadside vendor selling melons. A blue plastic tarp, giant crates of produce, and a homemade sign. Cyrillic writing. When did Hakan cross the border into Serbia? He can't remember.

His Panasonic rings again on the passenger seat beside him. A number with a Turkish country code blinks on the screen. Hakan can taste the dust on his tongue.

"Hallo?"

"Ey, man, where are you?" It's Peri's irritated voice. "I thought you were coming last night. I called you a thousand times from every fucking pay phone in the city."

Hakan fishes a cigarette from his fanny pack. "I missed my flight."

"What? You too?" Peri demands.

"What do you mean, *you too*?"

"Sevda," Peri explains. "Sevda forgot her passport. She's just landing today. But she's too late."

"Shit!" Hakan exclaims, already imagining how his mother will flay Sevda alive later that night. He lights up. Maybe Emine will be too exhausted to do the same to him if Sevda gets there first, he thinks, and he immediately feels ashamed of this thought.

"And you? When are you landing?"

Hakan considers a moment. "At nine," he throws out haphazardly.

"At nine? Tonight? Hey, guy, wasn't there an earlier flight? You only need a single seat. Go back to the airport and wait till something frees up. There's always bound to be some no show," Peri instructs him over the line.

"Yeah, good idea," Hakan says, staring through his windshield, searching for some point of reference to figure out where exactly he is right now. But there's not even a street sign. Middle of nowhere. Hakan can only see the sleepy melon salesman scratching his belly while car after car whizzes past him on the road.

"Are you going somewhere right now? It's so loud," Peri exclaims.

"Yeah, I've gotta take care of something."

"At six in the morning?"

"Ey, Peri, I've got shit to do, yeah?" Hakan stalls.

"None of your bullshit, Hakan. Don't leave me here alone. Anne's flipping out. I can't take it anymore . . ."

"Yeah, man. It's all good. But, Peri . . ." Hakan trails off, trying to think of what he should say next.

"What?"

"Ey. You think Baba ever got beat up by the police?"

"What? Where are you getting that from?"

"I've just been thinking the whole time. He got so weird whenever it had to do with the police. Like he was scared shitless of them, y'know?" Hakan suggests.

Peri snorts. "Aren't all foreigners scared of cops?"

"Nah," Hakan says. "But that's not what I mean. It was more than that. You know, like he already knew exactly what could happen. Like he'd already been through it with the pigs himself."

"Yeah, well," Peri says. "Baba was in the Turkish Army. He was stationed in Kurdistan . . ."

"What do you want now with Kurdistan?" Hakan interrupts, shaking his head stubbornly. "Why do you always have to bring that shit up, Peri? I asked you a completely different question."

"Nah, man," Peri hisses. "You asked me precisely that: Why was Baba scared of men in uniform? Maybe because he used to be one himself. Just think about it."

"What does that have to do with Kurds, Peri? You talk such fucking bullshit sometimes."

"Ey, fuck off, Hakan, okay!" Peri exclaims. "Talking to you's like pissing against a fucking wall. Now get your ass to the airport. Go."

Hakan wipes his forehead on his jersey. His whole body feels empty, like a useless, sweaty shell of meat. He really fucked up now. There's no way he'll make it to Istanbul before nine. He wishes he could just turn around now and drive back to Lena. Back to her perfect little world. Put on some romantic comedy and fall asleep before the lovers' first clumsy encounter. Wake up two days later. It would feel every bit as useless as arriving four hours after his father's funeral in Istanbul. But he can't do that. He's gotta make an appearance. Peri will never forgive him if he doesn't. Nor will his mother.

Hakan takes a fresh pair of socks out of the duffel bag behind the passenger seat and swaps them out for the nasty things he's currently got on his feet. The feel of the fuzzy cotton on his heels is almost as good as a shower. He sprays himself under the arms with his deodorant and starts the car. He pulls a little closer to the melon stand.

"Komshija," Hakan yells out the window. "Bulgaristan, what way?"

The salesman chews his gum in boredom. Then he raises two fingers like a peace sign. "Dva marks," he says.

Hakan buys a melon for two marks and drives off in the direction the chubby fingers of the salesman are pointing. Against the sun.

Peri's been on the same kick now for months. Somehow, she's convinced herself that she's Kurdish. It's ridiculous. Like that's something you can just decide for yourself. Hüseyin's father wasn't Kurdish. He was an orphan from the Caucasus. He'd just been raised by a Kurdish family. Or something like that. So, Peri can't be Kurdish because that's something you inherit from your father's side. Everyone knows that. And no one in Hakan's family speaks a word of Kurdish. Not even Sevda. Even though she grew up in their village in the mountains. Hakan had only heard his parents speak Kurdish a few times when he'd been really little and they'd spoken over the phone with relatives. But Hüseyin had never said that they were Kurdish. He'd also never said a word about the Kurds whenever they were on TV. Any time a few soldiers got offed somewhere. Hüseyin just slumped there silently in his chair, watching the news. He never said a word. He didn't want anything to do with it. So why the hell does Peri want it so badly?

As if it weren't enough to be a kanake in Germany. Did you have to suddenly become a kanake in Turkey too? Peri sometimes says Hakan should quit making everything about being a kanake. *You're so much more than that. Why don't you take some agency over who you want to be? Why do you just accept the role they force on you?* Yeah, yeah. And maybe she was right. Maybe Hakan is more. But if he could choose what he was and what he wanted to be for himself, Kurdish wouldn't even make it on the list.

Hakan's seen what that means on TV. Squatting somewhere in the mountains with your gun and trying to take out a couple of soldiers even though it's way more likely you'll get killed yourself. Like fighting with a homemade slingshot against the second most powerful army in NATO. Where's that supposed to take you? Yeah, exactly: six feet under the dirt. And no, Hakan's not some fasci, either, even though Peri had said he was just because he'd hung a Turkish flag on his rearview mirror. Hakan's just a realist. And the reality is simple: everyone needs a flag that means something to them.

And if you were to believe the other men in Hakan's favorite café, Kurdish people weren't even a thing. They did not exist. They were all just Turks. Turks who had been lurking for so long in isolation in the mountains they'd made up a few traditions of their own and taken to speaking some unintelligible dialect. The whole idea of a separate Kurdish people was just a conspiracy made up to undermine the Turkish state. An American plot. A Greek one. Whatever.

To be honest, these theories seem ridiculous to Hakan too. They sound more like the amcas in the café had puffed down a few too many doobies and were getting paranoid. But at the end of the day, Hakan doesn't care whether there are Kurds or not. He doesn't care what other people say about it either. At the end of the day, Hakan just wants to live a normal life. Take the woman he loves out to a nice dinner every now and then, pay his rent, and not answer to a boss. Yeah, just never have a boss.

It wasn't like Hakan had chosen to be a kanake. Like he wouldn't rather have just been some inconspicuous nobody who could manage to make it on time to his father's funeral because the cops didn't decide to accuse him out of the blue of being a junkie or a dealer. Someone with a degree or some certificate to show for himself. Someone who didn't get fired after a year by his Nazi shift manager with the nose hair. Someone who didn't get prodded and provoked day in and day out at work until he finally lost it and threw his cigarette butt into the dumpster after all. The one with the chemical waste.

Hakan can still remember sitting on pins and needles at home, wondering how to tell his father he'd been fired. It was the holiday season; Hüseyin just assumed Hakan had some time off. Sevda was living with them because her apartment in Salzhagen had burned down. Now that he thinks about it, it was a funny kind of coincidence that first Sevda's house and then his factory had burned. Even if the fire in the factory hadn't been as big of a deal because his Nazi boss had caught wind of it in time. But Hakan wasn't thinking of Sevda when he flicked his cigarette into the dumpster. Not about little Cem or Bahar either. He hadn't thought of anyone or anything; his body acted entirely on impulse, as if it were the most natural thing in the world to want to see the whole fucking place go up in flames. As if this fire were Hakan's one opportunity to not become like his father. Like it was an act of self-defense.

Hakan crept back to his workstation, and a few minutes later there was a huge bang and the fire alarms went off. No one was injured. No one had seen Hakan. But it didn't even take two days before they put him in their sights at work anyway. There were enough asshole coworkers to report that Hakan hadn't been at his station right before the fire broke out. And others who'd observed him constantly breaking the no-smoking rule in the courtyard.

To keep his head above water after he got fired, Hakan had taken to selling various things that had fallen off delivery trucks. Entertainment centers, televisions, that kind of thing. He got his hands on a big fancy video camera just before New Year's. The kind news reporters carried around. He wanted to test it out a little bit before he sold it, and so he started filming his family.

This is not a New Year's dinner. We do not celebrate New Year's, Emine said into the camera before noticing Hakan was filming.

She'd heard at the mosque that a devout family shouldn't celebrate New Year's. And so she'd forbidden them from mentioning the term at home and decided to make a goose instead of the roast turkey every family on Turkish television seemed to eat on New Year's. She said it wouldn't be the classic New Year's dinner then, just an ordinary evening. But because she'd never made a roast goose before in her tiny, dimly lit ground-floor apartment—of course it was more special than an ordinary evening. When Emine finally did notice the camera, she turned her back to him and grabbed two bottles of cola from the fridge. Not Topstar Cola, but two bottles of real Coca-Cola that she carried out into the living room to where the others were already gathered around the table. Another thing that would never happen on an ordinary evening. Hakan recorded everything, hoping to capture a few moments he could later cut into a little movie. But the recording only showed still, silent figures. People who neither spoke nor moved. All of them sat there stiffly as if they were posing for a complicated photo shoot. Hüseyin laid his arm awkwardly around Ümit. Ümit shouted *cheese*, Sevda tugged erratically at Bahar's hair, pulling her onto her lap while glaring daggers at Cem for sticking out his tongue. Peri hid her face behind one hand just like she always did in pictures before eventually cutting herself from the printed photograph entirely with a pair of scissors.

You could hear Hakan's voice saying over and over again to act *natural*. And the more often he said it, the stiffer and more artificial their smiles and their upright postures became. At some point, the room filled with smoke, and you could hear Emine screaming from the kitchen before the video ended. Hakan should have kept filming. Shown the scorched goose and Emine's foul mood. That would have been the real deal, perfect for the movie he'd wanted to make. His mother, frantically casting poisonous accusations in every direction, until everyone silently left the table and she sat there by herself with her burned goose and her misery.

∼

Hakan only has half of his supply of ten-mark bills remaining when he arrives in Kapıkule. He gave away his last pack of Marlboros to a Bulgarian officer just before the Turkish border who claimed he actually needed a translation of his car insurance forms. What a load of crap. The excuses cops make up to hassle you never stop, no matter where you go. But Hakan prefers adhering to an unwritten law that everybody follows over obeying a written law that applies to some but not to others. Hakan parks his Alfa and enters the first mosque after the Turkish border to freshen up in the washroom. An attendant shuffles past him, responding to his greeting with a murmur. The smell of chlorine in the washroom reminds Hakan of his mother's desperation. When he hears the azan, Hakan has to think of his father's helplessness. He hurries back to his Alfa, hoping to make the last spurt in two hours. But when he reaches the first gecekondus outside the Istanbul city limits, the darkening sky is already staining purple, the color of those shoes Musti used to have to wear. The shoes Hakan had ridiculed him for mercilessly.

After his disappearance, Musti called Hakan a couple times. But he always sounded so sad on the telephone. His voice started to quiver after the first couple sentences, and eventually, it always grew silent on the line.

"Ey, guy, what are you sniveling about? Are you some kind of girl now or what?" Hakan asked. It hadn't really been an accusation. It was just the way they used to talk when Musti was still living in Rheinstadt. But it didn't work anymore over the phone. The exchange of faces and hand gestures that could have explained away the brutality of the words was missing. There wasn't a fist to punch Musti affectionately on the shoulder to tell him: *Ey, man, pull yourself together, I've still got your back.*

After those couple calls, Hakan didn't hear from Musti again for years. Maybe because Musti was ashamed. Or maybe because he didn't want to hear about Hakan's life or Rheinstadt anymore. The narrow confines of that place he and Hakan had hated together for so long. A place he probably missed terribly now because it had still been his home. A home he could no longer return to after he turned eighteen because his residence permit would expire. And what would Musti have had to report anyway if he had called again? He was probably just moping around in the oppressive heat of some Black Sea village, listening to the soul-sucking buzz of invisible mosquitos around his ears. Musti couldn't possibly have known that Hakan was every bit as bored to death in Rheinstadt. Because a place was only home if you had someone there who understands you.

But now, Musti had turned a page. He didn't live in that little village anymore. He lived in Antalya. Lived a life Hakan could only dream of. They talked two or three times a year on the phone. Musti sent Hakan pictures stuffed in a plastic Fujifilm photo album. He looked good. Muscular and tanned in oversized Karl Kani shorts and the newest Nike sneakers. Pretty girls on his arm in triangle bikini tops. Some of the pictures showed them posing at night on boats with beer bottles in their hands, hot red lights, and dilated pupils. Musti had opened a shop in downtown Antalya, an internet café. When he first told Hakan about his plan a few years back and asked if Hakan wanted to invest—buy a couple of computers—Hakan had waved him off and said it was all just a pipe dream. Hakan could not have imagined then that now, only two summers later, the whole world would be hanging out in these cafés. But he was happy for his friend. Musti rented an apartment on Lara Beach. He drove to work shirtless on his moped, breathing the salt air.

Musti had invited Hakan to visit a million times. Hakan was only waiting for the right time, when money wouldn't be as tight, because he didn't want to just show up in Antalya like a loser and mooch off Musti's wallet. He wanted to buy a couple rounds himself at night if he was gonna do it. But now, after everything that's happened, Hakan can only wonder: What if the right time never comes? What if something always comes up instead and Hakan misses his chance to visit Musti and remember the good old days together with boat parties and crowds of half-naked girls?

Maybe now is as good a time as any. Maybe Hakan can take off after a few days in Istanbul and just keep driving to Antalya. That would do him good after this whole ordeal with his father. Of course, it would have a bit of a weird aftertaste. Of course, you weren't supposed to be out partying while you were in mourning. How was that going to look?

But on the other hand, everyone mourned differently, in their own way. Just for once, couldn't you just say fuck it to what everyone else was always expecting from you? Couldn't you finally just stop with the theatrics, now after your own baba was dead: stop putting on this show for the whole world and finally just do what you wanted to do? Hakan didn't want to have to play the eldest son whom everyone depends on. The one who had to be strong. The one who had to assume the role as the head of the family now that Hüseyin was dead. The one who always had to say the final word before every decision. Hakan doesn't want the last word. No, he really doesn't. The night before last, after Peri called his Panasonic and explained the news about Baba in a few barren sentences, he rushed home clear across Rheinstadt. Rushed back to Emine. And Emine sat there stiffly, all alone amid the furniture in their living room. Hüseyin's chair just sitting there beside her. And she said: *Hakan. Do you think it is a good idea to bury him in Istanbul?*

And Hakan, standing there breathless in the doorway, staring down at the convoluted flower pattern on the carpet, would have loved to just say: *I have no idea, Anne. I'm so terribly afraid of standing at his grave. I can't do it. I don't want to go.*

But instead, he'd just stared down at the carpet and said stolidly and as if reciting the words from memory: *Yes, that's a good idea. Verily he belongs to Allah, and verily to Allah shall he return. Allah is with Baba, wherever he may be.*

Empty words for Emine to nod along to, as if entranced. That was just what she'd wanted to hear. And that was what Hakan had given her.

～

Hakan has to circle around the block three times before he finds a parking spot. He exits the car, and the humid air of the city slaps a new layer of sweat across his face and neck right there on the spot. He extends his arms toward the murky nighttime sky, knots his fingers together, stretching his body after thirty-three hours folded together in the same position.

A group of men are seated in front of a café watching him. Inspecting his Alfa. Puzzling over his foreign license plate in the varying cadences of their different dialects before moving on to discuss the car's Italian craftmanship. Their faces are dried out and worn. Hakan thinks how these old men probably know everything there is to know about their world and yet Italy remains as unattainable to them as the surface of the moon. He stares at the crumbling facade of the building, at the multicolored ornamental curtains hanging from the open windows. Sees the piercing glare of the uncomfortably white light bulbs passing through the fabric. His eyes sweep back to the withered men on the sidewalk. Had Hüseyin consorted with them when he chose his apartment? Had they chatted, exchanged tips about this neighborhood that looked a little shabby but not nearly as decrepit as the gecekondus he'd passed through on his way into the city? He'd like to take a seat with them himself now, call them all Amca, and smoke bitter Samsun cigarettes with them until his stomach turned. He'd like to sit with them here the way he never sat with Hüseyin. But Hakan pops his trunk instead, empties the vehicle, slings his gym bag over one shoulder, takes the Serbian melon in his other arm, and heads for the door. He can't afford another detour now.

Hakan presses the top buzzer beside the last name Yılmaz on the nameplate. The windowless stairwell is as cold as a refrigerator. The building seems old but well built, with only one suspicious crack in the inner wall that needs to be plastered over. Hakan carries his bag up to the fifth floor, wondering how his father had planned on climbing this steep staircase every day with his busted knee. Whether Hüseyin had simply believed his knee would heal on its own after he stopped working and started taking care of himself again.

Hakan pauses for a moment at the top of the stairs before pushing his way through the already half-opened door. It's strangely quiet behind this door, considering how many shoes are piled in front of it. He knocks on the doorframe, opens the door wider, and sees Ümit standing forlornly in the hallway in front of him. His eyes are red, and his skin is as pale as his faded T-shirt.

"Abi," Ümit says and nothing more. But the way he says it, it's like he's pleading with Hakan to take him away from here.

Hakan puts his arm around Ümit quickly, slaps him hard on the shoulder twice, and proceeds into the apartment, although his feet would much rather turn around and hurry back the way he came. He can feel the muscles tightening around his heart. He treads carefully. The darkened hall of the apartment constricts until Hakan feels like he's tumbling down the sweaty muzzle of some colossal beast.

Hakan doesn't want to be here. He doesn't want to think about his father dying here. Where he lay on the floor. Where his heart first seized up. Where he realized that he would never see his family again. Hakan's stomach is in knots. He wants to run back down the stairs, hop into his Alfa, and just drive away. Keep driving. But he puts one foot in front of the other, and soon enough, the apartment swallows him and spits him back out in the middle of a battlefield.

Sevda's sitting on a giant sofa, staring up at him with glazed eyes. She only greets him with a blink. She doesn't seem capable of anything more. A few loose hairs are peeking out of her bun, frizzing upward toward the ceiling. Her blouse and the matching pants she's wearing in the same shade of beige are wrinkled from her journey. She doesn't look like she's been here for very long. There's a giant handbag at her feet with a shiny black finish.

Peri and Cem are sitting beside Sevda. How old has Cem just turned? Ten? Eleven? Cem's eyes light up when he catches sight of Hakan. His scrawny upper body stretches upright hopefully. They haven't hung out since spring. Hakan had to pick up a car somewhere close to Hanover and actually only wanted to stop in real quick to see his sister in Salzhagen on the way back. But Sevda asked him to stay the evening and watch her kids. They'd stayed up till midnight playing Gameboy and eating ice cream. When he left the next morning, Cem had begged Hakan to take him with him to Rheinstadt. Sevda stood by silently. *Next time*, Hakan had promised Cem. Hakan feels like he can read the words, *Next time is today*, in Cem's eyes now.

Slowly, Cem's eyes sink and hover about Hakan's left arm. Hakan follows his gaze and remembers the Serbian melon. He walks two paces into the room to an enormous wooden table and carefully places the melon in the center. He looks at Peri. She forms a silent *Hallo* with her lips followed by a half smile. She looks more awake than she did yesterday morning when she departed for the airport with the others. But she still looks stressed. She's sitting stiff as a statue, like she's on high alert. After a moment, she abandons her half-attempt at a smile and rolls her eyes and arches her brows in Emine's direction, as if trying to convey a secret warning to Hakan.

Hakan's eyes wander slowly across the room to Emine. She's glowering in the armchair in the corner of the room. She doesn't even look at him. But it's not like she isn't there. More like she's purposefully ignoring him, stroking the hair of Bahar, who's seated reluctantly in her grandma's lap. She can probably hardly even remember Emine, she was so small the last time she was in Rheinstadt. Hakan feels sorry for this little girl. Her gloomy expression reminds him of the boredom of his own childhood, those miserable Sundays spent with one acquaintance of his parents or another who came to visit. People Hakan couldn't stand, with their sloppy kisses and their shriveled mouths and the wrinkly hands with which they shoved some piece of peeled fruit in front of his face.

Hakan can sense someone standing behind him. It must be Ümit. He's stayed behind in the hallway and was now hiding behind Hakan like a protective shield. Hakan juts his chin and tries to make some kind of greeting, but there are no words in his mouth.

The silence of this room hurtles around his ears like a screaming siren, like a fire alarm. Like the sound of rolling tanks. Hakan knows this silence. This family never argues out loud. In this family, fights always happen this way: with meaningful glances and diverted eyes, with all those things that can never be said and so hang all the heavier in the air between them. Because despite all the words that remain unuttered, everyone knows exactly what's being said and to whom. Silence is the weapon of Hakan's mother, just as it was also the weapon of his father. Silence is the soundtrack of his childhood, Hakan suddenly realizes. And maybe that's why Hakan eventually fled into the thundering beats of

Larry Smith, found so much strength in the clear delivery of Rakim's rhymes. Maybe Peri is right, maybe it does all have to do with Hüseyin's past. With the things he experienced. The things he was never able to communicate about. Something must have happened. Something so terrible there were no words for it. And now that Hüseyin is gone, now here they all are—those whom he left behind—sitting around with his only legacy. Silence.

"Selamın Aleyküm," Hakan says to break the silence, and he can hear the echo of his voice fly back at him from across the still half-empty room.

A murmur ripples across the circle of his family, counters his greeting, suffocating it with inarticulation. Hakan pulls himself together and crosses the room to Emine. He bends over her, breathing in the scent of her rosewater. He takes his mother's hand, kisses it, lays his forehead against it. The hand does not resist, it allows all this to happen, but it remains deliberately lifeless.

"Anne. I'm so sorry that I've come too late. I wanted to be with all of you at the funeral so badly. But fate wanted things to be different."

Emine's hand whistles through the air, just once, as if warning Hakan against misusing the word *fate* as an excuse for his own incompetence. Hakan opens his arms to hug Bahar, but she's still trapped on Emine's lap. The little one wraps her arms around his neck, throws herself against him. He lifts her up and sits with her on the sofa. Ümit plops down beside them.

"My condolences, Abla," Hakan says, turning to Sevda.

She nods at him in exhaustion.

This silence is a formidable foe. Hakan looks around himself in the room and says: "This apartment. It's so . . ."

"It's so big," Peri finishes, grateful for the opportunity to speak. "Bigger than the one in Rheinstadt, right?"

"No," Ümit chimes in. "You only think that because the living room is bigger. But all the other rooms are tiny. I think it's exactly the same size as the one in Rheinstadt."

"Really?" Hakan asks, sighing with relief.

"But it's much lighter. You have to see it in the daylight," Peri says. "The way it glows."

"But somehow . . . ," Ümit begins, but he doesn't finish his sentence.

"Somehow what?" Peri demands.

"Somehow this apartment is strange. It has such a weird feeling about it."

Peri nods, and Hakan follows her lead.

"That's because of Baba," Sevda says, and Hakan stares gratefully in her direction because he's missed her voice. "You only came here because Baba . . . well. You associate it with that now, Ümit. But when a little time has passed, maybe you'll come to associate this place with other things. And you'll also think of Baba differently."

"I'm going to sell it."

All eyes turn to Emine. She's sitting in her corner, casting her unflinching gaze about the room.

"I am going to see a realtor first thing tomorrow."

Emine is glaring at Sevda now, as if the message was just for her.

"What?" Peri stammers. "But why, Anne?"

"Because this apartment is cursed," Emine says obstinately. "It took your father from you."

"Anne, what does this apartment have to do with that? Baba had a heart attack!" Peri's voice sounds urgent, like she's trying to talk Emine down from a dangerous flight of fancy. But her frightened face betrays her own misgivings about the apartment.

"Yes, but why?" The words escape Emine's lips, and her face softens before growing hard again. "Tell me, why? Why does a healthy man like Hüseyin die so suddenly of a heart attack? He never had a single problem with his heart!"

"Maybe he did, but he just never told us," Hakan suggests. Emine stares at him, shaken, as if he'd just made an outrageous accusation.

"Why would he not tell us this, Hakan? It is nonsense what you are saying!" she cries, clawing at her pale-green nightgown.

"I'm going to the hospital tomorrow. I want to speak with the doctors," Sevda announces. She seems to be returning to her senses now. She fixes her hair, pets Cem, then straightens his T-shirt.

"What for?" Ümit asks quietly.

"I want to know what went wrong. No one is supposed to die from their first heart attack. That would never have happened in Germany."

"And then what?" Hakan asks, staring at his big sister in surprise. "What do you want to do with the knowledge that it was the doctors' fault? What does that change? Nothing!"

"I don't know." Sevda shrugs. "Then maybe we can sue the hospital." She places both hands on her face and begins massaging her temples as if she has a headache.

A groan erupts from Peri before she can cover her mouth.

"What are you laughing about?" Sevda asks irritably.

"Abla, don't get the wrong idea. But the life of a simple man like Baba isn't worth much in this country. No court is going to rule in our favor here. And even if they did, what good would it do?"

"Then she will get some money from the hospital," Emine's offended voice cries from the corner of the room. "And now I understand why you have come here at all, Sevda Hanım. You want to make a little money, do you not?"

"Tövbe, Anne!" Peri cries, outraged. "What are you trying to do? Stop it!"

"Am I not right? All these years she did not care in the least about her father. Now he is dead, and even this did not move her enough to show up to his funeral. But now here she is. And why? Ha. Why, indeed!" Emine points one finger at her forehead to demonstrate that she's seen through Sevda's intentions.

"Anne, you know exactly why we haven't spoken for the past years. Don't make me dredge it all up now in front of everyone!" Sevda's words only elicit Emine's bitter laughter. Seated between them, his eyes roving back and forth between the two, Hakan is suddenly struck by how similar they look. They look more like sisters than mother and daughter. Emine's smooth face distorts with a wicked snarl.

"What, and now you threaten me too? Do you really think there is any excuse for turning your back on your own parents? To not so much as ask them how they are for years? We did not raise you this way, Sevda."

Emine's embittered words pound inside Hakan's head like an awful Eurotrash dance beat. Like a song that's been stuck in his head, haunting him for more than two decades. Like a horror movie seen at a far-too-tender age—the memory of which still follows him through every sleepless night, every unexpected sound, and every eerie silence. It robs him of his breath, crushing him down.

This fight between Sevda and Emine spins around and around in circles. Hakan wants them to talk it out. To finally let it out. But his exhausted brain can't handle it. He could be lying on the couch with Lena right now. He could just get back into his Alfa, rush to the safety of the fast lane on the motorway. He can't keep up with Sevda and Emine anymore. The ragged shreds of their words fly past him, and he feels like he's sitting on a carousel. Everything around him grows blurry, everything but the faces of Cem and Bahar. Their dark little button eyes, searching for an exit. Their tiny bodies cowering against the stiff fabric of the sofa, as if seeking protection.

Hakan feels his shoulders tightening, feels the muscles in his back propelling him back up. He feels himself rising from the couch and striding to the center of Hüseyin's living room as if entering a cypher. He feels himself waiting until all eyes are fixed upon him, until his family is finally straining to hear what he has to say.

"I'm going to Antalya. Who's coming with me?"

Emine

You unroll the sajada on the bedroom floor and close your eyes, Emine. The last azan must have sounded at least three hours ago. But if you're still wide awake long after midnight, you might as well pray a sixth time. You hope this nighttime prayer will carry you closer to God, protect you from misdeeds. Just like back then. Do you not remember how you lay awake for many nights because of all the things weighing heavy on your heart back then? They might have pushed you into an eternal desperation if you had not held fast to your belief.

You hear the clock ticking, Emine. It's one of those old-fashioned models with a pendulum of brass inside a thick, wooden house. You used to like these kinds of clocks. It comforted you to watch the movement of the pendulum, how it swung to and fro. But you can't abide this anymore, Emine. Now it seems like every stroke of the pendulum just pushes you a little further from your life, second by second. Further from Hüseyin. Until one day, it will be as though he had never been.

The clock is merely leaned against the wall, waiting to be mounted. But they never got that far. You already told him back then, when one family after another had begun moving out of your neighborhood: *Hüseyin, let's take our money and go. Like the others. The German state will give us 10,000 marks if we go back. That is a good amount of money; back home we can buy ourselves a piece of land with a nice house. Maybe even some animals.*

We can retire, Hüseyin, and finally be back among people we can share our life with. People who do not treat us like the last vermin.

But no. Hüseyin wanted to stay. For the children. Everything was always for the children and their futures. He wanted to keep working. Keep saving. *We're vermin there too, Emine.* Until the seagull of bushy hair above Hüseyin's eyes slowly grew sparse and gray. Until he had to take a break at every park bench along his walk because his knee could no longer keep up with him.

And now what, Emine? Now, Hüseyin is gone. Now, he's left you. Hüseyin's left you alone with your four children and this apartment here. Yes, the children are all grown, but what does that matter? Such things mean nothing to a mother. It's not like you will worry any less about them now. It's not like this means the end of your motherhood. Because these things, they do not end. Mothers cannot just call in sick. Mothers do not retire. Your children remain your children. Even Sevda should have realized this by now. Sevda, who once threw those words in your face: *Anne, how would you understand me, you've never worked.*

And now this apartment too. This goddamn apartment. Hüseyin was obsessed with it. For months, he could only speak of this. And what did it bring him? Had he managed to spend even two nights in this place? Could he take it with him to the other side, his precious apartment? No. It was all for nothing. All his hopes, these hopes that finally infected you, too—all of it was swallowed up by that deep hole they filled in today with earth and bugs and tears. Right in front of your eyes: they wrapped Hüseyin in a white cloth and interred his body. You should never look forward to anything too much in this life, Emine. You know this all too well. Only the Almighty knows what tomorrow will bring. You can only depend on His grace. You say, *Allahu Akhbar*, as you sink to your knees.

All this is just a test; you've been telling yourself this for days. You know you can't be weak now; you cannot lose faith. Faith that you are a true believer. Because the very first and very last thing that defines you as a Muslim is your faith that Allah is the one true God and Muhammed is His servant and prophet. You cannot bend from your belief now. You cannot damn your life. Because you don't need to understand everything, Emine, but deep inside yourself you already know: everything must be as it is.

God forbid you start to doubt this now, doubt that the things that happened to you in this life did not need to happen as they did. Doubt that you could have influenced or prevented them. If you started down this path now, the last threads still holding you to your being would be severed. You would lose the ground beneath your feet. You would have nothing left to hold on to. No hand. No branch. Nothing.

The clock is ticking. Dishes are rattling in the kitchen. What is Sevda doing now? Wasn't everything already washed? This snoopy girl. Surely she's sticking her nose into all the cupboards, assessing what Hüseyin left behind. Why did Sevda stay in the apartment at all? Why did she not drive to the seaside with the others? She stuffed her two children into Hakan's car in the middle of the night, alongside Hakan and Peri. And this, although Hakan had already apparently been driving for two days. You would have liked to beg Hakan to stay. To sleep here for just one night before departing. But you know how he is once he's gotten something in his head, Emine. At least he promised Sevda to stop somewhere along the way if he got tired.

Sevda had said she'd follow the day after tomorrow. That she still needed to take care of something. What did she want to take care of? She didn't think she could hinder you from selling the apartment, did she? Or that she would see some of this money when you did? As if Sevda needed money. Sevda already has everything. What more could she want?

You feel something. A tickle on the back of your neck, Emine. Wasn't Sevda just standing teary-eyed in the living room, every bit as dejected as the others? Every bit as desperate as you? Had she not just lost her father too? Was she, too, not fighting the emptiness that overwhelms you when someone so suddenly and so unexpectedly vanishes from your life? When you realize the life you've always known will never return? Does Sevda not know perhaps, too, that she shares some guilt in Hüseyin's death? Because she turned her back on her father this way: ice-cold. It must have broken his heart, Emine. Just like it broke yours too.

And still, you wish you could have held yourself back a little earlier. You wish you hadn't attacked your daughter so quickly. You have not seen each other in five long years, and the first thing you do is scream at her? You're sorry for this now, Emine. But you can't be any different; you cannot control this thing inside of you. Whenever you see Sevda, your first impulse is to put her in her place. It's always been this way. Or has it? You can't really say. All you know is that so much sadness entered your life with Sevda that it's always seemed impossible to feel all right in the presence of your eldest daughter.

They say the second birth is much easier than the first. But that isn't true. For you, your second birth was the most painful thing you ever experienced. Even today, you sometimes feel like your body can remember this pain. Your abdomen begins to throb, and a gaping wound splits open. It feels like your insides are tumbling out of you. Organs. Blood. Excrement. Everything. Until there's only a pained silence. You still wonder how you survived that night in the barn. And how you still managed to bring three more children into the world after. But it was all so different with them. Because after that night in the barn—after the weeks and months that followed while your tattered body finally grew back together again—it was like that thing between your legs no longer had anything to do with you, Emine. As if it didn't belong to you anymore. Remotely operated like a television. Because a TV never belongs to itself either. It was like your body was just following external commands. You simply leaned back and waited for what would happen next. You were always prepared for anything. With every birth, you knew that you could die, but you also knew it could never be as bad again as what you suffered that night in the barn.

Your first birth, on the other hand, had been precisely like what others meant when they say having a baby is the most wonderful thing in the whole world. It began with light cramps. They reminded you of your period. By the time these cramps grew stronger and finally became labor pains, your mother-in-law had already called the village midwife. You floated in the waves emanating from your body, concentrated all your power on your breathing—the inhale, the exhale—and just three or four hours later you exhaled that tiny creature with one giant wave. They laid the baby on your chest, warm and pulsing with life. It was such a beautiful child, more beautiful than any you had ever seen, Emine. It found your breast all on its own and began to nurse without anyone having to teach it how. It was like this child brought its own wisdom with it. It was magical. When you rocked it to sleep at night, sang it a ninni, it seemed like the little one was smiling. Although everyone knows that infants can't smile so early on. But maybe your child was different, Emine, or maybe you were just in love.

Sevda was the complete opposite. She wasn't beautiful. She didn't laugh. She didn't nurse from your breast, nor could she be rocked to sleep. Sevda did only one thing, night and day, without interruption: Sevda screamed. She screamed until her tiny head was red and then blue. She screamed until her whole body shook. She screamed until her voice broke and her vocal cords could only produce a hoarse, rasping croak. She screamed until she woke Hüseyin, your mother-in-law, and even your half-deaf father-in-law. She screamed until everyone in the house wondered why you were incapable of quieting your child, Emine. You rocked and rocked her, while wiping away your own tears. It was all but unbearable, but your arms held out. They rocked the child harder and harder until she turned green, until she was completely out of breath and had screamed herself unconscious. Only to awaken two hours later and scream again. Sometimes Hüseyin took over for you, took the little one stiffly in his arms. And this would calm her for a little while. Hüseyin then began, each time, to explain to you with confidence what you'd been doing wrong. How you should be gentler with the child, how you should walk carefully up and down the room with her. *Like this: one-two, one-two, one-two* . . . But by then, Hüseyin's magic would already be dispelled, and Sevda would begin to scream again. Would grow irreconcilable. And then Hüseyin would lay the child back into your arms. Take his pillow and go off to sleep in the kitchen.

Those screams. Those heart-rending, shrill, upsetting, simply unwilling-to-come-to-an-end screams. They drove you to the point of madness.

Something in you boiled over. It wasn't rage; no, it was bitter desperation. You choked and swallowed it down. Kept it inside of you, so you
wouldn't take it out on Sevda. So that, in a moment of weakness, you
wouldn't just drop her onto the stone floor. Or bash her tiny body
against a wall. Or smother her with a pillow. Or carry her out into the
snowy forest and simply leave her there. To keep yourself from doing
all the things that haunted your mind, Emine, when the screaming
began anew after only a short moment's respite, you began to pull out
your own hair. One single strand at a time. And already, the very first
time you did so, this burning pain in your scalp numbed you. And you
couldn't stop. Every night, one strand of hair. Some nights, even two.
Until one night you saw the horror on Hüseyin's face when you removed
your headscarf. And no, you still couldn't sleep with him yet, either. At
first, because of the damage to your lower body, and then later because
of all those things that filled your mind. But you still wanted to please
your husband, like any wife would, regardless of whether she loves her
husband or not. Whether she desires him or not. These things do not
matter. Because far worse than the feeling of losing your own attraction
to your husband is the knowledge that he is no longer attracted to you.

Sevda screamed into the early morning hours. She hadn't begun to
nurse at your breast until the fourth day. And from then on, she did
so for only a few minutes. You thought something about this child
wasn't right. But your mother-in-law was certain that the problem lay
with you. She cooked you buttery erişte each day and buttery bulgur.
She brought warm halva and warm cow's milk to you in bed so that
your own breasts would produce more. But this didn't help. Sevda was
not getting enough. Finally, they found a different young mother in the
village whose breasts produced sufficient milk, and Sevda accepted this
other woman immediately. And you, Emine, you had to carry Sevda
several times a day past all the other houses in the village and give your
daughter to this other woman to nurse.

The screaming lessened just a little. And slowly, you came to understand how to rock a screaming baby to sleep. You no longer looked your
daughter in the eye. No way. Because you learned that this attention
was what kept the child awake. Even when Sevda lay her tiny hand on

yours, light as a feather, you had to be stubborn, Emine. You pushed this little hand away. And your body continued rocking. Always with the same rhythm. Because if you stopped this rhythm, if you caressed your daughter, if you looked into Sevda's eyes, if you reciprocated her touch—it would all be in vain. All your hard work. The child would never sleep. And so, you kept rocking, Emine. Even when it took hours upon hours. Even when your rocking turned to trembling. Even when your rocking almost turned to shaking at some point. The rhythm stayed the same. You could not break from this rhythm, not till the very bitter end. No eye contact and no affection. No indulgence. Because she needed sleep. She just needed to learn. To finally learn she needed sleep.

And despite your wounds, you soon began to do housework again. You were much slower than you had been before. You couldn't carry heavy weight, but still you carried on at your own speed. So Sevda's grandmother could watch over her instead. Your mother-in-law wrapped your child in a blanket, tied the bundle with a bit of cloth, and rocked it lovingly in her arms or in a wooden cradle. Sometimes you would say you were going out to check on the cattle, just so you could stay away for a half hour. Your mother-in-law nodded knowingly. You'd spread a cloth down on the hay in the barn and catch up on a few minutes of the sleep you lost out on in the night.

～

You turn your face to the right.
Peace be upon you and the mercy and blessings of Allah.
You turn your face to the left.
Peace be upon you and the mercy and blessings of Allah.

You brace your hands against the sajada to rise. But your arms lack the necessary strength. So, you remain sitting, Emine. Your eyes pan the darkened bedroom into which only a frail bit of light falls from the hallway. You stare at the bed in which Hüseyin never slept. At the mirror in which he perhaps saw his reflection only one single time while hanging it. You've covered this mirror with a headscarf so it does not disturb your prayers. The heat of the city is still brooding; it did not let up overnight.

You can feel the pearls of sweat on your temples, but your feet feel cold. Like they always do. You are just about to cover them with the hem of your nightgown when you stiffen. It's like someone is standing behind you. It's like someone is watching you. But it isn't Sevda because you can hear Sevda's footsteps on the creaking wooden-plank floor of the living room. It can't be Sevda, and so this means no one is standing behind you. But there is that feeling again. It's been with you since the first time you entered the apartment. That feeling someone is follow-ing you. That if you could only turn around fast enough, you would see him or her. But you don't want to see anything.

The evening of your arrival, it did not scare you yet. Because last night, it was only one of a hundred competing feelings tearing through you, overwhelming you, until you could do little more than wring your hands around some handkerchief and rock your upper body back and forth as if you were holding an infant child in your arms. Even Ayşe's presence was merely an afterthought; you could not even feel outrage at your sister-in-law's audacity. The audacity of showing up now, thirty years later: thirty years after she had driven the great wedge between you and Hüseyin. Now, of all times, when Hüseyin was gone forever and your struggle to lead a happy life with him was finally over. Because yes, Emine, you had clung to some hope that everything could still turn out okay now. Now in the shared twilight of your lives. In your new home in Istanbul. But now some things were clearer. Finally, now, you were able to make peace with certain things. And so, when Ayşe returned this afternoon, showed up again in the hospital parking lot and wanted to speak with you there alone, this was enough. *Go to hell*, you'd told her, and *I do not want to see you at the funeral*. After all those years Ayşe had hidden herself away from you and from Hüseyin. Those years in which she had not so much as given you proper notice when Ahmet died, so that Hüseyin first heard about his brother's death after the funeral. After everything that had transpired, you told Ayşe she could continue on as she always had and keep her distance. If you had not been so utterly beside yourself, so broken, you would have liked to tear that ugly scarf from Ayşe's head and box her a good two or three times around the ears. She deserved it, Emine. But now you have no other option left than to simply continue placing all your trust in Allah, as you have always done. To go on believing that all mortals will one day atone for their sins. For all the hearts that they have broken and the lives they have destroyed.

Ayşe, too, has grown old. She looked so soft and fragile from the out-side; she no longer had anything in common with the proud snake she had already been at your first meeting—when she disturbed the peace of your wedding day. At first, you had liked Ayşe's different colored eyes: one light brown as weak tea, the other green with a brown pattern in it like a pretty frog. For this was something special. But soon enough, you could feel the force behind the glances she constantly cast after you. The poison in her eyes. Perhaps there was something in Ayşe's manner, her way of speaking loudly and assertively. Of taking over every room where no man was present. In retrospect, you believe that you already knew thirty-three long years ago that Ayşe had had something up her sleeve. But maybe you had not known anything. Maybe you had only been afraid of this strange woman and her pretty eyes. Of this much older and much wiser woman who had already been married to Hüseyin's elder brother for almost ten years and yet had been unable to bear him a child. The two had traveled all the way from Austria, where they had been living now for a few years. They'd come especially for your wedding, although people had not done such things during those times. Weddings back then had been little more than humble village gatherings. Yes, sometimes they had lasted for three days, but only be-cause no one in the village had anything better to do. Things then were not like they were in Germany—where everyone only sits at home alone, counting every coin three times over and living only between their workplace and their bed. Everyone was always together in the village, at least that's how it seems now to you, Emine. People in the village liked having something to celebrate. But for someone to travel from another country to join in a simple village wedding: this was something new. And yet Ayşe and Ahmet had come. They'd given you five golden armbands. Because Hüseyin and Ahmet had no sisters, Ayşe had told you she wanted to help you take care of all the *important* things. And so it was, on the morning after your wedding, that Ayşe had come discreetly to change out your bedsheets and to check if there was any blood.

The following year, when you were already heavy with child, Ayşe and Ahmet came again to visit, bearing further gifts: coffee and cremes, chocolate and nylon stockings. Ahmet must have made plenty of money in the factory in Austria, for their train tickets alone must have cost a small fortune. But as much as you were overjoyed at their many presents—the smell of the coffee, the brightly colored packaging on the cosmetics—you were not pleased to see Ayşe and her green eye appear again so close to the birth of your child. Without moving your lips, you had repeated the Surah Al-Ikhlas over and over in your head, each time Ayşe appeared. Which was incessantly in the little house you shared with Hüseyin and your in-laws.

Thank God everything had gone well. This first child came into the world healthy, and everyone in the house—your parents-in-law, Ahmet and Ayşe, Hüseyin and you—delighted at the presence of this tiny new being among you. You were so unbearably exhausted, Emine, but you were also bursting with joy. You only wanted to hold this child in your arms and smell its scent, but your mother-in-law warned you this would not be good for the child. She was always taking it away from you, wrapping it up, laying it back in its wooden cradle. At night, the child awoke only once or twice to nurse and Hüseyin got up with you to pet the baby and snuggle it, something he didn't do during the day in the presence of his parents. You longed for these nights, Emine, the three of you lying together in your bed in the soft candlelight when your happiness was all but overflowing. Your future lay before you.

But as long as Ayşe remained in the house, you also continued your silent prayers. You only wanted to know when Ayşe and Ahmet would leave again for Austria, but this wasn't something you could ask. And even if Ayşe recited Maşallah forty thousand times a day to protect your baby from the evil eye, still you could not trust Ayşe's own eye for even one second. Your instincts told you you needed to protect your child, and your heart told you to protect it from Ayşe most of all.

One night, you dreamed of a great black serpent, slithering toward your baby, snuggling up to it, only to suddenly strike. This snake had different colored eyes. Drenched in sweat, you jolted awake, Emine, staring anxiously in the direction of the cradle. But your child was sleeping soundly. You held your hand under its tiny nose anyway just to be sure it was still breathing.

And the next morning at breakfast, when you heard that everyone but your mother-in-law would go to visit Ayşe's elder brother in the neighboring village, you said: *Anne, why don't you go too?* Your mother-in-law told you one did not leave a new mother alone with her child until it was forty days old. But you pointed to your baby, saying: *Look how healthy it is, we are well here, and the fresh air would do you good, Anne. Just go.* You watched the five of them departing from the window, watched until they disappeared between the pines that had already shed their covering of snow and were slowly returning to a bleached-out shade of green. Frantically, you searched for a pencil and a bit of paper, Emine, and you wrote down the words *power of attorney*, before pausing to consider what else you had written for your aunt who could not write herself and was always asking for your help with such things. Finally, you simply wrote Hüseyin's name on the paper and pulled on your overcoat.

With the warmly swaddled baby in your arms and the paper in your coat pocket, you walked to the only neighbors with a car. Their eldest son sometimes drove down to the city when someone from the village had business to do there. You yourself had only been to this city once before in your whole life, Emine. Only the men undertook such journeys. But you handed the neighbor's son a gold coin you had received for your wedding. You said only a few sentences, clearly and carefully, and not at all like you were trembling with fear. The neighbor's son seemed pleased, not so much about the gold as he was about an excuse to travel back down to the city after the long winter. As did his little sister, who slipped excitedly into a dress to accompany the two of you as chaperone so that the whole affair did not appear like something it was not.

When you returned exhausted, shortly before nightfall, Hüseyin was standing in front of the house, his hands clasped behind his back, his whole body one fraught question: *Where had you been?* You handed him the birth certificate you'd received after much waiting in the city, much talking, and much haggling. The child was there. It was yours and Hüseyin's child. You had it now in black-and-white, Emine. But Hüseyin only stared past the document at the child in your arms. The seagull of his brow folded its wings together sadly.

∽

"Anne?"

Sevda is standing in the doorway. You're still seated on the floor with your back to the door. But you can see her shadow falling long and thin over you and the sajada.

"Is it your blood pressure?"

You take a corner of your nightgown and fold it over your cold feet. Carefully, you turn your head and look back at Sevda. She's wearing pink pajamas and her curly hair is tied back in a bun. The light from the hallway flows around her silhouette, and she looks like an angel. You nod to her; Sevda nods back.

"I'll bring you some water, okay?"

She disappears down the hall.

You remove your headscarf and drape it across your shoulders. It's not your blood pressure pinning you to the floor, Emine. And it's not your sadness, either. No. It's something different. You are seated there on your sajada as you have done so often before: surrendering yourself to memories from back then, back when . . . Yes. Your first child's name was Sevda too, but no one ever called it by that name. And so, this name never really belonged to that child. That's why you always simply call this child *o* when you speak of it. Or no: when you wish to speak of it, because you never do. Well, perhaps not never; a few times over the years you spoke of it to Hüseyin, but these conversations were always short because Hüseyin had always stiffened, he'd always been unable to speak another word. And you, Emine, you could only ever scream.

You give yourself over to your memories of *o*, as you so often have, and to the memories of how *o* was torn from your life. And as always, you find someone to blame. Usually it's Ayşe. Sometimes it's Hüseyin.

Sometimes, your mother-in-law, God rest her soul. She never so much as mentioned it again, but still, she had been there, and she could have done something about it. But she had not. But be that as it may, despite the guilt of the three others, you also know in your heart that you can never absolve yourself of the blame. Even if you were barely sixteen years old at the time. Even if you were naive and timid and perhaps only a child yourself. *O* was still your child. You were *onun* mother. And no matter what happened to *ona*, it was, above all else, your responsibility to protect *onu*. Half-victim, half-accomplice, as Perihan would say? No. There was no such thing as half-motherhood. And even if you never wanted to admit it, this realization had established itself inside your body over the past hours like a fully grown fetus. You'd brought the greatest guilt of all upon yourself, Emine. And nothing could ever change that.

"Here, Anne."

Sevda squats down beside you and hands you a glass of water.

"Sağol, Kızım."

You drink the glass, sip by sip, taking your time. You can feel the water slowly flowing through your body, how it dissolves the bitter knots inside your chest. How it cleanses you, cools you. How it softens you.

Sevda is still squatting beside you, and you turn to her. Sevda opens her hand to take the empty glass, but you put it on the floor instead. You lay your hand in Sevda's. Sevda's hand pulls back at first, but you take it and caress it. Sevda does nothing. She only looks down at the floor. You continue to caress her hand. Slowly, Sevda's head sinks. For a moment, it rises again in resistance, before sinking finally onto her anne's shoulder. Her body relaxes on the wooden floor.

"You . . . ," Sevda whispers, but she doesn't finish the sentence.

You inhale the scent of Sevda's curls. They smell like flowers and hairspray. Like woman and child. Like yesterday and today. You wrap your arms around your daughter, and your two bodies sink into the embrace from both sides. You can feel Sevda begin to cry. She does not make a sound, but her back is trembling.

"Shhh . . . ," you whisper into Sevda's curls. "Shhh," just like in those nights in your village, when Sevda had screamed her soul from her tiny, rebellious body. "Shhh . . . ," as if you want to tell her: *Everything will be all right, Kızım.* Although you know this is not true. Things will not be okay. But Allah will give us the patience to live on, the patience to look after the ones who have remained. And the patience never to forget the ones whom we have lost.

"Shhh . . . ," you whispered then in *onun* ear, while *o* had been nursing and you'd bent your body over *onun* body. You whispered "shhh" even though *o* never cried. It was you who cried. Those were the final days before you would lose *onu*. You already knew what would happen then, and you buried your face in the folds of *onun* neck to keep the sour perfume of *onun* body with you in the tip of your nose forever. Even weeks after *o* had departed, you continued whispering your prayers while wandering aimlessly about the house. Although Ayşe's eyes had long since vanished, taking with them everything your prayers should have protected.

Sevda slowly loosens herself from your embrace and fixes her hair.

You push yourself up from the floor with your fists, finally finding the strength to stand. You take the sajada, fold it twice, and lay it at the foot of the bed.

"Let's go to the balcony, Anne. Maybe you could use some air," Sevda says, taking your glass into the kitchen to fetch more water.

You tie your headscarf back around your head, open the balcony door, and step out into the thick darkness almost humming with humidity. Below you, a few people are still walking the night streets. You wonder how long Hakan and the others have already been driving at this point. An hour? They will not arrive in Antalya before noon.

"Should I bring you a chair?" Sevda asks, two glasses in her hands.

You shake your head and lean heavily against the railing. You have already sat enough. Your backside is numb.

Sevda places the glasses on a stool and fishes a cigarette from her pajamas. She lights up like it was nothing and takes a long drag, exhaling the smoke with relief as if she had wanted nothing more for hours than this first inhalation. She's staring at you.

"What is it?"

You only shrug your shoulders.

"Anne, you don't seriously expect me to hide from you anymore, at my age? I'm a grown woman."

"Do what you wish. It is your health," you say soberly, slipping in a quiet "You will only age more quickly," after.

Sevda laughs. "Believe me, my body already feels like I was ninety."

"What does this mean?" you ask.

"Work. Every week some other part of my body hurts."

"Pff," you snort, unimpressed. If Sevda only knew the kind of heavy labor you did back in your village. How you tended the animals and cleaned out the barn and had to toil in the fields all while taking care of Sevda and your two in-laws. No one had paid you money for this. Or given you a restaurant with your name on a shiny sign.

"Did you know Baba caught me smoking once?" Sevda asks you, amused.

You click your tongue indifferently.

"It was on my engagement day. I never smoked back then. But I was so nervous that I stole one of Baba's cigarettes and went down to the cellar to smoke in secret and just be alone. Suddenly, there he was standing before me. He was looking for the extra folding chairs. I panicked, and I dropped the cigarette. I burned a hole in my dress. Baba acted like nothing happened. He just said: *Get upstairs and help your mother; hurry up.*"

Sevda giggles quietly like a naughty child. The kind of child she never was. She ashes her cigarette down onto the street below. She's still watching you. But you turn away and look up at the starless sky. The moon is almost full.

"How was he at the end?" Sevda asks, her voice suddenly grown dead serious.

You're wondering why there are no stars in the sky here. It's probably because of all the exhaust fumes in the air. This city is so polluted, you can feel it in your body any time you stand outside for a short while. It makes your throat burn. You cannot grasp what it was that Hüseyin saw in Istanbul.

Sevda repeats her question. "How was Baba at the end? What was he up to?"

"He was not up to anything," you answer. "He wandered around like a little kid excited about his trip."

"He was happy, right?" Sevda asks expectantly.

You shrug your shoulders. Happy. Why do these children always speak of happiness? Perihan does this too. Why do they always want you to be happy? Why can a person not simply be? Why is this not enough?

"He only spoke of this apartment. He was obsessed," you say, shaking your head.

"You didn't want the apartment?"

You take your arms from the railing and cross them over your chest. You think.

"It is not about what I want. It was not necessary," you say. "We did not need this apartment here. Everything was fine the way it was."

"So, did you want to stay in Germany forever?" Sevda asks.

"No! Of course not!" The words burst out of you. You take your glass from the stool and take a sip. "But some day, when Ümit was finished with school and had made a life for himself, then maybe we could have returned to the village."

"Anne, what do you want to do in the village?" Sevda asks in irritation. "There's no one left there!"

"What do you mean what do I want there? That village is my home. My earth. Surely someone is still there . . ."

"Nonsense," Sevda says, taking another drag. "Everyone has long since moved down to the cities. Your village doesn't exist anymore."

"How would you know?"

"I just know it. Those are dreams, Anne. Dreams and longing for what used to be. Nothing more."

Sevda flicks her cigarette from the balcony. You watch it as it falls down to the street below. How sparks from its embers hang in the air, spiral, then go out.

"Do you want to go to sleep?" Sevda asks.

"I cannot sleep."

"Me neither."

"Then make us a çay," you command her gently.

You enter the living room and lie down on the big sofa. Everything around you is throbbing: the walls, the floor, the ceiling. Your body is spent and feels like it's melting away like syrup. Thoughts whirl in your brain like the tiny embers of a cigarette. The moment they blow too far off course, they return to you with renewed force. Hüseyin. It feels like a blow to the head. What will you do without him now, Emine? You don't have the strength left to come up with something new. You want only to remain lying here in the roaring silence and surrender to your sadness. What would this even be: a life without Hüseyin? How should it work? You can hardly remember a time before him, that's how long it's been. As if there was nothing before Hüseyin. Only an endless field of white.

Your memories begin on the first day you saw Hüseyin. He had come from the neighboring village to visit someone. Normally, you did not raise your eyes when you encountered a man in your village. Normally, your eyes stayed glued to the mud, to the gravel, to the weeds that lined the footpaths from the moment you noticed the body of a man approaching out of the corner of your eye. But for some reason, things were different that day. Hüseyin's gaze pulled you in like a magnet, and he had looked into you and you had looked into him. It could not have lasted for more than two seconds, but it felt like an eternity to you, Emine. Hüseyin had smiled and you had held your breath. And before you had the chance to sink your eyes again and hold one end of your headscarf over your mouth, before you had a chance to rush past Hüseyin and save yourself in the house of your aunt, before you had the chance to hide inside the kitchen and finally set your own smile free—you'd caught a glimpse of Hüseyin's sadness, seated there in the same face with Hüseyin's smile. It belonged to him so naturally. And it had remained even much later; regardless of whether Hüseyin was happy or tired or whether he was asleep, his sadness was always there. He hid it away inside himself like a precious secret. One might guess at its presence, but Hüseyin never revealed it, no matter how many years you tried, Emine. No matter how deeply you bored. Somewhere, you always encountered a lock he'd closed before the secret to his sadness. A lock to which there was no key. It shut you out forever, leaving only your own loneliness behind.

Already in the first nights after your marriage, Hüseyin began to murmur in his sleep. To cry softly. You could never understand what it was Hüseyin was saying. And finally, at some point, it ceased again. But now that you think of it, you remember he had also begun to talk again in his sleep much later in Germany. And to cry. *Hide yourself, they are coming!* he called out during one of those sleepless nights in Rheinstadt when you lay beside him with the Quran in your lap. He struggled and writhed in his sleep, made terrible expressions, as if he were in pain. You could still remember it so well because it shook you so. And not because of what it was he said but because of how he said it. In your mother tongue.

Hüseyin had forbidden you to speak Kurdish with Sevda many years before, even before he'd left for Germany. Later, he had done the same with the other children, explaining that it would make their lives easier if they never learned this language at all. He'd said, *I want my children to have a good life, Emine, don't you want that too?* And it was not as hard as you had expected it to be, especially after Hüseyin moved you and his parents and Sevda from the mountains down to the city shortly before his own departure. You're thinking now about the crumbling little house he rented for you there. *It's safer down here,* he'd said. Most of your neighbors there only spoke Turkish anyway. Turkish was spoken on the radio. They spoke Turkish in the government offices. And your Turkish was good, Emine, for you had gone to elementary school. Only your in-laws had trouble speaking Turkish, but they grew increasingly silent in Karlıdağ anyway. And so, at some point, Emine, the Turkish language had shaped your life to such an extent that you began to dream in Turkish too. And so, the fact that Hüseyin of all people years later still spoke Kurdish in his dreams, long after the death of his mother—the last person he had spoken Kurdish with on the telephone or during your rare visits back—that hurt you, Emine. Hurt you deeply, down to the very marrow of your bones. First, Hüseyin had taken your mother tongue from you, and then he had taken you away to a country where you did not have any language at all. It felt like a betrayal. As though he had betrayed you each and every day since your first meeting because he had been hiding his own innermost self away from you.

Sevda returns and settles onto the other sofa. Hakan's melon is still lying on the table behind her, like an unintelligible greeting. You wait silently for the çay to steep. The lightbulbs above you glow a penetrating white, casting a pale gray veil over the lotion on Sevda's face.

The silence between you is still uncomfortable. You fear Sevda could say something at any moment. She does not do it, but her silent presence fills the room with unspoken questions. What does she want to ask you? What can you say to her? You do not know any nice stories, Emine. You only know the truth. And the truth is not pretty.

"Anne," Sevda murmurs suddenly into the empty room.

You turn your head to her, while the rest of your body remains lying on the sofa, still heavy and slow.

"I have to tell you something, Anne."

Sevda looks down at herself, smooths out her pajamas. She looks like a nervous little girl. And as if she can hear your thoughts, she lifts her head and clears her throat.

"I've separated from Ihsan," she says, jutting her chin.

You nod and stare back at the ceiling. You have already heard about this from Perihan. You were not surprised that Ihsan had left Sevda. Sevda is hard to take. Sevda is never satisfied with anything.

"Anne?"

"Yes?"

"Why aren't you saying anything?"

"What do you want to hear from me?" You're still looking at the ceiling. You're wondering whether Hüseyin had new molding installed or whether it's only been touched up well.

"I dunno. Something? You always have something to say about this kind of thing . . ."

"I believe it is not my place to say. This is your thing," you respond.

"Oh, is that so?" Sevda asks in surprise. "Then it seems you've changed a lot." Her voice sounds a bit like she's making some kind of little joke.

You can feel the warm air gathering in your chest. You exhale slowly and deeply before the heat can bottle up. You do not want to offend Sevda.

"But even if you say it this way, Anne, it's still obvious that you don't like me getting a divorce. But you are right: It is my thing. It's my life. And I make my own decisions. For myself."

You are still nodding silently. But now the question is burning on your lips. "So, it was your decision and not his?"

"Yes. Why?" Sevda asks.

"Just wondering."

"You thought *he* left *me*?"

"Does it make a difference?" You are exhausted.

"Seems like it makes a difference to you."

You look at her and sigh. "I only want the best for you, Kızım. That is all."

"So, you don't think my life can be good without a man, Anne?" Sevda will not let go.

"That is not what I said, Sevda. Do not put words in my mouth I did not say."

"Well," Sevda says, raising her manicured eyebrows. "I wanted to leave Ihsan before, five years ago. And you did not support me then."

You shake your head. "Are you not a grown woman, Sevda? Do you need to ask my permission for such things?"

"Of course not. And that's why I left him now. But back then . . ." Sevda falls silent. She looks around herself in the room as if seeking to put the proper words together for what she has to say. You know what is coming now, Emine. The same thing that always comes. Accusations. Reproach. Ugly little needling quips. You know your daughter. You know how she is. All the bad things in her life are your fault. And all the good things are the result of her own labors alone.

"What was the problem back then? What are you talking about?" you ask, to help relieve Sevda of whatever she is brewing in her mind.

"I was really hurting then. I needed help. And you weren't there for me."

"I was not there for you?" you ask. "The way I recall it, you and your children spent many weeks with us until you had found a new apartment."

"The way I recall it, Anne, you threw us out. Even though you knew I did not want to go back."

"What is this, Sevda? You always overexaggerate. Nobody threw you out!"

"Whatever you say, Anne," Sevda chokes on her laughter. She crosses one leg over the other, one foot wiggling nervously in the air.

"Yes, you said you did not want to go back. And I told you to think hard on this decision. *Sevda, this is not something to take lightly*, this is what I said. Nothing more. Just the way a mother should. Perhaps I need to remind you that this is my task."

Sevda is shaking her head again, a sad smile on her face.

"What are you laughing about?"

"Nothing, Anne. You're right. It was just like that. Let me check on the çay."

Sevda rises and walks over to the corner where the different-sized nesting tables are fitted together. Hüseyin even thought of this. He knew just what you would need to have your routine here. To feel good, Emine. The hair on your arm prickles at the thought. Sevda places the largest table in front of you, the mid-sized table in front of herself. She shakes her head again on her way to the kitchen. She still has this strange smile on her face. What the devil does she want from you anyway? For you to take all the responsibility? For you to say, yes, of course, it's all my fault, I'm guilty of all the bad things that have happened in your life? Yes, I alone sent you back to your husband, back where you and your children belong?

You rub your eyes and take a deep breath. You place your hands over your face, asking Allah for the strength you will need to keep yourself from screaming at Sevda once again.

Sevda returns in her pink pajamas with a tray and places a tea glass on the table in front of you. You're still lying on the sofa. She passes you the sugar bowl. You raise one hand to wave it away. Sevda does not know that you have long since sworn off sugar. That you have grown so used to the taste of unsweetened tea now that you drink your tea pure—now that you *must* drink your tea pure because of your diabetes—

that you wonder how you could have spent your whole life tucking a sugar cube inside your cheek for each of your four or five daily glasses of tea. The taste of pure çay is so much better. If someone had only told you when you were young that you were destroying your health in this way you could have stopped this nonsense so much earlier. You wouldn't have to think five times now about every meal, about whether your body can handle it or not without losing a toe or an entire foot. Sevda stirs two sugar cubes into her glass with relish. Sevda is still young. She cannot yet imagine all the things that are still to come. How one day she will have to make a weekly visit to the doctor because of such unnecessary habits. But if you were to warn her about this, Sevda would certainly interpret your intentions differently. She would say: *You don't want me to be happy in this life*, or something else equally absurd. It is better for you to hold your tongue instead, to only listen to the sound of the metal spoon while Sevda stirs an early death into her glass of tea.

"I need to tell you something too, Sevda."

The sound of the stirring spoon ceases.

Sevda fixes you with her skeptical eyes.

"I do not know why you have separated from your husband, Sevda. This I do not know. But I am sure you have your reasons."

Sevda nods, unimpressed, and continues stirring with her spoon. The sugar must long since have dissolved. This stirring is just musical accompaniment.

"It was wrong, what I said to you back then," you begin, and Sevda finally sets her spoon aside. She takes a sip of her sugar tea and stares at you attentively. "What do you mean? What was wrong about it?" she asks defiantly.

"It was wrong for me to say that Ihsan is a good man simply because he does not hit you. This does not suffice to make a man good."

Sevda nods wordlessly. She's waiting for you to continue speaking. You fold your hands over your stomach, and you close your eyes.

"Maybe you are wondering whether your father was a good man. I think much on this, Sevda. For the last two days, I have thought on it. He took away and gave me everything, your father."

You can feel your body lighten. With each word you let escape your mouth, you can feel a new spark glimmer in your mind.

"I have suffered so much in this life, Sevda, and I have often thought I suffer because of Hüseyin. But I know now that it is not so. Hüseyin was a good man. Sometimes I wish he had mistreated me. Yes, I do. Because then I could say clearly: Hüseyin was bad, and this is why I have suffered. But I cannot say this because it was not so. Whatever things have happened to me, I did these things to myself. Your father simply allowed it to happen. Does this make him a bad person? No, I do not think so."

"But, Anne . . . ," you can hear Sevda begin. Your eyes remain shut, following the sparks. You're moving through a dark, vibrating tunnel; roving points of red light illuminate the path in front of you. Sparks or fireflies or cigarettes. It is the path back into your past.

"What happened to you, Anne?"

∾

"Shhh . . . ," you say. "Shhh . . . ," in *onun* ear, more to comfort yourself than to comfort this little creature that still has no idea about what is happening. Those were the last days before Ayşe and Ahmet returned to Austria. They had extended their stay so *o* could continue nursing from your breast. Until they could take *onu* with them. *O* lay ever more often in Ayşe's arms now so the two could grow accustomed to each other. Your mother-in-law did not say it this way out loud, and yet she arranged things so the child spent more and more time with Ayşe. Your mother-in-law was not cruel to you. On the contrary, she spoke kindly to you, almost as if she could understand your pain. But could she truly understand it? Would she really have permitted you to give away your firstborn child if she had truly understood your pain?

Your nightmare had come true. The same evening you and *o* came back from the city with the birth certificate, Hüseyin brought you into the bedroom and sat despondently beside you on the bed. His forehead spread the wings of the mournful seagull of his brow. He told you how he had given his brother his word. Told you of the sacrifices Ahmet had made for his parents and his brothers for so many years as the eldest

son. Of the money he had sent from Vienna in order to ease their lives.
Of the youth that would still help you and Hüseyin to bring many
other healthy children into the world. How it would be impossible for
Ahmet and Ayşe to ever have a family of their own without your help.
You did not cry. You did not say anything. You only rocked your baby in
your arms. You only breathed. As if you could inhale *onu* back into your
body if only you could concentrate enough, just as you had exhaled
onu out into the world only a few short weeks before.

You had nothing to say. You could only grow silent. Pray that this
was only a bad dream and you would soon awaken. That something
would disrupt the others' plan. But nothing did. They took your child
away and you never saw *onu* again. Even today, you ask yourself how
you could have let it happen, Emine. What had prevented you from
hiding *onu*, from not surrendering *onu*, at the very least from raising your
own voice against this injustice. Perhaps you did nothing because you
were too young. Because you had never learned how to object. Not
to the aunt who raised you. Not to your mother-in-law under whose
roof you lived. Not to your husband. The journey you and *o* made
to the city without anyone else's knowledge or permission, this was
surely the greatest insurrection you ever permitted yourself, Emine.
You believed you needed to hold onto *onun* existence, that you needed
to prove that *o* belonged to you should *o* ever be taken from you. But
all this had meant nothing. You had only received a scrap of paper the
rest of the world ignored. Ahmet and Ayşe and *o* simply returned to the
city and had a fresh document made. They made *onu* into their own
child. Gave *ona* their own name. They abducted *onu* with your own
husband's permission. And yes, somehow, also with yours. Because you
did nothing to prevent it, Emine. The morning of their departure, *o*
had been sleeping in *onun* wooden cradle. You sat in your room, watching *onun* peaceful face. You smelled *onun* little head. You gave *onu* to
Hüseyin. You leaned back against the wall, Emine, and you quietly shattered into a thousand broken pieces while the others said their good-
byes at the door.

∽

Sevda's eyes are glassy. Her hand lies over her mouth defensively. As though she needs to keep back words that have no place in this living room. Her other hand clutches her tea glass so tightly it could break at any moment.

"O is alive?" Those are the only words she manages to say while you are speaking. Then she remains quiet, allowing you time to finish.

You've sat back up in the meantime. You reach for your glass and take a sip. The çay has grown lukewarm; you only like it piping hot. But your preferences have little to do with the current situation. In the moment, you, too, simply need something to hold onto. However fragile that might be. Everything is stronger than you are.

"I don't understand this," Sevda mutters finally, allowing her shoulders to begin to quiver. "I don't understand it!" she cries out a bit louder. Her voice grows shrill. "I've brought two children into the world myself, and I can't comprehend how someone could do such a thing."

You nod in exhaustion. "Yes, you cannot understand such a thing, Kızım. But those were different times."

"Excuse me?" Sevda casts you an angry glare, as though you've just said something completely inappropriate. "What do you mean, different times?"

"Things were the way they were, Sevda," you say cautiously. "We did not know any better."

"What didn't you know better?"

You exhale, your breathing strained. It's as though Sevda is asking you questions she already knows the answer to or can at least guess. "Our elders told us something and we obeyed, Sevda. We did not object to things the way you do today. Such things did not happen then."

"Anne!" Sevda exclaims, raising one hand in the air as if to comfort herself. "Can you hear what you are saying?"

That look in her eyes is gone now. Replaced by something as raw as the unfinished wall behind her.

"Of course, people acted this way. I know that!" Sevda continues. "And you taught me the same. Exactly this same nonsense. But damn it all." Sevda slams her tea glass down onto the table. "This was about a child! A human being. How can you give away another human? Your own child?"

You exhale again, depleted. "The elders decided it in this way, Sevda. It was not our place to disagree. We did not say: *But I want . . . I want* was not an option for us then."

"I thought Baba told you to do it. Why do you keep talking about elders?"

"I know your grandmother imposed this upon him," you say. "Hüseyin was so sad. It was not his decision. This I could see."

Sevda rises and takes a few steps toward the dinner table. Then she returns. She paces back and forth, as though she was lost.

"No, no," she exclaims. "I'm thinking and thinking and yet I still can't understand. Nothing you say makes any sense. Nothing!"

"You can think and pace and yell all you want, Kızım. These things you are doing now, I have done them my entire life. And believe me, I still do not understand. This will not help."

Sevda stops pacing. She lays one hand in exasperation on her curls in the bun atop her head. "And now?" she asks.

"Now? What do you mean?"

"I mean where is *o*?" she asks. "Are they both here? Wasn't Ayşe at the funeral?" Sevda's eyes grow wider as she asks these questions.

"Yes, Ayşe is here in Istanbul," you say evasively, and you point at the spot by the wall where Ayşe sat yesterday between her two nieces and the other women, crying so dreadfully. Slowly, you begin to rock your body back and forth, trying to calm yourself, so as not to curse Ayşe a second time today. Because you know those who curse others are bound in the end to be cursed themselves.

Sevda considers for a moment longer. Then she nods, as though the answer has just come to her.

"It all makes sense now!" she says. "Of course: why we never saw Ahmet Amca and Ayşe Yenge all those years. While the rest of the clan decided everything. You didn't want to see them. You wanted to keep living your lies!"

"No," you say calmly but decisively. "Actually, it was Ayşe who did not want to see us."

"Even better! Your lies were far more dangerous for her . . . She never told the child, did she?"

You look at the ground.

"How could you keep this a secret from us? Did you think it would be like it never happened if no one ever found out? How could you ever live in peace? You had four more children. Four! Didn't you ever feel even the slightest bit bad?"

~

The weeks after *onun* departure felt like a fever dream. Your ears rang at the slightest sound, Emine, and you were always cold. You wore your woolen vest even though it was already May. The slightest movements exhausted you, as though you were carrying weights on your body. At the same time, your mother-in-law took care of you as best she could to help you get back on your feet. Hüseyin wrapped his arms around your feeble body in the nights, pressing himself to you, whispered in your ear things would be better soon. But these were empty promises. You knew that. For they had torn a wound into your throat that could not be healed. All these things you wanted to hurl back at Hüseyin or your mother-in-law or your father-in-law where he sat silently in his corner only passively observing everything. All these things sank into your wound instead. There was nothing left to say. For what words could describe something that wasn't there? Was *missing* the word for this feeling? Had you known *onu* long enough to miss *onu*? No, you had not. For it was not so that a child simply came into the world and you loved it immediately. One had to learn to love it with time, just as a child required time to learn to love, even if it learned to love its mother first. But they had taken all these possibilities away from you. And there was no word left for their absence. It only felt cold and heavy, like an old blanket, forgotten outside on the clothesline in the snow. This sodden blanket draped over your shoulders.

Toward the end of that summer, Hüseyin went west to Rize to work on the tea plantations as he did every year. He returned with cracked hands and only a few lira with which you would have been unable to survive the winter had it not been for the money from Austria. When the first snow fell, already a new child was growing inside of you. You knew this instantly. You were neither nauseous again, nor were your breasts swollen, Emine. And yet your body felt different. It was fuller, your appetite returned, and Hüseyin's touch no longer filled you with aversion. It was almost like you were back home inside your skin. At first, you kept this to yourself. You fasted for Ramadan, so no one would catch wind of it. Because this fasting gave you strength, a strength you needed desperately. You would bring another healthy child into the world, and this time everything would be different. You would not let anyone take it away from you. On the second day of Bayram, your mother-in-law took the heavy bag of coal from you and whispered knowingly: "Do not be afraid, Kızım."

It was an easy pregnancy. The fuller you became, the fuller grew the smile on your mother-in-law's lips and under your husband's moustache. Up until the final day, you felt as light as if you were walking on a field of pillows. When your water broke that morning, you stood up, slipped on your mantle, and went for a walk in the forest, hoping the contractions would follow soon. You stood in a clearing, enjoying the warmth of the sun. A butterfly flew by and landed on your outstretched hand.

Several hours later, you lay on your mantle in the barn, overcome with cramps. You'd spread your mantle out over the hay beneath you. And although, during your first pregnancy you had breaks between the labor pains, breaks that had allowed you to recuperate, this time there were no breaks. The contractions came again and again, melding into one tremendous, unending agony stretching from your back into your womb and then down to your knees. Stabbing, tearing, ravaging. Your mother-in-law came again and again to check on you, Emine. She brought you blankets and a pitcher of water. But hours passed and still you were barely dilated. The baby simply did not want to come. You screamed and writhed. You changed your mind. If you could have stopped and turned the time back now, you would gladly have done so. The moment you had realized you were pregnant you would have boiled a huge pot of parsley and drunk it all. You would have jumped rope like a wild thing. You would have run through the forest and thrown your body against the pine trees. You would have starved yourself, denied your body water. You would have done anything to stop this wrenching, tearing pain inside your body that was unlike any pain you'd ever felt before. Anything.

The midwife did not arrive until evening. She'd been at another birth in the next village. She must have found you white as snow, unconscious from the pain, Emine. Lying there in your own vomit with your mother-in-law and a few neighbor women standing languidly around you. The midwife called for a bucket of warm water, screamed at you, struck your face until you awakened with a terrible scream.

You must push, child. It will not work this way!

But I am pushing . . .

You must push harder! Don't be so pathetic.

I can't anymore.

And what should this mean?

I can't.

But you must. Don't you know what will happen otherwise . . .

I can't.

Your child will die! Because you gave up. Listen to me! Because you are lazy, both of you will die.

I can't. I can't.

And then, at some point—it felt like only minutes later, and yet hours must have transpired for the sun had almost risen again—the midwife sprang onto your belly, pressing and striking and shoving like mad. You had long since sunk into the apathy that overcomes those who have accepted that their end has come. Had given yourself over to fate because this was your only release from suffering. You gave one final push, pressing with every fiber of your being. Your mother-in-law bent between your legs to receive the child, pressed out in a final bout of cramps. But the eternal labor pains did not end there; they continued. Your ears listened until you heard the cry, the cry of the baby, and then you pushed again. Someone lay the crying child on your breast, warm and slippery and quivering like a little frog. You begged them to take it away from you, for the birth was not yet over. The wrenching and the tearing continued. On and on. The never-ending labor pains. And still there came more blood and mucus and more tattered lumps of flesh. Until in the end, there were only tears. Thousands of tears.

Sevda's face looks like it has been turned to stone as she listens to the story of her birth night. And then hears of the months that followed. The months before she finally stopped screaming and your wounds began to heal, Emine. Listens as you tell how Hüseyin grew ever more distant. How he returned to Rize to pick tea at the end of the following three summers, and how, each time, he returned with even less money than before. How at the end of the fourth summer, Hüseyin finally decided to depart for Germany. How he promised it would only be a year. And how that year became another. And another. Because in Germany he earned more money in a few days than he earned in two months on the plantations in Rize. How for years you only saw him in the summer when he came to visit. How you missed him like mad and how then, when he was finally there standing before you with his gifts— stainless steel pots, a radio, little cremes that smelled like chamomile— how angry you were when you finally saw him. Because it was always Hüseyin who decided when you would see each other. Because it was you who was always left behind waiting. How six years passed after the birth of your second child, a child you had also named Sevda. Six years until your body was able to be pregnant again. And how much easier it was with Hakan and with Perihan and then later with Ümit.

Sevda's hand taps nervously against her thigh.

"So, I was a difficult birth. And that's why you hate me?"

The question cuts through the air like a knife.

You blink at your daughter. "How could I hate my own child?" you ask. "Are you crazy? Why do you say this now?"

Sevda's hand forms a fist into which she seems to have balled up all her rage. Her eyes are wet again, as if she might burst into tears at any moment.

"Oh, right. So you don't hate me? Then why didn't you ever send me to school?" she asks.

"What do you mean?" you ask in return. "There was no school in the village."

"But there was a school in the city. Don't you remember, Anne? I was only eight when we moved there. Why wasn't I allowed to go to school?"

You think back, trying to remember. "I think Hüseyin did not want this."

"Oh, that's a bunch of crap. Baba was already in Germany," Sevda retorts, drawing a long line in the air as if tracing Hüseyin's route on a map. "You could have easily enrolled me. But you didn't. And I begged and begged, but you didn't budge. You told me I was too old for school. Too old! I was eight years old!"

You shake your head in exhaustion. Sevda's accusations never stop, not even in mourning for her dead father. "Things were different then, Kızım," you say patiently. "And I was naive. Girls did not go to school as often then."

"That's such bullshit," Sevda hisses, wrapping her arms around her head. She rises, wanders across the room again forsakenly. The floor creaks under her heavy footsteps. "Even you went to school! Up to the fifth grade! How could you not have known any better?" Sevda's index finger points at your forehead like an arrow.

"I do not know what you want to hear from me," you begin to defend yourself. Sevda's affectations are starting to be too much for you. What does she even want? Sevda already has everything she's ever wanted.

"I'll tell you what I don't want: To listen to your sob stories, Anne. How Baba went to Germany and left you all alone. Did you think I would feel sympathy for you? Hello? You went to Germany and did the exact same thing to me. And I was just a child."

The arrow strikes its target right in the middle of your forehead. Your head is pounding. You'll endure a lot of things, Emine. But you won't let her tell you that you were a bad mother. Not after everything you've sacrificed.

"What do you mean you were a child?" you ask in disbelief. "You were thirteen years old, Sevda! Do you know what I had to do when I was thirteen?"

"Oh, please, Anne. Spare me," Sevda says, fluttering a hand in the air as though she were driving away an unpleasant odor. "And I was twelve, by the way. But that doesn't make any difference. Even if I had been thirteen, you don't just leave your child behind and move to a different country. You just don't!"

You can feel the fire welling up inside your chest. Your hands begin to quiver. You've done your best tonight to extend Sevda your hand, Emine. But Sevda doesn't understand. Sevda tears your whole arm off instead, and the other one after it, the first chance she gets. Just like always, she's taking things too far. You're at your wits end, Emine.

"Who are you of all people, Sevda, to say this to me?" you snarl. "Was it not you who was off doing God knows what in the middle of the night while your children were at home in a burning house? They almost died, Sevda. And for what? Because you can never be content with the things you have and are always off somewhere else instead chasing after other things!"

"Ha!" Sevda manages a fake laugh. "How good of you to throw these words at me a second time, Anne. Did you think they didn't hurt me enough the first time?"

"You are simply ungrateful, Sevda. Do you know this?" You can feel your face grow hot, Emine. You can literally feel the redness, like a stovetop left on burning unattended. "You have money, you have a car, you have a restaurant. You have everything. And now you come to me with your accusations and tell me I did not give you enough. What are you still missing, Sevda? What did I not give you?"

Sevda's eyes are filling now with tears of rage. She shakes her head as if she could shove them back down inside of her.

"Love, Anne. That's what I'm still missing. A mother's love. Do you even know what that is? It's the thing that you never gave me, Anne. But I wonder if you're capable of loving anyone at all. It's no wonder Baba died so young. You made his life a living hell with your constant misery. Are you finally happy now?"

Sevda's voice sinks back into a dreadful silence. You stare at her. You want to look her in the eye, but Sevda turns away and marches off to the kitchen.

And there it is again. This oppressive feeling you get every time you see Sevda after a long absence. The same feeling you had when Sevda first came to Germany. The same feeling you had each time she brought her children to visit from Lower Saxony. This feeling that you're staring at a younger version of yourself. Your daughter looks just like you, Emine. Even you can't help but marvel. Just like you, only with less fear and better clothing. And the headscarf is missing. Otherwise, it's like one and the same person. Each time you look at her you feel like you're staring into your own face. Staring at your own self, just eighteen years younger. And it scares you. It reminds you each time of your own life eighteen years before. And that's not a source for happy memories. Because you've never had the luck Sevda's had in her life.

Eighteen years ago, it was 1981. The year Sevda came to Germany. You were thirty-one. Sevda was fourteen. You left her behind when she was still a child. She is right about that. Sevda was only a child when you left the village, and when she came to Germany, Sevda was already a young woman. You'd marveled at her beauty then when she stood in your doorway in Rheinstadt, Hüseyin behind her, tall and slender as a pine tree, their suitcases in his hands. She'd worn a blue, ankle-length dress with a little stain on it. Her long hair had been tied back into braids. She'd been so beautiful: just like you were at that age when you were promised to Hüseyin. You sat around the kitchen table and Hakan and little Perihan had drilled Sevda with questions about the airplane, the airport, and everything to do with the flight. Sevda had seemed so timid. A stranger. But then, in no time at all, she was raving about her two days in Istanbul with Hüseyin. He'd taken her to Kapalı Çarşı, bought her an ice cream and a handbag she'd apparently forgotten in their taxi. They'd even ridden in a taxicab!

You watched Sevda, gesturing wildly with her bare arms while she told of their adventure. Her pale skin glowing, her braids swinging behind her. And you were unable to escape your own feelings of anger at never having made such a journey with Hüseyin yourself. Never in your entire lives had the two of you enjoyed such a moment for yourselves alone. Not one single day. There were always others there with you. First your in-laws. Then the children. There had always been something to do. You had always been too busy or too tired, you and Hüseyin. Hüseyin would never have so much as thought of taking you out somewhere, Emine, or of buying you ice cream. And so, you sat there at the table, seeing the excitement in Sevda's eyes at finally being allowed to follow after the rest of you to Germany. You listened to her, the way she could barely contain her excitement, her desire to go out and explore and discover everything. And you shifted impatiently in your seat, staring down at your own dry, cracked hands. You still remember the thoughts that flitted through your mind then like it was yesterday: *Sevda had too much time with her grandparents to dream. She thinks she is free now. That she can be and do whatever she wants. Poor Sevda. Soon enough she will learn that no one is free. That no one can ever be and do what they desire. Not there and not here. Nowhere. Never.*

You are ashamed now of your feelings then. Now when they return to you, Emine. You are ashamed of having been jealous of your own daughter. Ashamed, perhaps, that you still are. Jealous of Sevda's lightness of being. Jealous of her naive belief that she is free. Jealous of her desire to make something of this life. Jealous that she can want something at all. Because you've never wanted anything, Emine. You could never have even thought about the possibility of wanting something. You thought this only happened in the movies: A woman who wanted a different life and was willing to leave her husband to achieve it. A woman who could do so because she can take care of herself. Because she can take care of herself well.

The warmness of the air inside the room is making it hard for you to breathe, Emine. You feel like everything is swollen: you yourself, the walls, the house. As though a great pressure lies over the night, capable of destroying everything if one makes the wrong move. Sevda returns from the kitchen, this time bringing the entire kettle of tea with her. Divorced. Businesswoman. Independent. She has her own bank account and a bank card made of hard plastic she can put into machines and make them spit out brightly colored paper bills. How did it happen? What did Sevda have that you did not? What was it that had carried her so far while you had remained trapped in the same place for the past fifty years? You've never once in your life put a plastic card into an ATM,

Emine. You don't even know how it works. What will you do now, alone, without Hüseyin?

Perihan will teach you, Emine. It's different with Perihan. Perihan who once told you: *If you ever ask me when I'm going to marry again, I'll shave my head, Anne.* Perihan is like this. You would never dream of comparing yourself with her. She was only three years old when she came to Germany with you. Everything was always different in her life. There was hardly a girl around her in the neighborhood who did not go to school. But there were also very few who made it into the college-prep high school like Perihan. Who went on to university. Perihan had taken this path effortlessly. It had opened up before her, smooth as glass. And you could stand back, Emine, and bathe in her glow. But there had not been such a path for Sevda. Sevda and you, you came from the same village. You marched along the same stony path of thorns, marched in the same direction. How then can it be that your lives are separated now by such great mountains?

Sevda's eyes have grown soft again. Carefully, she refills your glass with tea and then hot water. You look at her and find yourself staring back at your own face. You see the way Sevda feels bad now for the things she said to you a few minutes before. The way you, yourself, feel bad about the things you've said to her. You are so much the same. The way you drive yourselves into a rage and cast things about the room that you immediately regret. The way you have such a hard time apologizing after. Because you think apologies seem insincere, unserious, when they are merely spoken aloud. Because what are words? It really wouldn't be like you at all to accept such an apology right away, Emine. Not without first pulling a wry face and coldly repelling every attempt at reconciliation for three days. But you have no strength left for such games now. Nor do you have the time. You cringe at the thought. How long do you plan to keep avoiding your daughter? How long do you intend to keep pushing her away? How much more time do you still have on this earth, Emine? Will you tend only to the bitterness inside your heart forever? Do you want to be remembered one day only as a wicked, sorrowful, and eternally aggrieved old woman?

"Anne, I didn't mean to say it the way I did before," Sevda says.

"I know," you respond sheepishly.

Sevda looks up, visibly surprised at your reaction. You nod with half-closed eyes, as though to reassure her that it is truly okay.

"It's just . . ." Sevda drops her head into her hands, then hastily undoes her hair. Those awful blonde streaks she has her hairdresser bleach in. She looks like someone who wants to appear German. And somehow this insults you, Emine. Sevda's shoulders sag. She looks battle-weary. "It was a real shock with that story right now. And I want to know where *o* is now. Please just tell me."

Now it's your head that sinks, Emine. You take a deep breath. As though you're preparing yourself to climb a long, steep flight of stairs.

"Is *o* here? Have you seen *onu*?" Sevda is asking.

"No. *O* is not here," you say, folding your hands, twining your fingers so tightly together that they begin to lose feeling. "*O* is dead."

"What?" Sevda exclaims. "When? What happened?"

"A few months ago," you say. Your mouth is dry. You run the tip of your tongue over your lips; they feel like an old stale piece of bread.

"How do you know this?" Sevda asks.

"Ayşe called us. For the first time in thirty years. She told your father."

"But what happened. *O* was so . . . young," Sevda says, bewildered. "Just a year older than me, right? Just one year."

"Car accident."

Sevda sinks back into the sofa. You unknot your hands and open them toward the sky. Instinctively, your lips begin to recite a silent Al-Fatiha. In memory of your dead. Very little noise is rising up now from the street below. Only this strange, oppressive heat. Perhaps Istanbul, too, this brutal, strange, sleepless metropolis, is thinking of its dead. Of those who have gone and those who will still follow. Ten million souls jumbled together in the high rises, the luxury villas, the gecekondu shantytowns. What is it that connects them all? All of them will taste death, sooner or later. All will return back to Allah. And those among them who did not give themselves to Allah during their time here on this earth, those who pursued their own pleasure instead, they will face the same fate as the spider who built itself a house. For truly there is no house more flimsy and unstable than the spider's house. If only they would know this.

"You know . . ." Sevda's voice seems to reawaken the city. You listen to the nervous sound of honking vehicles in the distance. A madman is screaming on the street below.

"You know what I don't understand," Sevda continues. "Why you're telling me all of this."

You run your hand over your face to conclude your prayer. Only then do you look back at your daughter.

"What do you mean?" you ask.

"Well, everything. The story of *o*. You didn't have to tell me that. Baba is dead. *O* is dead. You could have kept the secret to yourself. You didn't need to tell me that your child didn't die immediately after it was born but that you gave it away. You and Baba kept this secret from the rest of us for so many years, but now . . . why now all of a sudden?"

Sevda does not sound angry. She doesn't even sound sad. Her face is wan with disappointment.

You just shrug your shoulders, Emine. You ask yourself how late it is. Maybe two in the morning? That would give you only four more hours until morning prayer.

"Are you telling me now to make yourself feel better? Are you trying to clear your conscience?" Sevda asks.

"No," you say. "I am telling this now because I must."

You can feel the dryness of your eyes, Emine. Every blink burns from the tears you shed at the funeral, from the missing sleep over the past days.

"For whom? For yourself?"

"No," you say. "For Hüseyin."

"For Baba? But why?"

You think about the mirror in the bedroom, Emine, the mirror you covered with a cloth before your prayers. You still haven't uncovered it again. What would you see if you got up, walked over, and uncovered it now? Would you see yourself, or would you see your daughter Sevda? And what difference would it make?

"He was thinking of *o*. When he died," you say at last.

"How would you know?"

"Halime said it. The neighbor from the floor below. She called the ambulance. She was here."

Sevda rubs her eyes, sits up a little straighter. "And what did she say?"

"That he said only one word. *Divan*."

"Divan? He wanted to lie down? Is there even a divan in the apartment?"

"No. Halime misunderstood. He said a different word." You hold your peace for a moment. You know what Hüseyin said. You've known it from the first moment Halime told you in the kitchen after you arrived in Istanbul. It's circled round and round inside your head all day. And when Ayşe came to you in desperation in front of the hospital, you were finally certain. Certain when you looked into her eyes again after all those years. You finally knew for sure what Hüseyin had said at last.

"He said *Ciwan*."

"Ciwan?" Sevda furls her brow.

"That is *onun* name."

"Really?" Sevda asks. "But that's . . ."

"Yes, it is a Kurdish name."

"No, I mean . . . sure, that may well be. But I meant . . . I thought, *o* . . . I thought that was the reason I could use *onun* birth certificate . . ."

"Yes. We thought so too," you say.

The years in Germany slipped past you. You lost your feeling for time, Emine. Only in the growth of your children could you recognize that the world was still turning, at all. For everything else remained the same. The eternal grayness of the sky. The eternal sadness in the faces around you. The eternal path along the river you walked day in and day out carrying your shopping bags. The dark smoke rising from the metal-works. The air that tasted like tin cans. Hüseyin's silence. The hole that grew between the two of you from the moment after your first child's birth. This abyss, growing ever deeper the longer you stared into it. You did your best to look away. You still shared a bed each night, but it never felt like your husband was sleeping beside you, Emine. It was only a sad, worn-out body that rose each morning and dragged itself back to the factory only to return each evening more depleted than it was before. Only to lay earnings on the table at the end of each month from which you could easily have lived for a year in Karlıdağ. But in Rheinstadt it was only ever just enough. Enough for the shopping: for the little yogurts the children took with them to school, for the shoes that they were constantly outgrowing. For the Marlboros Hüseyin smoked at night on the balcony until he collapsed exhausted into bed. Too tired to even speak, much less make decisions.

And so, you took on those responsibilities, Emine. How the children spent their time, what purchases were necessary, what television channels were allowed, what the family ate. You decided all these things, Emine. One might think this would have pleased you, after all the years you spent with your in-laws, living in the shadows of their wishes and needs. But it did not please you, Emine. Not one bit. Because these responsibilities also meant a responsibility for you to function properly so your family could function too. You were the one link holding everything together. That's the way you saw it. Making all the decisions wasn't something that made you happy. No. On the contrary, it was a burden because you could never please everyone at once. Sevda or Hakan or Perihan or even Ümit later always had something to say about the decisions you made, punishing you with their long faces.

More and more you simply felt like another one of the machines Hüseyin operated at his work. Your home was nothing more than another factory. The laundry, the food, the cleaning, bathing the children, shopping, brochures and catalogs, time for breakfast, time for bed, time for prayer, canning, freezing, thawing, replacing your supplies, the mountains of garbage. Trash and still more trash. The children had great respect for Hüseyin. But they only came to you when they needed something. It was you they loved and feared, you whom they obeyed or cursed. You took care of them when they were sick or when they argued or when they needed comfort. In truth, Hüseyin remained the stranger from their summer holidays, sitting silently in his chair at night in front of the television, rising occasionally to smoke on the balcony, returning with the stench of ice-cold ashes only to sit silently again in the same place.

You were exhausted too, Emine. Something always hurt. Sometimes your back. Sometimes your hand. Sometimes you had a headache. Sometimes everything hurt at once. The doctor said that you were healthy, that there was nothing wrong with you. The pain was only in your mind. *Just relax, Frau Yılmaz.* And so, you tried to relax.

In the evenings, you, too, sat before the television. Do you still remember? That autumn before you were pregnant with Ümit? The children were already in bed and Hüseyin was still at work. The first time you found out about what the Germans had done. That miniseries with Meryl Streep was on TV. You liked the tilt of her face. The story of the Weiss family. You'd only been in Germany for four years, Emine, and you couldn't understand much of what they were saying. And yet it was still crystal clear. It was like someone doused your face with cold water. What had they done in this country? They had exterminated people? Because they were Jews? And you and Hüseyin and your children and all your neighbors had come here voluntarily? How could this be?

Over the next weeks, whenever you had to leave the house to do the shopping, you studied the faces of the men and women on the streets and in the narrow aisles of the supermarket warily. You tried to imagine the older ones, whether they had looked the other way as young adults when they'd taken the Jews away. Or whether they themselves had called in the uniformed men to do it. Or whether they had worn those uniforms themselves. These were the Germans? You could not believe it, Emine. The way nobody spoke of it. The way no one seemed to know a thing.

And then you asked Hüseyin, but he only answered in riddles. Single syllables. Opaque. Hüseyin did not want to hear about it. You longed for a shoulder to lean against, somewhere to unpack all the thoughts filling your mind. But you only rediscovered the abyss yawning between you. You stared into it. You began to fill it up. Fill it up with all your fears, all your assumptions about what must really be going on in Hüseyin's

head at night when he cried out in his sleep. Or when he sat silently for
hours in front of the TV. Or just before bed when he decided to go back
out again.

It is late, Hüseyin. Why not come to bed?

I'm not tired. I'm going to go for a walk.

You watched him from the window then, Emine. The way Hüseyin
lit his cigarette on the street and then walked down to the river. His
long, gangly legs moved quickly, as though Hüseyin still had something
important to do. You lay awake in bed, waiting for the sound of his key
in the apartment door.

You imagined a thousand things that Hüseyin might be doing out
there in the middle of the night, Emine. You paid meticulous attention
to the time when he came home from work. You puzzled over every
minute of overtime, creating new theories in your mind. And then came
that one day in summer, shortly after noon. Perihan and Ümit were at
school. Hakan was God knows where. Sevda had already long since
married and moved away. You were vacuuming the apartment and had
just put a pot of soup on the stove. Hüseyin would be home in an hour.
The telephone had rung.

Alo?

The person on the other end of the line hung up.

You put the receiver down and went back into the kitchen to wash
lettuce.

The phone rang again. You walked back from the kitchen.

Alo?

Excuse me for disturbing you, a voice said in Turkish. *Is Hüseyin Yılmaz
at home?*

Your heart beat wildly.

Who wants to know?

There was rustling in the background. The voice said nothing.

Hello? I asked who I am talking to!

This is Hasan, a colleague of Hüseyin's.

You thought for a moment.

Hasan? Which Hasan?

Um, we know each other from work.

You grew so angry then, Emine. You started to laugh like you had gone insane.

Listen, do you think I am some kind of ass? Your name is not Hasan. And you are no colleague of my husband's! If you were his colleague, you would know Hüseyin works the early shift and is not home. Leave us alone. If you call here again, I will kill you!

You slammed the receiver down and stood there staring at the phone for a while, as if waiting for it to ring again. This time you wouldn't even ask who was calling. You could already guess. The voice had sounded so uncertain and strained. It didn't leave you any doubt. A strange satisfaction flowed over you. You had already suspected, and now you knew for sure: Hüseyin had found another! But this satisfaction was only fleeting. Soon, you collapsed onto the floor like a defenseless child and began to choke and sob. You cried like you hadn't cried since *onun* departure.

You bottled it back up until the evening. Then you confronted Hüseyin. He said he didn't know what you were talking about. He didn't know any Hasan. He ignored your questions. The seagull of his brow remained indifferent. Motionless. As if you were not in the room at all. Suddenly, you seemed so helpless to yourself, Emine, that you threw on your coat and ran from the house. The door slammed so hard behind you that it scared you. You ran out into the night, but you did not know where to go. Never in your life had you been out by yourself this late. You went down to the river and cried. The rush of the current swallowed your tears and your whimpers like the comforting of a friend. At some point, Hüseyin found you. He parked his car on the side of the road, got out, and stood there in the darkness without saying a word. A great scrawny ghost. You got into the car. The two of you never spoke of it again. But, of course, you never forgot about that phone call. Years later, you still pondered what had happened. Who had called. But even if it had been what you feared, even if it was another woman, and even if Hüseyin had admitted to it, would you have had any other choice but to accept this and keep on going, Emine?

And then there was the thing with the Clorox. Five years had gone by then. The metalworks was long since decommissioned, and Hüseyin was now working at a cardboard mill. One morning, you stood in the street staring at a tree. It had lost all its leaves in the middle of the springtime. And suddenly, you were overcome by fear. The air tasted like tin cans again, even though no smoke had risen from the factory in years. And then, only a few days later, you looked out your living room window and saw workers cordoning off the old metalworks' grounds, covering them with an enormous plastic wrap. Men in white hazmat suits came. They tramped through the neighborhood, removing the soil from front yard gardens and then from the fields and then from each and every strip of green along the roadways. They replaced it with new soil. You asked Hüseyin what the devil was happening. Some substance from the old factory, he'd answered, the city just wanted to be sure no one was poisoned. That final word echoed around your head, Emine. *Poisoned.* Why were these men wearing hazmat suits? Why had they come now, years after the factory was decommissioned? You had all been poisoned now for years! *Hüseyin, they made me sick!* But Hüseyin just waved you away. There were rules and regulations for such things in Germany. No one here was going to be poisoned. He'd worked himself in that factory for years, and he was fine. But you were not fine, Emine. You were not fine, at all. You could feel the poison. In your hands, in your back, in your head. Everywhere. And it was just a matter of time before the others felt it too. That whole summer, you did not let Ümit play outside. You told your neighbor, Feraye, she shouldn't let her kids out either. But Feraye only laughed. Feraye, who always cast her interrogating gaze in your direction each time they spoke of those terrorists on the news. Feraye, whose husband had just taken out a lifetime mortgage to buy an apartment in the house next door. She acted like all of this was completely normal: the new soil and the men in hazmat suits. As if you were just overreacting. *Everything is good here, Emine. Everyone is good. Everyone, it seems, except for you. You need to stop talking about this poison all the time. Otherwise, people will start thinking you are crazy.*

You were standing on the flowered rug at the window and staring out over the sealed compound of the factory when Hüseyin called to tell you he had to work overtime. Suspicion shot through you like a

stabbing pain in your temples, Emine. Hüseyin had never worked overtime at the cardboard mill. You decided to wait for a half hour and then
call Feraye, whose husband also worked with Hüseyin at the mill. You
prepared lunch for Perihan, who had just arrived home to visit from
Frankfurt. You made the call while Perihan was in the shower, so you
could talk uninterrupted.

Hallo. What are you doing, Feraye?

We're eating lunch with Osman. What is it, Emine?

*Oh, Hüseyin is still not home yet. Maybe Osman might know if he had to
work overtime today? He did not call. I am really starting to get worried.*

*You and your worries, Emine. But wait, let me ask him. Osmaaaan! Osman
says Hüseyin met a young man in front of the mill. They wanted to go into
town or something? Is he some relative? It doesn't sound like you need to be
worried, Emine.*

You hung up the phone and began screaming like a mad woman.
You did not know where your feet were taking you as you stumbled
blindly through the rooms. But this time they didn't carry you outside and to the river. This time they took you somewhere else, and you
allowed them to, Emine. Panicked, angry, you let your limbs guide
you independently, searching for a way out. A way to make it all stop.
You found yourself in the bathroom; you saw Perihan spring naked
from the shower, rush two paces to your side, and strike the bottle
of Clorox from your hands. A single drop burned its way down your
throat, Emine. You vomited all over the crocheted toilet lid cover you
had made.

That evening, Hüseyin got tangled in his own excuses. He had never
lied to you before, Emine. And so it was obvious this time that he was.
For thirty years, you could depend on this at the very least: Hüseyin
did not lie. Even after that strange phone call, at some point, you could
believe him: that he really didn't know who or what was behind it. Because lying and Hüseyin together did not work. Because you were convinced your husband was not like this. But this time, it was obvious.
You saw it in his downturned face, in his stiffened posture, in the frightened seagull of his brow. It nearly broke your sanity, Emine. Everything
you'd based your life on was meaningless.

Coldness mingled with the silence between you and Hüseyin over the following two years. From outside, it might appear little had changed. But it was in the small things, Emine, the small things where you showed Hüseyin you no longer cared for him. And wasn't it precisely those small things that made a home out of a mere couple of rooms, a couple out of just two people? There were still pots of fresh-made meals on the stove each day, Emine. But Hüseyin had to get his food for himself and eat alone. The laundry was still washed on schedule. But Hüseyin's things remained lying unfolded in the basket until he sorted them himself into his dresser. The shopping was done; the shelves remained stocked. But the walnuts and dried plums Hüseyin loved to eat at night in front of the TV—you did not buy these anymore. And the two of you got used to this kind of life together, in the same way you got used to so many things over the years. The discreet tenderness between the two of you in the house of your in-laws. The strangeness, the emptiness after the loss of o. The eight years you spent apart, separated by continents. The way you found each other again in Germany. The excitement you shared at Ümit's birth after all those years. And now this. There was such a coldness between you that you almost didn't look at your husband's face anymore. Until you did once again, some time, only a few months ago. And you saw the same sad seagull there, perched on his brow.

It took a lot for you to finally speak to him again. But you did it in the end, Emine, because the sight of your despairing husband's face grown suddenly ten years older was harder for you to bear than you admitted to yourself. And then one night, alone in the living room of your empty apartment—alone without Hakan, Perihan, or Ümit—he finally did it, in response to your questions. Hüseyin spoke. Spoke like he had never spoken before. And he told you the truth. Hüseyin spoke in broken pieces, moved in leaps and bounds. Labored, because he'd spoken so rarely of the things that occupied his mind. And while he spoke, digging his fingers into the fabric of his armchair, the pieces came together like the pieces of Ümit's giant puzzles with the pictures of galloping horses against the lush, green landscape of dreams.

O is dead.

Your eyes grew wide; they clung to Hüseyin, entreating him not to spare you a single detail. Begging him to tell you everything he knew. Everything that he could tell you. And when Hüseyin began to tell, his face only half-turned away; you saw again the young man you had smiled at thirty years before in the face of the old man who was now speaking. How *o* had first tried to reach out to Hüseyin; how *o* had called him at the factory only a few days after that strange phone call at home. How Hüseyin came down to the pay phone in the staff room and listened as *o* made introductions and explained how *o* already knew everything about *onun* adoption. That was 1990. *O* had said *o* would like to come to Rheinstadt and meet *onun* family. How Hüseyin told *ona* no, don't come, never call here again. How Hüseyin had been afraid because he hadn't known what would be right or wrong. Hadn't wanted to reopen your old wounds, hadn't wanted to turn everything on its head. How he had only wanted everything to somehow just keep going like it had.

How one day, last year, *o* had simply been standing in front of the cardboard mill, waiting to collect Hüseyin. How *o* had formally extended a hand to Hüseyin in introduction as Ciwan. How Hüseyin had had to ask over and over again until he'd understood. How he'd wondered at *onun* clothing, *onun* hair, and everything: this oversized leather jacket, a man's haircut, the beard on *onun* face. How *o* had struggled with explanations that only confused Hüseyin more. How *o* had finally said: *I'm like Bülent Ersoy, only the other way around.* How Hüseyin had simply known that *o* had left Ayşe and Ahmet. Had had to leave Ayşe and Ahmet. Because Ayşe and Ahmet could never accept *onu* this way. How Ayşe and Ahmet had apparently dragged *onu* to every hodja in Vienna in an attempt to heal *onu*. How, in the heat of the moment, they had said *o* was not even their own biological child. How *onun* eyes had shone with expectation, with hope, waiting for Hüseyin's comfort. For Hüseyin's welcome. How Hüseyin had, instead, been unable to say anything because he could only marvel at *onun* perfect Kurdish. And at the new name *o* had chosen for himself rather than the name Ayşe and Ahmet had chosen for *onun* second birth certificate. How Hüseyin had bought *ona* a meal, how he'd withdrawn *ona* 400 marks from an ATM, laid this in *onun* hand, and clapped *ona* on the shoulder. How he hadn't hugged *onu*, but just kept patting *onun* shoulder. How he had begged *onu* not to contact you, Emine, until he had told you himself. How *o* had nodded and smiled with disappointment in *onun* eyes. How *o* had laid the money back in Hüseyin's hand and simply turned away, left him there, disappeared. How *o* had vanished and never contacted Hüseyin again. As though *o* had never been there in the first place. How Hüseyin had always asked himself, over and over and over again, whether now might be the right time to talk to you. How he had never found the words. How time passed, and he had begun to wonder whether it had really happened at all, or whether this had all been in his head. How now, two years later, while you had been drinking çay with Feraye, how Ayşe had called. How she had told him, after all those years, without so much as a greeting, that *o* was dead. Killed in a car accident in Berlin. How Ayşe had sniveled over the telephone and begged him to pray for *onun* soul. Pray that Allah would forgive *ona*. How Hüseyin had prayed incessantly since that moment. Prayed and prayed uninterrupted. Prayed not for *onun* absolution but his own.

You could not believe it, Emine. How you could have had the chance to see *onu* again. How *o* had been here. Not in some other life behind a wall in Vienna insurmountable even in your mind like all those years before but right here, in Rheinstadt. *O* had wanted to come to you, Emine. *O* knew about you, had wanted to see you, to talk to you. You could have held *onu* in your arms, just held *onu* in your arms as long as you could, if only Hüseyin had not kept all this a secret. Maybe *o* would not be dead, you had thought, if only you had known about *o*. If Hüseyin had only told you, if he had only taken *onu* home with him that very day. If only. Always if only. All those ifs spiraled into such an endless line it made you dizzy, Emine. And in the end, you always landed right back at yourself. At your own guilt.

The sorrow tore at your skirt, Emine, pulling you down, just like it tore at Hüseyin. And you found each other there again, in your common tragedy. You stood shoulder to shoulder propping each other up. And the apartment in Istanbul enticed you like a promise of a new beginning. Hüseyin spoke incessantly of this. A new life together in a new place. A place without a past.

∿

You stand and open the balcony door, allowing the warm night air to waft into this stuffy room. The floor rolls with it, but that's only your own footsteps, Emine. Sevda cowers on the sofa, her fingernails digging deep into her forehead. You close the drapes in front of the open door and remove your headscarf.

"And then Ayşe came here. She came here to mourn. She waited for me in the hospital parking lot. Can you believe it? How could she? Ever since this afternoon I can think of nothing else, Sevda: How dare she? I gave her my firstborn child. My blood. My likeness. My baby. And she promised to love it even more than I ever would have. But what did she do? She threw it away for . . . For a name and a haircut! For such a thing, she chased my baby from her house. Threw it away!"

You collapse back onto the sofa. You slap both hands against your thighs as if to drive away an evil spirit.

Sevda takes her hands from her face and stares at you with a coldness that pierces through you.

"What makes you think she threw it away?" she asks.

"Ayşe drove *onu* away. In a moment when *o* needed all the support in the world. She told *ona*: *You are not my child*. In such a moment! Instead of being patient and trusting in Allah's grace . . . And for a name! For nothing more than a name!"

"Anne, I don't think it was only about a name," Sevda replies, rolling her eyes.

"Are you trying to say Ayşe was right? That she made the right decision? Is this what you are saying?" you ask Sevda in dismay.

"No, Anne," Sevda counters decisively, shaking her head. "I'm saying it was about more than just that."

"What then? A haircut? A jacket? Pants? What does any of that matter if *onun* heart was pure?"

Sevda shakes her head again, stares at you skeptically. "No, Anne. Don't you understand? *O* wanted to be who *o* was. And *o* wanted to be respected this way."

"What difference does it make, Sevda? Whether *o* wore a dress or a leather jacket. What is the difference? If I had not given *onu* away, none of this would have happened."

"Nonsense!" Sevda cries out impatiently. "That's only easy for you to say because it didn't happen to you."

"What do you want from me, Sevda? I pour my heart out to you, lie here helpless on the floor, and you kick me while I am down?"

"No, Anne, I'm not kicking you. I just want you to stop lying to yourself and playing the poor victim. Do you truly believe it all would have been different?"

You throw your hands in the air. "If o had stayed with us? And if I believe it!"

"Anne, what would you do if Ümit came to you tomorrow and said: *Anne, I'm a girl.*" Sevda tilts her head to one side. She looks at you like she's just asked you a question she already knows the answer to.

"Tövbe, Sevda, what are you talking about now?" you cry, aghast.

"I'm serious, Anne. Tell me. What would you do if he suddenly started wearing dresses?"

"Ümit would never do this," you say, waving your hands in the air angrily. But you feel something on your neck. A slight twinge. A faded memory. The nail polish on Ümit's fingers. Feraye's words of warning that she should take better care with the boy.

"And what would I do, if Cem did the same? Honestly, I don't know, Anne. I don't know what I would do. But I don't think I could just accept him with open arms and act like everything's okay. And with *you*, Anne, I believe it even less . . ."

"You do not understand anything, Sevda," you hiss. "They took my child from me. I would do anything to hold it in my arms again. I would not care what it looked like or what it was called."

"Oh yeah? Then why don't you say *Ciwan* when you speak of this child? Why do you always insist on saying o if the name means nothing to you?"

She looks at you expectantly. You rub your hands together, wring them as if you were washing them clean under a faucet.

"For me, it is still my baby, Sevda. Do you not understand? A baby has no name; it was still so small. We never called it by its name. We never had the chance to call it anything. It was gone so soon. Oh, Sevda . . ."

You feel the thick tears running down your cheeks, over your chin, falling down onto your hands. You don't wipe them away. You just sit there, crying silently.

"Anne, please," you hear Sevda's voice. It sounds resentful. "I can't listen to this anymore." You can feel her standing up. You look up and see Sevda pace toward the open balcony door. You watch her light a cigarette in front of it, without going outside.

"What are you doing?" you ask her, but Sevda ignores you. She pulls open the curtain just a bit and exhales her first drag luxuriously. Then she turns slowly back to you, holding the cigarette in the air between her outstretched fingers in demonstration.

"You're not going to like what I have to say, Anne. But if o, I mean Ciwan, had grown up with us, it would not have been different. And if you could just be a tiny bit more honest with yourself, you'd recognize this too."

"Do not be stupid, Sevda!" you wail, rubbing your hands across your cheeks now after all to dry the tears. "How would you know this? Do you think you are the Prophet now, or what?"

"I know it because you did the same to me, Anne." Sevda is speaking slowly, overarticulating her words as though she were reading you the diagnosis of a fatal illness. "You pushed me away and slammed the door in my face in that moment when I needed you most."

"Oh, do not start with this again, Sevda. Did I not just apologize? What do you want from me now?" you ask helplessly.

"It's not about apologies, Anne. And you know that. I told you then, after the fire, what I wanted and how I wished to live, and you could not accept it. You sent me back, sent me away, knowing that I never wanted to go back to Ihsan."

You tug at the collar of your nightdress, shaking it until a bit of air comes through. Everything in your body is quivering. You sigh with exhaustion. "Everything always has to be about you, Sevda! This is not about you now."

"Yes, it damn well is about me, Anne," Sevda says. "Because I'm the one you raised instead of o, I mean, instead of Ciwan. If you're going to look me in the face and tell me everything would have been better for Ciwan with you than it was with Ayşe, then you're also going to have to hear this from me. Because it isn't true. And I know it. No one knows it better than I do."

You let go of your collar, sinking slowly into the back of the sofa. Sevda is still standing with her cigarette by the balcony door, but her voice echoes as loudly as if a monster were towering over you.

"It seems you did better with the others. With Hakan and Peri and Ümit. Maybe you learned from your mistakes, Anne, you came to understand your children are their own people. That they aren't just separate branches growing out of you. That they make decisions not with or against you but for themselves. And for themselves alone. Maybe Peri is just stronger than I am and knows how to assert her will against you, I don't know. But listen to me now! With me, with me you did precisely the same thing that Ayşe did with o. With Ciwan. When I tried to show you who I am—without the lies, without the games—when I just wanted to be myself, you refused me. You drove me away."

The sofa groans beneath you. You can't bury yourself any further back in the upholstery. You wish you could crawl away and hide between the folds of fabric. Lie there in peace, alone just by yourself, without the outside world.

"You betrayed us," Sevda says. "For some bullshit you picked up somewhere—from your own mother and father, from your neighbors, in your mosque, on your TV. You picked them up and you imposed them on us, no, you forced us into them like a prison. You just accepted all these things without so much as ever once asking yourself if this was good for you. If this would be good for us! This ignorance, it's driving me insane. I want to scream every time you pretend you're even the slightest bit better than Ayşe because you're not!"

Your head began silently reciting Surah Al-Fatiha, completely of its own accord, starting the moment Sevda mentioned mosques. You pray for forgiveness for your daughter. You run your hands over the stiffness of your tearstained face and begin the prayer anew.

"You know, Anne, it's easy to say that it was everyone else's fault they took Ciwan from you. Or that times were different then and that's why I didn't go to school. That girls didn't go to school back then because they were girls. But it wasn't Baba who forbade me from going to school. It wasn't Baba who wanted me to marry at any cost the moment I turned eighteen. That was you, Anne. Do you think I don't know? It might well be that the men still called the shots; for fuck's sake, it's 1999 and things still haven't changed. But for this to happen, for them to stay in charge this way forever, that requires people like you. Women who do nothing but hold other women down. Women who force their children to lead the same fucked-up life they had to lead themselves. And I see it in myself too. I see it whenever I yell at my own kids or punish them. I constantly have to remind myself to do differently, that I don't want to be like you. But I could never, ever be as deceitful and hypocritical as you!"

Sevda's voice is slipping away from you; slowly it becomes nothing more than background noise. You're thinking of the dirt, Emine, the dirt they shoveled over your Hüseyin today. Over his white cloth. The earth was loose, dry. You hadn't seen a single beetle in it. But still, you wonder how long it will be before the maggots start to gnaw on Hüseyin. You're wondering whether any light will penetrate the soil, down deep where he lies buried. Whether his burial shroud can still be warmed by the sunlight. Or whether it's dark and cold down there, even in August. Down in that in-between world.

"You just didn't send me to school. And that's nothing but a harmless omission to you. You just say things were like that then. Your husband, your mother-in-law, God knows who supposedly wanted it to be this way. You think you can just push it all away from you and it's over and done with. But it's not that easy, Anne. It's never that easy. Do you even know how much the consequences of your decision affect my life? Do you know how it feels to be the only person in a room who can't read right? How it feels to have to ask your employees to write your letters for you? Do you know? Sometimes I see a movie that takes place in a school or university and I just start to cry, Anne. Do you know how hard it is for me that I can't even help Cem with his homework? Because I don't know how? Because I have no idea. Bahar has to write her own sick notes when she stays home from school, and I can only sign them. Because a second grader can do it better than I can, Anne."

You run your hands over your face again. You're praying for Hüseyin's soul, and that he will soon come to deliver you as well. The here and now just feels so wrong. If your time came this very night, you would be ready, Emine.

"You're going to say now that you can't even speak German. And that it just is how it is. But that isn't true. You're my mother. I'm your child. You could have made all this possible for me. You should have. I wanted it so badly. But instead, you sent me for a couple of months to German class, and even this, only because you got money for doing it. And then you married me off to the first available man you could find. To get rid of me. Even though I didn't want to get married! I can tell you don't want to hear this, Anne, but who else should I tell? Should I tell my employees? My German customers and neighbors? So they can nod at me in pity and say: *Yes, your people oppress their women, don't they? You poor thing.* But I don't want their pity, Anne. I don't want to reconfirm what they already think about us anyway. I just want you to understand that you are not the victim here. That you're responsible for this too. And also responsible for what happened to him, to Ciwan. And not because you gave him away. But because you would have done exactly the same thing that Ayşe did. Because you would not have accepted him. Yeah, yeah, just pray now like you always do. But pray for yourself this time, and not for Ciwan or for me. The best thing that ever happened to Ciwan was that he never met you. Baba did everything right."

Sevda is gasping for air as though she isn't finished yet. As though there are still things she can throw at you and hang around your neck. But you hold up your hand, Emine. You say nothing, you just hold out your palm. Like a shield. Or a stop sign. This is enough. Go no further. Sevda throws back her head in exasperation. She exhales.

You rise slowly and walk to the bedroom. Everything around you teeters as you go. You turn off the light in the hallway, the hallway where

Hüseyin died. You take one step after another, sparkling embers are falling toward you—blue and yellow and red—you wave them away with your hands as you keep walking. You're listening to your breathing. You can't fall down now, Emine. Not now. You want to at least make it to your bedroom first and be alone if you're going to collapse. You enter the darkened bedroom and remain standing for a moment because you feel dizzy. Or because something else isn't right. You look toward the corner where a bit of light is falling from the window. The mirror you covered up. You go to it, and you take the cloth away, thinking of Hüseyin's burial shroud. A haggard face appears in the wan moonlight.

Yes, Emine, it's true. Not Ayşe alone has grown old. Just look at yourself. Your face is like one of Hüseyin's unironed shirts. One of the shirts you smelled this morning. Crumpled and pale. You've become an elder, Emine. Do you remember how they spoke of them when you were still a child? How they taught you always to obey them, to listen to their every word because wisdom came from their wrinkled faces? How can it be that no one listens to your words now when your mouth is ringed by such wrinkles too. Can it be that the alleged wisdom of the elders was nothing but an illusion? Can it be that you have not earned this respect that you demand from others? Could Sevda be right about all these things? Oh, Emine. Your daughter's broken your heart, isn't it true? Oh, Emine. Each word was like a stabbing wound, like a thousand tiny paring knives, not sharp enough to kill you outright but more painful because each new wound was followed by another. Because nothing can deliver you from this pain. What will you do now, Emine? You can't do anything. You must live with this truth. Sevda is right. You could not have saved *onu*. There's no difference between you and Ayşe. At one time you were healthier, but this, too, is long since past.

But if you could go back now with this knowledge, Emine. If you could go back and live the same life over anew, then you would do things differently, wouldn't you? You would have to do it differently. And this, this then would be the wisdom people so like to speak of.

But you know it doesn't work this way, Emine. There are no second chances; there are no second lives. There's only one life and one God, and nothing changes anything about this. Not even you, not even now. Now in this moment, with your fifty years. Here in the freshly painted apartment of your dead husband. Now when you want something for the first time in your life, the first time since you can think. Want something so badly your chest is heaving with excitement at the thought of it. You want to relive everything; you want this second chance. You want to rewind it all like a VHS tape. Rewind back to the evening when you and *o* returned to your village from the city with *onun* birth certificate. Rewind back to that New Year's Eve in Rheinstadt when you sent Sevda away. But it doesn't work that way, Emine. Life is not a cassette tape you can fast-forward or rewind as you see fit. Your fate has long been written, and you know this all too well.

You think about the shirts in the dresser. Walk over and remove them, smell them one more time. Imbibe the scent of Hüseyin into your body, as long as it still clings to this cloth. How long will it take before this sweet, woody smell vanishes from his shirts? Until their fabric only smells old and full of dust? Until you can no longer remember how Hüseyin smelled, how Hüseyin sounded, how he tastes? Can you not vacuum-seal these shirts like you do the meat you divide up in little portions and freeze after Eid? To take it out again throughout the year and thaw it, to make soups and stews to feed your family? Who will you cook for now, Emine? Only Ümit still lives at home, and not for much longer. And Ümit does not even like to eat meat. Who will you take care of when Ümit, too, has moved away in a few years to study? Who will take care of you?

You are exhausted. Come. Lie down in bed, Emine. The sun will be rising soon. And you need a bit of sleep before the morning prayer. Lie down now, finally, and sleep. Even this day, too, must have an end. The floor trembles beneath your feet. Did you forget to take your blood pressure medicine? The pills are in your purse, there on the floor. Perhaps you should turn on the light to help you find your bag. You take another step, but the floor is vibrating so intensely now, you grow afraid. What is wrong with you? This quaking is something new. This quaking is different from the trembling inside you. It sways, and everything sways

3333333333

around you. Something almost knocks you to the floor. You stretch out your arms to keep your balance. *Anne!* You can hear Sevda screaming. Your child is calling for you. And then you hear a heavy thud and the sound of breaking glass. Ten, twenty glasses. Your feet carry you over the rolling floorboards to the wall with the light switch. You flick it on. A great rend tears across the wall above it. There was not a crack here in the wall before, was there? The crack is growing, becoming blacker; it spreads across the wall and down to the floor. Racing on before your eyes. You look around you, and you see the wardrobe wobbling. See yours and Hüseyin's bed literally bucking and shaking. You cast your eyes to the window and watch as it begins to shatter, the collapsing building overhead. The sky before the dawn. Everything topples. How can this be?

Anne! Anne. Earthquake!

You turn, and you see Sevda at the end of the hallway. You see the look in her eyes: the fear and yes, maybe also the love. You rush toward her, but a tremendous power throws you back against the wall like you were nothing.

Anne!

Something caresses your head. Something flutters above you. Is that dirt? Is it dust? Sevda is running toward you. You reach for your own shoulder, the one that just struck the wall. It hurts you. The rustling transforms into hail. Then into noise. A noise that deafens you. A noise that moves through your entire body like an electric shock. Sevda is drawing closer. Everything above you collapses in on itself. It's pitch black now. Completely dark. A darkness like the dark of the night back in your village when you were a child. So dark you cannot say whether your eyes are open now or closed. Whether you are awake or dreaming. The darkest darkness that has ever befallen you. And your left hand remains there where it was on the opposite shoulder. There is a heaviness upon your limbs so that you can no longer move, Emine. Not an arm. Not even a finger. Nothing. Your heart pounds so wildly you want to tear off your nightgown to give it room. But you cannot do this, Emine. Your hands seem to be bound. Your feet. And even your throat. A thought shoots through the darkness like a newly sparked ember. *Sevda!* Your lips form the word: *Sevda!* But does the word leave your mouth? Or does it remain inside of you? Is it also bound, bound like everything else? *Anne!* you hear someone call from a great distance.

Anne, can you hear me? They're going to find us. Don't move!

You want to say: *Sevda, this is the first time in my life that I will do what you say. I will not move. How could I?* And you think: *Who are they? Just who exactly are they? Who is going to find us?* The thoughts whirl quickly through your mind like a spinning top. But the real question should be: Do you want to be found, Emine? *Hide yourself, they are coming!* you think you hear Hüseyin whispering. You remember how he used to come back to Karlıdağ during the summers with his brightly wrapped presents from Germany and a smile over the sadness in his face.

Did you not just recite the Spider Surah in the living room, Emine? Surah Al-Ankabut?

The parable of those who entrust themselves to others than Allah is like that of the spider who builds itself a house. For verily, the frailest and most unstable of houses is the spider's house, if they but knew.

Were these not the words you so often repeated? The words whose meaning you know in Turkish because this is your favorite surah? And now you yourself sit in the spider's house, Emine. In a house more frail and unstable than any other. How can this be? You and Hüseyin entrusted yourselves to Allah all your lives. How can it be that you are now caught in the rubble of the spider's house? *Hide yourself, they are coming.*

Do you still remember that autumn when you were pregnant with Ümit, Emine? That miniseries with the Weiss family, the Holocaust series? Do

you still remember what your neighbor Latife said to you when you
told her about this show? She and her wild daughter Havva were still
living in Germany back then. It was just before they returned to Hatay.
Latife slurped her Nescafé slowly and said her grandmother had told her
similar stories when she had been young. Not stories about the Jews in
Germany but stories about the Christians in Turkey.

What are you talking about, Latife? you demanded, outraged. *This cannot be,* you said. *I do not know what you are talking about.* And yet, more
and more often you had lain awake in bed at night beside Hüseyin and
listened to him sleep. You wondered why Latife's husband wished to
return to Turkey if such things had happened there. You wondered
why you and Hüseyin wished so badly to remain in Germany now that
you knew such things had happened here. And then one night, when
everything inside your mind was swarming in contradiction like an ant-
hill, one night you woke your husband and you asked him questions,
Emine.

What did you do in the army, Hüseyin?
   What do you mean, Emine? What anyone does in the army.
   Yes, and what is that? What does a soldier do in Hakkâri?
   *A soldier protects his country, Emine. And sometimes a soldier just peels
potatoes. It always depends.*
   And who does a soldier protect his country from?
   *From robbers in the mountains. And from enemies who want to destroy the
country and break it up in pieces.*
   Who are these enemies, Hüseyin? Did you ever see them?
   *What do you want from me, Emine? What do you understand about such
things?*
   Tell me, Hüseyin. Who are these robbers you fought against?
   I did not fight against anyone, Emine. I only fought to come back alive.
   Why did you forbid us to speak Kurdish?
   *Because it was dangerous, Emine. Because they taught us in the army that
there are no Kurds. Because we were to spit in the faces of anyone who called
themselves that. There are only Turks in this country and nothing else.*
   And why did we have to leave our village?

Because it was safer in the city. Because the army passed through these villages to free them from the robbers. But the people in the villages protected the robbers instead. They suffered under their rule and yet they stuck by them anyway. You could tear out their fingernails and still they would never betray them. Do you understand? They died for them, Emine. Do you want our children to die too?

Your throat is dry, Emine. You want to cough. You open your mouth with all your strength and yet you open nothing. It stays shut. Your coughs stick in your throat. You gasp for air. But it is useless. Sevda's voice has grown silent. Has she made it out? Is she going for help? In the silence and the darkness, there is nothing but you and your wheezing and the sudden certainty that it is too late to hope for help. But there is something else, Emine. Are you wondering who I am? This is not important, Emine. The real question is: Who are you? For I am only a part of you, Emine. I am the hole between your belief and your action. I am the contradiction between the image you hold of yourself and the face you show to others. I am the void between what you hold to be right and wrong. The thin crack in your morality, the discord between your expectation and your being. I am merely a voice inside your head, Emine. I am nothing without you. So, tell me: Who are you?

The ticking of the clock. Everything is shattered, broken, blind. Everything but the time. Time still marches on. It carries you away from here, second by second, Emine. It carries you closer to Hüseyin. He's waiting for you, Emine. He raises the seagull of his brow with joy as he smiles upon you. And you are ready. You're saying your final prayer, and suddenly it no longer smells of rubble. It smells like something else. You know this smell; you know it from somewhere. Just think, Emine, remember. It smells like sizzling fat, like braised vegetables, like meat. It smells like home. You're standing in your kitchen in Rheinstadt. Sevda's children run past you; they're playing tag in your apartment. You watch them, and you smile. They're children, Emine. Children are this way. Carefully, you open the oven. The goose looks good. Juicy. It's glistening, golden. It's just right. You take it from the oven, and you carry it to the table in the living room. Everyone is already seated, waiting for you there. All of them greet you with patient eyes. *İbo Show* is playing on the television. İbo is singing an uzun hava. The audience in the studio claps as if on command. Hakan puts down his camera, makes room on the table so you can put down the roast. Hüseyin turns down the television. Perihan is pouring cola into the glasses. Ümit cannot wait and empties his in one big gulp. Sevda seats her children on the chairs beside her. You adjust the roast and ask Hüseyin to carve it. He says: *The food smells wonderful; you did such a good job, Emine.* You nod to him and smile. Ümit asks: *What language is that, Baba?* Hüseyin pats his head and begins telling Ümit of his childhood. You pour Ümit another glass. Hakan rises and says dramatically: *I'm quitting my training program. I don't want to do it anymore.* You and Hüseyin, you hesitate a moment; you exchange a look. Then you both say: *That's your decision, Oğlum. You're a grown man.* Perihan is wearing all black, as usual. She smiles with concern and asks: *How is your pain, Anne?* You look into her eyes and see she's carrying her own pain too. You tell her: *Where there is pain, there is also healing, Kızım.* She nods gratefully. And then you go around the table to Sevda and bend down to her ear. You place both hands on her shoulders and you whisper: *You don't have to go back to Ihsan, Sevda. Stay here with us, Kızım. This is your home too.* Sevda's eyes fill with tears and joy. She kisses your hand. And just as you are about to take your seat again, the doorbell rings. Sevda stands up, but you tell her: *I've got it, Kızım.* You take a few steps through the darkened hallway. You find the door, even without a light. You know the way. This is your home, Emine. Your own place in the world. The place where all the people you love are together. The people who love you. The place where everyone always forgives each other. Because forgiveness is the only thing that helps against our loneliness. Because forgiving others is the only way to find forgiveness. The only way to forgive yourself.

You open the door. Your heart is racing. And you say:

Ciwan.

Glossary

abdest—(Turkish) ablution; ritual washing and purification
abi—(Turkish) brother
abla—(Turkish) older sister
Alman—(Turkish) German; also a slang word in contemporary German for a
 stereotypical German or stereotypically German behavior
Almancı—(Turkish) slang for German-born or German-socialized people of
 Turkish descent
amca—(Turkish) uncle; also a title of respect or endearment
anne—(Turkish) mother
anneanne—(Turkish) maternal grandmother
Ausländer raus!—(German) "Foreigners out!"; common rallying cry for xenophobic, anti-immigrant movements in the German-speaking world
Azaab—(Turkish transliteration of the Arabic) anguish, torment; divine
 punishment
baba—(Turkish) father
babaanne—(Turkish) paternal grandmother
bacı—(Turkish) sister; also a title of endearment
bağlama—(Turkish) a long-necked lute used in traditional folk music
Bayram—(Turkish) a national or religious holiday; particularly used inter-
 changeably to denote the two Eids
Bu oğlan hiç adam olmayacak—(Turkish) "This boy will never be a man."
canım—(Turkish) darling
cin—(Turkish) djinn
-cım—(Turkish) a suffix denoting endearment
çay—(Turkish) tea

dede—(Turkish) grandfather

delikanlıs—(Turkish) boy, lad

dva—(Serbo-Croatian) two

elif be te—(Arabic) the first three letters of the Arabic alphabet

Elternhaus—(German) parental home; literally, parental house

erişte—(Turkish) noodles

Eşhedü en la ilahe illallah . . .—(Turkish transliteration of the Arabic) the opening words of the Shahada, the Islamic Profession of Faith: "I bear witness
that there is no God but God [Allah] . . .)

gecekondu—(Turkish) shanty or shack; used to describe the makeshift or
unpermitted houses built along the periphery of cities

Grüß Gott—(German) used as an informal greeting in the southern German-
speaking world (particularly in Austria and Bavaria); literally, "God's
blessings / greetings"

günah—(Turkish) sin

hanım—(Turkish) woman

haydi—(Turkish) colloquial for "come on" or "all right" (let's)

hingel—(Turkish) similar to mantı (see below); a type of dumpling associated
with Eastern Anatolia and the Caucasus region

İncil—(Turkish) Bible

Jungs und die Straße—(German) "Boys and the Street"

kahve—(Turkish) coffee; also used metonymically for café

kanak—(German) slang, used as a term of racialization to denigrate people of
perceived Mediterranean, Middle Eastern, Muslim, or North African heritage; also used increasingly as a term of self-empowerment within these
minoritized communities

kara sevda—(Turkish) sea of love

kilim—(Turkish) a traditional handwoven, woolen tapestry or carpet often
used as a prayer rug

kıro—(Turkish) slang for an uncouth or unrefined man; a farmer

komshija—(Serbo-Croatian) neighbor

korn—(German) short for Kornbrand or Kornbranntwein; a cheap, colorless,
high-alcohol liquor distilled from grains

Kristallweizen—(German) a filtered Hefeweizen (wheat beer)

lahmacun—(Turkish) a thin flatbread topped with a sauce of minced meat,
vegetables, and herbs, also known colloquially (especially in Germany) as
"Turkish pizza"

lan—(Turkish) slang term of endearment for a friend; also used as an exclamation at the beginning or end of sentences

mantı—(Turkish) small, typically lamb-stuffed dumplings, sometimes described
 as Turkish ravioli or tortellini
Maşallah—(Turkish transliteration of the Arabic) "God has willed it"
mersi—(Turkish spelling of French) merci; thank you
Meryem Ana—(Turkish) Mary, Mother of God
ninni—(Turkish) lullaby
o—(Turkish) he/she/it/they (singular); also declined as *ona/onu* (him/her/it/
 them) and *onun* (his/her[s]/its/their[s])
oğlum—(Turkish) son
oğlum benim—(Turkish) my son
Rabbim—(Turkish) "My Lord" or "My God"
sağol—(Turkish) informal: thanks
sajada—(Turkish) prayer rug
Saldır! Koş oğlum!—(Turkish) "Attack! Run, son!"
Selamın Aleyküm—(Turkish transliteration of the Arabic) traditional Islamic
 greeting: "Peace be upon you"
Swabian—from Swabia (German: Schwaben), a highly industrialized region of
 southwestern Germany associated with the German virtues of hard work,
 orderliness, and economic fortune; also negatively associated with stinginess
 and petite bourgeois values
şekerleme—(Turkish) candy; confectionary
tamam—(Turkish) okay
tövbe—(Turkish) repent; forswear; shame on you
Tövbe estafurullah—(Turkish and Turkish transliteration of the Arabic)
 colloquial: "I'll never do it again!"; literally, "Repent, Allah forgive me!"
Tu Kurmancî zanî?—(Kurdish) "Do you speak Kurdish?"
teyze—(Turkish) auntie; also a title of respect or endearment
uzun hava—(Turkish) a style of Turkish folksong; "long melody," literally:
 "long mood/atmosphere"
yakışıklım—(Turkish) cutie; literally: "my handsome one"
yani—(Turkish) well; so
yaramaz—(Turkish) naughty, mischievous
yenge—(Turkish) aunt, sister-in-law

FATMA AYDEMIR is an author, playwright, and journalist. She was born in Karlsruhe, Germany, in 1986 and studied literature at the Goethe-Universität in Frankfurt am Main. Aydemir's 2017 debut novel, *Ellbogen* (Elbow), received numerous literary prizes in Germany. Together with Hengameh Yaghoobifarah, she edited the 2019 essay collection *Eure Heimat ist unser Albtraum* (*Your Homeland Is Our Nightmare*), which is now available in English translation. She is also coeditor of the literary magazine *Delfi*. *Dschinns* (*Djinns*) is her second novel. It has been awarded several German literary prizes as well as been adapted for multiple theater performances. *Dschinns* was shortlisted for the German Book Prize in 2022. Aydemir is a columnist for *The Guardian*. She lives and works in Berlin.

JON CHO-POLIZZI is a literary translator and assistant professor of German at the University of Michigan. His research and translation work focus on the polyphony of the contemporary German literary scene. Originally from Northern California, Cho-Polizzi studied literature, history, and translation in Santa Cruz, Berkeley, and Heidelberg, Germany. In addition to his book-length publications, his translations have been featured in numerous anthologies, exhibitions, newspapers, and journals. He lives and works between Michigan, California, and Berlin.